INTO SUMMER

Dawn of a New Age

INTO SUMMER

Dawn of a New Age

-A Novel-

Larry Landgraf

Fresh Ink Group
Guntersville

Into Summer: Dawn of a New Age

Copyright © 2018
by Larry Landgraf
All rights reserved

Fresh Ink Group
An Imprint of:
The Fresh Ink Group, LLC
Box 931
Guntersville, AL 35976
Email: info@FreshInkGroup.com

Edition 1.0 2018

Book design by Amit Dey / FIG

Cover by Stephen Geez / FIG

BISAC Subject Headings:
FIC000000 **FICTION / General**
FIC055000 **FICTION / Dystopian**
FIC028070 **FICTION / Science Fiction / Apocalyptic & Post-Apocalyptic**

Library of Congress Control Number: 2018912311

Hardcover ISBN-13: 978-1-936442-67-6
Paper-cover ISBN-13: 978-1-936442-68-3
Ebook ISBN-13: 978-1-936442-69-0

Table of Contents

Prologue

Into Summer is book four of the Four Seasons Series and begins where *Into Winter* left off. But first, let's take a look back at the first three books of the series.

In *Into Autumn*, Lars Lindgren is getting up in years and longs to retire in the country. He buys a plot without his wife's knowledge and builds a small cabin. His wife doesn't go along with the move, but Lars sells his business and moves anyway. Lars struggles, alone in the dystopian environment, but over time he learns the ways of the woods.

Eileen Branson flees San Antonio a few years later when the grid shuts down, and government and the economy crumble. She finds herself way over her head, but fortunately, she runs into Lars. They band together and along with their neighbors scratch out sustenance and fight off predatory intruders. They eventually name their little community Peaceful Valley even though it has been anything but peaceful.

Reggie is Lars's best friend. Lars's son, James, and Reggie's daughter, Melissa, find their way to Peaceful Valley amidst the chaos. They marry and have twin sons, Robbie and Ronnie Lindgren.

In *Into Spring*, Robbie and Ronnie grow up with their Asian neighbor's kids, Sean and Debra. They are all about the same age and Debra is just one of the boys. Young men need women, and Debra is the only female. Debra chooses to marry Ronnie, and Sean and Robbie head to Corpus Christi to find women for themselves.

They leave Peaceful Valley for the first time and are captured by the ruthless dictator of Corpus Christi, Sandra Hawkins. Sandra takes a shine to Robbie, but he doesn't like the situation he's forced into, though he is treated very well. She is quite brutal to everyone else, but it is due to her ruthlessness that the economy of Corpus Christi thrives under her leadership. The fact that Corpus Christi is a coastal town and has a refinery helps too. Much of the country has fared much worse.

Robbie eventually escapes with two of Sandra's ladies, Beka Livingston and Florence Ingalls, and Sandra is pissed. Sean escapes from Corpus later with two more of Sandra's ladies, Brenda and Kim. They are both pregnant with Robbie's kids. This brings us to *Into Winter* where Sandra has blood in her eyes as she plans her revenge against Robbie and Peaceful Valley.

Lars died when Robbie and Ronnie were young, but Eileen taught the boys his ways. Robbie and Ronnie grew up as Davy Crockett types from head to toe, with coonskin hats all the way down to their leather moccasins. Their woodsmen skills were remarkable even compared to Lars, who became quite the expert. Thanks to their grandmother, Eileen, and their parents, James and Melissa, the boys also grew up book smart. Lars left a treasure trove of books, and they read every one.

Sandra and her army were no match for Robbie, Ronnie, and the rest of the members of Peaceful Valley. The boys' grandfather, Reggie, played an integral part in their survival not only with Sandra but in the early days with Lars and Eileen. He's an ex-army contractor who built a bunker when he first moved to the valley and filled it with an exorbitant stash of weapons and explosives. He loved making stuff that went boom!

Together, they rid the world of Sandra Hawkins and created a stable democracy in Corpus Christi. The boys liked what they built and decided to expand their success in Corpus to the rest of the country. This brings us to *Into Summer* where Robbie Lindgren and his twin brother, Ronnie, are about to head off on their quest to establish a new, peaceful, and stable democracy over south Texas. Their significant others, Florence and Brooke, respectively, hold down the fort in Peaceful Valley.

Sean Lin is now the mayor of Corpus Christi after the demise of Sandra Hawkins and her brutal dictatorship. This is where the central government of the new regime will be located. Christine is Sean's right-hand gal and Chief of Police.

Brenda and Kim, Sean's two ladies, have joined him in Corpus and they reside at the Farm, one of six compounds into which the city is still divided. Christine also stays at the Farm. The other compounds are the Hospital, the Bayfront, the Contractors, the Airport, and the Police.

Marcia Nguyen, the thorn in Sean, Robbie, and Ronnie's sides in Corpus Christi, is behaving herself after the disappearance of her husband. Sonny has been missing for two months and is presumed dead. Little Lola, their daughter, keeps to herself much of the time.

John Wimberley, his wife Kathy, and their five kids, Brooke, Charlotte, Kira, Lance, and Zack came to Peaceful Valley in *Into Spring*. John is working hard to help Robbie and Ronnie get a communications system set up with the help of his boys, Zack and Lance. They are doing this through a string of cell towers.

John has given up on his dream of building a church in Peaceful Valley. His wife, Kathy, has given up on life itself after the loss of her daughter, Charlotte, during the war with Sandra Hawkins. Her youngest daughter, Kira, tries to help but spends much of her time with the neighbors.

Sam and Sally Lin work daylight to dark every day, trying to get their homestead and their lives back in order after the war. When their neighbors need a hand, however, they are ready and willing to do whatever is necessary. They visit their daughter, Debra, when they can. Their son, Sean, is always on their minds. They keep hoping he'll come home for a visit, but he's too busy in Corpus Christi. Zack Wimberley has offered to take them to Corpus several times. Sam keeps saying he'll take him up on the offer, but his hogs take a lot of tending. Sally won't go without Sam.

Beka Livingston and Lance Wimberley are getting along better every day and continue to share a home with Zack Wimberley and Debra Lin. Beka wants a baby and Debra thinks she's pregnant.

James and Melissa Lindgren are just trying to keep their heads above water with all the work it takes to care for the Lindgren homestead. They are the backbone of Peaceful Valley. Their sons, Robbie and Ronnie, are always on their minds.

Reggie and Emily, the senior citizens of Peaceful Valley and Melissa's parents and Robbie and Ronnie's grandparents, do what they can. Emily spends most of her time keeping tabs on the pregnant and soon-to-be pregnant women in the valley. Reggie spends his days in his bunker keeping his weapons in perfect order and devising new explosives to keep everyone safe.

Introduction

"Shit!" Ronnie yelled. He instinctively put his hand out as his body slammed forward. He gave Robbie a glance, who was struggling with the steering wheel to control the Jeep. The tires smoked when he locked up the brakes. The first shot ricocheted off the hood. The second shattered the windshield.

Ronnie, with his hand on his AR-15, riding shotgun, scanned for a shooter. There were no houses, no buildings of any kind nearby, yet someone had shot at them. There! The puff of smoke from the top of a nearby water tower, then the pain in his right arm, and finally the report of the rifle. *Why is he shooting at us?*

Ronnie scrambled out of the Jeep, but the pain from his wounded arm slowed him down. Robbie was already out and behind the vehicle yelling at him.

"Get your ass around here dammit!"

"I'm coming!"

Ronnie winced at another sharp pain, this time in his neck. His rifle slipped through his fingers. He grabbed at his throat and went to his knees, then his hands. He tried to crawl around to the back of the Jeep, but his body plowed into the asphalt.

Chapter 1

Four days earlier in Peaceful Valley . . .

Robbie and Florence arrived home from Corpus Christi. Ronnie and Brooke were pleased with their uneventful trip. The boys spent one more wonderful night with Florence and Brooke. They packed their gear in the Jeep that evening. All they would need to load in the morning were a few personal items, consisting mostly of drinks and food, and then they could be on their way.

In the meantime, they had the whole evening to look forward to. Each boy took his lady's hand and led her off to their bedroom and a night of intimate goodbyes.

"You come back to your son and me safely, you hear?" Florence said.

"My son?"

Florence smiled. "You mean more to me than life, Robbie. We're going to have lots of kids. I hope the first is a boy, for you. Every man needs a son, but even if it isn't, I'll give you sons, many of them. I love you."

"I love you too."

Robbie laid his head on her shoulder and snuggled up close to her, his hand on one of her breasts. He traced his hand down her body to her tummy. He felt the baby kicking.

At the crack of dawn, Florence and Brooke fixed the boys a substantial breakfast consisting of eggs, plenty of bacon so they'd have leftovers to take along to snack on, and gravy—lots of gravy. The boys loved gravy. It usually took four or five biscuits to sop it all up. They all ate their fill.

When they were finished, they strolled out onto the porch, and the guys each gave their gals a final kiss. Robbie wiped a stray tear from one of Florence's eyes.

"That's the first I've seen in a while," he said.

Florence met his eyes with a steady gaze. "You don't have to worry about me. I'm learning to stand on my own two feet. I'm not the innocent girl you rescued from Corpus. I'll be fine, and I'm looking forward to telling our son about what a brave man his father was, making the world safe and secure for him. Now you two get going. The sooner you leave, the quicker you return to me." She gave him a kiss he would be thinking about halfway down the road. "Make us a better world."

Robbie and Ronnie climbed in the Jeep and looked over at each other with big smiles on their faces and fist-bumped. Robbie cranked up the Jeep and eased away from the house. He waved at Brooke and Florence as his eyes caught them in the rearview mirror on the porch.

"We have a couple of wonderful women," Robbie said.

"You know it, Bro! Now let's go make them proud."

⌁⌁⌁⌁

A few hours later, Robbie and Ronnie sat staring at the warning sign bolted to a steel post driven in the middle of the road: "Keep Out!" They'd made it to the farm a man named Jake directed them to earlier. They had to pass all the way through Kenedy and travel a dozen miles or so out a farm-to-market road, away from the city to get there. 'You boys do exactly what they said to do' their grandpa told them. 'In these days and times, they'll kill you just like we would intruders around here'.

Ronnie stuck his rifle out the door and fired two shots into the air, while Robbie stuck the pole with a white flag on top into the dirt alongside the roadway as Jake had instructed when they first met. Robbie hopped in the Jeep, turned around, and headed back up the road. At one mile, he turned around and switched off the ignition.

Thirty minutes later, a blue SUV approached with the white flag sticking out of its window. The twins got out of the Jeep and stood alongside. The SUV stopped thirty feet away, and the passenger door opened.

Robbie and Ronnie glanced at each other, then turned their attention back to the blue vehicle.

The big man got out and smiled. "Welcome."

Robbie returned his smile and stepped forward. "Thank you for coming."

The man walked around the door of the SUV and toward Robbie. "What can I do for you?"

"I'm Robbie. This is my brother, Ronnie," he said pointing his thumb.

Ronnie gave Jake a quick nod.

"We're from Peaceful Valley. Our Grandpa Reggie talked to you last year when you caught us looting Kenedy. My grandpa and dad were driving the bus. You're Jake, aren't you?"

"Yes, I am. I remember your grandpa. So, what brings you out this way?"

"We're on our way to some of the surrounding communities. We're going to get a new democracy going in south Texas. Grandpa said we should stop here first."

Jake squinted his eyes. "I'd like to hear how you plan to do that, son. Might be a little more curious about how you think we might be able to help." Jake took in a deep breath of air then slowly let it back out. "Well, Robbie, come on back to our farm, and you can tell us all about it."

They followed the SUV down the winding road. Two men stood guard at a gate at the edge of the farm. They opened the gate and waved the vehicles through.

Robbie pulled up alongside Jake's SUV in front of a large log cabin and killed the engine. Robbie and Ronnie got out and looked around. A few curious bystanders stopped what they were doing to watch the newcomers.

The boys followed Jake up on the large porch which wrapped around the side of the well-built structure. Jake pointed to a table and chairs just as a lady stuck her head out of the door. Jake gave her a wink. "Mary, won't you bring us some tea and then come and join us?" Jake sat down. "Come on, boys, have a seat."

The man who had been driving the SUV returned followed by a group of people. They gathered around the table. Other bystanders also made their way to the porch.

Mary came out with a tray. She eyed the crowd that had gathered and forced a smile. "I'll get another pitcher. This isn't going to be enough."

Jake made introductions while he waited for Mary. When she returned, he stood up. "This purdy lady is my wife. Mary, this is Robbie and Ronnie." He pulled out a chair for her, and they sat down.

⎼⎮⌐⎮⌐⎮⌐⎮⎼

Robbie looked around the group, their curious and eager faces staring back. ". . . and our valley was peaceful, just like its name, until Sandra Hawkins brought a terrible war to us. We won the battle at home, then went on to finish it in Corpus Christi. Corpus is stable now, and Sean Lin, along with the new Chief of Police, Christine, are working hard at controlling hostilities. We're going to expand our start there, to end the bloodshed throughout the region.

"We're tired of the fighting and want to stop it once and for all. We think others might be of a like mind. Our parents told us how it used to be decades ago. We want to bring back the sanity that once existed in this country."

"Mighty brave and ambitious of you boys," Jake said. "We all know how dangerous it has been out there for what seems like an eternity—how we can't let our guard down for one second. The men from here who ventured to Corpus years ago were my friends. We wanted seafood and salt. No one came back."

Jake sniffed and quickly stifled his feelings. "So, what are you fellas doing here?"

"We're looking for volunteers to help us," Robbie said, looking over the group. He turned back to Jake. "We can't do this alone."

Jake stood up and walked over to the edge of the porch, his eyes lost in thought. He turned around and scanned the men and women attending the meeting.

Jake stepped back and took a deep breath. "I don't know what we can do, Robbie. We're not as young and energetic as you two boys. Our community consists of mostly older folks like me. We'd like to help though. Is there anything we could contribute other than bodies?"

"Do you have any vehicles other than the SUV?"

"Nothing that runs."

Robbie shook his head. "Then there isn't much you can do. Other than a commitment from people to help, it's going to take transportation and fuel."

Jake sat down. "I'm sorry, boys."

"If you can't, that's all there is to it," Ronnie added. "We don't blame you."

Robbie stood and put his hand on Jake's shoulder. "No, we don't blame you at all." He looked around at some of the others. "If we can get you a vehicle and fuel, would any of you be willing to help?"

A couple of the men nodded but said nothing, more contemplating than agreeing.

Jake turned back to Robbie. "I can't make any promises, but I think we might be able to locate another vehicle and fuel, given the time."

Robbie smiled. "That's good enough for me."

"Have you seen any cell phone towers around here?" Ronnie asked. "This task is going to take communications too. We're working on the problem, but we're not finding enough towers."

"I know where one is," one of the men said.

Ronnie pulled out his map, and the man pointed at the location. Another man also pointed out the site of a second tower.

Mary offered their guests a late lunch, which they readily accepted. Jake also asked them if they'd like to stay the night and get an early start on their trip in the morning. They agreed to this too.

Jake, Robbie, and Ronnie continued to chat on the porch while Mary and one of the other ladies went inside. Most of the younger men and women had chores and got back to whatever they were doing before the boys arrived. A few of the older gentlemen and their wives stayed and listened in while Robbie and Ronnie took turns sharing the details of the battle with Sandra and her men, both in Peaceful Valley and later in Corpus.

The boys then shared some stories about their home life. To the twins, stories of home weren't that interesting, and Robbie moved on to the one of him and Sean going to Corpus.

That they weren't killed piqued the interest of one of the ladies. "My name is Susan . . . Susan Mitchell. My son, Timothy, went with one of the scout groups to Corpus about ten years ago. Have you heard his name mentioned?" She glanced back and forth between the boys with hopeful eyes.

Robbie looked over at his brother, then back at Susan. "I'm sorry."

"How about Mark Cross?" another man asked.

Jake added a few other names and Robbie shook his head to each.

In Corpus Christi at the Hospital compound . . .

A doctor and two nurses stood over a bed, the nurses taking vitals and the doctor looking at the chart. The doctor hung the chart back on the foot of the bed. "I can't see why he won't wake up. Everything seems normal. We can't keep him in here any longer. We've already kept him too long, but with the new program . . . dammit, two months is too long."

"Give him another day or two, doctor," one of the nurses pleaded. "We'll get him up even if we have to slap him around a bit."

The doctor shook his head and walked out. "Two more days," he said over his shoulder.

"Why are you so concerned, Jen?" the other nurse asked.

"If he dies, I'll never know his name. I hate it when a person dies, and his name is Doe. Too many Johns and Janes in the cemetery now."

"Are you really going to slap him around?"

She walked over and looked at the scruffy face. "No! We can't do that. . . we're nurses . . ." *Or can we?* She grabbed his shoulder and shook hard. "Wake up, damn you!"

Chapter 2

Robbie and Ronnie pulled out of Jake's compound before the sun made the horizon. They both got a good night's sleep and were ready to take on the new day. From here on out, they would be in new, never-before-traveled territory. The real adventure was beginning.

After a few turns, Robbie pointed to a road sign indicating Highway 181. "Next stop, Beeville. From there, we'll get on 59 to Goliad."

Ronnie was quiet but kept twisting and turning in his seat to see everything that caught his eyes along the highway. It wasn't long until he spotted a cell tower. He scrutinized his map and made a mark.

Robbie drove at a leisurely pace and made numerous stops. They found oil tanks, commercial buildings that hadn't burned, and of course the occasional pee break. All the while, Jake's final words stuck in his head, 'the world has been nothing but chaos the past couple of decades since the grid shut down. You two be very careful . . . you don't know what you're going to find out there'.

Robbie kept the speed between thirty and forty miles per hour, depending upon what they were seeing. Mostly there was the road ahead and brush with a few dilapidated houses here and there, but every so often, something that interested them showed up.

Robbie stopped and focused on a group of oil tanks he just barely spotted through the dense brush. He figured they would be worth checking out since they were well-concealed. Ronnie got out and cut the fence wires. Robbie handed his brother the machete, took his pliers, then followed while Ronnie trimmed a few tree limbs.

Of the five tanks, three had a liquid in them. One was nearly full and the others half full. Robbie took samples of each. He held the glass vials up to the sunlight and smiled. His Grandpa Reggie, who gave them the bottles for sample collection, would be proud. His grandpa would test the contents when they got back to Peaceful Valley.

Ronnie marked the location on his map and Robbie pulled back onto the roadway. When they got to the outskirts of Beeville, Robbie slowed to a crawl. His brother readied his AR-15. When they got closer to the buildings, Robbie stopped to take a good look around. The leaves rustled on the trees and dust blew around, but otherwise, he saw no movement and no signs of life.

The map indicated this had been a decent size city at one time. The road turned into a major freeway. Robbie put the Jeep in gear and eased forward, his gaze focused on the town ahead. The highway only skirted the city. *There have to be people here. They couldn't have all died.*

Ronnie pointed to the road he thought was Highway 59 to Goliad. Robbie stopped again at the top of the overpass. "I have the feeling we're being watched."

Ronnie nodded. Both boys scanned the area with the scopes on their rifles. They saw no cars, no smoke, and the only sound was the wind whistling across their ears. The city appeared to be a ghost town.

Ronnie poked his fist at his brother's arm. "Let's get on toward Goliad."

They made their way down to the access road and onto 59. A few miles away from the city, Robbie stopped, killed the engine, and turned in his seat to watch the roadway back toward town. "I feel like someone saw us and will be coming after us."

"It really gives me the creeps when we expect to see people, and there is absolutely no one."

Ronnie grabbed a nutrition bar out of his backpack and handed it to his brother. He got one for himself, and they nibbled on the bars while they waited and watched. After fifteen minutes, no one showed up.

Robbie turned the ignition key. He eyed the gas gauge, put the Jeep in gear, and headed on. At the edge of the little community of Berclair, Robbie stopped and eyed a very tall tower. "That's too big to be a cell tower. And it has round dish thingies instead of vertical bars."

Ronnie smiled. "Yeah, like satellite or television dishes. And one that looks like a space capsule!"

Ronnie pulled his map back out. "I'm going to mark it anyway. If it's not a cell tower, maybe we can add the antennas we want and make it one."

Robbie shrugged, put the Jeep in gear, and eased forward. They were on high alert as they rode through the vacant crumbled houses and commercial properties. Robbie let out a sigh of relief as they put distance between themselves and Berclair.

There were miles of nothing after that, and it was getting late. The sun was going down soon, and the early color hinted at a beautiful sunset to come in an hour or so. Robbie pulled off the road, and Ronnie hopped out to cut the fence wires. Ronnie masked the tire tracks with his feet as he followed the Jeep into the brush. Robbie stopped, and his brother got back in. They drove further into the bush until they could no longer see the road.

The boys got out and made a big circle around the area to check their surroundings. When they got back to the Jeep, they relaxed a few minutes while they watched the sunset.

They started to set up camp. Stretching a rope between two trees, they threw their tarp over and secured the bottom, then rolled out their bedrolls. Ronnie grabbed a couple of extra blankets and tossed one on each bed. "You should have stopped a little earlier. Maybe I could have gotten us a fresh rabbit. Now we're going to be eating jerky."

Robbie smiled. "Let's get a good sleep tonight. We're getting close to Goliad and the San Antonio River. There have to be people there."

Ronnie handed his brother a piece of jerky and a canteen. "Yes, there most likely will be. Let's hope we can get in without getting shot."

Robbie nodded. "And hopefully they can be reasoned with."

In Corpus Christi at the Hospital compound . . .

The next day, the coma patient was conscious but unable to move a muscle. *I'm awake, or am I? Nothing seems to work except my ears. I hear someone walking around. I am awake! But why won't my eyes open? Try your legs. Nope! Arms? No! I think a finger moved. No, I must have imagined it.*

What's the matter with me? Am I dead? Do dead people think? I've gotta be alive. Then why the hell can't I move? Relax and listen. Yes, I still hear someone. There is someone here other than me. What's that beeping? A monitor. Yes. I'm in a hospital. It feels comfortable here—quiet, restful, someone watching me. Yes, I'm alive, and someone is taking care of me.

Me? . . . Me! Who am I? Oh shit! I don't remember who I am. Relax . . . relax. It'll come to . . .

Someone touched me . . . touched my face. The bed moved, someone sat down on the edge, then she . . . probably she . . . touched my face. Yes, she. A man wouldn't touch . . .

Owww! What did she do?! She hit me. Yes, I heard it . . . and I felt it. The damn bitch slapped me!

He struggled. He blinked his eyes. *Yes! I see color. My eyes are working . . . trying to work. Try harder dammit!*

He blinked over and over, and his eyes slowly focused on a young girl. He mustered all he had to reach his arm out. He tried to say something, but nothing would come out.

She fell to her knees, tears of relief in her eyes that he was awake. "I'm sorry I hit you, but you're awake now. Relax. I know it probably doesn't look like it, but I'm a nurse." She smiled and scrambled to her feet. "I'm going to help you."

He looked into her glassy blue eyes. *She's pretty!*

Not far from Goliad, Robbie slowed the Jeep and held a steady twenty miles-per-hour pace. The San Antonio River bridge was coming up soon. *There will be people in Goliad . . . I know it.* If there were indeed people, they needed to see them first. Robbie saw the bridge from afar and stopped. He looked behind him, around, then back ahead.

Ronnie looked over. "Well?"

"Well, what?"

"What did you expect?"

Robbie took a deep breath. "I don't know. I guess I just expected to see some people."

Robbie proceeded to the bridge but stopped just short of the ramp. "If there is anyone here, they should be near town and the river. It's only a couple of miles farther to the edge of town according to the map, maybe three if we follow the river. The San Antonio River has to be the snakiest one I've seen. I think we should ditch the Jeep and go on foot. We'll have a better chance of seeing someone first that way. We can't let anyone get the drop on us."

"I'm with you. There's plenty of brush around here."

Robbie found a spot to hide the Jeep, and they packed enough gear for two days. They made their way back to the bridge on foot, crossed the river, and headed into the brush along the stream.

"It's been dry here too," Robbie remarked. "Not much water flow."

Ronnie nodded.

The boys followed the river to the point where the map showed it to be closest to town. There was no one along the way, and they passed up two run-down homes near the water, but at a third house, they heard voices.

Robbie knelt down behind a stump. His brother moved over behind a tree. Robbie gave him a hand signal indicating maybe three people and took the lead. The voices grew louder as they neared the third house. Robbie spied a woman and three nearly grown kids, but they weren't like any people he'd seen before.

The woman hung clothes to dry on a line. The kids chopped wood and stacked it alongside the home. A trickle of smoke snaked into the air from a roof pipe and faded into nothing.

Robbie looked over at his brother and shrugged his shoulders. They were both at a loss at what to do. Could they communicate with these people? Surely they spoke English, but they weren't certain. If there was a man, he had to be around somewhere. Was he nearby? The boys were careful and knew they hadn't been spotted. If there was a man, they had better keep their eyes open. These people could be aggressive toward strangers.

Robbie waved his brother to conceal himself better, then turned his attention back to the family. Robbie scrunched down and chattered like a squirrel. He watched as the woman stopped what she was doing and turned an ear toward him. Robbie chattered again, and the woman's eyes honed in on his position, but more toward the top of the trees than straight at him.

Robbie watched the woman as she turned toward the kids. "Joey. There's a squirrel somewhere up the riverbank. Get your gun."

The young boy who appeared to be the oldest of the three went in the house and came back outside with what Robbie thought looked like a .22 caliber rifle. The woman pointed the direction, and he headed up the river toward them while his brother and sister stayed behind.

Robbie waved his brother back, and the two moved farther away from the riverbank and the people.

Ronnie grabbed his brother's arm. "What the hell are you doing?" he whispered.

"We now know they speak English. We're going to capture one and see if they are reasonable."

"What?"

"Keep your voice down." Robbie pointed to a large oak tree. "Get behind that one. I'll lead him by you, and you grab him. And cover his mouth."

Ronnie followed his brother's instructions. The boy was coming with a gun, and he didn't have time to argue the point. Robbie headed farther away from the river and got behind a tree so he could still see Ronnie. Robbie chattered again and watched for the boy.

Ronnie laid his rifle on the ground and watched for his brother's signals.

Soon, the boy came into sight. Robbie chattered once again, and the young boy moved toward him with his eyes upward trying to spot the squirrel. Robbie signaled to his brother that the kid was coming on the left side.

Ronnie grabbed at the rifle as it appeared around the tree and jerked the kid toward him. Ronnie wrapped his arm around his neck and over his mouth, then took him to the ground and held him down with his body. Robbie was there in a flash, laid his rifle down, and pulled the gun from the kid's hands in order to help Ronnie hold him.

Robbie turned the kid's face so he could see his eyes. "We're not going to hurt you. Stop fighting dammit!"

The kid relaxed a little, and Robbie repeated, "We're not going to hurt you."

He waited a few seconds to let the boy settle down. "The only reason we jumped you is so you wouldn't shoot us before we had a chance to talk. We just want to talk."

Ronnie pulled his head around so the boy could see him. "If I take my hand off your mouth, will you calm down?"

The boy nodded.

Ronnie removed his hand but wasn't about to release him just yet. "We're travelers looking for peaceful people to help us rebuild this once great country. My name is Ronnie, and this is my brother, Robbie. Your name is Joey, right? That's what your mama called you."

"Yeah, I'm Joey. I might be more obliged to talk to you fellers if you let me up."

Robbie stood up now that Ronnie could easily hold on to Joey, who wasn't struggling any longer. "You're not going to run or yell out, are you? We'd like to talk to your mama too. Once again, we're not going to hurt any of you, and we don't want anything from you other than a little conversation."

"I'll talk, but you've got to let me up first."

Robbie picked his rifle up, and Ronnie released his hold. Joey got up and wiped off his clothes. "Can I have my gun back?"

Robbie shook his head. "Not just yet. How many people are there around here?"

"Five-hundred more or less."

"Are they all the same color as you?"

"No, we have white boys and girls here too."

Robbie looked over at his brother.

Joey started laughing. "You haven't ever seen a black boy, have you? I can tell the way you look at me. Well, you better get used to us, 'cause there's a lot of us around here."

Ronnie walked over to the big oak tree and picked up his rifle. "We don't care what color you are as long as you're friendly. We've read about black people, but we've never seen any. Just a little surprised, I guess. We weren't sure you folks were still around. We do have Asian people back home."

Jooo . . . eeey drifted melodically through the trees. Joey quickly glanced back in the direction of his home, then back at his captors.

"So there was no squirrel over here?"

Robbie smiled. "No, that was me."

"Mama's going to be a little upset that we're not having squirrel for dinner. Come on, I'll introduce you."

⌁⌁⌁⌁

In Corpus Christi at the Hospital compound . . .

Sonny remembered his name when he relaxed after a while and introduced himself to Jen. An orderly brought in his breakfast, and he ate everything. Though it was only liquids, Sonny imagined it was prime rib with all the trimmings. His vocal chords were not working a hundred percent, but enough that he could chit chat with Jen while she checked his vitals and tried to make him more comfortable.

The doctor came in and checked on the patient. "I was just about to give up on you. You can thank your nurse. She talked me into giving you a couple more days."

The doctor looked at the chart. "Get him up tomorrow. He's got to walk, and as soon as he has a BM, I'll release him." He walked out.

Jen looked over at Sonny. "You heard the Doc. If you eat well this evening, I'll start you on solid food tomorrow, and we'll get you up to walk. Then you can go home."

Sonny's lips curled up into a weak smile. *Where is home? How did I get here? I remember a girl . . . a pretty girl. Then darkness. The water . . . cold water . . . salty water . . . I was tied up. Lucky for the knife . . .*

"You okay, Sonny?"

Sonny looked over at the nurse. "I don't remember your name."

"Jen."

"Oh yeah . . ."

⌁⌁⌁⌁

At Goliad . . .

Josephine pointed toward her youngest two kids standing by the woodpile. "This here's Marcus and Samantha. Franklin left yesterday. The old coot's usually gone fer three or four days. He'll bring a hog or deer back. Sure wish you'd been a squirrel. I've got me a real hankerin' for rodent. Thank you for not hurting Joey.

"If you'd have come into town on the highway, someone would have shot you fer sure. Usually, when people come 'round, they're up to no good, hungry, or just plain sorry. Good thing you snuck up like you did."

Robbie and Ronnie couldn't get a word in edgewise since they sat down on the bench in the yard. They just kept nodding their agreement as Josephine rattled on. Once they'd introduced themselves and she learned of their intentions, she started talking and wouldn't shut up. But the boys were just fine with that. She was giving them the information they needed.

Josephine checked her laundry. It was dry. She started taking it off the line and piling it in her basket as she continued to talk. "Tucked way back here away from the highway, we hardly see anyone except town folk. The no-gooders blaze in on the roads and are shot immediately. If there's too many fer the one sentry to handle with his rifle, we have explosives. Doesn't happen often, but they always work.

"I think most folk around here would be happy if we didn't have to worry about outsiders anymore. There are a lot of things we don't get these days too. I miss coffee and chocolate.

"We have a few cars, trucks, and farm vehicles. We have diesel and gas, but it's used almost exclusively fer the tractors and such."

Maybe Josephine realized she was giving out too much information, or that she wasn't letting Robbie or Ronnie get a word in. She suddenly got quiet and stared at the boys.

Robbie uncrossed his legs. "Well, at least you have vehicles that work. If we can find a couple of guys to help us, maybe we can supply a little extra fuel from Corpus Christi. We have enough for our needs now, but are working on expanding our production for the new democracy."

Joey had squirmed a bit, but sat and listened up to this point. "Maybe I can go. I have a couple of friends who I bet would love to get out of this hole. There's nothing to do 'round here. We hunt, eat, and sleep."

"What about Gloria?"

"She's just a friend."

"Maybe to you, Son, but I see how she looks at you."

Robbie looked over at his brother. He nodded. Robbie turned back to Joey. "I tell you what, you discuss this with your mother and your friends. It may take us a couple of months before we can get back this way, but if you want to join us, be patient. We'll be back."

"Yes, I want to help."

"By the way, how old are you?"

"S-sixteen."

Robbie looked over at his brother. "Old enough for me."

Ronnie nodded.

Robbie continued. "When we come back, we'll come through this way so as not to be mistaken as marauders. Now that we know each other, we'll call you by name.

"Joey, find a car you and your friends can use. It needs to be dependable. And you'll need bigger guns than the .22 you have now. Josephine, you and Joey talk to the rest of the townspeople. Let them know what we're doing. We need everyone on our side. We're headed up to Refugio next. If we can get a few groups familiarized with what we're doing, we'll come back through and tie everyone together."

"We have relations with the city of Refugio," Josephine pointed out. "They have more fuel there. One of the big ranchers set up a mini-refinery after the grid shut down decades ago. There's a lot of crude oil there, and those rich boys had the means and ingenuity to turn it into gasoline and diesel. We've got more fish and a few other things that they don't, so we trade back and forth."

Robbie looked over at his brother. "Maybe we can bypass Refugio then and head on to Sinton. It will certainly save us some time and danger if you'll have your townspeople let them know what's going on."

"We'll do that," Josephine replied.

Ronnie pulled his map out. "By the way, do you know if there are any cell towers around here. Some of our folks back home are working to get communications going so everyone can keep track of what's happening. That's the only way we can effectively monitor the region. If people are going to stop shooting at everyone else, they need to know that someone is watching out for them. For that, we need a unified police force that can patrol and respond to any threat. For the safety and protection of everyone, communication is essential."

Joey looked over at his mother, then back at the twins with a quizzical look on his face.

"Tall towers with what looks like vertical bars on top," Ronnie said.

Joey's eyes lit up, and he reached for the map. "Let me see that. I know where two are."

Ronnie showed the map to Joey. He pointed to the locations.

Ronnie and Robbie shook hands with their new friends. "Be patient, Joey," Robbie said. "We'll be back."

In Corpus Christi at the Farm . . .

Kim and Brenda worked diligently in the kitchen preparing dinner for Sean. They had both been cooks at the Farm under Sandra's reign, so they moved the existing cooks back to the barn when they returned to join Sean. The temporary kitchen in the barn during the construction of the new farmhouse became the primary kitchen for the remainder of the farm hands. Kim and Brenda only cooked for Sean.

Cooking was probably the least strenuous job on the farm, and only cooking for themselves, Sean, and Christine gave the girls time to take care of the remainder of the vast house. The farmhouse was built initially with twelve bedrooms, but most were now empty. This arrangement also gave them more privacy between themselves and even with Sean when he was there. Christine was gone most of the day and stayed to herself after breakfast and dinner unless she had business to discuss with Sean.

Both Brenda and Kim loved Sean and shared him equally. In the bedroom, they all worked together to the satisfaction of all three. Tonight was a special night for the girls. It had been exactly a month since they moved in with Sean, and they decided it would be the first of many celebrations they would have with him.

Sean spent lots of time at the Contractors compound, primarily making sure fuel production was progressing, but also dealing with their communications problem, so he didn't have a lot of time for the girls of late. For the new government to work across south Texas, they needed security and this required adequate communications. They still hadn't located nearly enough cell towers. Sean hoped Robbie and Ronnie would add significantly to their short list of tower locations.

These and numerous other problems always exhausted Sean. He usually slept in on Sundays, and tonight the girls would make sure he had a good reason to sleep in even a little longer tomorrow.

Brenda would soon be having her baby, so sex would be out of the question for a while. She wanted one more pleasurable night with Sean before the baby became her primary concern.

Kim had fully recovered from her injuries sustained during the battle in Peaceful Valley. She had lost her baby, and while she didn't want to get pregnant again, her desires for sex had returned. Since Sean couldn't provide her with another baby because Sandra Hawkins had castrated him, Kim wasn't sure she even wanted to get pregnant again. She imagined being an aunt to Brenda's child was all she needed. But tonight, she intended to ravage Sean's body.

Kim strolled to the front door when she heard Sean's car drive up. She was waiting for him at the door with a big smile. The girls always made sure they had their smiles on when he got home. Kim gave him a quick kiss and hug, leaned back to sniff the air, and hurried him off to the bathroom for his shower. "Dinner will be ready when you get out." She patted him on the butt and pushed him onward.

The girls were putting the food on the table when Sean came in. Brenda ushered him into his seat and gave him a nibble on his neck. Kim poured the drinks, and the girls sat down.

When Sean had his fill of baked chicken with potatoes and gravy, creamed corn, and a fresh green salad from their greenhouse garden, the girls escorted him to the living room to relax with a glass of tea and some music while they took their showers. They found him snoozing on the sofa when they came out. They gently got him up and led him to the bedroom.

The girls stripped him down to his underwear and settled him into bed. Sean closed his eyes and presumed he was going back to sleep. But he was mistaken.

The girls snuggled against him on either side and giggled. Brenda took one of his earlobes between her teeth and tugged playfully. "We worked hard in the kitchen today making all your favorite dishes."

Sean pushed the hair back from Brenda's neck and nibbled at her shoulder. "I hope you saved something for me for dessert."

He could feel Kim's hand run up his thigh. "We never forget dessert," they sighed almost in unison, as Kim massaged him.

Brenda's lips fell to his nipples, and she licked and pinched alternately until he fisted her hair and pulled her lips to his. The hard day he had was melting away with each lick, kiss, and touch of his ladies' hands and mouths. He groaned in response to Kim's ministrations down below, and when her head popped out from under the sheet at his waist, he licked his lips in anticipation. "I might just have a little dessert for you two ladies as well." It had been a long time since their last encounter, and Sean's mood fired up quickly.

Kim teased Sean like a cat playing with a mouse, both knowing she would devour him before the evening was over. Brenda squeezed her breasts against him while she pinched and toyed with his nipples. Her tongue caressed his lips, then probed his mouth with careful precision, while she ran her fingers through his hair.

Sean was a prisoner to their affections and cherished every second with them. The girls did things to him he couldn't have imagined a few months back. He now gave himself totally to these women and couldn't imagine life without them.

Sean couldn't hold back his emotions or his accumulated energy, and he didn't want to. His body heaved, and the air was forced out of his lungs as he was thrust into ecstatic convulsions of relief and joy. Brenda and Kim both held on tight for the ride. They waited for the giggles to follow, which signaled Sean's total satisfaction.

Sean got his breath and always felt anxious to return the favor for the girls. Even tired, he couldn't get enough of playing with their bodies. They were always willing and readily accepted his affection. Two on one, the girls climaxed in minutes, after which they melded into a pile of one and drifted off to sleep.

Chapter 3

In Peaceful Valley . . .

Brooke had the stove fired up early when Florence scooted into the living room. "Coffee will be ready soon."

Florence smiled and went to the pantry. "I'd like to get a pot of soup going this morning if that's okay with you."

Brooke looked over. "Yeah, I'm fine with that."

Florence pulled out their big pot, then headed outside to grab some onions and veggies out of the root cellar. Florence returned with her basket of goodies and put them into the sink.

"You going veggie this time?"

"I think so. Beans too if that's okay with you."

"I'm fine with it. I'll grab a ham in a little bit. Mutt's scratching at the door. I need to fix breakfast for him before I go back out to the smokehouse. I'm fine with vegetable soup as long as I have some meat alongside. It doesn't have to be in the soup."

Florence smiled then turned back to her cutting board.

Brooke breathed in a whiff of the accumulating aroma. "The boys have been gone three days, and I haven't heard you say a word about them . . . and no tears."

Florence turned around, her bawling exaggerated with tears running down both cheeks. Brooke was surprised. Florence burst out laughing and held up the onion.

Brooke grabbed a cup and poured her coffee. "You can fix your own coffee for that."

Florence stuck out a lip in a fake pout.

Brooke set the cup down beside Florence. "Just kidding. I'll get the ham."

She returned with the meat and sat down at the table. She closed her eyes and squeezed her eyebrows with her middle finger and thumb.

"Something the matter, Brooke?"

"No. I'm all right. I didn't sleep well last night, and now I have a bit of a headache. Just not feeling well. My stomach is a little upset too. I don't know what it could be. I'll feel better after I get going."

"Just take it easy. You might be coming down with something."

"I don't feel like I have a temperature. Just feels like one of those bad days you have from time to time. Tomorrow will be a better day."

Florence hid her grin with her cup, then downed the contents. *Better get used to feeling like this for a while, girl.*

Over at the Lindgren homestead, nearly a mile away, James kissed Melissa, took the last sip out of his coffee mug, and headed out. He'd plowed the garden yesterday and wanted to run the row-disc over it, before planting their early corn tomorrow.

He cranked up the tractor and smiled. The new-to-him tractor he'd gotten from the neighboring town a while back, to replace the ancient one his dad had, was a welcome addition to his farm equipment. The old tractor was all but worn out before Lars died, and James had put many years on it since then. He removed the plows and hooked up the disc.

He opened the gate into the two-acre garden, lined the tractor up with the rows, and eased forward, back and forth, with little to do but drive and think. This was his favorite job. 'Men need to have time to think,' his dad had told him many times. Working the garden on the tractor provided this time because everything he was doing was so automatic.

James's mind drifted off to his sons. Robbie and Ronnie could be dead for all he knew, but James trusted in the boy's abilities. They were good at most everything they did. Helping to defend Peaceful Valley against Sandra Hawkins's army, then going to war in Corpus Christi against her remaining men, the boys learned new skills. Each also gained a lifetime of experience from their grandpa, Reggie, along with everything James had taught them. The boys would be okay, he imagined, but what they were doing was dangerous, and he couldn't help but worry some.

With his mind so consumed with thought, James felt like he'd finished the garden in minutes rather than the two hours the task really took. He drove the tractor back to the shed, parked, and got a drink of water from the wellhead.

Melissa brought him a biscuit with a slice of ham inside for a snack. "You planting tomorrow?" she asked.

"Yes, *we* are," he snickered. "You're late on getting your beets and carrots in."

Melissa frowned and headed back to the house. "Now I'm missing the boys again."

"I heard that!"

In Corpus Christi at the Hospital compound . . .

Jen came in early to check Sonny's vitals and disposition. Today he would get solid food, go for a walk, and hopefully have a poop. She walked in with a big smile on her face. "Good morning, Sonny."

"Good morning . . ." Sonny rolled his eyes. "Sorry, I've forgotten your name again."

"Jen . . . it's Jen. Don't worry about it. You've got better things to think about."

"Like what?"

"Getting some exercise so you can have a BM."

Sonny sighed.

"But first, some solid food. Well, relatively solid compared to what you had yesterday."

Seconds later, an orderly came in with a tray, set it down on the mini-table, and rolled the food over to the bed. He lifted the lid on the plate and left.

Sonny looked down. Potatoes with gravy, cooked carrots, crackers, and what looked like oatmeal. There was also tea and gelatin for dessert. "Yummy," he said, but his face said otherwise.

"You eat up, the more, the better, and I'll get you walking. You'll poop it out tomorrow, and you'll be ready to go home." Jen smiled.

Sonny smirked and took a bite.

⌁⌁⌁

Robbie decided it would be easier to go back to Beeville to get to Sinton. They wouldn't have to find a way around Goliad to get on 183, and they wouldn't have to find a way around Refugio to get on 77. Ronnie agreed. They could zip back to Beeville. They'd take another look at that large city. They figured there had to be some people there somewhere and since they were going back there anyway, they needed to take a closer look.

After that, there would be only one small town before Sinton. It was a no-brainer for the boys. They got an early start, and Beeville was just as dead as the last time they were there. Shortly after that, they sat in the middle of the road, a quarter of a mile out, staring at the community of Skidmore. It wasn't a large town, but smoke was curling out of a roof pipe on one of the buildings.

Robbie and Ronnie used their rifle scopes to check it out. The boys spotted a few people. They didn't appear to be paying any attention to the boys parked in the middle of the roadway.

Robbie looked over at his brother and shrugged. "Maybe they don't see us."

He set his rifle back in the rack and eased the Jeep forward. As they got closer to the people, they stopped and paid attention to the boys. They also all wore gun belts and had their hands on their pistols. While the men seemed to be on alert, they hadn't drawn their guns. Robbie pulled the Jeep to the curb and cut the engine.

He got out first, keeping a close eye on what the men were doing. They stood with their hands on their pistols but made no aggressive moves. He decided to leave his rifle in the Jeep and walked around to the other side where Ronnie was waiting.

Smiling, Robbie walked up to the two men nearest to them. "Howdy."

One of the men nodded.

"We're just passing through," Robbie said extending his hand.

Hesitantly, the man shook it.

"My name is Robbie, and this is my brother, Ronnie."

The man didn't offer his name back. The other man didn't say anything either. Two men came up from behind them. A sudden uneasiness overcame him. "Are we in trouble here?"

"Nah," the man said, "you two don't seem to be a threat."

"I can assure you, we're not here to cause any problems. In fact, just the opposite is true. We're on a mission to bring a new democracy to south Texas."

The man smiled and chuckled. "Just the two of you?"

Ronnie nodded. "How many citizens do you have here?"

"It varies. We come and go as we please. There's probably thirty of us here now. We all know each other and watch out for the others. There are probably a half-dozen guns pointed at you right now."

Robbie looked around, then back at the man. "We took out Sandra Hawkins, who was the dictator in Corpus Christi, and we're trying to expand on the democracy we've set up there. That way everyone can be more secure and safe. Maybe you can help."

"We heard ol' Sandra was gone. You the guys who did that?"

"Yep."

"We're liking you two more all the time," one of the men said. "We don't dish out any crap, but we certainly don't take it either. We did work for Sandra on a contract basis for a while and a little trading as well. She needed us when she was getting her regime started, but later she didn't want us around. Always too much of her shit to deal with. Had a lot of right pretty gals there though."

Robbie smiled. "We didn't care for her ways much either. Maybe we should have a meeting—see if we can work together. We could really use some help. We came from Goliad and made contact with the folks there. I think they're going to give us a hand. A group outside of Kenedy will join us if we can get a vehicle and fuel to them. We're just getting started. We have a long way to go and could use your help."

"If you're going around in that Jeep with that badass machine gun on the back, you should be flying a flag to identify yourself . . . to show people you're friendly."

"Good idea but we don't have a flag. Know where we can get one?"

"We can spare an old USA flag. We have several."

"If you'll spread the word about what we're doing and how to distinguish us from marauders, that would help. Maybe when we come back through in a couple of months, some of you guys can lend us a hand. If you can find more flags, fly them to show you're on our side."

"Maybe we'll do that. We'll see."

Robbie let it go at that. A 'maybe' was certainly better than a 'no'. They shook hands, and when one of the men returned with a flag, the boys walked back to the Jeep and attached their new colors to the antenna. The men actually waved back when the boys drove by. One stood at attention and saluted them. The boys couldn't help but smile and gave them a quick wave.

Robbie drove onward to the east toward Sinton. The sun was high in the sky now, so he was no longer driving straight into its bright light. He pushed through what appeared to be a small community at one time—it even had a river a mile or so further down—but they didn't see anyone.

Ronnie rechecked the map. "It won't be long before we should see Sinton. It's so damn flat out here. Not many trees either. This must have all been farm-land at one point. Guess there's no one to farm it anymore."

"Guess not. When we get to Sinton, if we find people there, I don't think I'd feel comfortable staying in the city, strangers and all."

Ronnie put the map back in his pocket. "Yeah, I was thinking the same thing. Great minds, huh?"

Robbie looked over and smiled. "Maybe we can go back to the river behind us. That's the only place I've seen with enough brush and trees to conceal the Jeep. Besides, we need to boil some more water."

Robbie slowed to a crawl when he spotted another vehicle. "Someone's coming."

Ronnie looked up. "Want me to get on the turret?"

Robbie stopped. "That might not be such a bad idea."

Ronnie crawled between the seats, swung the gun forward, and took the safety off. "Ready."

Robbie pulled ahead slowly, not taking his eyes off the vehicle a quarter-mile away now. *This is the first vehicle we've seen on the road. Has to be bandits to be out here. But we're not!*

At two-hundred yards between them, the other vehicle stopped. Robbie did the same. The passenger in what appeared to be a modified truck got out, stepped around the door, and walked up to the front bumper.

Ronnie climbed down off the rear of the Jeep and walked around to the driver's side beside Robbie. "They don't look hostile."

Ronnie walked around the front of the Jeep and pulled the flag upright so the men could see it.

The man waved, got back in his vehicle, and they drove toward them.

Ronnie looked back at his brother. "We're either gonna make some new friends . . . or we're gonna die."

"That was my thought."

Robbie got out and raised his arms in a sign of peace. Ronnie looked over and did the same.

The truck pulled to within thirty feet of the boys. Robbie slowly put his arms down. "Howdy!"

The man who had gotten out before got out again and took a few steps toward them. "I haven't seen anyone flying a flag around these parts for a long time, fellers. You supposed to be the good guys?"

Robbie grinned. "Well, we're certainly not the bad guys. How about yourselves?"

"We can be bad if we want to. I guess I woke up on the right side of the bed this morning. Haven't had a mean streak in me all day. We're the Protectors in these parts—just another name for police." He smiled and took a few steps forward.

"I'm Robbie, and this is my brother, Ronnie." He walked forward admiring the armor on their vehicle. "We're on a mission to bring some sanity back to south Texas. Corpus Christi is now a democratic society. We have a long way to go, but we're working on it."

"Democracy in Corpus? You have something to do with that?"

"Yes, we did. A friend of ours is the new mayor. What do you think about not having to look over your shoulders all the time and wondering which day you're going to die?"

"Sounds like a dream to me."

By this time, the driver of the truck got out and approached the boys. "Just the two of you going to turn this country right-side up?"

Robbie extended his hand. He reached over and gave it a shake. "We're looking for recruits to help us. We have access to fuel and vehicles in Corpus, and we're working on getting a communications grid going over the area. We want a unified police force to keep law and order within and from without."

"Fuel, huh? Gas has been tough to find around here."

"Work with us, and it won't be nearly the problem. Help us establish some law and order and maybe you won't always be watching over your shoulder. Find yourself an American flag and fly it to show you're on our side. You don't have to decide now. We'll be back through here in a couple of months to check on all the people we're talking to over the region.

"If you're with us, we'll see your flag. If you have some buddies who are also interested in our new democratic future, tell them to fly the flag, and we'll have a meeting to discuss the plan."

Ronnie pulled his map out. "By the way, did you guys come from Sinton?"

"Yes," the driver replied.

"How many people there?"

"Maybe a thousand or so. Don't know exactly, we never counted."

"That's a lot. We haven't seen many people behind us. Just a small group a ways back up the road, and some in Goliad. Do you think we'll have any problems going through Sinton?"

"Maybe not if you fly the American flag. Can't guarantee it though. Stay off the machine gun. We were about to take you out until you showed us the flag. Come around here."

Ronnie followed the man around to the back of his truck. On the end was a platform with a man seated comfortably on it who had not revealed himself to the boys. A cutout in the roof had several sniper rifles lined up in gun holders. "This is our secret weapon. One word from me and you're dead. You'd have never seen it coming."

Ronnie headed back to join his brother. "Where are you guys headed?"

"We're going to Beeville."

"We went through there yesterday, and it looked like a ghost town."

"It is pretty much. The place is a leper colony. You don't want to go there. Driving through is okay, but don't stop. You know about the armadillo around here, don't you?"

"Yeah. Dad told us about them carrying the disease. We eat them back home, but we're cautious about cleaning them, and we always overcook the critter. Mighty tasty. Just have to be careful with them."

"That's for sure. A couple of decades ago when the grid went down, armadillos were plentiful around here and were a ready food source. No one knew about them causing leprosy back then."

Robbie nodded. "So why are you going to Beeville?"

"I take a few supplies to them once a month that they can't get over there. Salt and a few medications mostly. Terrible disfiguring disease. Some of my family are there."

Ronnie shook his head. "I'm sorry."

He gave Ronnie a nod. "We better get on our way. We need to get there and back to Sinton before dark."

Robbie and Ronnie both extended their arms for a handshake. "Well, nice meeting you guys and tell your friends about us. Hopefully, we'll see you in a couple of months."

The men grasped their hands firmly. Robbie got back behind the wheel, and the strangers pulled around their Jeep and went on their way. Robbie just sat for a few minutes discussing their next move. They also wanted the men to be out of sight before they turned around and followed them toward the river for the night.

Robbie looked back, and there was no sign of the men. He cranked up the Jeep and turned around. He eyed the instrument panel. "Gotta put the last of our gas in this thing tonight."

Chapter 4

The river turned out to be more like a stream due to the lack of rain recently. It took longer than expected for the boys to boil enough water for the next leg of their trip. It was nearly midnight before they finished.

Robbie checked the Jeep's fluids after he emptied the gas can into the tank. "This will get us to Corpus."

Ronnie stretched out on his bedroll. "Maybe we should take a run into Beeville while we're so close. The lepers there don't seem to be driving cars and using gas."

Robbie sighed. "They can still shoot though. Might not like us stealing their gas whether they use it or not. Or maybe just not like us being there. Might not be able to make it to Corpus if we go to Beeville and don't get gas."

"Always tough decisions! So, on to Corpus then?"

Ronnie was up first the next morning. Robbie wasn't asleep, but just lying on his bedroll in thought. "You still wrestling with which way to go this morning?"

Robbie raised up rubbing his eyes. "Yeah. I think we should head on toward Sinton. We'll check the gas situation in Beeville the next time we come through here. No sense riling up a bunch of lepers unless we need something terrible."

"I'm with you, Bro. Get your shit together and let's get out of here."

Robbie loaded the gear into the Jeep, and he cranked her up. The bypass around Sinton made the trip quick and easy. One more small town between them and Gregory where they'd hit Highway 35 and head north.

Ronnie marked two more cell towers on his map. "I didn't think the land around here could get any flatter, but damn!"

Robbie chuckled. "We can sure see a long way. The only problem is we can be seen too."

Ping.

"Shit!" Robbie's eyes opened wide and focused on the gouge in the hood made by the bullet as he wrestled the Jeep to a stop. Beads of sweat instantly formed on his face. His hand shook as he grabbed for his rifle. The windshield shattered. He rolled out of his seat and behind the Jeep. "Get your ass around here dammit!" Robbie yelled.

"I'm coming."

Robbie peeked around the Jeep looking for a shooter. Another report and he homed in on the direction. "Ronnie!"

The landscape was flat, and there were no nearby buildings. Another shot. The puff of smoke from the top of a water tower. *That has to be a thousand yards.* "Why is this guy shooting at us?

"Ronnie!" he yelled again.

Robbie leveled his AR-15 toward the tower and looked through the scope. The man crouched on a walkway that circled the tank. Robbie squeezed off a string of shots guessing at the amount of bullet drop at the distance and elevation of his target.

Robbie removed the empty clip and quickly inserted another. The man scurried along the walkway headed to the other side of the tank and out of his line of sight. Robbie fired another string of shots aiming a little higher this time. The man's rifle fell first. He slipped to his knees and hung on the railing.

Robbie emptied the remainder of his clip at the man until there was no movement. He wasn't sure he'd hit him again, but he appeared to be dead.

Robbie was so intent on getting the shooter that he didn't realize until now that Ronnie hadn't fired a shot. "Ronnie!"

Fear gripped him when he heard no response. He crawled over to the rear of the Jeep. When he didn't see Ronnie, he frantically moved around the fender searching for his brother. "Ronnie!" he screamed.

He was lying beside the Jeep in a pool of blood. Robbie reached for him with raw terror. Heart pounding, he rolled him onto his back, drawing Ronnie's head into his lap.

Blood! Too much blood! It was everywhere. Robbie put a hand over Ronnie's neck, desperate to stop the flow, but deep down he already knew he was too late. There was nothing he could do.

Robbie's throat tightened with tears as Ronnie's lifeless eyes flickered open, his lips parted with a gurgling attempt at words. He strained a second more, then fell limp.

"No!" Robbie shouted, hands clutching at his brother's shirt. Tears seared his eyes, slick red coated his quaking hands, and over it all, his heart pounded cannon fire in his ears as his brother's heart stopped. "No! No!"

Chapter 5

Jen grabbed Sonny by the arm and helped him sit up on the side of the bed. "See, that wasn't so hard, was it?"

Jen pulled the walker and the IV caddy around next to him. She knelt down and slipped some walking socks on Sonny's feet. "We're about ready."

Sonny looked up. Her eyes were bright and cheery, and her smile was as broad as the Pacific Ocean. The vibrant blue color of her eyes was just as deep as the water and caught Sonny's attention. He couldn't help but manage a small smile.

Jen gave his arm a tug. Sonny wobbled a bit but managed to stand upright. He looked at her with a sense of hope.

"Work your legs up and down a few times; then we'll see how you walk."

Sonny barely got his feet off the floor as he stood trying to walk in place. Jen knelt down and massaged one leg, then went around and worked on the other. "How's that feel?"

"Better."

"Now let's see how high you can lift your legs."

One at a time, Sonny lifted his legs.

"Higher . . . higher . . ."

Each time, Sonny managed to get them up a little more. When he reached a foot high, Jen put her hand on his. "That's good."

She took the wide belt from around her waist and strapped it around Sonny. "Now, let's go to the door. You won't fall."

Sonny worked his way to the door with Jen at his side. She kept hold of the strap. When they made it to the door, she reached out and flung it open. Sonny gave her a quick look. She motioned ahead with her hand.

He stepped through the doorway and looked both directions. He started to turn left, the shorter distance to the end, but Jen guided him in the opposite direction. She was going to do her best to get him the hundred and fifty feet down the hallway and back.

Sonny stopped and looked down the long corridor, then back at Jen. "Clear to the end?"

"After that hearty breakfast you just ate? I bet you could walk twice that far if you really wanted to. You could do it for me." She smiled, gave his arm a squeeze, and fluttered her eyelashes at him.

He shook his head, but he couldn't help the small smile that escaped. At the speed of grass growing, Sonny and Jen made their way to the end of the hall. They turned around, and by the time they closed the distance to the room, their speed had nearly doubled.

"I'll make certain you get a good lunch for that effort. After you eat, we'll do it again, but next time I want you to make two trips down the corridor. I know you can do it if you eat well."

Sonny tried to make his way back to the bed, but Jen had different plans. She corralled him into the bathroom. "You're doing so well, Sonny, I think it's time for a shower." She pulled the ties on the hospital gown and removed the dripline from his hand. A little tug at the gown and suddenly wide-eyed Sonny was naked, the embarrassment showing in his face.

Jen looked into his eyes. "I've seen a million of them. Nothing to be shy about."

"Easy for you to say. You're not the one standing here without your clothes."

Jen adjusted the water, put Sonny under the stream, and lathered him up from head to toe. She cleaned every crevice and cranny and halfway down, his embarrassment was nearly unbearable, but he did manage to survive the ordeal.

"I'll get a razor and give you a shave when we finish. You'll feel much better."

〜〜〜〜〜

Robbie didn't know how long he'd been holding onto his brother, but he'd lost all feeling in his legs. He blinked his now dry eyes trying to focus on his surroundings. Robbie looked around, then down at Ronnie. Nothing would change no matter how long he sat there holding him.

Robbie got up and looked up and down the roadway, then toward the water tower. If the shooter had had accomplices, they would have had no trouble killing him. At this point, he didn't care.

He got out the tarp they'd used for shelter and stretched it out on the ground. He gently rolled Ronnie onto the tarp and fastened it around him with some leather cordage he found under the front seat. It took some effort to place his brother in the back seat. They were twins. They were identical in weight. He didn't think he had any more tears to shed, but once Ronnie was secure in the back, his brother's once smiling face concealed below a layer of plastic, he couldn't help himself. Robbie leaned against the side of the Jeep and cried.

When he crawled into the front seat, what had to be at least two hours later, he just sat holding onto the steering wheel, and he laid his head on his hands. From time to time, he butted his head against the wheel.

Robbie was impervious to the passage of time. He just knew he had to move. He had to do something. He got out to relieve his bladder and noticed his brother's gun lying on the pavement. He put it in the gun rack between the front seats and cranked up the engine. Eying the gas gauge, he thought he had enough fuel to get back home, but he wasn't sure.

It was a much shorter distance to Corpus Christi, but he'd have to go through Gregory and Portland. There were too many uncertainties in that direction. If he didn't have enough gas to get back home, maybe he could find some in Kenedy. Jake only had diesel.

Finally, he decided he couldn't take the chance of running out of gas and decided to risk going to Corpus. He could get there in no time if he didn't have any problems. He stared at the map he retrieved from Ronnie's pocket. *I'll have to go through the heart of Gregory and Portland. I could skirt Gregory, but not Portland. May as well shoot straight through both. Then cross the bay, and I'll be there in thirty minutes.*

Robbie crammed the gearshift into forward. The Jeep jerked a few times as he let the clutch out a little too fast. It didn't take long to realize eye protection was needed and he stopped again. He searched through the toolbox and found a pair of clear welding goggles. They weren't comfortable, but they were necessary for the remainder of the trip.

Robbie eased forward and adjusted the goggles as the wind in his face increased. He looked down at the speedometer as he approached Gregory—sixty-five. He pressed a little harder on the accelerator. *By the time someone realizes I'm there, I'll be gone.*

The miles zipped by. Robbie noticed smoke coming from some of the rooftop chimneys. There were people here, but he only saw one vehicle on the road, and he sped by so fast, they probably didn't even see him. He just got a glance of them.

There were a lot of buildings between Gregory and Portland; he could hardly tell where one stopped, and the other began. When he went under the overpass at Portland, someone was standing overhead with a rifle. Robbie waved and smiled as he flew underneath. He held his breath for the next mile. If the guy shot at him, he missed.

When Robbie reached the hump in the causeway, he stopped at the top and got out. It was a short distance to the harbor bridge. *There will be a barricade there.*

Robbie looked back behind him toward Portland. No one had followed. He took a deep breath of the salty air; then another tear rolled down his cheek. He looked down at the bundle in the back seat. He wiped his arm across his face and climbed behind the wheel.

At the top of the harbor bridge, there were junk cars stacked three-high across all lanes except one in either direction. A pipe gate secured the openings. Robbie stopped and cut off the engine.

"Who goes there?"

Robbie's eyes jerked upward. He stared down the barrels of two rifles trained on him from a small cubicle within the cars.

"Robbie Lindgren."

"I'll be right down."

One lady disappeared behind the stack of cars while the other kept her gun on Robbie. He pulled his goggles off and got out to stand and wait.

The woman who came down from the lookout no longer had her rifle, but she had her pistol out and trained on him. "You alone?"

"More or less."

"What's that supposed to mean?"

"My brother's body is in the Jeep."

The woman turned and looked at her partner in the cubicle. She then motioned with her pistol for Robbie to move back over toward the Jeep. She followed and looked in the back seat. She looked over her shoulder toward the cars. "It's clear here."

She turned her attention to Robbie. "Welcome back to Corpus. Sorry to see it isn't under better circumstances."

"You were expecting me?"

"Yeah, but Sean said to keep an eye out for twins. We had to make sure it was you." She motioned toward the back seat.

"What happened?"

"A sniper at the edge of some little town back there. A few hours ago. I didn't think I had enough gas to get home. I need to refuel and get back to Peaceful Valley."

"I'm sorry about your brother. We're all grateful to you two for what you did for Corpus Christi."

She opened the gate to let Robbie through.

"Thanks . . ."

"Judy."

"Thanks, Judy."

Robbie pulled up to the front of the main house at the Farm. Sean was halfway to the house where Brenda was standing in the doorway when he heard Robbie coming up the driveway. Sean turned to see the busted windshield, and his heart jumped into his throat when he caught a glimpse of the tarp-wrapped body in the back seat. He ran toward the Jeep.

When Robbie stopped, Sean slowed to a walk. He wasn't sure he wanted to hear the answer to his unspoken question. He turned back toward Robbie with a questioning look, the tears already starting to form.

Robbie choked out: "Ronnie."

Sean wrapped Robbie up in a big bear hug. "I'm so sorry!"

Brenda called out to Kim, and both gals made their way to the boys. They weren't sure what was going on, but it didn't look right. They saw the tears, then the body. Both girls immediately wrapped them up in a comforting group hug.

Chapter 6

After very little to eat and a nearly sleepless night, Robbie stood watching while four ladies carried Ronnie's body out of the barn and put him back in the Jeep. They fueled Robbie's Jeep up first thing, and he was set to head back to Peaceful Valley.

Sean kissed Brenda and Kim at the door and joined Robbie. "We'll be there later this afternoon. You know we wouldn't miss the funeral. I have a few things to take care of while the girls are packing. We'll load up right after lunch and be there as soon as we can."

Robbie checked the ropes securing the tarp and crawled in the front seat. With teary eyes, he gave Sean's hand an open slap, waved at the girls at the front door, and headed out.

After Robbie made his way through the checkpoint at the city limit, there was nothing to occupy his mind but yesterday's events. He went over and over every second of what had happened. They were just at the wrong place at the wrong time.

He felt otherwise though. Ronnie was his younger brother. Robbie had taken the lead in this adventure. He was responsible for his brother, and it weighed heavily on his shoulders. *What am I going to tell Brooke? I've let Mom and Dad down. Why Ronnie? What would Florence do without me . . . and our baby? Brooke without . . .*

Robbie slowed down. He was having a hard time seeing the road through his heavy tears. *Why couldn't it have been me?* Robbie reached over and slipped the gearshift into neutral and pressed on the brake. He closed his eyes and laid his head on the steering wheel. He pounded his forehead on the wheel, easy at first, but then harder and harder. Blood splattered onto his hands. He stopped and looked at the blood. "Ronnie!" he screamed.

In Corpus Christi at the Hospital compound . . .

Sonny finished off all of his lunch this time. He was already feeling stronger, but his memory was still shattered. Bits flashed back from time to time, but it was all so confusing. He remembered being out in the bay and he wasn't alone. He had a vision of Sean standing over him with a girl. Sonny's hand circled his wrist where the new pink scars from the rope were still healing. He had been tied. Why?

Jen came through the door with her perpetual smile. She looked at the tray. "You've made my day. You ate it all." Then she noticed his mood. "What's the matter?"

"I'm having a hard time remembering what happened. I remember some things, but it's all jumbled up."

"I wouldn't worry about it too much. Some things are coming back. That's good. In time, you'll remember the rest, and you'll be as good as new."

He looked up at her. "The optimist!"

She grinned, pulled the serving stand out of the way, and grabbed his arm. "The doctor told me to take the IV out if you ate well. You've certainly done that."

Seconds later he was free of his feeding tube. He stretched his arms, then ran his hand over his face. It was smooth as a baby's behind. Jen grabbed the walker and the waist strap. Seconds later, they were off to the races.

"Those exercises I gave you helped, Sonny. You'll be walking by yourself tomorrow, and you'll be out of here the next day for sure."

Sonny ate a good dinner followed by another and more-lengthy walk that evening. His strength was coming back quickly. Years of hard work had toughened him, and his muscles were like hardened steel. If he could only remember . . .

In Peaceful Valley . . .

Robbie pulled up to the edge of the clearing and stopped. The road into the place was much smoother than he'd ever seen it. The homestead looked quiet and peaceful though he was churning inside now that he'd arrived. Robbie signaled with a wolf howl and waited.

He slipped the Jeep into gear when his dad walked around the side of the house and returned the signal. Robbie waved, drove up to the porch, and got out.

James' smile faded immediately when he saw the broken windshield and only Robbie in the front seat. He hurried over. When he saw the tarp laying in the back, his legs almost gave out. He had to catch himself by gripping the side of the Jeep. James put his hand on the bundle, his distraught face turning back to Robbie for answers.

"I'm sorry, Dad." That was all Robbie could say, as he made his way to his father's side.

James wrapped his arms around Robbie with clenched fists. He fought back the tears as he screamed, "Melissa!" He yelled again louder, "Melissa!"

Melissa opened the door and saw Robbie and James. Her eyes lit up, and she ran down the steps, her arms flying and ready for a big hug, but the men's faces told an unpleasant story. Melissa screamed when she saw the bundle on the seat. James grabbed at her as she went down on her knees screaming Ronnie's name. "Ronnie! My baby! No!"

James helped her up and pulled her into his arms. He ushered her and Robbie to the porch. Robbie managed to get out a few bits and pieces of the story; then he noticed the sun on the tarp. The bundle needed to be moved to a cooler place until tomorrow. Robbie and James cleared the workbench off in the barn and placed Ronnie there for the night.

"Dad. I need to tell Brooke."

"I know. Go ahead. I'll take care of your mom."

Robbie ran back to the porch and gave his mom another hug. Then, as soon as James made it to the porch, Robbie headed for the Jeep and the horrible task of telling his brother's betrothed that they would never marry.

ᚷᚢᚢᚢ

The new road to his house made the trip quick and easy. His grandparents needed to be informed today too. But first, he had to tell Brooke. He dreaded this most.

Mutt started barking as soon as Robbie got to the clearing around the house. Brooke and Florence were already on the porch when he pulled up. He could see the confused looks on their faces. He was not supposed to be there. He and Ronnie were supposed to be on their adventure, but destiny had smacked them all in the face.

Robbie got out, and he couldn't hold back the tears. Brooke knew immediately. There was only one possibility for Ronnie to not be there with his brother. Brooke collapsed on the porch. Florence tried to catch her, but as pregnant as she was, there was nothing she could do. Brooke hit the floor hard, but it didn't seem to faze her. The real injury was deep in her heart.

Robbie ran to her and scooped her up to help her inside. Florence followed them in. When Brooke was safely on the sofa, Florence wrapped her arms around him and covered his face with a quick and already salty wet kiss.

Florence immediately turned back to Brooke and wrapped her up in a hug while Robbie knelt by her side on the floor. Brooke couldn't talk for crying. Florence's own tears mixed with Brooke's on her blouse.

Robbie didn't have the words. Only time would help. Robbie held her hand and patiently waited.

Time had no meaning and Robbie's leg cramped, but he changed position and stayed where he was. He waited for Brooke to do something, anything, to tell him he needed to do something other than hold her hand and stay close.

Mutt barking outside brought everyone back to reality. Florence got up to look out the window. They all heard the wolf howl. *The Carstons.* Florence returned the signal, and Reggie and Emily headed toward the porch.

Florence waited at the door. When they stepped up on the porch, they could see the tears.

Robbie looked up when his grandparents came in. Emily glanced at Florence.

"Ronnie," the young woman replied in a word.

Emily rushed to Brooke. Reggie collapsed in one of the dining room chairs, his hand to his chest.

$$\dashv\hspace{-2pt}\vdash\hspace{-4pt}\vdash\hspace{-4pt}\vdash\hspace{-2pt}\vdash$$

At the Lindgren homestead . . .

James and Melissa were still on the front porch when Sean drove up. Sean helped the pregnant Brenda out first, then Kim. The girls hooked theirs into his, and with a lady on each arm, Sean made his way to the porch.

Brenda and Kim hugged Melissa. "We're so sorry," Brenda said.

Sean shook James's hand, followed by a sincere hug; then he turned to Melissa and gave her a squeeze and a kiss on the cheek. "I'm sorry."

Melissa broke down into tears again, and Brenda and Kim joined her. James pointed at chairs, and they all sat down.

Sean glanced over at Kim holding her stomach, her head hanging down. She got up abruptly, her eyes turning to the sycamore tree. "Abigail," she uttered and hurried off the porch.

Brenda stood and watched Kim heading toward the cemetery. Melissa rose as well and reached for Brenda's hand. "The sycamore tree is a good place for crying. Let's go help Kim."

Brenda gave Melissa a loving smile. "Of course."

Sean looked over at James. "What can I do?"

James put his hand on Sean's shoulder. "We'll have to wait and see when Robbie gets back. He's with Brooke and Florence now; then he's going to see Reggie and Emily."

"Has anyone gone to Mom and Dad's?"

"No, and your sister and the Wimberleys need to be told too."

"When is the funeral?"

"I'm assuming tomorrow . . . first thing."

Nearly an hour later, the girls made their way back to the porch and joined the men.

Sean stood up. "I'll make a swing by Debra's; then I'll go tell Mom and Dad. I'll make sure Lance or Zack go tell their parents. I'll be back as soon as I can."

Sean gave Brenda and Kim a big hug and kiss, then headed out toward Debra's.

Melissa wiped her tears and looked at Brenda's belly. "I need to make some sleeping arrangements. Brenda, you can't be making that long walk to Sean's parents' house." She stood to go inside.

Kim followed her. "I'll help."

Brenda squirmed in her seat but didn't rise.

James smiled at her. "When are you due?"

"Not for another month, but he sure seems to be fighting to get out sooner."

James chuckled. *Life goes on.*

Robbie hardly slept at all. He was up and dressed before sunrise. Brooke was still asleep. Florence got up with Robbie. She quietly put the coffee on while he rummaged around outside for a shovel. Neither of them wanted to wake Brooke. He leaned the tool against the wall beside the front door and went back inside.

Florence was as quiet as she could be, but couldn't help clinking coffee cups together. "When Brooke gets up, I'll help her get dressed, and we'll be over to your parents' as soon as we can."

Robbie nodded as he stirred some sugar in his coffee. His mind was racing with bits and pieces from the previous day's events, but his mouth couldn't formulate a coherent sentence. He looked up at Florence, and the tear trickled down his cheek. He left his coffee untouched, got up, and wrapped his arms around Florence. "I've gotta go. We need to get the grave dug."

He squeezed Florence a little tighter, and she gave him a peck on the cheek. He sniffled and turned toward the door.

Mutt came up on the porch as Robbie stepped outside. He gave him a quick scratch on the back, grabbed the shovel, and headed down the steps. He turned to take a quick look at Florence, still standing in the doorway. "Since I'm walking over, I'm going to take Mutt—if that's okay with you?"

Florence nodded. "The keys in the Jeep?"

Robbie reached into his pocket, pulled out the keys, and jingled them in the air for her to see. He stuck them in the ignition and shut the door. "Come on, boy." He and Mutt headed toward the Lindgren homestead.

Mutt ran ahead, darting in and out of the brush in hunting mode, barking merrily. The dog didn't know any better. Robbie had no way of telling him the hunting days with him and Ronnie were over.

Robbie's mind drifted back. It wasn't just his brother who had died. A part of him had died as well. After all, they were twins, and besides, the only time they had ever been apart was when he and Sean went to Corpus Christi, while Ronnie stayed behind in Peaceful Valley to be with Debra. That wasn't even an entire year. For the rest of their lives, they had been inseparable.

He saw how Kathy had withdrawn into herself when young Charlotte died during Sandra's invasion of their valley. For a long time, she seldom spoke and often seemed to be in a daze. He didn't know back then how she had felt with the loss of her daughter, but now he imagined he understood. He had killed many men in his short life, and he felt no remorse for what he did. The thought that they might have been loved by someone else had never crossed his mind. Losing someone dear to your heart is painful, but to Robbie, losing his brother was like having his own heart ripped from his chest. He now understood how Kathy felt. He also realized what his mother and Brooke were feeling.

He could feel himself changing. He never had an ounce of compassion for Sandra or her men. He was a killing machine and was doing what he needed to do to secure a future for himself, his family, his parents, and friends.

He had never lost anyone close to him. He had feelings for Jade and for Florence's mom when Sandra executed the both of them, but that was different. You don't get closer to anyone than you do your twin brother, and this was especially true in their close-knit community, and when one loses the other—Robbie was feeling it deep in his bones.

He thought back to what his grandpa had told him many times. *The world is still a dangerous place, and when dealing with adversaries, you have to be ruthless. You can't consider them as men, but only as targets. Feelings cause hesitation, and hesitation will get you killed.*

I've got to be strong . . . for Mom . . . for Brooke . . . but he was my brother . . . my only brother. Nothing I can do will ever bring him back. Why weren't we more careful? But we were careful . . . How could we have known there would be a sniper on a water tower taking pot shots at the highway. There was no one else on the road. He couldn't have been waiting just for us. He couldn't have known we would be there.

Robbie stopped and sat down on a log near the path. He wiped at his eyes. He wrapped his arms around his chest. The ache was real, and it hurt badly. No matter how tight he squeezed, the pain wouldn't go away.

Mutt came over and licked at his face. Robbie didn't try to push him away. The dog sat and stared at Robbie. The tears now flowed freely as the loss of his brother sunk in. His cries grew harder and louder, even more than right after Ronnie's death. Mutt whined and laid his head on Robbie's knee.

Robbie grabbed a handful of rocks from the ground and began pelting the nearby trees as fast as he could, screaming obscenities. His heart pounded, and blood pumped heat through his arms as he threw the rocks wildly. Mutt backed away and cowered. Dizziness overcame Robbie, and he fell wallowing in the dirt, still screaming. When he finally became still, Mutt came over and laid at his feet. The dog's whines chimed in with Robbie's moans.

His tears eventually dried up, and Robbie heard a squirrel chatter at him from the treetops. He looked up and quickly located the red-tail rodent. It reminded Robbie of when he chattered at Joey. How Ronnie knew precisely what he was doing. Like they could read each other's minds. He would never have that again. He would *never* be as close with someone as he was with Ronnie.

He didn't know how long he had lain there but knew he had to get on his way. He had things to do. *Mom . . . Dad . . . I'm not the only one hurting.*

〰〰〰

Mutt started barking again when Robbie reached the edge of the Lindgrens' meadow. Robbie let out a wolf howl, and his dad came around the side of the house with two shovels over his shoulder.

Robbie threw his shovel back over his and met his dad halfway to the house. James gave him a brief hug, and they both headed toward the sycamore tree.

They had the grave half dug when Zack and Lance showed up with Debra and Beka following close behind. Mutt went running toward them when the wolf howl echoed through the woods. The girls headed toward the house. Zack and Lance followed Mutt back to the sycamore tree where James and Robbie were waiting, taking a break from the digging.

Lance made a grab at the shovel Robbie held, but he jerked it back.

"Don't make me smack you," Lance said. "I loved him too."

Robbie handed him the shovel and Zack relieved James, but James smiled and picked up the third shovel, which the boys hadn't seen leaning against the tree. Robbie sat on the bench and watched them work.

It had been only minutes when he heard the horn on the Jeep. Robbie glanced toward the edge of the clearing. Florence and Brooke were in front with Reggie and Emily in back. They parked by the house, and then Reggie made his way toward the men.

"Damn good thing you left a little for me," Reggie grumbled. "I'd have been pissed. Now give me one of those damn spades."

By the time the grave was finished, and the men had made their way back to the house, the Lins and Wimberleys were there. James and the younger men went to the barn to get Ronnie's body, while the others waited on the porch. James had constructed a stretcher with three handles sticking out on each side. When they came around to the front of the house with an empty handle, Reggie filled the space. John followed the men with the procession of ladies.

Reggie took his position and began the ceremony, but it only took seconds to realize he couldn't deliver the eulogy. His heart was broken. Reggie was just barely able to give the tribute when Lars, his best friend, died years ago. Now, losing his grandson who was so close to his heart—it was more than he could handle.

John quickly stepped in to lead the service.

He took a deep breath and looked over at Brooke. "We don't always know God's plan, but there is a reason Ronnie was taken from us. Ronnie was a strong and courageous man . . ."

John hit on all Ronnie's strong points, frequently comparing him to Grandpa Lars. He then finished the service with a passage from the bible. ". . . though I walk through the darkest valley, I will fear no evil, for you are with me; your rod and your staff, they comfort me . . ."

When John finished, Robbie stood up. "I'd like to say something." He took a deep breath as he looked over the gathering. "Ronnie and I had a dream to reclaim and unify this country once again." He glanced over at his mom and dad. "To get this country back to what you have told us it once was—a great country where life isn't an everyday struggle to just survive and where everyone isn't always trying to kill everyone else. That dream has not died with him. I may end up buried right beside him, but in his name, I will complete our dream."

When they got back to the house, Kathy helped Melissa make more coffee and some snacks. Most of the ladies fussed with Brooke around the sofa, consoling her, while the men gathered on the porch.

Robbie discussed the cell tower situation with John, Zack, and Lance. John assured him they were making progress. Sean filled Robbie in on the fuel production in Corpus Christi. "Everything is moving along great. I even went shrimping once. It's too early in the year, but we managed to catch a few. It was fun to be back out on the water again."

"I always knew you'd like getting back to Corpus," Robbie said with a smile. "There is so much there for you, and especially the girls. And by the looks of Brenda, you're going to be a daddy soon."

Sean grinned as his face flushed.

Kim came out, grabbed Sean's arm, and pulled him up from his seat. "Brenda needs you inside."

"But . . ." he resisted as Kim pulled him toward the door.

Robbie got up. "We'll chat later, Sean. I need to be with Ronnie anyway. I need to have a talk with him." With that, he trudged back to the sycamore tree and sat down on the bench.

I'm sorry I let you down, brother. We weren't careful enough. Just like Sean and I in Corpus Christi, we got caught. We, I, didn't learn the lesson from Corpus. We always thought we were ten feet tall and bulletproof. We weren't.

At the snap of a twig, Robbie glanced up. He watched silently as Brooke made her way toward him. He scooted over to share the bench with her. She wiped her tears and caught Robbie's gaze. "I know you two. I'm sure there was nothing you could have done to prevent this."

Robbie sighed, leaned over, and put his face in his hands. "That's what I keep telling myself, but on the other hand, we could have been more careful. We just didn't expect the sniper . . ."

She put her hand on his neck. "You can't always anticipate everything. There will always be something which will put you at risk. That's life."

Robbie raised up and turned toward Brooke with a newfound strength in his voice. "He will not have died for nothing. I will make this country safe, or die trying."

Brooke felt of her stomach. "That's the first time I've felt him. I will have Ronnie's son." Then she teared up and couldn't speak. *He won't ever see him.*

Robbie put his arm around her and pulled her close. They were quiet for some time, both just staring at the freshly heaped mound of dirt.

Sean got up and went inside the house to get the girls. Brenda and Kim were chatting away with Debra and Beka on the sofa. It had been a while since they had seen each other and they were catching up on all the stories.

Sean walked up to the back of the sofa and put his hand on Brenda's shoulder. She turned and looked up at him. "Time to go?"

"Yeah, it's a long drive back to Corpus."

"You should stay another night," Sally said.

"Yes," Melissa agreed.

Sean winced and looked back at Sally. "I would love to Mom, but Corpus needs me. Though the work there is coming along nicely, there is still so much to do. The crews are lost without me, and if I stay gone for more than a day, the work will stop. I can't let that happen after what we went through to get to where we're at."

Kim walked up behind Sean and gave him a squeeze on the butt. He gave her a frown for her ill-timed pinch and turned red in the face. He stepped forward and wrapped his arms around his mom. They said their goodbyes to everyone.

Sean turned to Brenda and Kim. "I've got to tell Robbie and Brooke goodbye. You girls can wait in the car if you want. I won't be long."

The ladies headed for the car, while Sean jogged up toward the cemetery.

Robbie and Brooke were both hunched over on the bench when Sean walked up and put his hand on their shoulders. "I've got to get back to the city, Robbie."

"I wish you could stay the night."

"You forced me into this job. Now you've got to put up with the drawbacks."

Robbie smiled. "I didn't think that far ahead." Robbie rose and gave Sean a big man-hug.

Brooke got up and wrapped her arms around Sean once Robbie had released him. "Thank you for coming."

"You going to be okay, Brooke?"

"Not in the next week or so, but yes, I'll be fine. I haven't been too keen on God, but I've had a change of heart. I need a place to talk to Him. I've decided I'm going to help Dad build his church. If we're going to be civilized around here, I think we need a place of worship. I haven't told Dad yet, but I think he will be both surprised and happy."

Brooke looked over at the headstones. "It seems like our cemetery is growing too fast. With Charlotte, little Abigail, and now Ronnie . . ." She sniffled and wiped her tears again. "There will be more. I hope not soon, but we can't all live forever. None of us have prayed much for some time. Maybe that will help. I think too that gathering to build a new church will bring us closer together."

Sean looked over at Robbie. Robbie shrugged his shoulders. "This is news to me too."

Sean gave Brooke a hug. "Well, I hope you get it done. I think Mom and Dad would like to have a church too. I don't know if Mom can get Dad to come regularly, but I know she'll try.

"Brenda and Kim are waiting. We need to get on the road." Sean gave Robbie a shake and another quick hug.

"I'll see you next week, Sean."

Sean turned toward the grave. "See you, Ronnie. Rest in peace."

He headed back to the car. He turned looking toward the sycamore tree. Sean sniffled, wiped his sleeve across his cheek, and climbed inside.

Chapter 7

All the following week, Robbie was up early each morning. He had breakfast ready by the time Brooke and Florence got up. By the end of the week, he had all his gear packed in the Jeep and was prepared to head back out on the road.

Florence yawned, stretched her arms high, then wrapped them around Robbie. "You sure you want to do this?"

"You know I have to. I have to complete Ronnie's and my dream. We will have a civilized country once again, and we'll all sleep better at night. You know I have to do it, don't you?"

Florence smirked. "I know you do, but now I'll be more afraid for your safety. I'll try not to cry, but I will worry more."

Robbie hugged her a little tighter. "Now let's eat before everything gets cold."

Between mouthfuls of dewberry pancakes, Brooke talked about the new church. "I still haven't told Daddy, but I will later today. I think he will be quite shocked, actually. I'll get Zack and Lance to help me."

"Aren't they busy with the cell towers?" Robbie asked.

"Yes, but that's not a full-time job. I think they can spare a day or two here and there, and maybe I can get Reggie to help too. He can get me started on the layout. I can do as much of the work as being pregnant will allow. I won't be able to do any of the heavy stuff, but my brothers will help with that, I hope. I'll do what I can, and I'll get stronger too, both physically and mentally. It's not like we're building a big house."

Robbie took a drink of his grape juice to clear his mouth. "And where do you think you're going to build the church?"

"I was hoping in the trees behind the cemetery. Your parents' place is centrally located, so I thought near there would be best, but I need to talk to James and Melissa about it first. I want it to be close enough that everyone can attend services if they want to."

On that note, Robbie finished his drink and got up. "I have to get going. I need to find Hank, the oyster guy in Corpus, and see if he's willing to go with me. I know he wanted to get back to Seadrift, but if I can actually make it happen, he may change his mind about going."

Florence stood up and gave him a warm hug. She gave him a soft kiss which left no doubt about what he was leaving behind. "Don't stay gone too long. I don't want you to miss the birth of your son."

Robbie smirked. "You know I'll be back as soon as I can, but I'm going to be taking things a little slower now. Safety first."

Florence looked into his eyes and squeezed her arms tight around his midsection. Her arms didn't even come close to going around him. They both looked down. It was like they had a basketball between them.

He kissed the tip of her nose. "He sure is getting to be a big boy!"

She gave him a smoldering look that would melt ice. "I love you."

"I love you too, baby. I'll be back in a few weeks."

He patted her on the fanny, then pried himself from her arms and gave Brooke a final squeeze. He took a deep breath and headed for the door. Mutt was waiting on the porch. Robbie gave him a nice back scratch and headed for the Jeep. As he opened the door, he gazed back at the house. *Damn, I'm such a lucky guy. I hope Brooke will be all right. She's strong. She'll be fine. And Florence doesn't cry much anymore. She's toughened up a lot the past year. They'll both be fine.*

Robbie cranked up the Jeep. He gave the gals another wave, and he was off. He looked over at the empty passenger seat and felt the tears welling up in his eyes. *For you, Ronnie.*

〜〜〜〜

Robbie stopped when he reached the main road and got out to get some relief from all the grape juice he drank before he left the house. The roadside was in full bloom with wildflowers. He noticed a large patch of the dark red Winecups that were one of his brother's favorites and a tear trickled down his cheek. *I guess there'll always be something to keep reminding me of him. Dammit, I've got to keep my mind clear, or I'll end up right beside him at the sycamore tree.*

Not far down the road, he found himself humming a tune Ronnie hummed. He shook his head. *If you're going to always be on my mind, you better help me keep a lookout. You don't want me to get killed too, do you?*

Robbie stopped at the barricade at the edge of Corpus Christi and chatted with the gals at the guard station for a while. He recognized both ladies, though he could never remember their names. He quickly remembered when they told him, but he just didn't see them often enough anymore to put a name with the pretty faces.

"You certainly break up the monotony around here," Charlize said. "We never see anyone anymore. You're the first soul who's been inbound through this checkpoint since the last time you came to Corpus. There have been a few police cars out fifteen or twenty miles just to check on things, but they never see anyone."

Robbie pushed his hat back. "That's good to hear. Don't let anyone sneak up on you though."

"We won't," the other replied. "We heard you coming a mile away. By the way, sorry to hear about your brother."

Robbie nodded. "Thanks."

She gave him a loving smile.

"Guess I better get on my way. It was good to see you two again."

He figured he would most likely find Sean at the Contractor's compound. He met a couple guys coming out as he was going in. "Sean around?"

"He's in his office," one of them replied.

Robbie knocked on the wall of the already open office.

Sean looked up. His face spread into a wide grin. "Well, lookie what the cat dragged in!" Sean pushed his chair back and stood to greet him.

Robbie looked around the large room as he strode over to the desk. Numerous framed news stories with pictures adorned the walls. Many had Sean in them, and this caught his attention. Some were photos taken on shrimp boats out on Corpus Christi Bay. In all of them, Sean had a big smile on his face. In others, Sean was working with men on cell towers and drilling rigs.

Robbie shook his hand. "Looks like you've been out and about getting things going around here. You got your own 'Press Photographer'?" he teased.

"Yeah." Sean grinned. "Isn't it cool? Actually, Sandra had a newspaperman and photographer on staff when she was alive. He came by one day looking for business."

Sean waved Robbie over to his desk. "I think we'll have the communications system up and running soon . . . at least between here and Peaceful Valley. Oil production is up to speed, and the Police Department is fully staffed. Yeah, I think we're doing well."

"I knew you could do it, Sean. And it looks like you've been spending some time out on the bay."

Sean looked over at the pictures on the wall. "Yeah, that's the fun part. It's still a little early in the season to get a lot of shrimp, but the oysters make up the difference."

"Speaking of oysters, is the 'oyster man' around?"

"Hank?"

"Yes, I'm going back up Highway 35, toward Seadrift. I thought he might like to join me."

"I think he spends most of his time over at the seafood plant. They're still getting a decent number of oysters most days. You're not going to take my best plant manager, are you?"

"I thought I'd try. He said he had a hankerin' to get back to Seadrift, it being home and all. I think he's missing someone there. Won't talk about it though.

"Anyway, he just might be able to help me get in there without getting shot. He knows the place much better than I do. You can't really tell a lot from a map."

"I'm through here. Why don't we head on over to the plant and we'll see if we can find him?"

"He's not really your best plant manager, is he?"

"Not really, but I let him think he is. That keeps him happy. He's been good to me. Brings me oysters regularly, and he's fun to listen to. He gets a little long-winded sometimes, but he always has a good story to tell. He loves to reminisce about the good ol' days."

"I'll bet. I got that impression the first time we met him. He could certainly shuck oysters faster than we could eat them, couldn't he?"

Sean patted Robbie on the back as they headed outside. "I'll be back tomorrow," Sean said to some men working on conveyor equipment.

⎯╱╲╱╲╱╲╱╲⎯

In Peaceful Valley . . .

Brooke checked her pistol, put it back in its holster, and headed out the front door. "I'll be back before dark," she told Florence.

"I'll have dinner ready when you get here. Beans and cornbread okay?"

"Works for me."

Brooke looked up at the sky as she stepped off the porch. The clouds blanketed the trees in gray, and there was a hint of mist in the air. The air was chilly, but not overly cold, just enough that she pulled her scarf tighter around her neck. "Stay, Mutt!"

She made her way to the Lindgrens', gave out a wolf howl, and told James that she was just passing through. That she'd be back later to have a talk with him and Melissa.

"We'll be here," he said and waved as she headed on to her parents' place.

Brooke signaled as she went past Debra and Beka's home, saying only that she'd stop in on her way back by.

"I'll hold you to that," Debra yelled from the door.

Brooke waved and continued on her way to the Wimberley homestead.

John stepped out to the porch. Brooke signaled again, and he waved her in. "What in the world are you up to? It seems like we never see you these days."

"I'm sorry, Dad." He gave her a big hug and led her inside where Kathy was finishing up the breakfast dishes.

Kathy dropped what she was doing and immediately came over to give her oldest daughter a long embrace and kiss on the cheek. "I've missed you so much."

"I'm sorry, Mom."

Kira came running in through the back door. "I saw you from the garden, Sis." She screeched to a halt when she saw how big Brooke's tummy was. She tried her best to wrap her arms around her big sister, but they didn't quite reach. "I don't see you enough. I've missed you."

"Things have been so hectic lately, Kira. I'll try to do better. You're growing so much. We're going to have to find you a man soon. Maybe in Corpus."

Kira smirked. "My body's been ready for a while, but I'm only seventeen. I think I'll wait a few years, Sis. Besides, men cause too many problems." Then she stood back and admired how big Brooke's belly was getting and changed the subject. "Looks like you've been doing some growing yourself. Mom and Dad keep me so busy around here that I hardly have time for myself, but I promise I'll make time to see you more. I'm going to be an aunt soon."

Brooke smiled. "Yes, you are, little sister."

John grabbed his drink off the kitchen table and held it up to Brooke.

"Yeah, I'll have whatever you're drinking, Dad, I think. Water is it?"

John nodded.

Kathy, Kira, and Brooke headed to the sofa. John got a glass for Brooke and joined them. He handed her the drink, sat down in his recliner, and looked Brooke in the eyes. "What do you have on your mind?"

"I thought I'd help you build your church," she blurted out.

John looked over at Kathy, then back at his daughter. His mouth hung open for a minute in disbelief as he stared at her. "I don't understand. I didn't think you believed in God anymore?"

"I didn't think so either, but . . ." The first of many tears trickled down her cheek. "I'm sorry. I wasn't going to cry."

Kathy put her hand on Brooke's, and she looked up at her mother.

"Since Ronnie . . . I don't know . . . I just feel so lost. I thought maybe God might help."

John leaned forward in his chair. "God can always help. You only have to give Him a chance."

Brooke looked up at her mother. Kathy nodded and smiled, squeezing Brooke's hand gently.

Brooke looked back at her dad. "I thought I'd do more than that. I thought I'd help you build your church. I know how badly you wanted that for a long time. Do you still want one?"

John was flabbergasted, and it took him a few seconds to gather his thoughts. "Yes . . . yes, of course, I do."

He hadn't had much to smile about these days with his heavy workload, and Brooke could see he was having trouble breathing from both his shock and growing excitement. He panted in short breaths, and his eyes darted back and forth between his wife and daughter.

"You okay, Daddy?"

John took a deep breath, then let out a long sigh. "Yes, I think I am. This is just such a surprise. I never thought you . . ."

Brooke reached over, put her hand on her dad's, and looked into his eyes. "I'm not sure, but yes, I think I want this . . . mostly for me, but I thought you might get some joy out of it as well."

John couldn't sit still any longer. He shot out of his chair and pulled his daughter up out of hers for a warm hug. Brooke could feel her dad's heart beating rapidly when he wrapped his arms around her.

When his breathing slowed, Brooke patted his chest and stepped back to sit down again. "I thought we'd build it near the Lindgrens'."

His eyebrows squished together as he sunk back into his chair. "What?"

"You know they're centrally located. If you want the church to be convenient for everyone, it has to be in the middle."

"But most of them don't believe in God," Kathy said.

Brooke took a deep breath. "I know Melissa does. I think she'll drag James along. Sean's parents will come I guess. Sally will get Sam to church eventually. Debra, I'm sure will go.

"What about your brothers?" Kathy asked.

"You know Zack and Lance always do what I want them to do."

Kathy smiled. "Yeah, I guess you've always been good at that."

John picked up his glass and took a sip. "Have you asked James and Melissa?"

"No, I saw James on the way over and told him I'd stop by on the way back home. I didn't say anything about the church because I wanted to talk to you and

Mom about it first. I told Debra I'd stop by their place on the way back too. If it's okay with you, I'll tell them all about it after we get through here."

John set his glass back on the coffee table. "I don't think they'd want to see the church right out front of the house every time they go outside. The cemetery is bad enough."

"Daddy, that's why I thought it should be a few hundred yards into the woods toward the highway. No one could see it routinely, but everyone would see it when they headed out to the main road. Maybe over time, Reggie and Emily would decide to drop by. But that's up to you."

John frowned. "Me?"

"You've got to come up with a sermon to end all sermons. I'll start dropping a few hints that'll get Reggie, the atheist, there because his curiosity won't let him stay away."

John laughed. "Yes, you do that. If you can get him there, I think I can come up with something that will keep him coming. I'm getting to know him fairly well. We worked well putting our early warning system together before Sandra came, and we've been doing well together with the cell tower re-vitalization program. Yes, I think I can pique his curiosity. I don't know if that'll be enough to get him to attend, but I'll do my best."

Brooke smiled. "I know you can. You can breathe fire when you want to, old man."

"Who you callin' old man, little girl?"

Brooke rose and gave her mom and dad a big hug. "I better get over and see if they're okay with the location. We'll need some help from Zack and Lance to build the church. I'll let you know how things turn out."

Kira hopped up and gave her big sister another hug. "Can I go too?" She looked up to her sis and then over to her mom and dad. "Please! I'm done in the garden!"

John looked over at Kathy and back to Kira. "Only for a couple of hours."

Brooke knew Kira would have questions, but her huge backlog was more than she could have imagined. She loved her little sister and missed her of late, so she patiently answered all of her queries as they ambled upstream. Some of the questions were about Ronnie, but mostly about the baby. Brooke reminded her that it would be five months before the little tyke made it into the world. They stopped first to visit with Debra and Beka.

Debra returned Brooke's signal and waited on the porch. She and Beka had lunch ready. Beka insisted they stay and eat with them. Brooke saw it as a golden opportunity to present her new idea.

Chapter 8

In Corpus Christi . . .

Sonny stood on the steps of the hospital, gazing across the parking lot. There were only two cars. He spotted a bench, walked over, and sat down. A mockingbird chirping in a nearby tree caught his attention. It felt good to be outside, and this warmed his heart as he drew in a deep breath of the fresh air. *Yes, much better than inside.* But Sonny had a predicament. *They said I could go home. But I don't know where home is. I told them, but they didn't have any suggestions. I had to leave.*

The sun was high above the horizon. It was just breaking through the clouds and residual morning fog. It was chilly outside, but not uncomfortable without a jacket. The slight easterly breeze was refreshing against his sun-warmed skin. He squinted and turned away from the brightness.

It's about ten o'clock. Sonny looked down at his wrist instinctively. He then felt his left wrist with his other hand. *I must have worn a watch at some point. History now. Anyway, it's ten-ish. Doesn't matter. I don't have anywhere to go. Doesn't seem right for the hospital to release me, me not knowing where I live. Maybe I don't have a home.*

Sonny stood up. The salty air made him smile. "Smells good that way," he whispered to himself and headed into the breeze.

An hour later, he stood staring at the water. Nothing had looked familiar so far. He walked down to the seawall and savored the familiar aroma. The water definitely smelled good. He could see the T-head and the boats moored there. That seemed to be the place which pulled him forward.

As he approached the boats, a familiar chord twanged in the back of his head. He looked around for a vessel which he might recognize, but none sparked a memory. Then he remembered being stranded on a beach. His boat was probably at the bottom of the bay somewhere.

There were some men on a boat up the dock farther. He drifted in that direction. He stopped and stared at a couple of brown pelicans floating in the harbor, then up at some seagulls squawking nearby.

As he approached the other men, one yelled in surprise, "Sonny!"

Sonny didn't recognize these men. He hurried toward them. They knew him!

"Where in hell have you been?" one asked.

"In the hospital," was his automatic response.

"We thought you were dead," another said. "We heard your boat left one day with your deckhand and a couple of gals but never heard anything else."

"I think I might have been close to death. I've been in the hospital for a long time. I don't remember much."

"Marcia never said anything either. She mostly kept to herself after you disappeared."

"Marcia?"

"Yeah, your wife." The man looked at him questioningly. "Didn't she come to see you in the hospital?"

Sonny stared with his mouth open, but nothing came out. His eyes scanned the men for clues. *Are they telling the truth?* They didn't seem to be playing a sick joke on him. *Have I been dead to everyone for the past few months? No one seems to have missed me . . . not even my wife! Who found me and why wasn't Marcia told if, in fact, she is my wife? She should have been the first to be notified. But I couldn't tell them who I was at the hospital. Who brought me in? Maybe whoever it was didn't know me.*

"I'm sorry, I was injured, and I've lost huge chunks of my memory. Do you know where I live?"

One of the men pointed at a tall building along the bayfront and Sonny turned. "Two blocks down the street behind that building on the corner. The red house with the swing set in the front yard. You can't miss it."

Sonny only said one more word, "thanks", then turned and walked away. He was going to get answers. He could hear the men mumbling as he left, but he didn't care about them. He only wanted to know more about who he was . . . and Marcia.

He stopped and looked up toward the top of the tall building. He could hear a couple of people arguing through an open window about halfway up. He walked right down the middle of the pavement, littered with numerous potholes.

He stopped and stared at the red house on the corner. *Needs a paint job. The yard needs cutting.* The swings on the yard set slowly swayed back and forth in the gentle breeze. *It doesn't look like anyone lives here!* Sonny took a deep breath and headed toward the side door.

He pulled the screen door open and knocked on the wooden one. Again and again, harder each time. It wasn't like he expected anyone to answer considering the condition of the property. He looked around, then jiggled the doorknob. He stepped back and let the screen door swing shut. He sat down on the porch and stared across the street. *Now what?*

Meanwhile, back in Peaceful Valley . . .

Brooke and Kira finished their lunch with Beka and Debra. Lance and Zack both said they'd help with the church. Kira gave her older sister another big hug and headed back home while Brooke started toward the Lindgrens'.

She signaled when she got there. James stepped around the side of the house and returned the wolf howl.

"Melissa's inside," James said. "Go on in."

"Actually, I'd like to talk to you as well."

"Yeah?" Brooke got his attention, and he took his cap off to wipe his brow. "And what would you like to talk to me about?"

"A church."

James squinted at Brooke. "A church?"

Brooke just stood and stared intensely at James, eyebrows raised, her blue eyes glistening in the sunlight.

Damn, why can't I ever say no to that gal? When she and Ron . . . Ronnie needed a stove for their new home, all she had to do was bat her eyes. Carrying my grandbaby doesn't hurt either. He sighed. "Come on in, and we'll talk to Melissa about it."

James gave Brooke his hand to help her up the steps. He couldn't miss seeing that her belly seemed to be growing exponentially these days. She'd be having his grandson . . . or daughter. A tear started down his cheek, and he quickly whisked it away with his shirt sleeve.

James opened the door and let Brooke through first. "Seems like Brooke wants to talk to us about a church, Melissa."

Brooke glanced at Melissa and gave her a knowing nod. She eased herself into the nearest chair and sighed in contentment.

Melissa put the lid back on her pot of stew and laid her steaming spoon down on a plate. "Really!?

Brooke just stared.

James and Melissa joined her in the sitting area.

Brooke squirmed to get comfortable facing her in-laws. "I think Ronnie's death is proof that I need God in my life. When Charlotte was killed by Sandra's men, I thought about this, but I fought it. Now with Ronnie . . . I'm having second thoughts. He has helped me deal with Ronnie's loss. He comforts me, and I can finally sleep at night."

Melissa put her hand on Brooke's. "And you think building a church will help?"

"It can't hurt, can it?"

James huffed, got up, and went to the kitchen. "You know what I think!"

Melissa turned on the sofa so she could see him. "And you know what I think, James. We have been on opposite sides of the fence in this department for a long time . . . ever since we got married, and we've gotten along just fine. I think we do need a church. We have for a long time."

Brooke got up and walked halfway between James and Melissa. "I didn't mean to start an argument."

Melissa rose and took Brooke by the arm. "We know you didn't." Melissa gave Brooke a hug; then she looked over and squinted her eyes at James. "James, you know this too."

James could see that even if they were arguing, there was no way he was going to win this one. He'd seen that look in her eyes many times. "Okay, where?"

Brooke threw him her sweetest smile. "Up the road a ways toward the highway. You just happen to live in the most central location for everyone to attend if they want."

Melissa turned to James. "Let's go see if we can find a suitable spot." She grabbed him by the arm.

Brooke led the way outside, Melissa pulling James along. James pulled back when they got to the porch. "I've got work to do!"

Melissa jerked on his arm again and gave him her best 'you're gonna be in the doghouse' look. "You've been fiddling with that tractor all morning. A little break will do you good."

James sighed. Melissa took Brooke by the hand, and they led the way. After a few steps, they both turned to make sure James was following. He was, not willingly, but he poked along.

⊣⊢⊣⊢⊣⊢⊣⊢

In Corpus Christi . . .

Sonny hiked up his britches and walked around to the side of the house. He found a window that was not latched, pushed it up, and crawled in, closing it behind him.

He tested the lights but flipped them off as soon as he found there was electricity. It was plenty light inside without it. The kitchen was reasonably clean, and there was food in the pantry. A few roaches scurried around. *Seen those before. No big deal.* He flushed the toilet in the bathroom and checked the bedclothes on the bed. *Not perfect, but way better than sleeping outside.*

He stopped and looked at some pictures hanging on the walls in the hallway and one of the bedrooms. He was in several of them with a woman and a little girl. *They both look familiar.*

He stretched his arms high in the air and couldn't hold back the yawn. He looked over at the bed. *Just a short nap.* He fluffed the pillow and stretched out. This was his first day out of the hospital, and he was feeling the strain. He still needed to take it easy until he got all his strength back.

The bed was inviting, and he dozed off no sooner than he closed his eyes.

A noise startled Sonny awake. It was dark. He raised up and blinked his eyes, trying to see something. He crept over to the bathroom and flipped on the light. He glanced over, and there was just enough toilet paper on the hanger.

Next stop was the kitchen. The clock on the wall read 4 o'clock, but Sonny doubted it was accurate. *It can't be four a.m.* The only thing he knew for sure was that it was dark outside.

He opened the refrigerator. It was nearly empty. A block of cheese appeared in relatively good condition. It had mold on the outside, but the inside was still okay. It tasted all right, anyway. He got a sip of water to wash it down and went back to the bedroom to lay on the bed.

Marcia and I are supposed to be living here. Then where is Marcia? And who is that little girl? Do I have a daughter too? The men didn't mention her. Papers! There have to be some papers around here!

Sonny got up a little too quickly, and his head began to swim. He grabbed at the bed to steady himself, but still went down on one knee. He took a deep breath and got back up a little more slowly this time. When he was steady, he flipped the light on and looked around.

There was nothing in the bureau or the closet. Sonny rummaged through the other rooms including the kitchen, scavenging for anything that would provide him with the information he so desperately needed right now to piece together his identity.

He had worked up a sweat searching the house, and his strength was fading again. He dragged himself back to the bedroom and lay down, where he quickly drifted off to sleep again.

The next time he awoke, it was light outside. The birds were chirping. He got up and checked the clock. It read 11 o'clock now, but the sun was sitting on the horizon. He guessed it to be closer to six, so he turned the clock back a little. *Why do I have such an obsession with time?* He felt his wrist.

Sonny yawned, stretched his arms up high, and headed for the front door. The air was damp, but not so cool. He would be fine dressed like he was. He ran his tongue around inside his mouth and went back inside to the bathroom. There was no toothpaste or toothbrush, but he found a clean washcloth. He wiped the inside of his mouth, rinsed with water, and spit it out.

He looked in the mirror. He needed a shave. There was a razor in the cabinet, so he took the opportunity. His mouth still felt dirty, but he did feel better overall. There was nothing in the kitchen pantry he wanted. He would find something outside to freshen his mouth, and something to eat too.

Sonny stood in the middle of the street. No direction seemed any better than the other. He'd already been to the harbor. He headed in the opposite direction, but the farther he went, the more rundown the houses were and the trashier the neighborhood became. He didn't see anyone. *Looks like I better get back down to the Bayfront where at least there are people.*

Sonny turned around to head back. He was already getting tired and dragging his feet along, his head wearily hanging down. He stepped off the curb and into the cross street.

Screeeeeech!

Sonny's head jerked up, his eyes popped open wide, and he raised his arm to shield himself. He was standing in the middle of the street, and a red truck slid to a stop a mere two feet from him. "Get out of the damn road, you son-of-a-bitch," she yelled out of the window.

The driver laid on the horn. *Beeeeeeppp . . .*

Sonny couldn't move his feet. It was as if he had stepped off in fresh knee-deep quick-set concrete.

"Get out of the road, dammit!"

Sonny put his arm down and stared at the woman. He looked down at his feet, turned, and stepped up onto the curb.

"Sonny!"

He turned and looked at the red truck again. The door opened, and a woman scrambled out. "Sonny," she yelled again.

Her face triggered a memory in the back of his head. *The pictures in the house. Marcia?* He just stood and stared. He didn't know what else to do.

She hurried over, tears streaming down her cheeks. "Sonny!" She wrapped her arms around him and held on.

Sonny gazed over Marcia's shoulder. A girl got out of the other side of the truck and headed over. *The little girl in the pictures.*

Chapter 9

Robbie awoke to the sound of roosters outside. It took him a few seconds to remember where he was. *The Farm.* How could he forget? He rolled out of bed and went into the bathroom. He quickly finished up in there, got dressed, and headed down to the kitchen to join everyone.

Christine, the Chief of Police, was sitting at the head of the table when he walked in. She pointed to an empty seat.

"Good morning, sleepyhead," Kim said with a big smile, then mouthed a kiss in his direction.

Robbie looked over at Sean sitting next to Christine. *Yes, he saw the kiss Kim blew him.* Robbie blushed. "Good morning."

Sean paid them no attention. He smiled and concentrated on his plate.

Brenda started piling food on Robbie's platter. He had to wave her off because she was overfilling it. "Thanks. That'll be plenty."

Sean nodded at her. "I could use a little more bacon, sweetheart." He looked over at Robbie, then back at Brenda, and almost in the same breath said, "Hank will be here soon. Maybe you should make another pan of biscuits and gravy. He can't ever seem to get enough of your buttermilk biscuits."

She waved her spatula at Sean with a pleased look, nodded, and turned back to the stove.

"You sure you won't stay an extra day or so, Robbie?" Christine asked.

"I'm sure. I need to get on the road. If I stay in one place too long, I have too much time to think. I need to stay busy."

"Okay, suit yourself. I'll make sure you have plenty of bacon to take along. Hank likes bacon too." Christine looked over at the Brenda. She was paying attention and nodding.

It got quiet when Hank's unique gravelly voice echoed through the kitchen. "Ahoy, mates,"

Sean got up. "In here, Hank."

The newcomer stopped and took a whiff of the breakfast aromas. Sean pointed at the seat he had vacated. Brenda was already dishing eggs, bacon, biscuits, and gravy onto a fresh plate.

Midway through his second helping, Hank slowed down enough to get a little conversation going. He looked over at Robbie. "So, we leaving when I get through?"

"That's the plan if you're okay with it."

Hank nodded. "What's with the American flag on your antenna?"

"The guys in Skidmore gave it to me. They said I needed something to distinguish me from marauders."

Sean got up and went to the broom closet. He rummaged around, and pulled out a broom handle. "Tie this on. Fly it high and stay alive."

Robbie grinned. "Thanks."

Sean went to the bathroom. Robbie sat and watched Hank eat. *We better get to Seadrift quickly. We won't have enough food to feed this guy if we take more than a couple of days. Man, he can put it away!*

Sean came back in and laid his hand on Robbie's shoulder. "I've got to get over to the office."

Robbie stood and gave him a firm handshake. "It's good to see you again, Sean. I'll be back through this way before you know it."

"Don't take too long. I hear my mechanics have your Cessna about ready for its first test flight."

A big smile spread across Robbie's face, and his eyes lit up.

Sean gave Robbie a 'thumbs up' and returned the smile. "When John and his boys were over last week working on the cell towers, I told him to ask your dad if they could get an airstrip set up soon. They took a hundred-gallon tank back with fuel for the plane. The next time you come here, you can fly home."

Robbie gave Sean another hug. "I can't wait!"

⌁⌁⌁

Marcia and her sister finished setting the dinner table. Her brother-in-law sat at the head of the table. Marcia took her seat across from Sonny next to her sister. Marcia had a lot to talk about with Sonny. She wanted to be able to look directly at him. Little Lola, who was not so little anymore, sat next to her dad.

"We've been staying here with my sister and her husband since you went missing. Now that we're all together, I want to know exactly what happened to you and who's responsible."

Sonny hadn't had much to eat all day and was starved. He paid more attention to the food than Marcia. He gave her a blank look and then washed down his mouthful of food with a swig of water. "I don't remember," he said and refocused on his plate.

"What do you mean you can't remember? If you don't know, who does?" She tapped her fork on the table, her impatience with Sonny showing.

Sonny washed another bite down. "Will you stop that! I woke up on a beach, cold and hungry. I could hear someone talking. They carried me to their boat. I faded in and out. Next time I woke up, I was in the hospital. I was there for several months before I finally woke up again. They fed me, got me walking, and kicked me out when they thought I was okay.

"I made my way to the harbor, and some guys recognized me. They told me where I lived, and I went there, but the place was locked up and empty. I broke in a back window and spent the night. Yours and Lola's pictures looked familiar, but I couldn't even remember your names. I still don't feel I really know you two."

Sonny took another bite, and Marcia just sat there flabbergasted. Marcia's sister finally spoke up. "And I guess you don't remember us either?" She looked over at her husband, then back to Sonny.

His mouth was full, so he just shook his head and kept on eating. Lola gave him a little elbow into his ribs, and he looked over. She was such a beautiful girl, her dark eyes, and long dark hair, but to Sonny, she was a stranger. Sonny, with a sad look on his face, shook his head.

With a look of disappointment, she turned back to her plate. She picked at her potatoes as the realization that her own daddy didn't know her sunk in.

"I'm sorry, but I don't remember you either. I wish I did, and maybe in time I will, but right now . . . no."

A couple of minutes later, Lola pushed back in her chair, got up, and stomped off toward her room.

Sonny sighed. *I don't blame her.*

⼀⼁⼀⼁⼀

Robbie headed across Corpus Christi for the harbor bridge with Hank riding shotgun. With his belly full, Hank seemed to be brimming with energy. He didn't stop talking until they reached the checkpoint on the bridge. Robbie got out and walked over to the sentry station. One of the women was climbing down the ladder. When she got to the ground and turned toward Robbie, he recognized her as the same one who stopped him when he brought his brother through here. "Judy, isn't it?"

She smiled. "Yes."

"Hank and I are headed up 35 toward Seadrift. He's from there."

Hank gave a wave.

"Again, I'm sorry about your brother. You be careful, you hear?"

"We will."

Judy kissed him on the cheek. "For luck."

Robbie couldn't help but smile. He touched the cheek gently where she'd kissed him. "Thanks."

She winked, and Robbie turned and headed back to the Jeep. Judy swung the gate open.

⌐√⌐√⌐√⌐√

When Robbie got over the causeway to Portland, he hit the gas. He didn't want to meet up with the rifleman on the overpass he saw there last time. Again, there was someone on the bridge. Robbie waved as he went under. He couldn't tell whether or not the guy waved back, but at least he didn't shoot at him. *If I make it back through here again, I'll have to stop and check this guy out. If he's the same guy, maybe he'll remember the Jeep.*

Hank was momentarily silent when they sped through Portland, but resumed his chatter past Gregory. Robbie noticed the temperature gauge creeping up toward hot, so he stopped. There was a leak in the radiator hose. It was close to the clamp and he was able to cut it off and clamp it back on, but he'd lost a lot of water. He refilled it with half their drinking water. He'd have to add more later if they could find a small stream.

Hank resumed his chatter the rest of the way to Aransas Pass. "My wife passed along many years ago before I left Seadrift. Died in a car accident. She left me with a five-year-old daughter. Clara was her name. She stayed with friends; then I got trapped in Corpus. I wanted to go home but got caught up in all the rioting. Then Sandra made it impossible to leave. I wonder if she's still alive? Maybe she found a husband. I could have grandkids. Wouldn't that be something?

"I had a couple of old buddies too. Homer was a mean son-of-a-bitch and about as tough as they come. He's gotta be still kickin'. I guess it's too much to expect for everyone to be alive and well? I can hope, can't I?"

At the outskirts of Aransas Pass, the highway skirted the city, and Robbie pulled up on top of the overpass there. Hank grew quiet as they looked over the scene.

Robbie turned in his seat. "What do you think?"

"There will be people. This is a fishing village. Some tough sons-a-bitches around here. These people will know how to take care of themselves. Whether or not they're friendly, that's another story."

Robbie took a deep breath. "Maybe I should get on the turret just in case."

"That's your call."

"You know how to drive this thing?"

"Of course."

Robbie pulled himself up behind the machine gun while Hank got in behind the wheel. Robbie then grabbed the American flag, tied the broomstick on so he could hold it high in the air, and told Hank to go back to the exit into town. "My AR-15 there in the rack is loaded if something happens. You do know how to shoot, don't you, Hank?"

"How? Of course! Can I hit anything? That's a different story. My eyes aren't quite what they used to be."

"That's okay. Just point and shoot. Maybe you'll get lucky."

Hank grinned and put the Jeep in gear.

They made it to what was left of a McCoy's Lumber Yard before they saw someone. Hank slowed to a stop. Two young boys about Robbie's age, each with pistols on their hips, drew their weapons when they saw the Jeep. They didn't point them, they merely held them up to let Robbie and Hank know that they were armed.

"Ease on ahead, Hank."

Hank slowly let the clutch out but kept his foot off the accelerator. The Jeep crept toward the boys. Robbie put his hand on the machine gun and waved the flag back and forth a little. He noticed the smile on one of the boys' faces.

"Close enough, Hank." Robbie never took his eyes off the boys, nor his hand off the gun. "You boys want to talk, or do you want to shoot?"

Robbie watched as the boys looked at each other and said a few words back and forth that he couldn't hear. They both turned their attention back to Robbie.

"Talk," one said.

"Holster your pistols then."

Hank killed the engine, and when the boys' guns were safely tucked away, Robbie climbed down from the Jeep turret and made his way toward the boys. He kept his hand on his pistol.

"We came from Corpus Christi. We're trying to get some law and order over the area so we'll all be a little bit safer around here."

"The only law in Corpus is Hawkins's law. We don't take to well to that bitch's law."

"Sandra Hawkins is dead. We're the law there now."

The two boys looked at each other. "That why you're wavin' that flag?"

"Yep. Good rules, freedom, a new police force, and equality for all."

"You ain't shittin' us are you, mister?"

"No, not at all. Are there others here we can talk to?"

"Yeah, there are a lot more. We're just the expendables."

"Expendables?"

"Yeah. There are two of us at each entry into the city. We may die, but so will you if our police force hears some shootin' out here."

"We would sure like to have a friendly conversation with your leaders if we may. It's getting late; can we come back in the morning? Tell them we'll be right here just after daylight."

"We can do that."

Robbie shook the boys' hands and eased back over to the Jeep, still not fully trusting the boys and not taking his eyes off them, nor his hand off his pistol. "Until tomorrow."

Hank cranked the Jeep up and turned around. When they were a quarter-mile away, Robbie breathed a sigh of relief. He pointed to a location from back behind them where he'd spotted a place to spend the night.

There was a shallow ditch to cross and enough brush that they could duck back into the trees to find a place to conceal themselves. Robbie looked both ways down the highway just before they drove through the ditch. A few minutes later he patted Hank on the arm. "This should be far enough."

Hank shut off the engine, and the first words out of his mouth were, "I'm hungry. What's for dinner?"

Chapter 10

Hank's snoring woke Robbie up before daylight. He reached for a stick and whacked his leg. Hank snorted, turned over on his side, and breathed a heavy but relatively quieter tone.

Robbie lay looking up at the stars. The clear night made the air a bit cooler than the night before. *It seemed a little too easy yesterday. Better pay attention today. Expendables? Can the lives of a few be so unimportant that they can be so quickly thrown away for their security? Maybe they don't have a security problem . . . perhaps they have been relatively safe over the years . . . maybe they have not had the intruder problems we've had. I think the flag helps.*

The eastern sky showed a hint of light. Robbie got up and grabbed some food out of the Jeep. He nibbled on some leftover bacon while he stretched his legs and relieved himself. A rabbit sat watching him nearby. "What are you lookin' at?" Robbie smiled. "Lucky for you, you didn't show up last night. We'd have had you for dinner with leftovers for breakfast."

Hank moaned and rolled over. "Who you talkin' to?" he mumbled.

"Just a rabbit. You about ready to get up? It's getting a little light in the east."

"Yeah, I gotta pee anyway. May as well get up. Do I smell bacon?"

"I saved you a couple of pieces, and there's one biscuit left."

"I'm going to need a little more than that, son."

"You'll have to fill up on water for now. This is all we have. Maybe we can find another rabbit this afternoon."

Hank grunted and farted. He took a big swig of water and burped loudly. Robbie shook his head, crawled into the Jeep, and waited for Hank to get himself together. Twenty minutes later, Hank climbed in the passenger seat and looked over at Robbie. "Ready."

When they got close to Aransas Pass, Robbie stopped and got in back while Hank got behind the wheel. The machine gun and Robbie's pistol were still ready from the day before. Robbie unfurled the flag with the broomstick attached, so he could fly it high when they found their welcoming committee.

As they neared the old McCoy's store, Robbie could see several vehicles in the parking lot that weren't there yesterday. "Slowly, Hank."

Hank put the gearshift into low and lifted his foot off the accelerator. The Jeep crawled forward. Robbie waved the flag a little just like he did the day before. A hundred yards out, he told Hank to stop. They rolled to a halt and he waved the flag again, holding it up a little higher.

There didn't seem to be anyone there. "This is a little creepy, Hank."

Robbie looked around at the other buildings and brush. He didn't see anyone.

Hank killed the engine and climbed out.

"What are you doing, Hank?"

"I'm going to give this a chance. You wait here and keep a hand on the machine gun."

Hank took off his baseball cap, wiped his brow with his sleeve, and walked forward toward the vehicles in the parking lot at McCoy's. Halfway there, he held his arms up high and kept on walking. He stopped ten feet from the closest car. "Anyone home?"

⌇⌇⌇⌇⌇

Reggie gave out a wolf howl at the edge of the clearing near Brooke and Florence's home. They were on their way to the Lindgrens' with some .30-cal. reloads for James, and Emily insisted they stop to visit with the girls for a while.

No one answered, so he and Emily headed on toward the Lindgrens'. His wolf howl produced the same result there. "I don't know what's going on, Emily, but there's something mighty strange around here."

Reggie and Emily both looked around, and there wasn't a soul stirring. Reggie took a deep breath, frowned, and scratched the back of his neck. "Mutt would have been near Florence and Brooke's if they'd been home. I expected to find them here at the Lindgrens', but this is queer."

"I agree," Emily replied.

Some pounding caught Reggie's ear, and he turned his head toward the old sycamore tree. "It's out past the cemetery. That's not a woodpecker. Someone's hammering."

Reggie headed that way, and Emily followed. Reggie stopped next to the sycamore tree and listened. He stared at Lars and Eileen's graves while he waited for the hammering to resume so he could home in on the direction. *Sure miss you guys these days.* He glanced over at Charlotte, Buster, and baby Abigail's gravestones and the hammering started again. It appeared to be coming from down the road.

They walked toward the noise. A few hundred yards down the road they heard voices. Reggie looked at Emily and grabbed her hand. He kept his other hand on his pistol. When he rounded the curve, he could see James and Melissa, Brooke and Florence, and others. Lance and Zack were down the road a piece, headed in their direction with a log on their shoulders. Reggie and Emily just stood and watched.

Melissa was the first to notice them and waved them over. "Hi, Dad . . . Mom."

Melissa met them halfway to the groundbreaking. "Surprised to see you guys here."

Reggie smiled. "What's going on?"

Emily elbowed him. "Say 'hi' first."

Reggie frowned. "Hi . . . and what's going on?"

Melissa smiled and gave her dad a brief hug and a kiss on the cheek. "We're building a church."

"A what?"

"You heard me . . . and we're building it for atheists too."

Emily snickered. "I'm not an atheist . . . just not a real believer."

Melissa hugged her mom. "I know, but I'm fairly certain Dad is. I talked to John, and he won't be preaching fire and brimstone. He wants everyone to feel comfortable attending his services."

Reggie huffed and left Emily and Melissa standing. He walked closer to the construction. Only one hole didn't have a post in it, and Lance and Zack walked up with the last one. Brooke, Florence, and the other girls were nailing stringers to tie all the posts together.

Reggie forced a smile when John saw him watching the construction. The younger man walked over to Reggie and gave him a firm handshake and an ear-to-ear grin.

"John."

"Reggie."

"Looks like you're finally going to get your church, huh?"

John's grin grew wider. "Looks like it."

"How'd you pull this off?"

"Actually, it wasn't me. I had all but given up on getting a church built in my lifetime. I knew one would be built eventually, but didn't think I'd ever see it. To tell the truth, Brooke came to me last week and said she wanted to build a place of worship to help her with losing Ronnie."

"Really?"

John nodded. "I thought she was lost, but now she seems to have found God again."

Reggie stood with a gruff look. "Still, I should have been informed before you started building. You know I like to know what's going on around here."

"Don't blame me, Reggie. That was Brooke's doing."

"Still, someone should have told me, dammit."

"I know, and I'm sorry, but Brooke wanted to get the walls up at least before you found out. Past the point of no return, so to speak."

Reggie glanced over at Brooke. Her hair was a mess, and she was standing there, hammer in hand, watching his and John's conversation. She flashed him a quick smile.

Reggie turned back to John. "She . . ." Reggie shook his head and looked down.

John gave Reggie a gentle shove. "How about I make it up to you?"

"And how are you gonna do that?"

"I'm going to write a special sermon just for you."

"You don't have to do that, John."

"Oh, I insist. You can stand outside if you wish, but you'll want to hear what I have to say."

Reggie frowned. "You're not afraid the place will spontaneously combust if you even mention my name?"

John laughed. "I don't think you're that bad a guy, Reggie. I'm not going to try to convert you either if that's your concern. I just think we need to be friends and respect each other's wishes with regards to God. We've been working really well together dealing with Sandra Hawkins as well as getting the communications up and going between here and Corpus Christi."

Reggie took a deep breath. "Maybe you're right . . . as long as you're not trying to change me."

"I'd never try to do that, Reggie. I have too much respect for you."

Reggie cocked his head a little and squinted his eyes at John.

John smiled. "Well, maybe I'd try a little bit, but I know that's a losing cause. You'll come to God when and if you want. You don't need me causing friction around here."

Reggie extended his arm and John grabbed his hand. "Holy Roller!"

"Devil Worshiper!"

They both broke out in a big laugh. All eyes turned toward them.

Hank looked around and then back toward Robbie on the machine gun. "Hello!"

"You don't have to yell," a voice from inside the shadows of the McCoy's building said.

Hank's head snapped in that direction. "You going to come out and say 'hi', or what?"

"Just seein' how you guys react."

"We don't mean you no harm." Hank looked back and called Robbie. "They're here. I'm waiting for an invite."

Chuckles emanated from the shadows. "Tell your boy to get down from that machine gun, and we'll come out."

"And you're not going to shoot us?"

"Not unless you do something stupid."

Hank looked over his shoulder. "They want you to get down off the turret, Robbie."

"Yeah?"

"They said they'd come out if you get down."

Robbie looked around 360° and then back toward Hank. *Guess we've got to take some chances if we're going to get anywhere. They could have picked me off with a rifle if they wanted to.*

Robbie shook his head, then climbed down. He stepped around to the side of the Jeep. He glanced over at his AR-15 in the gun rack and back to Hank. They would be dead if that's what the men inside the building wanted. *I hope we're doing the right thing, Ronnie.*

Robbie walked over beside Hank and waited. One by one, eight men came out. The first four carried rifles. The last four were older gentlemen and only carried pistols.

Robbie smiled and held up his arms to show he was at their mercy. "My name is Robbie. This is Hank."

The four men with rifles paired off on either side of them. One man stepped forward to introduce himself. "Hi, I'm Aaron. The others are the leaders in the city."

They stood and listened attentively as Robbie spelled out the situation in Corpus Christi and their plan for south Texas.

The men explained they didn't have any significant problems except with fuel. They relaxed considerably when Robbie told them he could help with that.

"Maybe we should discuss this further over brunch," Hank suggested. "You know where a guy can find a bite to eat around here?"

Aaron looked around at his associates. They nodded. "If you'd like to join us, we'll lead you into town. There won't be any problems that way."

"Thanks, Aaron, we'd like that."

Robbie followed Aaron, and one of the men with rifles followed Hank.

"I'm Buddy." He extended his hand and Hank gave him his best firm, yet friendly, handshake.

By late afternoon, Robbie and Aaron had a plan worked out. Aaron had his men find some old flags and put them on the vehicles which patrolled the perimeter of the city.

"So, Robbie, if someone comes to town displaying the American flag, we can assume they're friendly?"

"That's the word I'm spreading, but we're a long way away from that. Be cautious of all visitors. I'm just saying don't assume everyone to be aggressive. After I make it all the way back home, I'm coming around again. I'll have more information about fuel and, hopefully, about getting some communications set up around here.

"We're finding cell tower locations as we go. We have men working on them, so maybe one day we can communicate quickly and be able to respond to any emergencies. One more thing, tell everyone that if they see a small yellow plane flying over, don't shoot at it. That'll be me."

"You have a plane and pilots too?"

"I taught myself how to fly. That's a long story. I'll have to tell you about it someday. I've only done it once but will be going again as soon as the mayor of Corpus gets my Cessna ready for me. I see you have some long stretches of highway around here. If you designate one as a runway, I'll drop in on you from time to time. I can bring some spices and maybe tequila up from Mexico."

"We'd appreciate that. We don't get much booze here. What little some of the locals make isn't very good. Some honest-to-goodness real chili powder would be great too."

Robbie got to his feet. "It's getting late. If we're going to get out on the road, we better be going."

Aaron stood up as well. "We'd love to put you up for tonight. Are you in that big a rush?"

Robbie looked over at Hank.

Hank smiled and turned his gaze toward Aaron. "Does that include breakfast?"

Aaron stroked his scraggly beard. "Of course, it does."

Hank raised his eyebrows as he glanced back to Robbie, licking his lips in anticipation.

Robbie snorted his defeat and turned back to Aaron. "Looks like it's settled."

In Corpus Christi . . .

Marcia drove Sonny over to their old house. "Since you don't remember me, I think we'd all be more comfortable if we didn't spend the night together. I'll come back in the morning and pick you up. We can talk more then."

Sonny nodded but kept his eyes focused on the covered plate in his lap Marcia had made him for breakfast. "Yeah, I guess so." He picked at the packaging, his mind churning in the darkness, probing for answers.

They didn't say much as they drove. Sonny watched out the window when they got closer to the house, hoping he would recognize something. *I can't believe I've lived here all my life and don't recognize a damn thing. A wife and a kid. How do you forget stuff like that?*

Sonny took a whiff of the air. They were getting closer to the bay. His nose seemed to be working well, and he knew he liked the Bayfront, but nothing down there seemed familiar either. Maybe in time.

Marcia pulled up in front of the red house. She handed him a key. "There's no sense you having to crawl in and out a window, and I certainly don't want you leaving it unlocked."

Sonny took the key. "I'm sorry I don't remember you and Lola."

"You will in time. Your clothes are still in the closet if you want to clean up. I didn't get rid of them after you disappeared. Just didn't seem to find the time."

Sonny got out and shut the door. He stuck his head inside the window. "Tell Lola I'll be all right, will you?"

Marcia leaned over and patted him on the hand. "If you have dreams, try to remember them. They could be memories coming back. Ask me, and I'll try to help you get your past straightened out."

Sonny nodded and stepped away from the truck. He stood and watched until she disappeared around the corner. He held the key up, sighed, and headed toward the house.

Chapter 11

Aaron met with Robbie briefly the next morning before he and Hank left. "There are some mean sons-a-bitches over in Rockport, Robbie. It would be super dangerous for you and Hank to go there, especially the way you two confronted us. With the promise of fuel in the future, I think we can spare a little to go there and try to reason with them ourselves. They know us, and they won't shoot first and ask questions later."

Robbie pulled out his map and showed it to Aaron. He scrutinized the area. "You can cut across here," Aaron said pointing. "Then this road will take you to Bayside. You'll almost get to Refugio and take a right here. There's not much out there, and you probably won't see anyone. You can make good time and be back to 35 before you know it."

"Sounds good to me. Don't forget to tell the guys in Rockport about flying the flag if you can get them on our side."

Aaron smiled. "I won't forget. Fuel is too important to us, and to have even a small amount would be more precious than gold used to be decades ago."

They shook hands, and Robbie and Hank were off again.

Sean paced back and forth. "You've got to breathe, one, two, three . . . that's what they said you've gotta do! Where the hell is Kim?"

Brenda giggled at Sean's state. "Kim will be here as soon as she gets dressed. Now calm down. You're going to make me have this baby right here with you as the deliveryman."

Brenda pulled out her suitcase and went to the dresser.

Sean stopped in his tracks. "We've got to get you to the Hospital. And you shouldn't be lifting that."

"It's an empty suitcase, for Christ's sake. Now sit down and shut up for a minute. You and I both know there will be no one there until 8:00 a.m. That was one of Sandra's rules, and it hasn't changed."

Sean looked over at the clock. "Three hours! You're not going to have him here, are you?"

"No, babies take a while . . . most of the time. This will be my first, and they usually take even longer. It'll probably be afternoon before this one makes it into the world," she said trying to calm the expectant father down. "Now relax. Go get me some strawberries out of the field. I'm craving freshly picked ones."

"You're about to have a baby, and you want strawberries?"

"Yes, dear. And you know how I like them." She raised her eyebrows and tilted her head a bit.

Sean's eyes darted to the door, to Brenda's stomach, then back to the door. Brenda huffed. "Well?"

Sean kissed her on the cheek and headed out the door with Brenda's chuckle following him. *I'm the boss here now. I'm going to have to change Sandra's rule. Surely someone can man the emergency room around the clock. Most of them stay at the hospital anyway. Why do they lock down the place every night? This will never happen again!*

A few seconds later, Kim gave the door a couple of knuckle taps and walked in. "Where's Sean?"

"I sent him out for some strawberries."

Kim laughed. "What?"

"He thought I was going to have this baby in the next five minutes, the way he was acting. I had to get him out of here. He was making me nuts!"

"Yeah, I heard Christine yelling at him when he woke her up. She doesn't take to that shit in the middle of the night. She really likes Sean, but liking doesn't extend to her shuteye."

Brenda put the last of her stuff in her suitcase and set it by the door. She noticed Kim's glassy eyes. "You remember what we decided?"

Kim wiped her eyes and nodded. "I've been missing Abigail a lot the past few days." She wrapped her arms around her tummy and squeezed.

"I know you have. As soon as we get this little tyke out and fattened up a bit, we'll take a trip to Peaceful Valley so you can visit her grave. We'll take a few days so we can catch up with everyone else too."

Kim sniffled and ran her extended finger under her nose. "I'd like that." She leaned over and gave Brenda a hug. When she did, Brenda jerked and grabbed at her belly. "How far apart?"

"Uhhggg! About ten minutes and getting stronger."

Brenda straightened up a bit, and Kim loosened her hold on her. "I want you in the delivery room too, Kim. This will be your baby just as much as it is mine. You, me, and Sean are a family. Soon we'll be four . . . equally . . . just like we are with Sean. Got it?"

Kim pushed her hair back over her shoulder. "You're a wonderful partner, Brenda."

"I love you just like I love Sean . . . and Abigail, rest her soul."

Kim grabbed the suitcase, and they headed for the kitchen. She set the bag by the door. *May as well leave something for Sean to do to keep him busy. He can put it in the car.*

Sean came in with the strawberries. He washed them, picked out a banana, and cut them up just like Brenda liked. He was still breathing heavily from his rush to grant her request when he handed her the bowl.

Kim watched Brenda pick at the bowl of fruit. Sean paced around a few seconds until Brenda suggested to him, "Why don't you take the suitcase to the car?"

When he hesitated, she waved at him. "Go on!" she said, and Sean darted out, grabbing the suitcase on the way.

He was back in less than a minute and pulled a chair up beside Brenda. He leaned toward her. "You about ready?"

She forked another strawberry, looked up at him, and nibbled at the sweet, freshly picked fruit. "In good time."

Sean looked up at the clock. He sighed and rested his chin on his hand; elbow on the table. He jumped up when she screamed unexpectedly.

"Eeeyyoowweee!" She squinted at Sean. "I think your son is playing soccer with my kidneys."

"Maybe we better head to the Hospital."

Both Brenda and Kim looked over at the clock.

Kim shrugged her shoulders. "Some of the staff may be there early. It's a weekday, after all."

Brenda shook her head. "I'm not having this baby in the car. We'll wait." She then sucked in a quick breath of air and grabbed her stomach. "The contractions are getting much closer together. He seems awfully intent on getting out right now."

Another contraction and Brenda dropped her fork, grabbing the table edge. This was a long one. When it slacked off, she tried to get up with Sean's help.

He led her to a recliner in the living room. "If your son . . . or daughter is going to come before the Hospital opens, I'd rather have it here. Kim can help me while you run over and bring a nurse or doctor here to the house."

"But what can I do now?"

"Make yourself scarce until I call you."

Sean went back to the kitchen and made himself breakfast. He didn't care for oatmeal, but it was the only thing he knew how to fix. He could roast up a pig or raccoon over an open fire, but in the kitchen, he was lost.

After Sean left, Kim turned to Brenda. "You're not actually planning on having it here, are you?"

"Hell no . . . I just needed to get him out from under our feet."

When he peeked back into the living room to check on Brenda, she shook her head. He ran and took a shower, passing Christine on the way there. "You going to work?"

"Yeah." She put her hand on his arm. "Settle down. Babies are born all the time. Everything will be fine."

He managed a smile, nodded, and headed to the bathroom.

He didn't stay in the shower long before he dried, dressed, and returned to the living room. He looked at Brenda with a hopeful expression.

She nodded, and Sean slapped his hands together. "Okay, then."

He got Brenda comfortably into the car, then slid in behind the wheel. He fumbled for his keys and dropped them at his feet.

"Sean!"

The keys slid further away as he searched for them by touch.

"Sean, slow and easy," Brenda said with a smirk when he finally came up with the keys. "I believe we have nearly half an hour and it's only fifteen minutes to the Hospital."

Robbie started the Jeep. He looked over at Hank. "To the next adventure."

Hank smiled and dropped his head to scrutinize the map while Robbie drove north toward Rockport. It wasn't long before he pointed. "There's the road we want to take around Rockport."

Robbie slowed and took a left. Hank put the map away, having memorized the route, grabbed the AR-15, and laid it across his lap. Robbie watched as his partner's demeanor changed from navigator to lookout. The young man wasn't about to leave all this chore to Hank. Two sets of eyes were better than one, and you never knew when someone might be waiting in hiding. Robbie focused on anywhere someone could hide. He was especially tuned in for water towers.

The area was desolate and flat, only now they couldn't see very far because of the mesquite brush. They saw plenty of water when they got to Bayside on the back side of Copano Bay.

Robbie stopped, and he and Hank got out to stretch their legs for a while. They could see some old, rundown houses, but no people.

When they reached the road that would take them back to Highway 35, Robbie pulled over at the stop sign and glanced at Hank. There was no road straight ahead. Left would take them to Refugio and right where they wanted to go.

A shot rang out to the left. Robbie jumped in his seat, and the hair stood up on the back of his neck. He didn't see anything down the road where he thought the shot originated.

Hank gave Robbie a thumb signal to the right. "Probably someone hunting. Nothing to worry about." The young man didn't hesitate to follow the older man's suggestion.

A few miles up the highway, Robbie slowed when he saw something dark cross the road a quarter-mile ahead. As he neared it, he slowed even further. His eyes caught movement in the weeds. He pushed the clutch in and let the Jeep roll to a stop. He quietly opened his door and stepped on the side-bar. He could see something moving, but couldn't tell what it was.

"Hand me the .22 mag," he whispered.

Robbie checked the wind. It was in his face from the southeast. He went into hunting mode. He crouched down and moved slowly and silently. He could hear something grunting. Inch-by-inch, Robbie moved with the stealth of a large cat.

He leveled his rifle, took aim, and squeezed.

"What ya got?" Hank hollered.

Robbie walked over to the edge of the water that had accumulated in the ditch from recent rains. He reached down and grabbed the small pig by the hind leg and held it up. "Dinner!"

By the time Robbie made it back to the Jeep, Hank was already out with his knife in hand. "Hank, I'll do that."

"I may be a bit older than you, son, but I'm assisting you on this mission. Now let me help."

Robbie smiled. "How about I hold him for you?"

Hank nodded.

Remembering the shot earlier, Robbie watched up and down the road while Hank field dressed the pig. When he finished, they tied the carcass onto the rollbar at the back of the Jeep, and headed on. It didn't take long to reach the crossroads at Highway 35. Robbie stopped and looked both directions as well as behind him and the road ahead. They hadn't seen a soul since they left Aransas Pass.

"Think we can risk a fire?"

"Nobody gonna see the smoke if nobody's around. We haven't seen anyone all morning. Don't see why not."

Robbie eased forward to the edge of 35 where he could see down the road in both directions. "Well, let's get a fire started here where we have a good line-of-sight."

Hank was already headed toward the mesquite brush.

Robbie had the skillet out and as many pieces as he could fit in the cast iron pan when Hank returned. Robbie started the fire and put the skillet on. He skewered the remaining pig to roast over the open fire. The meat in the skillet was ready in no time, and they munched happily on that while they let the carcass cook for a couple of hours. Then they doused the fire.

They decided to head toward Austwell first. The map indicated the road to the east would wind around through the country about ten miles, but eventually get them to the bayside city. After they checked out Austwell, it was only a short hop to Tivoli.

It was still a couple of hours before dark when they reached the edge of the small village. Robbie stopped in the middle of the road and killed the engine. A small trickle of smoke was rising from the brush ahead and dissipating quickly in the southerly breeze.

Robbie's ears perked up when he heard the clanging of metal. He reached for his pistol. Goosebumps popped up on his arms. "Looks like there's someone here," Robbie whispered.

Hank, his eyes squinted and sharp, AR-15 squeezed tight in his hands, finger on the trigger, scanned the treeline for targets.

The metal clanged again.

"Sounds like someone is hammering on something, Hank. We're upwind. If I start the engine, they may hear us. They may be able to smell the pig we cooked and already know we're here. Stay here. I'm going to try to sneak up on them. Let me have the AR-15, and you get on the turret. Keep your eyes open."

Hank nodded and started to get out.

"Pssst!"

Hank turned around.

"Don't shoot me when I come back."

They both smiled and Robbie eased toward the sound.

⌁⌁⌁⌁

The Hospital didn't open until 8:00. Kim stayed with Brenda while Sean paced around the car, sticking his head inside the window every trip around the vehicle to check on the girls.

I'm going to be a daddy today. Are all new dads this nervous? Anything could go wrong. I'm glad we're here and not in Peaceful Valley. Melissa and the girls would do fine, but . . .

Sean focused on the car headed up the driveway in his direction. He recognized the big nurse from a couple of previous trips to the Hospital months back.

He ran over and greeted her. She looked up but didn't smile. Come to think of it, he'd never seen her smile. Sean slid up to her on the loose gravel.

"Something I can do you for?" she asked in her thick, matronly tone.

Sean turned his body halfway back to his car. "We're having a baby!"

She leaned around him and looked over at Brenda and Kim, who were getting out of the vehicle.

She rolled her eyes. "Hummfff!"

She didn't say another word. She walked over to the door, inserted the key, and pushed through to the inside.

Sean hurried over to Brenda and Kim to help the soon-to-be mom to the door.

Brenda jerked them to a stop and bent over. She pulled her arm away from Sean to grab her belly. "Mmmm!" She held the position for what seemed like an eternity to Sean, but it was probably only about thirty seconds. She relaxed and returned her steely grip on Sean's arm. "You better get me on a gurney!"

Other members of the Hospital staff began showing up, and most gathered around Brenda. Before he knew it, he was alone in the waiting room with Kim. The nurse assured them they would come to get them when Brenda was prepped and after the doctor had checked her out.

Kim was nervous, but she sat quietly waiting for the nurse to return. Sean, on the other hand, could not relax. For him, time stopped. Not slowed down, but stopped dead in its tracks.

⌁⌁⌁⌁⌁

Inch-by-inch, Robbie made his way toward the hammering. Every sense was on high alert. He'd done this before and knew exactly what to do. The first priority was to get to where there was a crosswind between himself and his target. The grass was green, no doubt from the recent rains, and the stalking was silent. His moccasins made sure of that.

Robbie caught some movement as the hammering started again. Like a gentle breeze, he slipped through the trees and brush to make his way behind the trunk of a large oak where he could get a better look.

Robbie spotted a heavyset man swinging a hammer at an anvil. He had a fire going in a large kiln into which he stuck the metal. He watched and waited until his project was red-hot, then hammered at it on the anvil. It looked like a plow blade.

The door gaped open on a large metal barn. Robbie could see every sort of junk both inside and out scattered around this man's yard. A short distance away was a weathered house. Remnants of old broken farm implements and cars were spread all around. A trickle of smoke wiggled out of a smokestack as it hit the light breeze and dissipated. *There might be someone inside. Maybe a wife?*

Robbie kept his eyes open for a second person as he moved directly behind the man. He wore no sidearm and there was no rifle around that Robbie could see.

He didn't want to startle the man, but he had to get his attention. Robbie picked up a rock. The instant the man stopped hammering, he tossed the rock some distance into the scrap metal off to the man's right. When he looked over, Robbie cleared his throat.

The man turned, dropped his hammer, and looked straight at him, his eyes so wide the color in them almost disappeared into a field of white. He immediately produced a knife from an arm sheath that Robbie failed to see and had it sailing at Robbie's head in a split second.

Robbie gasped when the knife flew by his right ear. In half a second though, Robbie had his AR-15 aimed at the man's nose. "Stop! I'm not here to fight. I don't want to hurt you, but I will."

The man, now unarmed, scratched his gray beard with one hand while he put the other on his hip. He squinted, then spit to the side. He inhaled a deep breath and stared at Robbie square in his eyes. "Why would you want to kill an old coot like me? And why'd you sneak up on me?"

"I didn't want to scare you."

"Well, that worked well for you, didn't it?" the man said in an exasperated tone.

"You here alone?"

"You point that gun in another direction, and we'll talk."

"You gonna stop throwing stuff at me?"

The man smiled, and Robbie lowered his rifle. "I'm Robbie."

"Nice to meet you, sonny. You can call me Phillip."

Phillip took a few steps toward him, and he held out his hand, but Phillip walked past him instead.

"Where're you going?"

"See if I can find my knife. I just made that thing, and I don't want to lose it."

Robbie followed the old man between a line of barrels and a row of old lawnmowers to a large trailer. Phillip leaned over and pushed some weeds over so he could see the ground. They both heard the rattlesnake at the same time. Robbie spotted the snake and drew his pistol. One shot and the rattler was dead at Phillip's feet.

Phillip looked at the snake, then at Robbie. "I would have been a goner if that thing had bitten me."

Robbie pointed. "That the knife you threw at me?"

Phillip stepped over and picked up the dagger, then the rattlesnake with the blade. "You saved my life and found dinner too."

Robbie's ears perked up when he heard the sound of a dog bark. Phillip returned the bark. He turned to Robbie with a grin. "The missus heard the shot and is asking if I'm okay."

"A signal?"

Phillip nodded.

"Yeah, we have a signal too. A wolf howl."

"Since you saved my life and all, I guess it's okay to take you inside to meet Jeanne, right?"

"I'd like that, but first, I left my sidekick out on the road. He only has the turret gun. Let's go out there and get him. I'll introduce you two; then we can all go in and meet Jeanne."

Phillip nodded and followed Robbie. Robbie let out a wolf howl and proceeded through the brush to the Jeep.

"Damned nice setup you have here," Phillip said.

Hank climbed down from the machine gun and lent Phillip a hand and smile. "That's Robbie's doing. I'm just a passenger."

Robbie beamed. "My grandpa, Reggie, was an army contractor. He has just about everything we need for warfare. We took out Sandra Hawkins's army from Corpus Christi when she tried to eradicate our little community."

"Don't know her and haven't heard of her. Bet you had your hands full though."

"To say the least."

"Well, nice to meet you guys. How 'bout we go see my wife?"

They followed Phillip to the house.

"Phillip, just you and Jeanne in this town?" Robbie asked.

"Yep, just us."

"Aren't you afraid to live way out here? Just the two of you, I mean?"

"Nah. Nobody ever comes this way. Not for a long time. Just a few Tivoli folks when they need something. Not much out here—deer, hogs, decent fishin', and me and Jeanne. No reason for folks to mess with an old coot and his woman. Besides, I can fix stuff. People comin' around usually need things or have something needin' fixin'. I've got a little bit of whatever you might need around here. Guess you noticed that by now?"

Robbie looked around the yard. There were old vehicles, boats, tractors of all kinds. He thought his dad had a lot of stuff in his barn, but Phillip . . . this was a junk man's superstore.

Phillip barked a couple of times, and the signal was returned from inside his home.

Phillip pushed the door open into the house. "We've got company, Jeanne."

"Yeah, I heard you and your bark."

Her look of surprise quickly turned into a big smile. "Wow, we haven't had any visitors since . . . uh . . . I can't remember when."

"I'm Robbie, and this is Hank. Nice to meet you, Ma'am."

"Likewise."

"Get us something to drink, will ya, sweetheart?"

Phillip extended his arm toward the dining room table. The men settled in as Jeanne poured water.

"I just pulled a rhubarb pie out of the oven. It's terrific when it's hot."

Phillip glanced over at their guests. "Hell yeah, sweetheart. These guys look hungry."

"I could eat a bite," Hank said. "I've never had . . . what was it . . . rhubarb? Never had a bad pie though."

Phillip turned to Jeanne. "This young man can shoot, I tell ya. I'd a been a goner. One shot and that snake's head went flyin'. Never seen anybody who could shoot like that. Nope. Never in all my life."

Jeanne served the pie and sat down next to Phillip. "I want to thank you, men, for saving Phil's life. We don't see many rattlesnakes around here, but with all of the equipment around, they can hide out. One nearly got me a couple of years back. You never know when one will show up in the wrong place."

Hank looked up. "Yeah, thank you, Robbie. Damn, this pie is good."

Jeanne grinned.

Phillip turned to Robbie. "So, what brings you to our neck of the woods?"

Robbie spelled out the details of his plans for south Texas. Thirty minutes later, their glasses were empty, the pie was gone, and the story told.

"That's a mighty big plan, folks." Phillip scratched the side of his head. "Maybe I can help you, men. There is a small group over at Tivoli. Maybe I can introduce you to them. They're friendly folk, but mighty suspicious of strangers and highly protective of their community. They know my truck, but I'm about out of fuel, and it's hard to come by around here. I only get a few tanks-full a year.

"The group at Tivoli provides me with gas from one of the local ranches. I have a welder and tools to keep some of their equipment running. I scratch their backs, and they scratch mine, if you know what I mean."

Robbie looked over at Hank, then back to Phillip. "We can probably spare a few gallons if you can introduce us. We don't have much, but have an extra can about half full."

Phillip hopped up like something bit him on the butt. "Well, let's do it."

Robbie and Hank joined him.

Phillip leaned over and gave Jeanne a kiss on the forehead. "I'll be back well before dark."

"You damn well better. You know how I hate being by myself after dark."

Phillip smiled and led Robbie and Hank outside. Hank grabbed the gas can. "We've got three gallons in here, and the tank on the Jeep is half full."

Robbie looked over at Phillip. "Will two gallons do it? We've got to have enough to get us to where we can get more. If we can't get some in Tivoli, then we'll have to make it to Victoria, and we're going through Seadrift first. Hank already told me that Seadrift wouldn't likely have any to spare. We'll have to see if we can locate some at an old service station or abandoned vehicle in Victoria."

Phillip took his handkerchief out of his pocket and wiped his brow. "I understand. You can't get stranded out in the middle of nowhere, and there is a lot of nowhere around these parts. By the way, what's with the American flag?"

Robbie took the gas can from Hank. "That's our calling card." He stuck the can in the Jeep and walked across the driveway. "Damn, Phillip, you've got a lot of stuff!"

Phillip stepped over and gazed across his junk. "Yeah, guess I do. But when the farmers break something, I can usually find a part. If not, then I have the forge to make a new one. That takes resources."

Hank joined them. "Looks to be no shortage of anything around here."

Robbie pulled at his scrubby beard. "You know, my dad always needs something—a plow blade, a new tool, something . . ."

Phillip drew in a breath of air and stuck out his chest. "I can fix or make pert near anything."

"I bet you can. Maybe I can throw you a little business if you'd like. Get a little trade going between you and Peaceful Valley. Corpus could benefit from your skills too. They do reasonably well, but there's always a shortage of specialty parts at the Farm. Could there be something you need in trade?"

"Jeanne and I don't need much. Plenty of resources around here. 'Bout the only thing I can think of is gasoline. That's always in short supply."

"And what about Jeanne? They grow a lot of strawberries in Corpus. She might like a few for her garden. They make fine desserts."

The mention of food caught Hank's attention. "Hell yeah. And maybe we can check back in on you folks from time to time."

Phillip smiled. "Dessert is always my favorite part of any meal."

"Done." They shake hands.

Sean held Brenda's hand on one side of the delivery table while Kim did the same on the other. "One, two, three . . ."

Brenda stared at a flower painted on the ceiling as she focused on Kim's counting and her breathing.

Sean was unconsciously breathing along with her. "You're doing great, baby!"

He looked up at the clock. "Doesn't look like we're going to make it by noon like we thought."

It was a quarter till.

The nurse glanced at the clock. "Don't be so sure about that. She's fully dilated." She nodded at the other nurse, who headed for the door.

She stepped outside and seconds later came back in with the doctor.

The doctor didn't say a word. He slipped on some rubber gloves with the ease of years of experience. He took his position. Looking first at Brenda, then at the two nurses. He nodded to each. "Let's do this."

"Push," one of the nurses said when the contraction began.

"Now relax."

Sean patted Brenda's forehead with a damp cloth. His eyes were fixed on her every move. He didn't even blink.

"AAhh!" Brenda screamed.

"Push! . . . More!"

Brenda held the strain as long as she could, then relaxed and looked wearily at Sean. Sweat dripped off his forehead. She reached up to wipe his brow.

"You'd think you were having the baby. It won't be . . ." And the pain grabbed her again. She caught his hand and squeezed hard as she pushed.

Sean winced. *Damn, she's strong!*

When Brenda relaxed, Kim said, "You're doing great."

Brenda smiled then screamed in pain.

"Push! Hard!" the nurse said.

"Whaa!"

"It's a boy!" The doctor clamped off the umbilical cord on the crying newborn. The nurse laid him across Brenda's chest. The doctor looked up at the clock. "Twelve, noon, on the dot?"

The first nurse extended her arm with a pair of scissors in her hand toward Sean.

"What?"

"Would you like to cut the cord?"

Sean looked first at Kim, then the doctor, and back at the nurse with the scissors. "I don't know."

"We haven't done this in a long time, but that used to be traditional."

Sean reached out, took the scissors, and snipped the cord. He had a son.

"You have a fine healthy boy, Sean." He looked over at Kim. "Now, if you two will step out into the hallway, we'll finish this up."

Sean and Kim hesitantly left the delivery room and pulled the door closed behind them.

Kim gave Sean a big hug. "We're parents now."

He just stood there shell-shocked. "I need to sit down." He slid down the wall to the floor.

"You all right?"

"Yeah, I think so. I got a little woozy in there. I thought it would be a little cleaner . . . in a hospital and all. I've never seen anything like that. That's almost as messy as cleaning a deer or hog."

Kim frowned. "The people that say 'birth is beautiful' don't have to clean up after it." She chuckled. "Now we need to settle on a name."

"Yes, we do. When they let us back in to see Brenda, we'll do just that. I know we've talked about a lot of names, but I can't settle on one."

Kim twisted her mouth and wrinkled her eyes in thought. "I still like Ben, from the book *Ben-Hur*, a marvelous story of a prince that was wrongly accused of treason and thrown into slavery. He escaped to sea and returned many years later and found redemption. Marvelous story. Sandra had the book in her little library at the Farm. I read the story several times."

"Benjamin, maybe?"

"That works for me, but we'll have to see what Brenda thinks."

〜〜〜〜

Phillip took a back road to Tivoli. The pavement zig-zagged all the way there, but it was only about six miles and didn't take long. At the edge of town, he stopped, and Robbie pulled up behind. Phillip laid on his horn—two short blasts followed by one long. He repeated it three times.

He shut off his engine and walked back to the Jeep. "Someone will be here in a few minutes."

Robbie killed the Jeep and settled in to wait.

Directly, two men came walking down one street and three from another direction. They waved. Phillip returned the greeting and waited for the men to walk over.

Robbie and Hank walked to the front of Phillip's truck with him. When the men arrived, Phillip made the introductions.

"Welcome, I'm William. I'll be the spokesman for the Tivoli group."

They all shook hands. William insisted they call him Billy. Robbie nodded and gave them a brief explanation for the visit to Tivoli.

While the men were skeptical about such a huge undertaking, master-minded by one young man, whom they perceived as still wet behind the ears, Billy assured Robbie that they would listen to his proposal. "But we'll have to take it to all the citizens of Tivoli. We don't make the decisions for the whole community."

These men had worked with Phillip for many years and trusted him, but this young buck and an old fisherman, formerly from Seadrift, were strangers.

After an hour, Phillip had to get back to Austwell so his wife wouldn't have a cat about him staying gone so long. She would start to worry long before dark. So Robbie and Hank were on their own.

Phillip gave Robbie and Hank a firm handshake and apologized for rushing off. He thanked them for the gas and off he went.

The locals invited the two to a café for some coffee and maybe a snack. A town with an operating restaurant was amazing, but what they found inside was even more of a surprise. As soon as they stepped inside, a big gal with flaming red hair caught Hank's attention. "I'm already liking this place."

The restaurant was quaint fifties style with booths, a bar with swivel stools, and worn linoleum flooring.

They pulled a couple of tables together so everyone would have a place to sit. The red-haired lady came over. "Hi, I'm Arlene. What can I get you fellers?" She kept her eyes on Hank, who sat staring with a sheepish grin on his face.

"Coffee all around."

"Now, Billy, you know the rule. One pot for the morning crowd. You're late."

"Okay, whatever you have then."

She returned a few minutes later with glasses of juice. "This is as crowded as it's been all week." She eyed Billy. "They are paying customers, aren't they?" she said looking over at the newcomers.

Robbie's mouth dropped open. He didn't know what they'd pay with.

Billy saw their young guest's reaction. "Don't worry about it, kid. We've got you covered."

Robbie smiled. "I thought we were going to be doing dishes this evening."

"Ha ha!" Billy looked over at Arlene, then back at Robbie. "I'm sure she'd find a task a little more strenuous than that. She charges double for outsiders. This time, however, the drinks are on us."

Robbie let out a sigh of relief and gazed at Arlene. "The sign outside says Joe's Café?"

"My late husband. I couldn't bear to change the name after he disappeared."

"So this place is yours now?"

"Lock, stock, and barrel."

"Maybe you'd like to join us. What we have to discuss concerns you too."

Hank pulled out a vacant chair next to him.

Her eyes crossed Billy's. He nodded, and she joined them. "So boys, what's up?"

Billy took a sip of his juice. "I don't recognize this one, Arlene."

"A new mixture. One of the fishermen found a new berry growing up the Guadalupe River. Not sure if it's poisonous yet. Guess we'll know a little later."

Billy choked a bit. Arlene let out a big laugh, and all eyes turned toward her. "Just kidding. I had some yesterday."

Billy inhaled deeply, set his glass on the table, and gazed over at Robbie. "Anyway, this young buck thinks he's going to turn our upside-down world right-side up again."

Arlene gave Robbie her undivided attention over the next hour as he spelled out his plan to the group. Only then, when Robbie's spiel got too technical for her, did she briefly glance over to Hank, who hadn't once taken his eyes off her.

By the end of the second hour, a pact was made with the Tivoli group, and Robbie held up his glass. "To the future."

They clinked glasses and Arlene got up. "You men hungry? We butchered a big steer yesterday, and I've been marinating some ribeyes for the evening crowd. It's not too early for dinner, is it?"

Hank slapped his hands together. "Hell no!"

Billy and the rest of the group had wives and left, but Arlene whipped up a couple of steaks for Hank and Robbie, with seasoning neither Robbie nor Hank had ever tasted before. They moved over to a booth, and Hank asked Arlene to join them. Her waitress showed up about the time the steaks were ready, and she scooted into the bench across from them.

Hank asked her about her husband, and he and Robbie ate and listened while she laid out the history of Joe's Café.

"Joe inherited this place from his dad, Joe, Sr. He died a few years before the grid went down. My Joe and I got married a few years before that. I was a waitress. When Pops, as we called him, died, Joe and I ran this place together.

"The spices for the steaks originally came from Seattle. It was a family recipe, and Joe was there visiting and replenishing the spices when the grid failed. He was supposed to come home that day but never made it. After a few years, I gave up hope. I haven't heard anything since.

"Joe loved to eat, and I loved to cook, so I kept the restaurant up. It just didn't seem right to change the name."

Hank handed her his napkin.

"I'm sorry. I shouldn't be . . ."

Hank reached out and put his hand on hers. "I think it's a wonderful story—sad, but . . . you still miss him. I think it's delightful that you still have the love in you."

Arlene sniffled and sucked it up. "Thank you." She glanced at his empty plate. "You remind me a lot of him."

"How's that?"

"You like to eat."

They both laughed.

Robbie washed down his last bite. "So, if you can no longer get spices from Seattle . . .?"

"It's not exactly the same, but I managed to find many of them locally. Close enough anyway. If you can accomplish what you say you're going to do, maybe Corpus Christi or Mexico can provide some. They're always a struggle."

"It would be a shame to lose this recipe, Arlene. Those were mighty fine steaks. We'll do what we can."

They were full of some of the best cooking they'd had in a while and ready for a good night's sleep. Arlene provided them with a spare room off the side of the restaurant for the night. Hank took his shower first and went back into the restaurant to talk with Arlene. Robbie finished up in the bathroom and peeked in on Hank and Arlene. They were still talking, so he went to bed.

Bright and early the next morning, Arlene insisted that Robbie and Hank stay for a cup of coffee and at least a couple of slices of bacon. She assured them they could pay her back at a later date. "If you guys do all you're planning on doing, you'll be getting free meals around here every time you pass through."

Robbie held up his cup of coffee. "As sure as this coffee is sweet and black, we're going to do everything I said last night and more. I noticed you have a cell tower here in town. We have men who are trying to get a cell grid set up over the entire area as we speak. It will work, or I'll die trying."

Arlene took their empty cups and extended her hand. "Again, I'm sorry to hear about your brother, and I know in my heart that if it can be done, you'll do it. You've done well so far. I wish you continued success."

Robbie stood up and gripped her hand. "Thank you, Arlene. We'll be seeing you again."

Hank nodded. "I'll be staying in Seadrift now. Thank you for your hospitality, the conversation, and I look forward to seeing you again. If . . . when . . . Robbie finishes his job, maybe you'll get a few steak customers from Seadrift. I'll definitely spread the word. Damn, those were good!"

Arlene smiled. "I look forward to it. I only serve the steaks up once a month now, but maybe if I can stir up a little more business, I'll make a weekly thing of it. How does Friday steak-night sound?"

Arlene stood on the front steps of her restaurant and watched Robbie and Hank get into the Jeep. She gave Robbie a 'thumbs up'. He returned it with a two-finger salute. Hank winked and just waved.

As they pulled away, Robbie looked over at his sidekick. "I saw that look in her eyes. Something I should know about?"

Chapter 12

Robbie eased up on the gas pedal and rolled to a stop just outside the curve in the road at the edge of Seadrift. He took a deep breath to take in the smell of the salty air. The bay was not far away now.

"You ready to do this, Hank?"

"I'm not sure. I hope someone remembers me. It's been a long time."

"Just how long?"

Hank rolled his eyes trying to come up with a number. "You know, to tell you the truth, I don't remember."

"Can you guess? More than ten? More than twenty?"

Hank took his cap off and wiped his brow with his sleeve. "Definitely more than ten. You know the years go by so fast when you're having fun?"

"Well, how old are you?"

"Hank scratched his forehead. "Sixty . . . two . . . five . . . Hell, I don't know. A helluva lot older than you, kiddo!"

Robbie was getting frustrated. *Damn, I hope I'm not this bad when I get old.* "Okay, don't worry about it. We better prepare for the worst. You drive."

Robbie climbed out and got onto the turret. He double-checked the gun and took a good look in all directions. "Ready . . . forward, slowly."

Hank looked back over his shoulder. "This place has certainly changed. I remember it looking a little nicer than this. Roads are still the same though."

He angled right at a burned-out gas station. "This'll take us down to the bayfront. If there's anyone around, there'll be someone down there this time of day. A business or two might even be open. This is Main Street I recall." Hank slowed to a crawl.

A dog ran out from the bushes to the right and barked at the Jeep. The pooch startled Robbie, and he swung the turret around. Hank stopped.

"What do you want to do, Robbie?"

Robbie whistled at the dog, and it stopped barking but stood its ground.

"Just keep the AR-15 handy." Robbie scrutinized each building. Most were rundown and appeared to be vacant . . . except one. "Hank, see that building over there?"

Hank looked back to see where he was pointing. "Yeah, what of it?"

"I thought I saw some movement. There may be someone over there. Ease forward."

Robbie turned the turret back forward and kept a sharp eye out. Fifty yards from the building, he told Hank to stop. "There is definitely someone in that structure."

"Yes, there is," said a voice from the right between two buildings. "But you don't have to concern yourself about them. Look over on the other side of you."

Robbie spotted one, then two, and three men with automatic weapons trained on him and Hank. He turned his attention back to the man who yelled at him. "You going to shoot us?"

"That's up to you."

"I know you," Hank yelled out.

"I don't think so, mister. I've never seen you before in my life."

"Yeah. You're a Helms. I'd know you anywhere. Can't remember your first name, but I've got your last name. I'm right, aren't I?"

Robbie stood frozen to the turret. He was afraid to make a move. *Please be right, old man. I hope you can remember your names better than your numbers. Maybe we won't die here today.*

"My name's Derek."

"Can't say I know a Derek Helms. But you are a Helms, right?"

"Yeah."

"Then I know your old man."

"My old man's dead."

"Sorry to hear that, son. He was a good man. I used to live here about twenty years ago or so. I had a shrimp boat and knew everyone. We had a bad shrimping season, and a bunch of us went to Corpus Christi. We heard they had some big green-tails down there. I got stuck when the grid shut down and never made it back here . . . until now."

Robbie looked down at Hank then back over to Derek. "So, are you gonna shoot us, or are we going to talk?"

"We're talking now. I'm still trying to decide whether or not I want to put a bullet in you."

Hank cut in. "I haven't even introduced you to my gunner. His name is Robbie. See this flag here? This flag used to represent this great country. This young man has it in his head that he can make this country great again.

"Robbie and his men destroyed Sandra Hawkins's dictatorship in Corpus Christi, and it is now a free democracy. They work together for the common good in an atmosphere of peace and camaraderie. They have a strong police force and want to consolidate all of south Texas into a peaceful and thriving district."

"You talk a good talk, but what proof do you have that you are who you say you are and your intentions?"

Robbie eased his hands high into the air and climbed out of the back of the Jeep. He stood straight with his arms raised over his head and walked toward Derek. He walked right up to his rifle until it was touching the center of his chest. "We are telling you the truth. My brother was killed nearly two weeks ago doing exactly what we're doing now. If you don't believe us, if you don't think you can trust us, if you want to throw away the chance we're telling you the truth, then pull the trigger. Just squeeze, and it'll all be over with.

"I don't know how happy you are, but you don't look content with the way things are now. You may never get there, but I promise you, I will put my life on the line to make your life better."

Robbie stood and stared Derek in the eyes. He didn't flinch; he didn't bat an eye, and he didn't budge.

Derek took a deep breath, then lowered his rifle. "Those men you saw going in that building," he said pointing, "they're some of the elders. We'll take you over, and they'll decide what to do with you."

Robbie smiled. "That works for me."

"And maybe they can tell me where I can find my daughter," Hank added.

⌁⌁⌁⌁

Derek and his men took Robbie's pistol and led them to the building down the street. Hank scratched the back of his neck. "I remember this building as a grocery store."

Derek went inside. He came back out with several elders a few minutes later.

"I'm Robbie. This is Hank. He used to live here before the grid shut down."

Hank stepped forward. "It's taken me this long to get back. I need to find my daughter, Clara."

A voice from inside the doorway. "Clara Keyes?"

Hank's face lit up. "Yes, do you know her?"

The man worked his way outside to Hank. "Know her? I married her. I'm Mark."

Hank reached for his hand. He couldn't stop the tears. "I need to see my baby. It's been so long."

"I'll go get her."

The elders invited Robbie and Hank inside. They got comfortable around a large conference table. Robbie put his hand on Hank's arm. He's trembling. "It's okay. You're home now."

Robbie outlined the basics of his plan to reorganize south Texas while they waited for Mark to return. The men and women listened and asked a few questions, mainly about fuel.

Nearly an hour later, the door opened, and an attractive lady came in carrying a baby. Mark followed.

Robbie gave Hank a hand up. "This is a great day. Go meet your family, my friend."

Robbie stood and watched as Hank introduced himself to his daughter and granddaughter. Mark walked over to him. "I want to thank you for bringing him home. This is truly a touching reunion."

"Yes, it is, Mark. Family is important."

Two hours later, Hank and a few of the Seadrift elders followed Robbie out to his Jeep. His gas tank was filled as promised by their hosts, and those close patted him on the shoulder, for his courage to take on the enormous task of consolidating south Texas. They wished him well and told him they would be watching for him when he returned.

Mark gave him a firm handshake, while Clara gave him a peck on the cheek. Robbie rubbed little Tiffany on the head, and she smiled at him. *Losing Ronnie was hell, but life goes on, and our dream goes forward with each person I meet.*

One of the elders' wives even packed Robbie a sack lunch consisting of shrimp tacos, smoked fish, and enough water to wash it all down.

Hank was happy to be back home, and he gave Robbie a farewell hug. "I don't know how I can thank you for bringing me along with you. I thought I would die in the hell-hole Sandra Hawkins created. You finish what you've started, and I'll see these guys erect a monument in your honor."

Robbie blushed and squeezed Hank's arm affectionately.

Hank smiled. "You take care of yourself."

Hank and Robbie shook hands, and Robbie crawled in behind the steering wheel.

One of the elders stepped over. "We are on good relations with Port Lavaca. We'll let them know what you're doing. We'll also tell them to fly the American flag. We have a few around here someplace too. Every post office, justice of the peace, and city hall had one. We'll dig them out, and the next time you come, you'll see one flying at the edge of town.

"And don't forget what we told you about Victoria. They have a lot of men, and they won't be nearly as friendly as we've been. Some are downright nasty. They think they're the center of the universe."

Robbie nodded. "Thanks."

He reached out, and Robbie grabbed his hand. His handshake was firm and sincere.

The young man cranked up the Jeep and headed for the city limits. He held his speed at 40 mph as he drove back toward Highway 35. He wasn't in any hurry though. It would be dark soon. He spotted a place to stay the night near the crossroads of Highways 35 and 185. He could hide the Jeep behind an old dilapidated building just down a side road. Victoria was going to be a significant obstacle with so many people, apparently ruthless hooligans who had their own way of doing things. They may not want a new government, as they'd apparently created their own, just as Sandra Hawkins had.

Five thousand is a lot of people. There are only three thousand in Corpus Christi. How in Hell did so many survive in this smaller city? The guys in Seadrift said there were several big ranches in the area with an ungodly amount of resources . . . fuel, their own electrical grid, livestock . . . and guns and ammo, no doubt.

Robbie took a deep breath and shook his head. *I've got to come up with a plan.*

He pulled the Jeep behind the old building and into the brush. He grabbed the food they gave him in Seadrift, opened the bag, and took a whiff. He had thought he wasn't hungry until the aromas piqued his appetite. He grabbed his water jug, found a shady spot, and sat on an old five-gallon container.

Robbie pulled out a taco and put it up to his nose. "Damn!" He pulled the side open to see what was inside. He then took a big bite. *I've got to remember to get more of these shrimp tacos when I get back to Seadrift. They're tasty.*

After he finished his meal, he needed to find a safe place to sleep before it got too dark. He peeked inside the old building. It wasn't inviting. The roof was already half caved in. He decided the back seat of the Jeep would be the most comfortable and safest place.

⎍⎍⎍⎍

Robbie awoke early to find the Jeep was shrouded in ground fog. He didn't sleep cold, but there was a slight chill in the morning air. He took a couple of bites out of the leftovers from the previous night and rinsed it down with a swig of water.

The sun will be up soon. May as well get going.

Robbie worked his way out of the brush and back onto the road. He kept a sharp eye out. It wasn't like he expected to see anyone, but there was always a chance. It was only another twenty or so miles from here to the outskirts of

Victoria according to the map. He eyed the gas gauge and smiled. It felt good to have a full tank.

He crept along at 30 mph. He wasn't in a hurry, and he hoped the hours' time it would take him to get to Victoria would give him enough time to come up with a plan. Last night he had fallen asleep quickly and had slept throughout the night. He felt well-rested, but he still had no plan.

He thought of maybe waiting until dark to enter the city but remembering way back when he and Sean got captured entering Corpus Christi, he decided against the option. *These people could have night scopes too. At least during the day, with my stealth capabilities, I'll have an equal or better chance of getting in and making contact with my choice and not theirs.*

According to the map, Victoria is a damn big city. So was Corpus, but . . .

Robbie saw some smoke off in the distance. He slipped the gearshift into neutral and rolled to a stop. He checked the landscape all the way around, then focused on the smoke.

He pulled his map out and looked at the little town. *Bloomington.* He remembered the small community but had forgotten the name. *Seems like someone is living here too.*

He spotted a thick grove of trees and drove the Jeep over what was left of an old fence to get there. He wiggled the Jeep into heavy cover, grabbed his AR-15, and got out.

From the edge of the trees, he scanned the area with his binoculars. The smoke was deeper into town. In full stealth mode, he made his way to the first building. Little-by-little, he worked his way in the direction he'd spotted the plume.

The grass was still soft from the fog and dew. Robbie was silent as he made his way into town. The smoke had disappeared. After two hours of searching for it, he decided to give up.

He made his way back to the Jeep. He retrieved his water and the last two strips of jerky from his backpack. He munched on them as he formulated a plan on how he was going to proceed. He would need to hunt soon, but could he risk it so close to town? What, or who would the sound of gunfire bring?

Robbie cranked up the Jeep and made his way out of the trees and brush. After he'd made it through Bloomington, he drove a little faster to get to Victoria. It was still at least a couple of hours before noon. It wasn't that he was late, he just wasn't early anymore. He always liked to get to places early. A good habit or bad habit, he didn't know, but a habit nevertheless.

Robbie found a place to park his Jeep and once again headed into the city. The big one this time—Victoria—the crown jewel on his map.

The grass and weeds made a little more noise now that they'd dried out, but Robbie was a master at stealth. Growing up in the country and the lessons he'd learned from his parents, grandparents, and the two wars with Sandra Hawkins's men, made him an expert at an early age.

The breeze had come up from the southeast, and this was a more significant problem than the plants. The sound of the wind would cover the noise from the weeds, but he would be upwind from anyone or anything he'd come across. He would not be able to detect any odors ahead of time to warn him of danger, and any sounds would be more difficult for him to detect. However, the situation was what it was, and he didn't have a choice. He just had to be doubly careful.

It took him an hour to find a home with smoke. He spotted some trees nearby and worked his way in that direction. He saw a large tree to hide behind. It was a well-built home with a perimeter fence and a well-manicured yard. He spotted several chickens scattered around within the enclosure. Robbie hunkered down behind the tree and watched.

Evidently, someone was inside. The smoke rising from a rooftop stack proved that. But who? How many?

An hour went by, and Robbie was getting a cramp in one of his legs. He repositioned but froze when he heard a voice—a woman's.

A young lady came around the side of the house with a small pail in her hand and a few chickens following. "Chick, chick, chick . . ." She tossed grain into the yard, and the remainder of the chickens came running.

Robbie slowly eased a little farther behind the tree, keeping only one eye focused on the gal. The young lady appeared to be about his age. Her long brown hair quavered in the gentle breeze. When her pail was empty, she reached up and pulled her locks over her shoulder.

Suddenly, she stiffened and looked around. To Robbie, it appeared as though she'd heard something. Robbie's sharp eyes could spot a tree frog at thirty yards in a moonlit night. In the daylight, he could see how beautiful she was. Her soft, moderately tanned skin, moist, tender lips, and blemish-free complexion made her a beauty.

She focused in his direction. Beads of sweat formed on his forehead from the tension, but he held still. He didn't dare move a muscle.

Unafraid, she took a couple of steps forward.

She sees me. She can't from this distance, yet she does. No, that's not possible.

With the voice of an angel she asked. "Is someone there?"

I can't answer her. I can't let her know I'm here. She'll scream, then all hell will break loose.

Her eyes scanned the area where Robbie was hiding. Again, she spoke. "I know you're there. Please answer me."

That's not possible. I'm too far away. The sun is in her eyes. She can't see me.

"If you're not going to reveal yourself, I'm going to have to come out and get you. Don't make me do that."

Everything that Robbie knew told him that she couldn't see him, that under no circumstances should he reveal himself to her, but for some reason beyond his comprehension, he couldn't stop himself. "I'm here."

Dammit! Why did I do that? I shouldn't have . . . I'm going to get myself killed.

"Then come out so I can see you better."

Slowly, Robbie pulled himself up using his AR-15 as a crutch due to the weakness in his legs from lack of circulation. He maintained his focus on her.

She stepped forward. "I'm not going to hurt you."

You're not going to hurt me? Robbie's lips formed a smile. He stuck his head around the tree. "I'm here."

"Well, then come out where I can see you."

Robbie gripped his AR-15 tight with his finger gently on the trigger, took a few steps forward, and stopped. He eyed the house and to his left and right. There was only this brave, young, beautiful girl in front of him.

She stood tall and straight as she strolled—no . . . floated toward the fence between her and himself. She made not a sound as she drifted forward. The pail she carried didn't rattle or otherwise make a noise that Robbie could detect. Her dress swayed in the breeze and the movement of her legs, but there was no sound whatsoever.

Is she a ghost? Am I seeing things? Is she really here? I must be dreaming.

Robbie took a step forward, then another and another. *Am I breathing? Breathe!* Robbie intentionally inhaled, paying attention. *Yes, I am.*

When she reached the fence, she hung her pail on one of the pointy pickets and crossed her arms over her chest. Her stare was intense. Robbie could feel her eyes burning into him. She appeared calm and without fear. It was as if she was invulnerable to anything he could do to her.

Thirty feet apart, her intensity turned into a welcoming smile. But it wasn't just a friendly smile. It was captivating. It tugged at him. Robbie felt his finger easing off the trigger of his rifle. She could have been the devil in disguise, and there would have been nothing he could do. He began to feel a calmness in her presence and that he had nothing to fear. This could have been just the opposite of reality, but Robbie felt as if he had no control over what was happening.

He wasn't even sure he was still walking, so he looked down to see if his legs were moving. They were. Yes, he would eventually get to the fence. He would be face to face with this angel, this monster, whatever this girl was who was drawing him toward her like a ball bearing to a magnet.

He stopped two feet from the fence directly in front of her and looked into her eyes. They were multicolored—the flecks of blue, green, and yellow sparkled in the sunlight.

Robbie was dumbfounded by her presence first of all, but also by her beauty. He couldn't understand why she had the power to coax him out of hiding so easily. All he could do is stand there and stare.

Then, with the voice of an angel: "I'm Freya."

He hesitated. Not to be rude or anything, but only for the fact that for an instant, he had forgotten his name. "I'm . . . R-Robbie."

She extended her long slender arm, her smooth hand that didn't look like it had ever been dirty or had felt work. Slowly, Robbie's fingertips met hers. She grasped his hand and gently gave it a squeeze. He looked down when he felt the electricity, or what he perceived as electricity, arc from her hand to his. It was more of a tingle than a jolt, and he wasn't sure as to whether or not it was real, but in his mind, he felt it.

"Come around to the side, and I'll open the gate for you. It's getting hot out here."

Robbie made his way along the pickets to the opening while keeping his eyes on her. She smiled her never-ending smile. *Is there something wrong with her? Now she won't stop smiling. I'm a stranger . . . and with a gun. Something's really wrong. And her name. I've heard that name before . . . in a book.*

She unlatched the gate. "You look thirsty. Would you like to have a cool drink? I have juice, milk, and water."

"Water will be fine."

Freya turned toward the side of the house. He followed but kept scanning the perimeter. He gripped his rifle a little tighter as they rounded the corner. There was nothing that he could see to be afraid of, but the hair had been standing up on the back of his neck ever since he revealed himself to Freya. There was quite a sizeable fenced-in garden with a wide variety of plants, some just getting started and some quite large, and fruit he could see.

"Nice garden."

She turned around and produced that smile!

The house seemed a bit too large for just Freya. It was well-maintained and looked to have been built in the last decade or so. Robbie glanced up at the pitched roof. The metal panels were in good shape as well. *She can't be keeping this place up herself. She's too . . . what's the word? Yes, frail.*

Freya turned the knob and pushed the door in. She stepped aside to let him go first. The thought of stepping into a trap crossed his mind, and he gripped the AR-15 tighter, and his finger found the trigger. *Venus flytrap. I'm the fly.*

A single light on the ceiling illuminated the interior. The furniture was minimal but sufficient—table, a few chairs, a sofa, and a unique large rug on the floor with an intricate design which he couldn't fail to notice. Robbie turned around as Freya closed the door.

She looked at his rifle. "You can lean that thing up against the door frame."

He didn't see any need for the gun, so he complied.

Robbie didn't see when her smile faded, but it returned quickly when he opened his mouth. "Do you live here alone?"

Freya didn't say anything at first. She walked over to the refrigerator and removed a pitcher of colored liquid and set it on the counter. She grabbed a couple of glasses and got ice out of the freezer compartment.

It suddenly dawned on Robbie that she had power. He was so enthralled with Freya that he didn't make the connection with the light bulb. "You have electricity!?"

"Yes, doesn't everyone?"

Robbie staggered back a step. "No! Some places have more than others, but . . ."

She interrupted him. "Well, we do here. And 'yes' I live here alone, to answer your first question."

She handed him his glass. "I know you said water, but you look like you could use a little sugar."

Robbie took a sip. It was sweet, something he wasn't used to, but it was cold and refreshing. After all, he wasn't used to ice all the time either, and this was pleasant as well.

He held the glass up to the light. "I don't recognize the taste. What is that flavor?"

"Persimmon."

"A fruit?"

"Yes, they grow wild around here."

"So tell me, why do you live out here alone?"

Freya turned. She put her finger to her temple and gazed upward for a second. She then locked eyes with Robbie. "Daddy left when I was about nine. The fights—Mom and Dad screaming and me crying in my bedroom. I don't know what they fought about. One day he left and didn't come back.

"Mom was strong. She worked hard. She was always mixing herbs for people's ailments. They bartered for her concoctions. She also saved up some gold and silver when Dad was here and hid it well. Dad never found out. She only told me where she hid them in case something happened to her. Made me swear to keep her secret.

"She loved gold and silver coins. Her treasure is mostly gone now. I kept a few to remember her by. Before she died, she made sure that I would have everything, well mostly, that I would need to live out here like she did."

"How long ago did she die?"

"Four years. I was fourteen then."

"An accident?"

"She had migraines. I think that's why she got into herbal medicine. One morning she didn't wake up."

"I'm sorry." Robbie took hold of her hand. "Who maintains this place? Surely you don't do it yourself. Your hands don't look like they do a lot of hard work."

"I wear gloves, but I don't have to do much. I take care of my chickens, garden, and the inside of the house, but I have people who regularly come to take care of everything else. Someone usually comes by every week to see what I need. I tell them, they do the work, and I pay them with herbs. They bring a list of what people in town want. Mom taught me how to mix all her best medications. It's as simple as that.

"My dad came by a couple of months after Mom died. I told him I wouldn't leave this house. He helped with getting maintenance men out here to do some of the things Mom hadn't thought about, like sewer and air conditioner work.

"He remarried, and I didn't like his wife. I ran into her one day at the library. She was mean and nasty to me. Said a lady shouldn't be staying out here alone. Dad wanted the two of them to move here. I told him I'd be tempted to poison his bitch of a wife. He let it go. They live on the other side of town, and my dad comes around from time to time, but not often."

"Maybe you should have let your dad and step-mom move in here. You . . . it's just not safe. Someone could hurt you living way out here alone."

"No one has yet . . . you didn't."

Robbie leaned back and finished off his second glass of persimmon juice. "How did you know I was out there?"

"I didn't really. I had a feeling . . . maybe I picked up your odor."

I've got to be more careful. I always think about that when I'm hunting. That's twice now. Robbie raised up his arm and gave it a whiff. "I guess I do need a shower. I don't recall when . . ." *I guess I'd better start thinking about it even in town. Maybe, especially if it involves a woman.*

Freya's lovely smile quickly returned. "You don't smell bad. People don't really smell other people . . . well, maybe when we're this close . . . I have a shower. You can take one now if you'd like?"

Robbie stood up. "Yes, I'd like that, but I have to get some clean clothes out of my Jeep."

"You do that, and I'll whip us up something to eat. When you get out of the shower, I'll have something ready."

Robbie had been so wrapped up in Freya that he didn't think about food. Now that she mentioned it, he was getting quite hungry. He hadn't had much of anything all day. "I'll be back in maybe ten minutes."

"Come on in when you get back."

He couldn't help smiling every time she did. That was often, even during their long conversation.

Robbie grabbed his AR-15 and opened the door. It was almost dark. *Damn! Where did the time go?*

┼┼┼┼┼

Robbie got out of the shower and dried. Then he noticed Freya had apparently laid out some things for him. There was deodorant, a razor, and nail clippers. *This gal is quite surprising, to say the least.*

Robbie walked into the living area and was hit by the aroma of the meal she had prepared. The table was set for two with a candle in the middle for lighting. *Romantic! Or maybe just practical. Florence and I eat by candlelight all the time. Perhaps she's just saving on electricity. I miss Florence. I wonder what she's doing right now?*

Robbie walked over, and his host pointed to a place at the table. "Can I help?"

"No, I've got it covered. You sit down." She grabbed his plate and took it over to the stove. She dished a helping out of each pot and put his in front of him and grabbed her plate.

Robbie leaned over and took in the inviting vapors, which made him more relaxed than he'd been all day. She served baked chicken, seasoned potatoes, and a salad. With the meal, there was iced milk with a purplish tint to it. He frowned but didn't say anything.

When Freya sat down, he held up the glass.

"Taste it."

Robbie took a little sip. This was a flavor he recognized. "Dewberry, right?"

"Do you like it?"

"Yes, we have a lot of dewberries back home." Robbie took another sip, set the glass down, and sat staring at her. He couldn't stop doing that.

She was beginning to notice his fixed attention. "Eat. Don't let it get cold."

He smiled and picked up his knife and fork. The food was as good as Freya was beautiful. There were a few glances back and forth, but the conversation was dead outside of some compliments from Robbie and the replying smiles and giggles from Freya.

When they'd finished, Robbie pushed his chair back. "Sorry I made such a pig out of myself, but that was just so good!"

"I didn't think you made yourself a pig. You're a big, strong, healthy man and men have appetites. I know that. I'm glad you liked my cooking. Some of the men who come around to work on things . . . well, I make snacks for them."

"That was the best meal I've had since I left home, and that was a while back. I don't know how I can thank you for such a good dinner."

Robbie helped Freya with the table and dishes; then she fixed him more persimmon juice and they resumed their conversation on the sofa. The conversation turned to Victoria.

"Outside of town toward Goliad, there is a reservoir where they generate electricity. Coleto Creek, I think they call it. After the grid shut down I'm told, another electric plant was built out of one of the chemical plants to the south of town. There is another on the north side on the Guadalupe River. So, we have plenty of electricity. The hospital has big generators. It's only partially used as a hospital though. With all the rooms, it was turned into housing."

"Where do they get fuel?"

"This area is rich in oil, I'm told. Another one of the chemical plants to the south was turned into a refinery."

"Do they make deodorant too?"

Freya gave him a smirk. "No, silly. We have manufacturing. Not on a large scale, but we have a lot of niceties and nonessentials. I make my own fragrances and share with some of the ladies in town. A place over near the library makes razors. I like to keep my legs and underarms . . ." She blushed a bit and changed the subject.

"Most of our trade is through barter, but gold, silver, and precious stones are also used. Some trade labor for goods."

"How did the city come out of the crisis after the grid shut down to become such a civil place? Most of the places I've seen have been brutal and are still a mess, even Corpus until we eliminated Sandra."

"I can't really say. I've only heard a few stories from my mom. The important thing is that Victoria is not such a bad place to live. The police force can be a little overbearing at times, but they keep the peace, not only from within but from without. But that's enough about me. I want to know more about you."

Robbie spent another hour outlining his plan to reorganize south Texas.

"After what the men in Seadrift told me, I thought I might die here."

"You'll be okay. Someone will be here to check on me in a few days. I'll introduce you to them and then they, in turn, can take you into town and introduce you to the leaders of our fair community. You can tell them what you told me and everything will be just fine. I'm sure they'll like what you have to say."

"Me stay here a few days?"

"Yes, that's best. If you barge into town, you might be killed. I can't have that on my conscience . . . when I can help you get in safely."

"And what do I do in the meantime?"

"Stay inside and out of sight for one thing. I'll find something to keep you occupied. Someone will be here soon. I know it can't be more than a day or two . . . that's all."

Robbie rolled his eyes, and Freya caught him.

"It won't be so bad, Robbie, really. I'll find you something to do, and we can talk some more. I don't usually talk much, but for some reason, you're easy to talk to. The workers who come out don't say much. They ask questions, but real conversation, no."

Robbie was excited and thoroughly enjoyed visiting with Freya, but the long day was starting to get to him. He couldn't help but yawn.

Freya smiled. "It's getting late, and you're tired. If you put the glasses away, I'll go prepare your bed."

She gave him a warm smile, got up, and strolled over to the entrance, giving him another glance, her eyes glistening with tenderness.

Robbie got up and headed toward the sink. He finally took notice of his surroundings in more detail. Up until now, his focus had been on Freya. He rinsed out the glasses and walked over to a window where on the sill, small dishes had things drying in them. Other plants hung from the ceiling.

He noticed three picture frames on the wall. The first held an old photograph of a woman holding a baby—Freya and her mother, he guessed. The second was a photo of Freya, maybe at twelve years of age, in a garden. She was holding a small basket in one hand and what appeared to be a squash in the other. The smile on her face was the same one Freya wore most of the time since they first met. The third was a picture of three men. They all carried rifles. Robbie leaned in a little closer. One had to be her father, but he could see no resemblance to the beautiful woman Freya had become.

Robbie looked around the room. There was little else which caught his attention. *Obviously she gardens. She cooks and cleans, but what else? Does she have any fun? It's so strange to me for her to be out here alone—living like a hermit. No, not a hermit. People come around. What's the word? Isolated. Secluded. Those fit. Recluse? Reminds me of home. Peaceful. There is still a troubled world out there, yet here, I feel as relaxed as I do at home. Maybe more.*

Robbie retrieved his rifle and walked over to the entrance to the hallway to meet Freya coming out of one of the back rooms. She stopped and held out her arm. "Come."

He walked toward her and again that smile.

"It's ready." She turned around. "Here across the hall is a bathroom if you need one during the night." She reached in and flipped the light on and then back off.

She looked down at his rifle, then his pistol, but she didn't say anything. The look in her eyes made it perfectly clear to him, however, that she didn't like guns.

Robbie walked into the bedroom and leaned his gun in the corner. A light on the night table illuminated a simple room similar to the living room and kitchen. The bed looked inviting and was turned down, ready for occupancy.

As Robbie walked in, he detected a light fragrance. He heard the door squeak and turned around. Freya had closed the door and was gone.

There was nothing to see or do. The walls were bare. Heavy drapes covered the one window. Except for the bed, nightstand, and table light, the room was empty. Robbie undressed, crawled into bed, and after a few moments turned the light off.

He lay on his back and took in a deep breath of air. He felt uncomfortable but unafraid. If anyone had anything to be afraid of, it was Freya. Living here alone had to be hard on her, but everything he'd seen so far said just the opposite.

He couldn't hear any noises outside, and the house was quiet except for the faint sound of water running. *She has to be taking a shower.*

Robbie closed his eyes, but though his body was telling him how tired he was, his brain would not shut down. The bed felt soft and comfortable, and part of him wanted to sleep, but details of Freya, her uncanny senses, and gentle ways kept him awake.

He could feel his mind fading away as its attempt to rationalize Freya's behavior proved futile. Then the door made a noise. He sleepily opened his eyes. The faint light from another room backlit the slender frame of Freya dressed in a nightshirt. The light penetrated the fabric, revealing the curvature of her body. As earlier in the day, she appeared to float across the room.

Robbie blinked his eyes to see better and to understand what was happening. He felt the covers pull back, and she crawled in beside him. The scent of her was more noticeable now—sweeter, cleaner, titillating.

Her skin was cool against his warm body. She was soft and cuddly, like a puppy. Her body wrapped around him, and she excited him. His body reacted accordingly. He was powerless to do anything about what was happening as Freya touched him and teased nerve endings in every erogenous zone on his body.

Her lips pressed against his, and her tongue flirted with the inside of his mouth. The taste of persimmon lingered on her breath, but now the sweetness of the nectar had multiplied a hundredfold. Robbie was under her spell. He couldn't do anything to counteract her erotic onslaught upon his body. His body felt the need for hers, and his mind couldn't argue the point, like a starving man being unable to refuse food.

Robbie wrapped his arms around her smooth body and pulled at her nightshirt. She did the same with his underwear. The heat of passion produced lubricating beads of sweat laced with their intoxicating aromas. Their arms and legs slithered over each other like boas squeezing, pulsating . . .

⌁⌁⌁⌁

Robbie's eyes opened slowly. A rooster crowed outside. Slivers of the sun's rays found their way around the edge.

He felt the bed. He was alone. *Freya!* The memory of last night forming in his head. He didn't know when she left. He'd apparently fallen asleep shortly after . . .

Robbie reached for the light. He dressed quickly and headed for the door, but stopped dead in his tracks. *Freya. Freya! The Norse Goddess of Love. She was in one of Grandpa's books. Damn!*

He looked at his rifle and pistol in the corner and decided they could wait. He needed to see Freya. As soon as he stepped into the hallway, his senses picked up the aroma of food, particularly the eggs.

Freya was sitting at the kitchen table eating. "Sorry, I was hungry. I couldn't wait for you, sleepyhead." And then the smile. She immediately got up and went to the stove. "Eggs and leftover chicken okay with you?"

Robbie nodded. *She's acting like nothing happened last night. Something did happen, didn't it? I wasn't dreaming. No, it did. My shorts were off when I got up. It did happen! Florence! Shit!*

The eggs and warmed-up chicken were ready in no time, and Freya added a little more to her plate, poured another glass of juice, and joined Robbie.

He took a couple of bites before looking up at her. "Something we should talk about?"

Her smile returned. She cocked her head a bit and shrugged her shoulders. "Not unless you want to."

She looked at him for a couple of seconds, then turned her attention back to her plate.

Robbie's mind drifted. *I don't guess there's anything to say. Water under the bridge . . . but what a scenic river! . . . Dammit! Get your head out of your ass, Robbie. You have a wife-to-be and a baby on the way. You've gotta get out of here. Last night can't happen again.*

They were quiet until they finished their meal and drinks. Robbie got up when Freya did and helped with the cleanup. He then retrieved his rifle and set it where he would have easy access to it during the day. The best spot he could find was next to the sofa.

"Do you have to have those things there?"

"Sorry. They go with me."

She frowned. "Okay, have it your way, but you make your own bed. I'm going to the garden."

"I'll go with you."

"No, you must stay inside."

"And why is that?"

"It might cause a problem if someone sees you before they see me. They could jump to the conclusion that you hurt me. I need to explain you to them first. I wouldn't want anyone to get the wrong idea."

"But I need some stuff out of my Jeep. It's parked in the grove of trees," he said, pointing the direction though he could not see the trees.

She paused a few seconds. "If you really need stuff, I'll go with you." She paused again. "What kind of stuff?"

"Well, clothes, for one."

"And two?"

"Not much else, I guess."

"So you don't need them right now. We'll go for them later." With that, she grabbed a large bowl and headed to the garden, leaving Robbie standing in the middle of the room.

Chapter 13

Back in Peaceful Valley . . .

Brooke and Debra nailed on the roof decking under the supervision of Zack. He and Lance had done most of the foundation and framing simply because Brooke didn't have the skills. She was able to drive a few nails at the bottoms of the wall stud, but had to leave the rafters to the boys.

When she and Ronnie built their home along with Lance, Beka, and the others, the girls did what they could, but the men did most of the work. The ladies were more adept at keeping the guys fed and hydrated. This time Brooke wanted to do more of the work. After all, it was her idea in the first place, and she wanted to feel like she had a more significant part in the project.

John helped supervise and made sure the structure was sturdy. Reggie refused to go near the construction site. He swore to John that he'd never set foot in the place, but John had a plan. John knew Reggie couldn't be converted in a million years, and that wasn't his intention. He only wanted to show Reggie that church was much more than trying to force the Ten Commandments down the throats of others.

Lance cut planks while Beka handed them up to Brooke and Debra. Brooke held up the can with the nails and rattled the nearly empty container. "I think we're going to need some more nails up here."

John stepped over and she poured the few nails left into her hand and tossed the can down to him. "I'll go see if James has some more," John said. "You guys and gals need anything else while I'm there?"

Debra wiped her brow with her arm. "I could use a sandwich."

The boys looked up. They were always hungry, and at the mere mention of food— "Yeah, me too!"

Brooke looked over at her dad. "May as well bring me a sandwich too, Daddy."

John shook his head and headed to the Lindgrens'.

Brooke and Debra used up the rest of the nails quickly. Lance continued to cut, and Beka handed up the planks. When they couldn't go any further for lack of nails, Brooke and Debra took a breather while Zack got down. He and Lance started cutting the metal panels so they'd be ready as soon as Brooke and Debra finished with the planks.

John caught James with a drink, taking a break on the front porch. James looked up and waved him in when he whistled.

John took out his kerchief as he walked up, wiping his brow. "Starting to warm up nicely around here. That ought to be good for the gardens now that the rainy season is over."

James nodded. "How about something to drink?"

"I'll certainly take you up on that . . . and I came to beg sandwiches for the kids." They went inside to give Melissa the kids' requests, then headed out to the shed to look for more nails.

"So, John, how is the construction going?"

"Good. The younger generation are really working hard. Brooke inspired them all to help make this world a better place. God is needed in our world. Brooke has seen the light and others will follow. I don't like a pregnant woman on the roof, but she wouldn't listen."

"Just don't count on me to 'see the light'."

"You know, if you and Reggie just give me a chance, I'll bet you will want to come back after the first sermon."

James laughed. "It'll be a cold day in Hell when you get Reggie to attend your church. You'll not be converting that old buzzard. Now don't get me wrong, Reggie and I are close. He was Dad's best friend, and Reggie and I have been through a lot ourselves . . . I'm just saying . . ."

"I know what you're saying, James. I'll tell you what, if I can get Reggie to attend, will you come as well?"

"Yeah, why not," James said laughing, not able to control himself. "Not gonna happen."

John turned around and held up a can. "I think I found the nails we're looking for. Now all I need is the sandwiches."

Melissa had the food and drinks ready by the time they made it back into the house. "I hope this is enough. Your boys certainly can eat a lot. And the girls, if they're working as hard as I know they are, they're going to be eating on the heavy side too."

John nodded. "Thanks, Melissa. I better get going before they starve to death on me."

"My pleasure. By the way, how are they coming along?"

"Quite well, actually. A few more days and it should be ready to begin having meetings. What day is today? You know I can never keep track. Tuesday, isn't it? I am going to prepare my first sermon for next Sunday. I think the place will be ready so I will be ready too. I hope you'll attend."

"I wouldn't miss it, John."

John smiled and looked over at James. He shook his head. When Melissa saw him, she frowned and whispered to John. "I'll see what I can do."

John nodded and headed back to the construction site.

Robbie was going stir crazy. He'd been cooped up inside the house for three days. The only reason he'd made it this long was Freya. While he was accustomed to doing housework, he wasn't used to doing quite so much. Three days of dusting, mopping, and cleaning bathrooms was a little too much for him.

Freya did feed him quite well—three square meals a day—much more than he'd been eating for weeks. But that was all she was feeding him. There wasn't a repeat of their first magical night together.

He actually thought a time or two that Florence might notice he had gained weight when he got home. He mentioned his concerns. Freya assured him, with that convincing smile of hers, that he wasn't out of shape.

On the fourth morning, while Freya was in the garden gathering vegetables for lunch, Robbie heard male voices. He looked out the window to see Freya talking to two men. They were dressed as workmen.

While he could hear them talking, he couldn't make out what they were saying. He stepped away from the window and over toward the kitchen when he saw Freya motion with her arm toward the house, turn, and lead them toward the back door.

He looked over at his AR-15 leaning in the corner next to the sofa. Freya warned him several times that the guns would only complicate things. That he should go with the workers, who would eventually come, unarmed and show no aggression toward them. She would explain things to them, and they would take good care of him as long as he wasn't armed.

This wasn't Robbie's way, and it hadn't been the way of Peaceful Valley for his entire life. The world was just too messed up. But Robbie decided he'd listen to Freya. She had a calming effect on him. He had no reason not to trust her. She lived out here all on her own without a weapon of any sort that he could see outside of her killer beauty and medicinal skills.

The second thing that made Robbie listen to her was that though going in unarmed was different, that is just the type of world he wanted to create—a new world where people weren't always killing strangers; where people could walk down the street unafraid; where the world was like the stories his mother, dad, and Grandma Eileen had told him about; how the world was so long ago, long before he was born.

Robbie silently stood his ground and stared at Freya and the men when the door swung open. He stepped toward them. They did not have gun belts or pistols. Instead of rifles, one had a hand pruner, and the other held a flashlight.

Robbie greeted them just as Freya had instructed him to. "Hi." He looked at her, and she smiled.

Freya extended her arm toward Robbie. "This is the man I told you about, Robbie."

The men lent their hands. Robbie shook each. They didn't offer their names, but it wasn't vital. They were only Robbie's path to the central government of Victoria. These men didn't need to know all the details of what he had in mind. They just needed to take him to their leader.

Freya had assured him long before they arrived and did so again now. "I want you to take Robbie directly to see the mayor. This is extremely urgent. Do you understand?"

Freya spoke to the men with an intensity Robbie had not seen up until now. And she had the men's undivided attention. It appeared to Robbie that Freya knew them well and they wanted to please her. Maybe the spell she had on him extended to all men.

While Robbie wasn't entirely comfortable without his weapons, he wasn't afraid of a man with a pruner and another with a flashlight. The men weren't aggressive in the least, and they bowed at Freya as though she was a priestess when she was giving them instructions.

It was almost comical how she seemed to have them under her influence, but maybe that was her weapon. She certainly had Robbie under her total control the past few days. *Have I been so pathetic?*

It wasn't that she'd taken away their free will, more like she won their respect and honor by her gentle spirit and peaceful ways.

Freya then told the men that she had no work for them today. That their only job would be to do as she had instructed and take Robbie immediately to the mayor.

Freya gave Robbie a quick kiss on the cheek. "Now off with you. I have chickens to tend."

Robbie looked back a final time as the two men led him away. He expected some sort of vehicle. According to Freya, Victoria had fuel among many other things. He expected a small car at the least. What he got was a two-hour walk to the center of the city.

The men stopped and pointed to a large granite multi-story building. *Well, at least they're taking me to see the mayor.*

—↕—

In Corpus Christi back at the Farm . . .

Sean kissed Brenda on the forehead. He'd missed several days with the new baby. Kim pestered him that he didn't need to do anything, that she'd take care of Brenda. He was a new daddy though. He wanted to be involved at least for a couple of days, but he had work to do. He finally decided work could wait. What was the worst that could happen?

Kim didn't know it, but Brenda had also read *Ben-Hur* way back when and was delighted with the name. It would be Benjamin for the birth certificate, but they would call him Ben. Then they decided that Ben Lin sounded funny, so even though most everyone else didn't have a middle name, it was agreed that Benjamin would definitely need one if he were to be called Ben instead of Benjamin.

The problem was that no one could think of a name that didn't sound funny with Ben Lin. They finally decided that they would call him Benjamin and make sure everyone else did the same.

Kim changed diapers, prepared meals, and washed clothes. She pampered Brenda and Benjamin to the point that they were quickly getting spoiled. This wore her a little ragged for a few days until she had the routine down, but the upside was that Brenda was recovering quickly, and the baby was growing stronger each day. By the end of the week, Brenda was getting around nicely and helping with the workload, while Sean took care of city business.

Corpus Christi was ramping up for the upcoming shrimping season. The oyster season was excellent, and the freezing plant was full. Wild cattle came through the winter healthy and the police who did the hunting and red meat processing, just as they had for decades under Sandra Hawkins's rule, were bringing in adequate supplies of beef and even some small game.

Spring crops were growing well after the early rains and sporadic rainfall since. Fuel production was at its peak, and word came in that they were getting very close to having cell phone service in Corpus Christi and most of the way to Peaceful Valley. They were having trouble with one cell tower but were confident they could get the problem resolved soon.

Regular trips to Brownsville remained on schedule though they had only one pilot, but he was training two more and expected to have them up to speed by mid-summer. They certainly needed the sugar, tea, coffee, textiles, and other essential products Brownsville could supply.

Sean was a happy man. He had two lovely ladies at home, and now a new baby. The city was running well, and there wasn't a thing he could think of that could ruin his day.

He thought of Robbie often and said a little prayer for him. Each time he thought of his friend, however, he was saddened by the loss of Ronnie. At the same time, he knew that Robbie would make his brother proud. Ronnie's force always traveled with Robbie.

Marcia picked Sonny up and decided to take him on a drive down to the Bayfront. She'd been taking him to different areas of the city to try to jog his memory. He seemed to do much better when they went to the seawall and sat to watch the boats, birds, and water.

"And you say I used to run a shrimp boat with you and Lola? I certainly like the salty air. And this guy, Sean, what kind of guy was he?"

"I didn't care for him at first. He was Asian like us, but there was something about him that rubbed me the wrong way. I don't know what it was, but there was something. Maybe it was because of the people he hung around with in Peaceful Valley. He was . . . more like Sandra . . . not mean like her, but sneaky."

Sonny took a deep breath. "I remember lying on the beach. My head hurt." He reached up and rubbed the back of his head. "I was doing something . . . not on the beach . . . long before . . ."

Marcia sat and watched the contortions on his face as he struggled to remember. She still loved him. She had always loved him . . . well, pretty much always . . . it was an arranged marriage by Sandra, but she already knew him and liked him a lot before Sandra made the match. She sat and held his hand and hoped his memory would return, not only for her but for little Lola.

"A pretty face, then darkness, but there's something else. Sean was there . . . on the boat. I didn't black out. He . . . Sean . . . Sean hit me with something. He's the reason I blacked out. But why?"

Marcia reached up and turned Sonny's face toward hers. "Sean took two of Sandra's top women with him. Kim and Brenda betrayed Sandra and somehow talked Sean into helping them to escape."

"Escape to where?"

"Peaceful Valley. I don't know if they wanted to be with Robbie or what, but for some reason, they thought Sean was their ticket out of here. Robbie escaped with Beka and Florence. That sent Sandra into a tailspin, but when Kim and Brenda skipped with Sean, she went psycho. That was her downfall.

"Robbie, those girls, all of them, and Sean destroyed this city. It's getting to where nobody wants to work anymore. The Farm is on eight-hour workdays. Production is only a fraction of what it used to be. They have split shifts and tea and coffee breaks. Bullshit! Water's not good enough anymore.

"The shrimpers should be here working on their boats, but look, there's hardly anyone around. And pink cops! That's a real laugh. You can see their pink cars and uniforms a mile away. They're targets! If there were a real threat from the outside like there has been from time to time, they wouldn't stand a chance."

"Calm down, Marcia." He patted her hand and smiled.

Everything she said was true, but she didn't need to have a stroke about it. Marcia drew a deep breath of the humid air and slowly let it back out. *He's right. I'm getting all worked up. I need to relax.*

Sonny smiled. "That's better."

She didn't tell him that Sean was now the mayor of the city. She wanted him to remember Sean before she shared this bit of information with him. Then, with Sonny's help, they'd take care of that little bastard from Peaceful Valley. *Damn right, we will. No outsider will run Corpus Christi.* The corners of Marcia's lips slowly curled into a stiff smile. *Not as long as I'm alive, Sean!*

✸✸✸

Sunday morning, James sat on the porch smoking a cigarette and finishing off his morning coffee when he heard a wolf howl. James returned the signal. Reggie and Emily appeared and made their way to the porch.

James took the last sip out of his cup and stood. "What's up?"

Emily looked up and pushed her hair back. "Going to church."

James shot her a smile and looked over at Reggie. "Want me to get you a cup of coffee? We can sit out here and catch up on things until Emily and Melissa get back."

"Nah, I'm going too."

James's jaw dropped. "What!? Say that again. I don't think I heard you right."

Reggie snorted. He looked over at Emily, then back to James. "I'm going to church."

"Are you being blackmailed? It's gotta be something like that . . . or worse."

"No! Nothing like that. John said he was going to write a segment of his sermon just for me. Said he wouldn't try to blow angel dust up my ass."

James pushed his hair back with his hand and blinked his eyes hard. "Dammit, John!"

"What's the matter, James?"

"That sneaky son-of-a . . . he tricked me."

Reggie smiled knowing James wasn't easily duped. "Now how in the world did he do that?"

"I told him that I'd attend one service if you went."

Reggie let out a big laugh. "That son-of-a-bitch _is_ sneaky! You going like you are?"

"There's no rule against work clothes, is there? If there is, I'm going to change that rule right now!"

Reggie shook his head and looked over at Emily. She shook her head as well. "Not that I know of, James. Well, guys, you ready for church?" She was grinning like a Cheshire cat.

Reggie grabbed her hand. "You didn't have anything to do with this, did you, darlin'?"

Emily put her free hand to her lips and zipped her mouth shut.

James followed them to the church without a word.

⌁⌁⌁

John stood behind the dais waiting for everyone to take their seats. He couldn't help his smile when James sat and looked in his direction. "I want to thank everyone for coming this morning, but especially to you, James and Reggie."

They both smirked.

John cleared his throat. "James . . . Reggie . . . none of us would be here today without you. Your bravery, James, and your ingenuity and explosives, Reggie, saved us all from Sandra Hawkins. Before that, you also had your trials and tribulations from which your heroism is duly noted. This is not to take away from the rest of you. You are all strong and courageous men and women. Without you, there would be no Peaceful Valley. I feel humbled in your presence . . . each and every one of you.

"But that's not what I want to talk about today. I just thought it should be mentioned. I want to talk about a special lady. That lady is Eileen Branson Lindgren.

"I'm sorry to say that I didn't know Lars, but I certainly knew Eileen. She was a city lady and quite beautiful at that. Her blonde hair and striking facial features were flawless. But she was much more than that. I could see a lot of Lars in her too. I'm told he tried to teach her everything he knew about living here in the woods. She was not only feisty, but she was also tough. Reggie, can you tell us a story about this remarkable lady?"

Reggie wasn't prepared to speak at this engagement, but he had no objection to talking about Eileen. He drew in a breath. He exhaled slowly as if in thought. Then a smile came over his face. He turned in his seat. "The first time I met Eileen was after a heavy thunderstorm. As many of you know, it is a little swampy in the meadows toward my home. Anyway, after a good rain, Lars and Eileen showed up at our doorstep covered in mud. He brought her to introduce her to Emily and me. We couldn't let them in the house as dirty as they were. She looked mighty fine in mud, I should add. You can't hide beauty with muck.

"Anyway, we found them some clothes to wear, and they took showers. Eileen went first, and Emily got her a dress to wear. She hadn't been here long, and I don't think Lars had ever seen her in a dress. When she came out, and Lars laid eyes on her . . . well, you should have seen his face. It was priceless. I think he fell in love with her at that instant."

Reggie turned to Emily. She smiled, and he leaned over and gave her a little kiss.

John gazed at James. "How about you, James. Would you like to share a story about her? I know you have to have a million of them."

"As a matter of fact, I do. Eileen was at Lars's grave not long after he died. His death hit her hard and she spent a lot of time talking to him long afterward. She would spend so many hours by the sycamore tree that I built a bench especially for her.

"Well, one day while she was out there, she heard a twig snap. She hid behind the sycamore and peeked around. When this intruder went for his gun, she drew hers first and put two bullets in his chest before he could get a shot off. He was dead before he hit the ground.

"I went running out to her, but by the time I got there, the threat was gone. Eileen didn't have a tear in her eyes, and the look on her face was that of a fierce warrior. Eileen turned to me and said, 'will you get this trash away from our cemetery?' She then turned and calmly walked to the house. She was remarkable."

Those that knew Eileen told more stories for another hour followed by a few songs. John closed the service with a prayer. Before everyone left, he asked

Brooke if it would be okay to tell a few stories about Ronnie at the next service. She hesitated only a few moments before agreeing. This was the way to keep the memories of the ones they loved alive.

⌁⌁⌁⌁

Melissa, Emily, and the rest of the girls headed inside to prepare a late lunch. Reggie and James pulled up chairs on the Lindgren porch and lit up stogies. John stood just off the porch talking to Brooke. When they'd finished, he gave her a generous hug and she went inside with the rest of the ladies. John followed her up the steps to where James and Reggie sat, having finished their smokes. "Mind if I join you two?"

James extended his arm toward an empty chair. He and Reggie were quiet.

"I can't believe you two still have tobacco."

James looked over at Reggie. "Yeah, it's not that hard to grow. Lars grew it every year and always kept plenty on hand. He showed me how to grow it before he died, and I always plant a row for Reggie and me. It's one of God's gifts."

John frowned and changed the subject. "The sermon wasn't so bad, was it?"

James glanced at Reggie and back at John. "No, but you tricked us."

John smiled. "Maybe so." He leaned back in the chair, crossed his arms over his chest, and looked over at Reggie, who hadn't said a word yet. "Awful quiet, Reggie."

Reggie looked over at James and motioned for another stogie. James lit another up too. Reggie took a big puff and tried to blow a smoke ring, but in the breeze, it failed to form. "I liked your sermon, John. You hardly mentioned God. It was about the family lost. I hate that you made me cry . . . I don't do that often . . . but I guess I was in good company.

"We have lost too many good people. I especially appreciate what you said about Lars and Eileen. Of course, I miss my grandson . . . he is our newest hurt . . . I still miss Lars and Eileen more than you know, but you were close." Reggie wiped at another tear. "Dammit! Get the hell out of here, John."

John drew in some fresh air and stood. He turned the knob to the front door and looked back. "Next Sunday, Reggie?"

"Maybe. I'll see . . ."

"James?"

"Oh Hell, why not!"

John smiled and stepped inside.

Chapter 14

In Victoria, Texas . . .

Robbie sat in a cell at the local police station. He was treated well, but they decided that they had to confine him. They assured him that he would see the mayor, but when? Tomorrow, he thought at first, but he'd been here three days already. Maybe next month, or even next year? Perhaps never. How could he tell?

"You don't just waltz in and get to see the mayor," Chief Hayes said.

The chief, however, did listen to an abbreviated version of his story and seemed to like what he was saying. *But did he? I could rot in this cell.*

Robbie was served three meals a day. They weren't great, but they weren't bad either. He guessed they took care of his dietary requirements. He asked each time he was fed, how much longer he would be confined. Even though the person delivering the food was different each time, the answer was the same, 'when the chief says so'.

On the fifth day, Robbie heard the rattle of keys about an hour after he finished breakfast. He raised up and sat on the edge of the bed. Someone unlocked his door, and two men entered, one with handcuffs. "Regulations," one said, "just like when you were brought in."

Robbie turned around with his hands behind his back. These weren't just men. They were big bastards, and there wasn't a lot of fat on their bones.

Robbie felt butterflies in his stomach as the men led him to an office and opened the door. Chief Hayes looked up from behind a pile of papers. The goons marched Robbie in front of the desk.

"You can take the cuffs off now."

The guards left as Robbie rubbed his wrists, stood straight, and waited for the chief to speak.

Hayes looked up at the clock on the wall to his right. "I'm sorry I had to lock you up and even more so that it took so long to get you a meeting with the mayor. I told him what you told me and he's interested. Not so much for here in Victoria. We have a good democratic system, and it works well, but every so often there is some trouble in one of the outlying cities. Some places are still relatively wild with little or no law and order. Anyway, you've got your date at ten o'clock."

Robbie relaxed a bit. "Yes, Sir. Thank you, Sir."

The chief smiled, then returned to the papers on his desk. "Give me five more minutes, and we'll be ready to go. Have a seat if you'd like."

Robbie looked around. He sat down in the closest of two chairs over near the wall. *Relax. Just tell them what you told the chief. Just a condensed version. If they want to know more, they'll ask.*

Robbie stood up when the chief did. He walked around the desk. "Follow me, son."

He led Robbie out to a police vehicle. It was painted much more professionally in black and white than the pink ones in Corpus.

Fifteen minutes later, Robbie followed the chief into an assembly room. Several men sat behind a long curved tabletop podium on a riser facing the audience.

Chief Hayes led Robbie down an aisle to the front row. There was a small lectern to his left. "Sit down here, Robbie, and wait for me," the chief said pointing.

Robbie watched the chief walk to the man in the middle of the group. The man he assumed was the mayor leaned over and looked around the chief, directly at him. Robbie felt the butterflies coming back.

His breathing was unsteady, and beads of sweat formed on his forehead, though the temperature was quite comfortable in the room.

A few people continued to filter in and take the empty seats on either side of the mayor. A handful of others came in and sat in the spectators' chairs to his left. Robbie guessed that the time had to be nearing ten o'clock.

Hayes slowly walked back over to Robbie, acknowledging some of the other people who came in. "When Mayor Rodriguez is ready, I'll give a short intro for the benefit of all the attendees; then it will be all you."

Robbie nodded. "Thanks for letting me see the mayor."

He looked over. "Don't thank me. Thank, Freya."

Robbie's eyes bugged out. "Freya?"

"Yes, Robbie. We found your Jeep, and I talked to my daughter yesterday. We also questioned the laborers who brought you to me. You have been totally honest as far as I can tell, and that is why you're here."

"Your daughter?"

The chief smiled. "Yes."

The butterflies went on a rampage in his stomach. The perspiration formed under his arms, across his forehead, and on his palms. Robbie looked straight ahead toward the mayor. He didn't want to make eye contact with the chief again.

Chief Hayes looked over at Robbie squirming in his seat. "Just continue being honest and everything will be fine. So, Robbie, you like Freya? She went on and on about you. Seems she's taken quite a liking to you. She doesn't care for guns though. I guess you gathered that?"

Robbie turned his head toward the chief, but not far enough to make eye contact, and nodded.

"Don't worry about your Jeep and guns. When you're ready to leave town, everything will be returned to you."

Hayes was saying all the right things, but Robbie couldn't seem to relax. *This was almost entirely because of Freya? She should have told me her dad was the Chief of Police. I wish Sean were here to explain everything. He's much better than me at this kind of stuff. Just tell the truth—the truth, the whole truth, and nothing but the truth.*

The mayor waved his hand in their direction. The chief stood up and walked over to the small podium on their left. He outlined Robbie's arrival, discussions with his daughter and the workers, and the newcomer's demeanor during his stay thus far. Then he turned and introduced Robbie.

He headed for the chief. He shook his hand and thanked him, then stood straight and cleared his throat. "Mr. Mayor, thank you for allowing me the opportunity to discuss the plan my deceased brother and I devised after setting Corpus Christi on the path to democracy. Yes, democracy . . ."

The mayor had a young lady take a bottle of water to Robbie shortly after he cleared his throat and began to speak. He wouldn't have made the two-hour speech with the occasional question without it.

Other than an intermittent muffled cough, there wasn't a sound in the room. The mayor and all attendees sat and listened to Robbie until well after lunch. At the end of Robbie's dissertation, the mayor thanked him and informed him that his proposition would be discussed and he would be brought back tomorrow for questioning.

Chief Hayes took Robbie back to the station. "I'm sorry, but I can't let you out and about on your own just yet. It's for your own safety."

"It would help if I had something to read, Sir."

The chief looked around. "There, on the table. There are some old magazines."

Robbie walked over and picked one up with a fish on the front. *Field and Stream.* Then he saw the date it was published. He smiled. *This thing's older than I am.*

The chief pushed a button on his desk that Robbie hadn't noticed before. Seconds later, two burly officers came in. One he recognized from earlier. "I don't think we need the handcuffs, do we, Robbie?"

"No, Sir."

The chief nodded at the men.

Robbie's breakfast was a little better this morning than the previous day. He didn't know whether the improved meal was due to something he'd said to the chief or the mayor, but the eggs and sausage were much better than the cold pancakes the previous morning. And juice instead of water.

The guard took Robbie into the chief's office at nine the next morning and sat him in the same chair he'd sat in yesterday.

Chief Hayes had Robbie in front of the Mayor by ten o'clock, and Robbie began answering questions the Mayor posed: When was the cell tower system going to be completed? How many citizens in Corpus Christi? How many planes did his community have? How often do you make trips to Brownsville? How many producing oil wells did they have? How much seafood could they provide?

Robbie answered every question to the best of his ability and added a few reassuring remarks about the willingness of Corpus Christi and Peaceful Valley to provide specific resources to Victoria and the surrounding communities, which might not be currently available to them. In particular, gas and diesel from the crude Victoria would provide, and seafood.

The questions started trailing off after a couple of hours, and the mayor wrapped up the interrogation after another hour. "Robbie, we—and I'm speaking for all of us up here—feel you are honest and straightforward in your quest for a better Texas. But be aware, we do not need you or the rest of the country. We've been doing quite well for a long time. However, we're compassionate people.

"I'm old enough to remember how it was before the grid shut down. Though it wasn't perfect, it was better than what we have now. We do desire a few things that you currently get from Brownsville . . . and I haven't had a good plate of fried shrimp in quite some time."

Some of the men alongside the mayor chuckled, and Robbie smiled. "I know we can help you with that problem, Mr. Mayor."

While Robbie had the mayor's attention, he had a few requests of his own, namely for help visiting some of the surrounding communities to elicit the cooperation of any people who might be out there.

The mayor agreed. "We have fuel, but it is limited. With the refinery in Corpus, we could do more, expand outward, and just maybe get back to some semblance of what our society once was.

"I remember going to San Antonio regularly. I really enjoyed the River-walk—the coolness provided by the water in the heat of the day, the ducks swimming in the river, the music, and some of the best restaurants known to man."

The mayor paused for a minute. He took a deep breath. Robbie smiled as he imagined the mayor was reliving one of his favorite outings there.

Then, Mayor Rodriguez snapped out of his dream. "Yes, Robbie, I like your vision of a new world. Maybe we won't make the same mistakes as last time around."

"I hope not, Sir. If you become Governor of Texas, maybe you can see to it that we don't."

He laughed. "I think we have a lot of work to do first, son. I do like the way you think though."

The mayor looked to the men on either side of him. They all had their eyes trained on him. "Well, gentlemen, are we all agreed that we should proceed with Robbie's proposal?"

The mayor was the boss. Robbie had gathered that, by the way the men had been reacting the past couple of days. He wasn't a dictator like Sandra Hawkins in Corpus Christi, but he did have most of the power.

He wasn't like Sandra at all—he was more genial. He was the one who pointed out that Robbie needed water and asked the young lady to get him some. Maybe that was why many citizens and even some of the police officers in his town didn't carry guns like they did in Sandra's world. They didn't need them. They were kind and courteous to visitors. Cautious, but not ready to put a bullet in someone as was the case in Corpus.

The police force had rules for their own protection. They were mostly well-armed and outfitted but seemed to show respect to outsiders. Robbie also assumed they were well-trained and would respond in a heartbeat should the need arise. That was the impression Robbie got, and he didn't dare test them. His entry into the city, with the help of Freya, unarmed and considerate of everyone he'd met thus far, showed others he wasn't a threat. And Robbie wasn't a risk. He wanted help. He wanted his and Ronnie's dream of a new world. It was too early to get his hopes up, but it appeared that his plan was coming together.

Chapter 15

The next morning, Robbie heard the jingling of keys. He'd been awake for an hour, just lying on the bed thinking about the coming day. The mayor told him that two teams of men would visit Port Lavaca, Edna, Cuero, Yoakum, and Refugio. Robbie's route was out Highway 59 to Goliad.

Mayor Rodriguez liked Robbie's idea of flying the American flag on the vehicles. He instructed the chief to locate some for the scout vehicles, but since they had too many police cars, the flag would be painted on them.

Robbie stood up when the cell door opened. The officer actually smiled at him. Robbie responded with a "good morning."

"And the same to you."

He nodded and followed him to Hayes's office.

The chief looked up when Robbie came in. "Have a seat."

Robbie sat down and grabbed a magazine, but the chief didn't go back to his papers. "Robbie, I have a confession to make."

Robbie focused on him. "Sir?"

"Normally when someone new comes to town, we take their guns, and they stay in a nearby boarding house. The fact that you and Freya . . . dammit, she seems to have taken a liking to you mighty fast. I don't know what went on between you two, but I didn't like it. We haven't gotten along all that well for some time, but recently things have been better. I guess I was the protective father. I didn't want you seeing her."

"But Sir, we just met. We hardly know each other."

"Freya seems to think she knows you well enough. I think I know you a little better now though."

He paused a second. "She's been asking about you. I thought you'd like to take a little tour of the city."

The chief glanced over at the clock. "Freya should be here any minute. I didn't tell her I locked you up. Can we keep that our little secret?"

Robbie nodded and stood up when he heard a tap on the door frame and saw Freya standing there. Her yellow sundress was almost as bright as her smile. She had her hair pulled back into a ponytail and looked to be ready for a day on the town.

Freya gave her dad a quick kiss on the cheek, then hurried back over to Robbie and grabbed his arm. They were out the door in a flash.

"So, how are we going on our little tour?"

Freya pointed. She walked over and leaned her hand on the bright red car.

Robbie ran his hand along the side of the vehicle. He opened the door and stuck his head inside the Volvo. *Yep, just like Grandma's.*

Freya smiled when Robbie turned and looked at her. "You approve then?"

"Absolutely! This is the same car my grandmother had. It's dead now just like . . ." Robbie winced at the pain in his heart. "I have a lot of good memories both of her and the car."

Robbie led Freya around to the driver's side and opened the door for her, then ran around to the other side. She drove him down the main drag, which was Laurent and not Main Street. He thought that was strange. The college seemed to be the center of the activity. The brick buildings surrounded by huge trees stood tall, unfazed by the passing years. It seemed reasonable that that was where the remaining people would gather. The nearby hospitals had also endured the test of time.

Freya drove out to some of the outlying areas of the city. "Outside of the business district, there's not much to see."

"I see that."

"The bigger buildings burned and weren't rebuilt. Those that are still standing are vacant."

"If there are so many people in Victoria, why is so much of the city empty?"

"Most stay on the ranches. There's a large ranch to the south and another to the north. The refinery is near the one to the south where some old plants are located by the Victoria water basin. The plants are no longer functional for the same purpose as before, but with the resources, one was turned into a refinery.

"The ranch to the north provides most of the red meat, though there is some on the southern ranches as well. Most of the work is outside of town, so that's where the people are. Those who stay in town are support-, manufacturing-, and distribution-oriented."

Freya made a pass down by the Guadalupe River, which ran around the west side of town. There was one spot where they could drive to the water's edge, and they stopped and got out.

Robbie looked up at the tall pecan trees. People wandered around in the forest and up and down the riverbanks. Then he realized what they were doing. *They're fishing.* Some people floated around on the water in makeshift rafts with rods and reels. Others fished off the bank. Children of the grownups played nearby. A lone woman sat at a park bench with her toddler, unafraid.

Freya didn't seem to be in any hurry, and neither was Robbie. There wasn't much to see in town, and there was less outside of the city. One thing Robbie noticed was that no one was wearing guns. There were heavily armed policemen everywhere they went, but the citizens were unarmed. *Is this how it was before the grid shut down? How Grandma told me it was? Police to keep the people safe where they didn't need to carry guns. This, I think, is what the whole country needs to be. Victoria will be our model city.*

Robbie and Freya strolled through the trees in the park, hand in hand. Robbie took a deep breath of the fresh-smelling humid air. It wasn't as hot here by the river as it was just a short way into town.

Freya's pace hurried when they approached the zoo. "You've got to see the animals," she said, her voice more excited now.

Robbie followed her inside. She introduced him to the zookeeper. "Hi, Pepe. This is Robbie. He's a friend. Mind if we take a look around?"

He reached out and gave Robbie a gentle shake but barely looked at him. Though he was an elderly black man, he seemed to be mesmerized by Freya as much as he was. "You know you're always welcome here, missy."

Freya gave him a gentle hug and slipped something into his hand. He squeezed his hand tight to not drop the gift.

She grabbed Robbie's hand and led him off through a heavy door. She led him through the reptile room first. Most of the glass enclosures were empty. Some had snakes, toads, and lizards, most Robbie had seen before, but that didn't matter. Freya was excited.

"I saw you slip something to Pepe."

"Yes, a silver coin."

"One of your mother's?"

"Yes. He needs it. Pepe struggled to keep this place up after the grid shut down. He still has a hard time feeding the animals. I love the ones he's managed to save. Many had to be put down because he couldn't . . . I just have to help him."

Robbie wrapped his arm around her and gave her a comforting squeeze.

Freya then led him outside where the big cats were. "I'm so glad he was able to save the kitties."

Robbie jumped when the king of beasts roared. He'd seen pictures in books but never imagined how ferocious the African animals were. "These things aren't scary in photos. Damn! I'm glad we don't have them in the wild around here. It'd be hard to sleep at night."

After they finished their tour of the zoo, they drove only a short distance, and Robbie held up his arm. She stopped. Men and a few women played on a well-manicured golf course. "I've heard of this game, but I've never played. Golf, isn't it?"

"Yes. Don't ask me how they kept this course going over the past few decades, but somehow . . ."

Robbie smiled. "I'd like to try to play one day."

"Ha!" Freya scoffed. "I tried it once. Daddy likes to play. Seemed like an easy thing to do. Fooled me though. Better practice a bit before you try to get out on the course."

"How hard can it be to get a little ball in a hole?"

"The holes are anywhere from a hundred to five hundred yards away from the tee-off spots. And the heads on those darn clubs aren't very big. When you stand, looking down at that little white ball, I think it shrinks up to half the size. Not just that, but if you don't hit it square on the club-face, it will go in the trees, water, or sand bunker every time."

"I could do it. It just doesn't look that hard," Robbie boasted.

"Well . . . that's not the worst of it. If you get it on the green, I think the holes move when you take your eyes off of them."

"Now you're ribbing me!"

"I'm just saying it's not nearly as easy as it looks."

Robbie frowned and turned back to the men in shorts as she slipped the car into drive.

The next stop was at the large ranch to the north. On the way, Robbie gazed at the many fields of corn, cotton, and grain. "Seems to be a lot of farming around here."

Freya looked over and grinned. "Yes, you can't live by meat alone."

When they reached the road into the ranch, cattle grazed in a seemingly endless pasture, and several cowboys rode their horses nearby.

Robbie rolled his eyes back, remembering a photo in one of his grandpa's books. "Just like the wild west out here."

Freya drove up to a large set of pens. A few cattle stood eating hay. They got out and leaned up against the railing, looking at the nearly grown calves. "These will probably be butchered in a day or so. They keep a few penned up so when there is a demand, they are slaughtered. That's usually once a week this time of year."

As there was no one around except a couple of cattle hands and they were taking care of their own business, Freya nodded toward the car at Robbie, and they headed out.

It was nearly dark by the time they got back to the Police Station. "Robbie, will you stay at my house tonight?"

"No hanky panky?"

"I promise. We're friends."

"Sure." *Certainly beats a cell.*

"Wait here." Freya hopped out and went inside. She was back in minutes, and they headed to her place.

"I expected more, but I really appreciate seeing your town. Loved the zoo though, and the park and ranch were fine. I just expected more in the city."

"I know. There aren't enough people to fix things up. Too many other operations are more important. Maybe tomorrow I can take you to my most favorite place, the library."

"Maybe on the next trip. I need to get on the road."

Freya's bottom lip pushed up into a pout.

"Don't do that! I've got a big job ahead of me." He gave her a hurt look. "The library can wait until next time, can't it?"

"And how long will that be?"

"Not long. You'll see."

"Okay, I guess." She gave him a stern look. "You better not be long."

"I promise."

"And next time we can go to the refinery too. That's a much longer tour, but Dad thought we'd save that for last. Maybe when we can start getting some fuel from Corpus Christi. There are storage tanks to hold the gas there at our little refinery. Maybe we can pump the oil to you guys, and you can pump the gas back here. I know there were pipelines between here and Corpus at one time. They'll need to be checked out and repaired first though."

Robbie's face lit up at the thought of getting some trade going with Victoria. "That's the plan, I believe."

⊣⊢⊣⊢⊣⊢⊣⊦

His Jeep was parked in front of the station the next morning when Freya drove him back. Chief Hayes handed Robbie his pistol, holster, a bag of cartridges, and his AR-15. "We unloaded them. Please wait until you get to the edge of the city before you reload."

Robbie nodded.

The chief shook Robbie's hand. "So, we'll see you in about a month then?"

"That's the plan . . . if I'm still alive in a month."

"You're a good man, Robbie. You'll be okay."

Robbie smiled. "It was a pleasure meeting you. I was really concerned about coming to Victoria, but you're good people with good values. We'll get along well."

Hayes smiled.

Freya gave Robbie a kiss, and he headed to his Jeep. His escort to the edge of the city got into the police car just in front of him. He held out his arm indicating he was ready, and pulled out. Robbie eased off the clutch. He threw a grin into the rearview mirror. Freya waved. The chief had a smile on his face too.

At the edge of the city, Robbie's escort eased over to the shoulder of the pavement and waved Robbie on.

⌁⌁⌁⌁

When Robbie found the edge of Goliad, he drove back away from the city limit a couple of miles and hid his Jeep. Then he readied himself for a long walk around town since he was on the opposite side from where he initially met Josephine and her son. Robbie needed to see them, and particularly Joey, her eldest son. It was time to see if he had rounded up a couple of friends to scout out the counties to the north.

There were a couple of areas where he didn't have a lot of brush cover. He spotted an old mission on the left side of the city and decided to check it out. He'd never seen this type of architecture before, and it interested him. Everything was built out of stone and tree limbs.

Rows of rock fences overgrown with weeds surrounded the property. They had deteriorated severely but were still identifiable as walls. These provided him with the cover he needed. As he neared the side of one of the buildings, he was startled by voices. They appeared to be coming from inside. The doors were open, but he couldn't see anyone.

Robbie decided quickly that he had seen enough. He didn't want to take the chance of getting spotted, or worse yet, caught. He needed to find Josephine's place.

The trees hid the sun now. He headed back to the road and followed it down to the San Antonio River. He continued along the bank, but it got dark before he found her house. He didn't want to barge in after dark, so he located a place to make camp and spend the night. He didn't dare build a fire. Instead, he ate a piece of sausage he'd saved from Victoria and chased it down with water.

⌁⌁⌁⌁

The sound of a flock of crows awoke Robbie at daylight. He sat up and leaned against the tree under which he had slept. It was a large live oak. He sat and stared at the river gently flowing by. A hint of fog hung over the ripples caused by an old dead tree stump. *Would be nice to be sitting down on the bank with a fishing pole in my hands, Florence sitting at my side. I really screwed up with Freya. I can't tell Flo. She'll kill me.*

Robbie checked his pistol, grabbed his rifle, and started to walk along the riverbank. His ears and eyes on high alert, he made his way through the sometimes dense brush. He wasn't certain how far it would be to Josephine's house, but he thought it wasn't too far.

In the distance, he recognized something and slowed his pace. As he neared the house, he looked for a concealed location from which to watch the residence. He got comfortable and waited.

He didn't have to wait long. The back door opened and Josephine walked out carrying a basket. She set it down beneath the clothesline and started hanging the wet clothing. He called out her name.

She turned and looked across the river, but not directly at him, so he hollered her name again. "Josephine."

Robbie stood up and waved. Her lips curled back in a big grin, her teeth sparkling in the sunlight. "Well, I see you've made your way back, young man."

"Yes, Ma'am, but I got myself on the wrong side of the river. Is it okay if I come over?"

"Yes, of course, but you're gonna get yo'self wet."

"If you'll turn your head a minute, I'll come across in my underwear."

She let out a laugh and waved her arm into the air as she turned around. She methodically hung each piece of the freshly laundered clothes on the line with care, happily humming away, not once looking in Robbie's direction.

He kept one eye on her while he slipped his shoes and britches off and slid down the steep bank. He slipped into the water, holding his rifle, pistol, backpack, and trousers high. The water was little more than waist deep, and he made it across easily. He quickly re-dressed on the opposite bank.

Josephine barely gave him enough time to get dressed before she finished hanging the clothes and turned around. "Well, you didn't drown anyway."

They both smiled as Robbie sat down on a stump to put his shoes back on. "Joey around?"

"He'll be back a little later. I sent him on an errand."

Robbie nodded.

"You hungry? I can whip you up some eggs, and I think there's a couple pieces of chicken left over from last night's meal."

"That would be nice. I could use a bite."

"You may as well come in and make yourself comfortable for a while. I'm not sure when Joey will be back. He's only been gone half an hour. It might be noon. He ate a light breakfast, so he won't be much later than that. That boy does like to eat."

Robbie followed her into the house. Samantha was on the sofa playing with her rag doll. Marcus came in from his bedroom to see who was there, said 'hi', and went back to his room.

Josephine went to the stove. "Where's your brother? That was your brother who was with ya last time, wasn't it?"

"Yes, Ma'am." Robbie batted his eyes, fighting back the tears. "He didn't make it. We ran into some trouble over on the other side of Sinton . . . a sniper."

"I'm sorry, son. I know that's going to hurt for a spell."

"Yes, Ma'am."

They were quiet for a long time after that until Marcus came running in yelling, "I'm hungry."

"I told you, you should have cleaned your plate at breakfast. The chickens done ate it. You'll have to wait until your brother gets back and I fix us all lunch. Maybe next time you'll clean your plate, young man."

Marcus pouted and ran over to plop down on the sofa.

It was nearly noon to the minute when Joey walked through the door. The grin on his face stretched his lips tight, exposing his teeth. He gave Robbie a man-hug and looked around for Ronnie. "Where's . . ."

Robbie shook his head. "He got shot."

"What! Nooo."

Joey and Robbie strolled outside to talk while Josephine put up the supplies Joey brought.

"Don't you boys stray far."

Robbie had a long story to tell, and except for his brother, it was good news, especially about Victoria. He left out the part about Freya and locked up that little bit of information in a secure place in the back of his mind.

"So, since you don't have your . . . brother, you needing a partner to ride shotgun?"

"Your mom might not like that after what happened to Ronnie. Besides, it looks like your dad is gone most of the time, so you're needed around here."

"Dad's here enough. Mama can take care of things. I want to help."

"And you will. I just don't think going with me is what I need right now. I'm headed home. There wasn't too much of a problem between here and there."

Joey took a deep breath. Robbie could see he was disappointed, but he would get his chance. "Did you find a buddy or two, and a car or truck to drive?"

"I haven't really talked to anybody about a car, but a couple of my friends are interested in going with you and helping. I didn't talk to anyone else though. I wasn't really sure if I'd ever see you again."

"I understand. I'll be back in a couple of weeks. See if you can get a car ready full of gas and at least one sidekick and a couple of guns with ammunition. The most important thing I want you to do is to talk to some of the leaders here in town. See if you can get them on my side, and when I come back next time, you can introduce me to them. Can you do that?"

"That's easy enough, I think."

Robbie told Joey about Hank and his trip to Seadrift, the guys in Sinton, and the leper colony in Beeville. He shared a little more about what happened with his brother, but broke down and changed the subject to Corpus Christi. Joey said he'd never had shrimp or oysters.

"Well, you're in for a surprise, especially the oysters." Robbie licked his lips at the mere thought of them. "My Jeep is all the way across town. Maybe you can help me get through the city and over to this side. I need to go west. It would save me a lot of time. It would also give us the opportunity to talk a bit more."

"Sure, let me tell Mama where I'm going."

Joey stuck his head inside. "I'm going to help Robbie get his Jeep over to this side of town. We'll probably be gone most of the afternoon."

"You be back before dark; you hear?"

"Yes, Ma'am."

Robbie put his backpack on, slung his rifle over his shoulder, and followed Joey's lead. "Do people carry guns in town?"

"Most. I only have my .22, and I carry it everywhere. Bullets are hard to come by. One of my buddies makes ammo for me. I get enough to kill a few rabbits and squirrels, but that's about it."

Joey led Robbie into the heart of the city. There weren't a lot of people out and about, but the few who were meandering around paid little attention to him and Joey. They looked, then went on about their business.

At least a dozen shops were open, and Robbie saw people inside. Most had the front doors to their businesses open. An American flag hung in front of one. *I think this is going to work out okay. People are tired of the way things have been. It's been a long time, more than a lifetime for me, since the grid shut down. The older folks have been through hell over the last couple of decades. They're ready for peace . . . for life like it used to be . . . like Grandma told me.*

Joey pointed out the road leading to Victoria. That's where Robbie parked his Jeep. It felt good for him to be walking about in a strange town, people he didn't know and didn't know him, to look and go about what they were doing; like he belonged there. It gave him a sense that progress was being made and that everything would eventually work out.

With the help of John and Sean, a communications grid would materialize. Then, all the communities in the area could come together and work for the good of all. Not just himself against the world, but droves of people all working together. He had felt so alone in his quest. Even with his brother alongside, it was still just the two of them. Now, there was Joey. Hank was back in Seadrift and familiarizing its citizens with his dream for a unified State. The men in Sinton would help, he was sure. And Victoria. Robbie smiled. *It's going to work. It is working!*

Joey noticed the smile on his face. "What's up?"

"Just thinking about things. Thank you for helping me, Joey."

The lad returned his smile. "I'm being a little selfish. It gets so boring around here most of the time. There isn't much to do. It feels good to have a little adventure to look forward to. You sure I can't go with you now?"

"Don't worry, you'll get your chance. I'm planning on coming back. I won't let you down. If for some reason I don't show up, you'll know I'm dead, because I won't quit until I see a new order around here." Robbie placed his hand on Joey's shoulder. "Maybe I'll take you flying one day."

Joey's eyes lit up like a Christmas tree. "Flying? You have a plane?"

"My best friend, Sean, is working on getting a Cessna for me in Corpus Christi. I had one that I flew home when I escaped from Corpus. Unfortunately, it was damaged. I crashed it. But, Sean found another and said he'd get it going so I could fly again.

"You can't imagine the feeling. I only flew that one time, but it truly was breathtaking. You can see for miles in all directions. Everything looks so different from high in the air. The world is mighty big down here, but up in the air . . . you realize how small and insignificant one person is. It makes you think.

"Victoria has an airport. Maybe one day I can take you there. You can see the city lights."

Robbie and Joey stopped and talked to the sentry on the road out of town. Robbie didn't notice him until Joey pointed him out. The outpost looked more like a deer blind than a sentry post, but he guessed that was the idea. Joey informed him that they'd be back through here in a Jeep.

Robbie glanced at the sentry's gun, a bolt-action hunting rifle, but remembered about the explosives Josephine told him about. He looked around and didn't see any, but assumed they'd be well hidden and protected from the weather.

After another hour, their surroundings looked familiar to Robbie. "I think we're getting close."

The trees cast a shadow across the roadway when Robbie finally located the spot where he'd parked. He recognized the large gnarly live oak tree close to the road and found the tracks where he'd driven into the brush.

"Nice gun," Joey said when he saw the turret. "I sure would like to shoot that thing someday."

"You may get the chance, but hopefully it will be just for target practice. I don't ever want to shoot it in self-defense again."

Joey hopped in the passenger side, and they headed back to town. The sentry waved the vehicle through without stopping them. In town, several people stopped and stared, but when Joey waved, a few waved back.

They stopped briefly at the edge of town, and Joey introduced Robbie to the sentry there before heading on. Robbie stopped again at the river bridge and let Joey out. He said there was a trail to his house along the riverbank.

"See if you can find some American flags too. That's important. The flag will be the symbol of who we are and what we're trying . . ." He stopped and corrected himself. He was more confident now. "A symbol of what we are going to accomplish."

Robbie shook Joey's hand and gave him a high-five. "Make sure everyone here knows what's going on."

Joey nodded. "I will. And I'll be ready to go when you get back."

Robbie waited until the young man disappeared into the brush. He looked down at the fuel gauge. *What I should do is turn around, get on 239 to Kenedy, and get my ass home. But why do I have the feeling I should go straight ahead to Beeville? It's a leper colony. Curiosity has always been my weakness . . . How can a disease be so severe that people are isolated? I'll have to find gas there, or I may not make it all the way home.*

Robbie looked down at the gas gauge one more time, took a deep breath, and put the Jeep into gear. *What the hell! I've never seen a leper. What do they look like?*

Robbie sat staring at the overpass he took the last time he came through here. He couldn't imagine what was drawing him to Beeville, but he was going to find out.

A nearly calm air and clear skies hinted at a beautiful day. His left cheek barely detected the breeze. The sun perched on the tops of the trees to his left.

Robbie drove under the overpass and spotted a place he could hide the Jeep. He got out, checked his guns, donned his backpack, and took a good look around before heading into the heart of the city.

He meandered through brush and dilapidated buildings where he thought he could stay relatively hidden. If there were people here, he wanted to spot them first.

After an hour, he'd still seen no one. He kept hidden between buildings and in the shade as he crept farther into town. It was only when he found the business district that he began seeing people. He found a sheltered place and sat, studying the area through the scope on his rifle. It appeared as though the stores were all closed, but there were also residential properties scattered among the commercial businesses.

The first few people he saw were sitting on the large porch of one such residence. They didn't appear to be talking to each other. Robbie was too far away to hear voices. His jaw dropped as he swung the scope up to study the folks closer. What he saw shocked and scared him.

One man's face was covered with what looked like blisters, and his eyes were red. They appeared to be bleeding. Another had a stump for one hand, and his skin was discolored and marred with splotches. A third person sat with his head down and appeared to be dead. He was missing an ear, and his skin was similar to the others.

Another person hobbled out the door, leaning heavily on a crutch. One foot was little more than an irregular remnant of what it should have been.

Robbie lowered his scope. He could look no more. He'd never seen anything like these people. *Lepers, the man in Sinton had said. Armadillos can cause this?*

Robbie stayed concealed and made his way around to another residential house. He found more people. Some did not appear to be as bad as the first ones he saw, but all bore the marks of the disease to some degree or other.

He didn't need to see any more. Careful not to be seen or heard, Robbie made his way back toward his Jeep. He drove to a couple of old service stations, and there seemed to be no one around.

He found gas in the storage tank of the first of the two gas stations he'd spotted. He filled the Jeep, then got out the spare can. He heard a noise just as he finished topping off the container, and looked over. A man was staring at him.

Robbie knocked over his gas can, spilling some on the concrete. He scrambled to get the cap back on. The man stepped toward him. The man's face showed signs of leprosy.

"Stay away from me." Robbie stumbled backward with his gas.

"I'm not going to hurt you," he said.

Robbie drew his pistol and pointed toward the unarmed man. His hand shook noticeably. "Get back, I tell you!"

He laughed. "You're afraid of me, aren't you? I told you I wasn't going to hurt you."

"But you're sick."

"Yes, I am. And you're a thief."

Robbie looked around. The two of them were alone. "I need this gas to get home." He moved around to the far side of the Jeep and put the can in the back, all the time keeping his pistol on the stranger.

"I don't care that you took the gas, but you could have asked. This damn disease is nasty, but it's not going to jump out and get you. We're people too. We're sick, but we still have feelings, desires . . ."

Robbie walked back around the Jeep and a little closer to the man. "I'm Robbie."

"I'm Steven. You'll excuse me if I don't shake your hand."

Robbie smiled. "So what do you want?"

"Just a little conversation." He set the bucket down he was carrying and sat on it. "I have a brother who comes around every month to bring us stuff, but he doesn't stay long. I've heard all the stories from the people who live here. So, what's going on in the world?"

Robbie reached over and grabbed the fabric of his flag. "I'm changing it."

"Enough to get all of us out of this hellhole?"

"Maybe."

Robbie opened the door of the Jeep and sat down. He spelled out his plan to reorganize the country, and Steven listened attentively.

"See if you can find a flag and hang it around here somewhere. You might also put up a 'leprosy colony' sign to forewarn any visitors. That way any future visitors will know that while you're friendly people, precautions need to be taken."

"So, you'll be back?"

"Yes."

He got behind the wheel and headed home. He tried to force the visions of disfigurement out of his mind and convince himself that they were still people. The only difference between himself and them was a disease.

Robbie slowed down after he got a few miles away from the Beeville city limits. He couldn't stop thinking about Steven and the other residents. He needed to concentrate on the road and his surroundings. Dwelling on the lepers could get him killed.

He thought about Florence. He would see her tomorrow afternoon. One more night in the field, and it would be an easy drive to Peaceful Valley.

As he tried to maintain his thoughts of reuniting with Florence, he found his mind drifting to his encounter with Freya. How she crept into his room and made him forget about everything else but her. She teased every sense and led him to the realm of every man's fantasy—to have your body ravaged by the most beautiful woman on the planet. Freya sucked every last bit of energy out of his body, and he lay afterward, totally spent and in a state of complete satisfaction.

But that's a dream. Life between your legs. We can be friends, but Florence, my son . . . that's what I want. Life is not just about sex. I could have had that with Sandra's girls. It was great, but that was not what I wanted then, and it's not what I want now. I love Florence. But that night with Freya . . . damn!

With the thought of Freya still fresh in his mind and his eyes trying to close, he decided to stop and take a break from driving.

He pulled deep into the brush so he could relax, close his eyes, and not have to be concerned with someone coming down the road, though this seemed unlikely. Over the many miles he'd driven, he seldom saw a soul on the streets. People were stuck in their communities, and unless someone was going out hunting or trading with another city, there was no one on the highways.

Robbie found a shady spot alongside a dried-up creek. He killed the engine, leaned back in his seat, and closed his eyes. He forced Freya out of his mind and thought about Florence for a few minutes. *Do I love Florence? Yes. That's a fact. But we're pregnant. Sure sex is lacking, but that can't be helped. Temporary. I do love her. I shouldn't have let Freya . . . but I couldn't help it. Dammit!*

Then he drifted off to John, Sean, his dad, and what they were doing. He hoped they were making progress with the cell towers. Hopefully, Sean would have fuel production maxed out by the time he returned to Corpus Christi again.

I hope Sean has the Cessna ready by the time I get back there. I hope Dad gets the runway built at Peaceful Valley. Sean sent fuel.

The stress and long hours driving finally got the best of him, and he drifted off to sleep. Visions of monsters with stumps for hands and covered with huge blisters, all pawing at him yelling for help, made him squirm in his sleep. He awoke dripping with sweat, afraid he would contract the disease that caused their disfigurations.

Robbie looked around. He was alone. The monsters were gone. It was all in his mind. But the people in Beeville were real. They were not a figment of his imagination. They were living the hell of what leprosy did to their bodies and minds. He wanted to help these people, but there was nothing he could do. They were banished from society. Though they did nothing to deserve their fate, their lives were essentially over. Life would never be normal. In fact, the complete opposite was true. They would spend their remaining days in misery in the company of others who shared the same fate. They had only one thing to look forward to—death.

Robbie cranked up the Jeep and continued on his journey toward home. He needed the rest, but sometimes staying awake was better medicine. Demons show up at night when you're vulnerable and even during the daytime if you doze off and give them the slightest chance.

By the time he got close to Kenedy, the trees had hidden the sun to the west. Robbie kept his eye out for a place to stay the night. He could make his way around Kenedy, and if he didn't run into any problems, he could be home by early afternoon. Florence would be surprised. The trip had gone much better than expected, and he was arriving home early.

Robbie spotted a place. He steered the Jeep off the roadway and into the brush near a small valley. There was likely an old creek bed there, and with a little luck, he could find a spot which held a little water. He had drinking water, but a water hole would be a magnet for wild game. He'd love to have a rabbit or small piglet for dinner.

Robbie killed the motor to listen to the sounds of nature. After a few minutes, he got up to hunt but found little game. The armadillo he did see he chose to ignore—he'd never touch armadillo meat again after what he saw in Beeville—but a nearby snake proved a worthy alternative. He shot the head off, skinned it, and wrapped it around a stick for roasting.

Robbie saved a little piece of the snake for breakfast and ate it on the fly. He got back on the road and concentrated on the pavement ahead. Once he got around Kenedy, he felt like he was mostly out of danger and sped up a little. The idea of home and his family were exerting a significant pull on him.

Just after noon, as he had expected, he turned off the highway and headed down the road into the property. He meandered his way along the dirt road but stopped short of the Lindgren homestead. He was surprised to see someone had built a new building.

He stopped to have a closer look. *No one can live here. It's not big enough for one person, much less a family.*

He checked the doorknob. The squeal of the hinges echoed through the structure as the door swung inward.

Robbie twisted his face up into a frown. He walked down the aisle between the four benches, two on a side, up to the dais and stared at the wall. *Well-carved cross.*

Robbie shut the door and headed back toward the Jeep. *Looks like John got his church. How in Hell did that happen? Brooke . . . well, I'll be damned. Guess she got it done.*

He got behind the wheel and continued on to his parents' place. He stopped there before heading home. Robbie tooted the horn as he drove into the clearing. His mother met him as soon as he stopped, yanked open the door, and smothered him with kisses.

"Mom!"

"We don't see you enough. We miss you." She drew back, frowned, and looked down at his stomach. "And you're not eating enough. Come on in. I just took a venison pot roast out of the oven."

Robbie looked up at the porch. His dad was standing there with a big grin on his face, watching his wife drag their son out of the Jeep and onto the porch. "May as well come on in. She won't quit until you eat a bite."

Robbie pulled away from his mother long enough to give his dad a hug. His mom then yanked him inside. She had a plate fixed almost before he sat down. Then as he ate, came the barrage of questions.

Most of the questions could be answered with a nod of the head, and Robbie quickly finished his plate. "Give me a day with Florence, and we'll have a meeting. I need information from John and Grandpa Reggie. I'll answer all your questions then. How about the day after tomorrow?"

James nodded. "I'll notify the Lins and Wimberleys if you'll get word to Reggie and Emily."

"I will, Dad."

His mother pinched him in the ribs. "You need to eat more."

He smiled and headed out to the Jeep.

Mutt started barking the minute Robbie drove out of the brush. Florence was already on the porch by the time he stopped in front of the house. She waddled down the steps, tears flying, and grabbed at her belly. She sat down on the bottom step.

Robbie took a moment to give Mutt a scratch on the back. As he headed toward Florence, he noticed the liquid running off the step. "What'd you do, pee your britches?" He couldn't help but laugh.

She looked up but wasn't smiling. "My water broke!"

Robbie hurried over and slid down on one knee. "Really?"

Brooke had followed Florence to the door; she came out just in time to catch the news. "Robbie, help me get her in the house."

He slipped his arms under his wife and carried her to the sofa. He knelt beside her and held her hand as the first contraction hit.

"Go get Melissa, Robbie," Brooke ordered.

Robbie gave Florence a small kiss. "I promise a better one as soon as I get back."

She yelled after him as he went out of the door. "Great timing."

He hopped in the Jeep and was back in a flash with Melissa.

"Run over and get your grandma, if she wants to come," his mom told him. They didn't need a man hanging around getting in the way. "You need to inform them about the meeting anyway. May as well get that done now."

Melissa took over the responsibility for Florence. She sent Brooke after towels. "Robbie, put a large pot of water to boil before you leave."

"Yes, Ma'am."

Robbie signaled with a wolf howl at the edge of the Carstons' meadow. Reggie came around the front from his bunker and returned the signal. His grandson ran up, huffing and puffing, and gave his grandpa a hug.

Reggie bear-hugged him back. He was so very relieved to see the boy. "Good to see you again, son."

By this time, Emily was on the porch.

Robbie caught his breath. "Florence's water broke. She's going to have the baby. Mama is over there now."

"Do you need me to come?" Emily asked.

"I think Mom and Brooke can handle things. Mom just thought you might want to go over."

I think I will stay out of the way," Emily said. "You come and get me if your mom and Brooke need me."

"Well then, I best be getting back, but I wanted to tell you we're having a meeting day after tomorrow. I'd like you guys at Mom and Dad's. We need to discuss my trip. I have to know things before I head to Corpus Christi to see Sean."

Reggie gave Robbie another hug. "I tell you what, how about we drop over tomorrow. By then there will be a new great-grandkid to say hello to. We'll have some time to visit then, and we'll see you again at the meeting."

"That works for me." Robbie hugged his grandparents and headed back home.

When Robbie got back to the house, Melissa and Brooke had their hands full with Florence.

His mom looked up when he walked in. "She's still a few hours away."

Robbie smiled and kissed Florence on the forehead. "Grandma and Grandpa will be over tomorrow."

Another contraction grabbed Florence's attention, and Robbie gave her some room. He decided to cook something. He could leave the women to their duties and have something ready for Florence when she was up to eating. He decided to make some stew. He ran out to the root cellar and smokehouse and grabbed what he needed.

Cooking helped keep his mind off his soon-to-be wife's agony, and his mind drifted. *Florence is going through hell for me . . . for us . . . I should have thought . . . Freya should never have happened. I've got to make sure it doesn't . . . never again. And I've got to tell Flo.* He closed his eyes and shook his head. *That's going to be fun.*

Two hours later he was at the table enjoying his meal. Florence screamed. In the middle of another contraction and yelling obscenities now, she caught his attention. He started to say something, but that was just the smartass in him, and he decided he'd stick to eating.

Florence relaxed and got a whiff of the aroma. "Sure smells good over there, honey."

Robbie smiled. "As soon as you have junior, I'll dish you up a bowl."

Robbie was so hungry he had another, cleaned up the kitchen, then took a shower and changed clothes. Florence was still in labor, but when he came out of the bathroom, they had moved her into the bedroom. Robbie went in to check on her progress.

Between contractions, Melissa looked up. "It won't be long now."

Robbie gave Florence a peck on the cheek. He had difficulty listening to her scream, so he retreated to the porch where it wouldn't be so loud. The sun was already gone, and only the orange glow remained. The breeze had died down. Mutt came up and lay at his feet. The dog whined when Florence squealed from another contraction. Robbie reached down and gave him a scratch. "It'll be all right, boy. If you stay around long enough, you're going to be hearing a lot of this."

I do love Florence. We will be a family. A big family. Maybe Flo will have twins. No, Grandma said they usually skip a generation. We will have more than one though. I wouldn't have wanted to be an only child.

Florence screamed again. Mutt whined. Robbie leaned over and patted the dog. *It's going to take some convincing to get her to go through this again anytime soon. Better not tell her about Freya just yet.*

The remaining light faded into darkness, and Robbie got up to go inside while he could still find the doorknob.

Robbie heard the baby's cry. He couldn't get in the house fast enough. He met Brooke coming out of the bedroom. She pushed him back. "Sit down and wait."

Brooke grabbed the pot of water off the stove and hurried back in. He could hear activity and now was desperate to see. He should have asked Brooke the sex of the baby. In her frazzled state, she didn't think to tell him.

Then Brooke came out with the sheets to take out to the tub to soak. "You can go in now."

Robbie hopped up and peeked around the corner. Florence looked up and smiled when she saw his face. "Come on in. Meet your son."

Robbie walked over and sat down on the edge of the bed. Florence pulled the cloth back so he could see the baby's face. His jaw sagged as his eyes focused on his son. He was speechless as he sat and marveled in the perfection he and Florence had created.

He leaned over and kissed Florence on the lips. He could feel the tears coming. "I love you." *Yes, I do love you, Florence. We will be a big happy family. Lots of kids, just like we planned.*

He nibbled on her neck and whispered in her ear. "Thank you for the wonderful son. Now, when can we get started on your daughter?"

"I'm sorry, honey, never again," and she bit him on the shoulder.

"Owww!"

She scoffed. "I didn't bite you that hard. That didn't hurt as much as my first contraction. I'll never go through that again."

Robbie raised up, his eyes wide, shock on his face. Then the smile returned to Florence's face as she could no longer contain her deception. Robbie sighed his relief, and they both laughed. They snuggled the baby together.

Chapter 16

The meeting convened on the porch at the Lindgrens' homestead. Florence and Brooke stayed home with the newborn; and since Debra, Beka, and Kira didn't need to be at the meeting, they made their way upstream to see the new baby.

Robbie called the meeting to order. "Thank you for coming. I want you to know that I've found a lot of support for our new democracy here in south Texas. But before I get to the details on that, I'd like to share the name Florence and I came up with for our son. We have decided on Lawrence."

There was a round of applause and a couple of cheers. James handed him an enormous cigar with a paper band around it. On the band in his mother's handwriting was 'It's a Boy'. "You can smoke it later with your grandpa." James held up the other cigar that had been made for the occasion with 'It's a Girl' on the band and handed it to Reggie.

Robbie laid the cigar on the table. "You know I don't approve of smoking, but I guess it's okay for this special event." He gave his grandpa a wink while he shook his dad's hand.

Robbie gave his mom a hug for the thoughtful bands on the cigars, then resumed the meeting. "Hank went with me to Seadrift, and he is now home and happy to be there. We found people who will help us. Hank will lay out the new plan to those folks.

"I think Hank might have found a girlfriend in Tivoli, and he was reunited with his daughter he hadn't seen since before the grid shut down. Clara had grown up, married, and had Hank's first grandbaby a few months back."

Robbie couldn't help the smile on his face, thinking about little Tiffany. "Originally, I was petrified about Victoria being such a large community. Not spread out far and wide as Corpus, but still quite large and with more people. There are a lot of folks in Victoria—thousands. I guess they didn't have someone like Sandra Hawkins to kill them off."

Reggie leaned forward. "How'd you get in there, Son?"

"I'll get to that, but first, I've got to tell you that they are going to play a significant role in getting the new country going. Some large ranchers and farmers in the area had a lot of money and resources to stabilize their region.

"They are a tight-knit group and don't associate with outsiders much unless they need to, but I got lucky and got in. They have an electrical grid, they built a small refinery out at one of the ranches, and they have a system of government not so unlike what I'm trying to build."

Robbie glanced over at his grandpa. Reggie had his arm propped up on the table and was leaning his chin on his hand. He was focused entirely on Robbie. "Sounds like it would be a tough place for you to get into. So, how did you get in?"

Robbie looked around at the others. You could have heard a pin drop. "I . . . er . . . there was this hermit I ran across at the edge of town . . ."

Robbie poured himself a glass of juice from the pitcher his mother had on the table for the meeting. His eyes roamed the group as he took a drink. "I told this old loner what I was trying to do. Some workers came there regularly to do maintenance for the hermit . . . this recluse introduced me to them, and they took me to town to the mayor of Victoria.

"It took a few days to get to see the mayor, but thanks to this . . . hermit, whom he knew to be trustworthy, he listened to what I had to say."

James lit up a smoke and handed a second to Reggie. He took a big draw off his stogie and blew a smoke ring toward Robbie. "Tell us more about this . . . hermit."

Robbie squirmed in his seat and took another drink. "Not really much to tell. I didn't stay there that long. I did most of the talking, so I guess I really didn't learn that much." *Leave this alone, guys!*

James leaned back in his chair and stared at Robbie. Robbie caught himself fidgeting, and James noticed.

Robbie changed the subject. "John, I need to know how the communications are going. This whole plan revolves around the cell towers."

Robbie tried to avoid eye contact with his dad and grandpa, but out of the corner of his eye, he could see their focus on him as he pried John for answers.

John looked over at his boys. "Robbie, you can thank Lance and Zack for a lot of the work that has been done. We've been working with a group Sean sent out of Corpus Christi. We found enough towers to make a connection between here and there. The hard part is we don't know the technology well enough.

"There is a group of people in Corpus going through every manual they can find to help the guys figure out how to make everything work. There are plenty of phones, and all the towers have been electrified, but getting the stuff to work properly has been difficult. We'll get it, but it will take a while longer.

"Lance and Zack have been up and down the highways between here and Corpus almost every day since you left. They had a few chores here at home, but every other day was spent on the towers. Maybe one of them can give you a better idea of when the service might be up and running."

Lance got up and took a seat nearer the table. "I've been talking to Sean and the men in Corpus who have been working on the towers. They seem to think the towers are working fine. The problem, they think, is with the phones. They have to be programmed, and no one has ever done this. And there are several different kinds of phones. They're all a little different and have different manuals. Someone will figure it out eventually, but in the meantime, if you'll ask around if someone can help while you're traipsing all over the country, that might speed things up a bit. Are they using phones in Victoria?"

Robbie shook his head. "I didn't see any, but I'll ask. He massaged his jaw with his hand. "Oh, by the way, I noticed a new building coming in here." He looked over at John.

"That was Brooke's idea. After . . . Ronnie . . . she decided she needed religion back in her life. Of course, I couldn't refuse her," he said with a cat-ate-the-canary grin.

Robbie looked around at the rest. He knew pretty much how they stood on religion. He could have understood a church being built near the Wimberleys', but this close to the Lindgrens'? "I hope you won't hold it against me if I don't choose to join your flock."

James laughed. "That's what we said. You watch out for old John. He's a sneaky coot. Got your grandpa there too."

Robbie eyed Reggie. "You, Grandpa?"

Reggie smirked. "Yes, even me. Wasn't so bad though. Not quite like I thought it would be. Maybe you'll go with me one day if I choose to go again."

Robbie shrugged his shoulders. "We'll see."

Melissa reached over and put her hand on Robbie's arm. "Speaking of new stuff, what's with the flag?"

"You didn't see it last time I was here?"

"No, I guess I missed it. That was when you brought Ronnie home. I didn't see much of anything after . . ."

"One of the guys over at some little town on the other side of Beeville gave it to me to fly. Said it might keep me from getting shot. But that's when that bastard shot Ronnie. The flag seems like a good idea since, but I guess there'll always be that someone around who'll shoot first."

"Or maybe that guy was using the flag to put a target on your back," Reggie said. "The next time you go through that neck of the woods, I'd be cautious. Maybe avoid that area altogether."

"We can't ignore them. They're right in the center of the region. If they're a problem, we need to take care of them as soon as possible." *Maybe the guy had a beef with the guys who gave me the flag. Perhaps he thought we were part of their group. I hope he was the only one.*

Robbie looked over at Sam. "You've been mighty quiet."

"Not much to say really. Looks like your plan is going to work out. I miss Sean a lot." He reached over and patted Sally on the arm. "We don't get to see our son much anymore."

Robbie saw the tears forming in Sally's eyes. "I'll talk to Sean the next time I go to Corpus. I know he's been swamped, but if we can get the communications system going, that will give you the opportunity to at least talk to him regularly. And who knows, maybe he'll have a plane going soon.

"And that reminds me, we need to get an airstrip marked off around here. Maybe something a little closer than the highway."

James pointed to the side of the house. "We already have the fuel tank. I wasn't sure where we could make the runway. We're working on that."

"There are some fairly flat stretches in the burn area not far from the new church." Robbie pointed out.

"If it can be mowed, graded, and flagged, maybe we can fly right into Peaceful Valley. We can have the church double as an airport terminal." Robbie laughed.

Reggie and James were the only two of the others who laughed at what they thought was a joke. Both Melissa and Emily poked them in the ribs. Reggie and James got up. James handed Reggie another smoke.

Robbie raised up his arms, questioning. "I'm not kidding. What's wrong with making the church a multi-purpose building? That way it's used more than once a week. That's only practical. I think it's a great idea!"

Robbie didn't seem to be making any headway with his suggestion, so he changed the subject.

Melissa, Sally, and Kathy went inside to prepare some snacks and to give the meeting a short break.

James sat back down beside Robbie. "How long a runway do you need?"

"I think the runways at the Corpus Airport are two miles long. The Cessna didn't even use a fourth of that. Do you think you can find a stretch that long out there?"

"Yeah, probably even more than a half-mile."

"More would be better for me. I'm still a new pilot, but anxious to continue learning. You just never know what you're going to need. The last plane

I flew here, I think I stopped it in less than a hundred yards, but I was fighting to do so."

Reggie smiled. "We don't ever want you to do that again. That was a close call."

"Yes, it was, Grandpa. Florence and Beka would agree with you. I'm certain of that. Maybe we should keep a water wagon nearby . . . just in case."

The ladies filed back out to the porch with plates of goodies. Melissa looked over at her son. "Don't be bashful. You need to put a couple of pounds back on your bones."

Robbie blushed. "Yes, Ma'am." He turned back to Reggie. "So, Grandpa, what got you in church, besides being tricked?"

"John kept his fire and brimstone under control for the most part, and he just talked about Lars and Eileen. Looks like future services will include Ronnie, little Abigail, and even Buster. I don't know where he got all the information, but we, and I mean myself included, just had a friendly talk about how much we love those guys and how much we miss them.

"We talked about some of the things they did and about how brave they were. They were pioneers, much like you, Robbie. They had their dreams, and they worked their fingers to the bone to make those dreams come true. They are the reason you are here and alive today. Their principles are probably why you are off on your quest as well.

"You have grown up to be a fine young man. I'm proud of you, and I know Lars and Eileen are proud of you too. This is what we talked about in church. If you want to join us one day, maybe we can continue that discussion."

Reggie looked over at John. Even John had a tear in his eye. He raised his glass to the old patriarch of the community.

Robbie stood up. "I think I've said about all I wanted to say. I'll be headed back out to Corpus in a day or so. There's a lot I need to talk to Sean about. Is there anything else you guys want to discuss?"

Melissa smiled up at Robbie. "Just eat more. That's all I have to say."

Robbie grinned. "I'll do my best. Now, if there's nothing else to discuss, I need to spend some time with Flo and Lawrence. With all those women over there, I'll be lucky if I get a chance to hold my son." He eyed his father and grandfather. "I will expect you two to keep them from spoiling him rotten while I'm gone."

"Hell, don't ask me to stop that," his grandfather said. "Spoiling kids is what grandparents are made for."

It was hopeless, Robbie thought. He might as well set his mind to the fact that he would be the disciplinarian when he came home. "I'll check with you," he said, tilting his head toward his Mom and Dad, "before I leave again. It's good to see the rest of you."

On the way back to the house, Robbie made a detour to where he knew, from his hunting days, a field of daisies grew. He picked as many as his arms could carry to take home to Florence as a thank you for his beautiful son.

It sounded like a hen party when Robbie arrived home. Florence was seated comfortably. She wasn't talking much, but mostly keeping an eye on all the other ladies fussing over his son. The baby didn't seem to mind the attention either.

Robbie strolled over and squatted down beside Florence's chair. He handed her the flowers and leaned over to give her a gentle kiss on the cheek. "Everything looks like it's going fine here."

"Yes, the girls have been wonderful. Nothing against Brooke, but I'm enjoying the new faces I haven't seen in a while. I can't remember when I saw Beka and Debra last."

As with most good husbands, though he and Florence weren't married just yet, Robbie was beginning to feel the protective husband and father role. "But you need your rest too."

Florence smiled up at him. "I'm doing fine. Your son hasn't cried all morning. And go look on the stove. The girls have been cooking all day. They even baked a dessert."

Robbie walked over. He smiled when he saw the confectionary delight. He couldn't remember when the last time he'd had cake. Cobblers were the usual dessert around here, as they had plenty of fruit for several months out of the year.

The cake hadn't been cut. Robbie looked questioningly at Florence. She pointed to the nearby pot. "You eat something that will stick to your ribs first; then you can have the cake."

Robbie wasn't sure what was in the pot, but he put a big smile on when he smelled the aroma. As he dipped some into a bowl, he saw the chunks of rabbit, venison, and pork all mixed together with the potatoes, wild onions, wild peppers, and carrots.

Beka came over and sat down at the table across from him. "That's my recipe. Do you like it?"

"It's a little unusual, but yes, I do like it. So, what have you and Lance been up to lately?"

"Just the usual—work, work, work . . ."

"Tell me about it."

She grabbed one of his hands and pulled it toward her. "All you're doing is running around all over the country. Driving isn't working. You don't even have any calluses on your hands. Look at how clean and soft those things are!"

"I can't argue with that, but . . ." He couldn't finish the sentence. What he was doing really wasn't that hard physically. After he'd dropped Hank off in Seadrift, he felt alone out in the middle of nowhere, but nothing he was doing was strenuous. Freya popped up in his mind again, and he quickly forced her out. ". . . if I don't get shot, I guess I don't really have much to complain about."

Beka punched him playfully in the shoulder. She probably felt guilty about teasing him after that comment. It was still too close to Ronnie's death. She should have known better. "Hey . . . just givin' you a hard time. We all know what you're doing, and we certainly know how much danger you're in. We appreciate your dedication to a new south Texas. You've gotta promise me one thing though."

Robbie smiled between mouthfuls. "And what's that?"

"If Sean is able to get that plane going in Corpus that you talked about before, I want to be one of the first to go flying with you."

"I think I can do that. Just you, me, and Florence. Like it was the first time, only this time without the fire."

"That works for me. Especially the fire part. You did do a great job and we were damn lucky!"

Robbie smiled. "Yes, we were."

Robbie kept one eye on Florence. He caught her glancing over at him and Beka a few times. *I better cut this off. Looks like she's getting annoyed at me talking to Beka. What's she going to be like when I tell her about Freya? The flowers helped. Better have a lot more than daisies when I tell her.*

Robbie glanced down at Beka's voluptuous breasts, took a deep breath, and closed his eyes. *If not for Florence, we could have been . . .*

He shook the thought and got up. *I've gotta have a slice of that cake.* "Who made this thing?"

Debra turned around, held up her hand, and smiled. "I did."

"It sure looks good, Debra. Is that some of Reggie's chocolate?"

"It is. He brought it over as a special treat for Florence. She said it would be fine if I made a cake and used it for icing."

Beka squeezed up against Robbie, pressing her breasts into his arm. "Will you cut me a slice too?"

Robbie looked down. *Is she doing that on purpose? Little obvious. Not good in front of Florence.* Robbie pulled away and grabbed a knife off the counter. "How big a slice do you want?"

When she took another step toward him, he quickly grabbed a plate and stuck it out between them. She grinned but didn't say anything.

Robbie cut a slice for Florence and Kira as well. Debra only wanted to hold the baby. He watched as Florence kept an eye on the girls, especially Beka, and as soon as Beka's plate was empty, she decided the party was over.

"I want to thank all of you for coming over, but it's getting late, and I'm getting tired. I think Robbie and I need a little alone time now. He's only been here a couple of days, and he'll be leaving again soon."

Debra turned and looked over. "When's that going to be, Robbie?"

"Day after tomorrow. I was planning on leaving today, but with Florence . . ." He turned and gave her a loving glance. "I almost missed this, and I promised Florence I'd be back in plenty of time. Now I have to get to Corpus Christi. Hopefully, soon we'll have phone service between here and there."

The ladies cleaned the dishes and changed the baby's diaper before they left. Robbie and Florence were nearly alone. Brooke turned into bed as soon as it got dark, and this gave the new parents some time to themselves.

Florence fed little Larry. Robbie marveled at how tenacious the newborn suckled her nipples. *A chip off the old block. Guess I'll be sharing now.* Robbie burped his son, and he was asleep in minutes.

Flo put him in his crib and crawled in beside Robbie. He reached up and pushed her hair out of her eyes. "You sure do make fine babies, girl." He gave her a peck on the cheek.

She leaned into him and pressed her lips hard to his. "I've missed you. It won't be long . . . when you come back . . . I'll be healed up."

"I'd like that. We're going to be a happy family." He turned his head toward the crib. "One down . . ."

"A girl next time. I need someone to help me in the house."

Robbie squeezed her hand. "I'll do my best."

"Beka was getting a little chummy today."

Shit! How do I answer that? Robbie turned to lie staring at the ceiling. "Ahh, didn't mean anything. She's always been like that." He glanced over at her.

"Yeah, I know. It's a little unsettling . . . but you're mine now." She grabbed his arm and pulled them close. "I know that. I know you love me and wouldn't ever do anything to jeopardize my trust in you."

They were quiet for a few minutes. Florence turned to lie on her back. She looked over at Robbie. His eyes were closed. "You're not asleep yet, are you?"

"No. Won't be long though. It's been a long day."

"It'll be longer tomorrow."

"Oh?"

"I have a 'Honey-do' list a mile long. We still have a couple of roof leaks. We almost ran out of firewood the last time you were gone, and you need to check the cistern. The water pressure is a little low. The weeds are starting to get out of hand in the garden . . ."

⌇⌇⌇⌇⌇

Robbie got an early start the next morning. He gathered and chopped wood just after daylight. He fed the chickens, checked the fruit trees, cleaned the solar array, carried out the trash, cleaned out the gutter to the cistern, and cleaned the water filter to the tank. Brooke had a late breakfast ready for him when he got through. Florence had another list of chores for him when he finished eating.

She was still moving a bit on the slow side this morning, but he was happy to see her up and about. She got up twice during the night to feed the baby, but all things considered, Lawrence seemed to be progressing as well, if not better, than Flo.

In the afternoon, Robbie fixed a couple of roof leaks, cleaned out the root cellar, and worked in the garden. The girls had been a little lax in keeping the weeds out. He couldn't blame them. There was a lot for them to do and Florence had been less than mobile the last few weeks. The garden was doing well, but with Lance and Zack so busy with the cell-phone towers, and a few other things they hadn't planned on like the church, the garden took a backseat to the work.

By late afternoon, Robbie got a little fishing time in but didn't catch anything. He'd thought the big fat worms he dug would surely get him at least a couple of nice ones, but after ninety minutes, the worms were gone, and his stringer empty.

He checked the fluids, belts, and tires on the Jeep before it got dark. He would leave at daylight. Florence had kept him so busy doing chores that she only had a couple of hours each night to really have some alone time with him. It seemed like he'd just arrived and now he was leaving again.

The good news was that she didn't cry. He remembered back. She was such a crybaby when they first met. She cried about everything that didn't go exactly her way. She was still girly, but she was now the toughest girly-girl he knew. Well, maybe Debra could give her a close race in that department, but he had no complaints about Flo.

After Florence fed the baby, she snuggled up against Robbie. He rubbed his hand over her nearly flat stomach. "You sure did a fine job. You've made me the happiest man in the world."

She squeezed his arm, then moved her hand down to his underwear. She slipped her hand inside and gave him a squeeze. "When you get back next time . . ." She gently massaged the tiger she'd aroused.

Robbie closed his eyes and took a deep breath. The next thing he knew it was getting light outside and the rooster was crowing.

—┤├—┤├—┤├—┤├—

Robbie drove with a new sense of appreciation for life. He was a daddy now. *I need to start thinking about Florence and me getting married. Our son will need a last name. Yes, when I get back home, we need to discuss it.*

However, it wasn't any time before Robbie was searching his mind and lining up questions he needed to ask Sean when he got to Corpus Christi. Questions about the cell towers, phones, gasoline, Cessna, seafood, and Marcia. He hadn't heard a peep about Marcia in quite a while. He hoped the old gal was behaving herself.

When Robbie reached the checkpoint into Corpus, Charlize was there once again. She had a different partner this time, but Charlize came out and greeted him when he pulled up. Her smile and pretty face always stirred a response from Robbie. He readjusted himself before she reached the Jeep. Good thing he did, because she leaned inside the window and her uniform gapped open wide with the top three buttons undone.

He could understand this with the temperature warming up nicely as it had been over the past month or so, but *damn!* She crossed her arms on the door's window frame. She wasn't even wearing a bra, and didn't try to conceal herself in the least. When Robbie looked over, she leaned down farther. He couldn't see her smile. His eyes fixated and froze on all her lusciousness staring at him head-on. He could feel the drool forming in his mouth and the flush on his face.

"Good morning," she said.

Robbie managed to break his stare and look up into Charlize's lovely eyes. He wiped at his mouth and swallowed the accumulated excess moisture. "Err . . . good morning, Charlize. You're looking well this morning."

"Good to see you back," she said in a soft and tender voice.

Robbie shook his head and scrunched his eyes. *Focus.* "Everything still quiet around here?"

She batted her eyes. "As a church mouse."

Robbie licked his lips again. *Change the subject!* "Good news . . . I'm a daddy!"

"No kidding?" Charlize seemed to lean in closer, and his eyes dropped back to her voluptuous equipment.

"Yeah, headed in to tell Sean and discuss some other developments with him." He managed to pull his eyes back up to her. "Permission to pass?"

Charlize's face turned somber, and she sighed. "You know you have a permanent pass through here."

"I know, but it's polite to ask, isn't it?"

She smiled and waved him through the checkpoint.

Robbie heard the laughter as he drove away and looked in the rearview window. *What the hell is going on back there?*

⌇⌇⌇⌇

Charlize slapped her hands together and turned to her partner. "Two more hours sleep tonight! I thought I almost lost when he told me about the kid."

"Remind me to never take bets with you. I've never seen anyone turn that red so fast."

Charlize turned back to watch Robbie's Jeep fade into the distance, a look of satisfaction on her face. "Yep, I cheated a bit. I knew he was easy to fluster. Now it will be even more fun with Florence and the kid to raise the stakes."

⌇⌇⌇⌇

Robbie decided to take a drive down to the Bayfront. It would be hours before Sean got off work and would be at the Farm. He drove out to the end of the T-head where all the boats docked, and pulled the Jeep up to the pilings at the edge of the concrete, killing the engine. When he took a deep breath of the salty air, it went straight to his toes. The sun was high, and the tall palm trees cast a little shade over the edge of the concrete bulkhead. Robbie sat down in one of the shadows and dangled his legs over the edge.

The water was green and clear. A jellyfish drifted by, its body pulsing and tentacles trailing behind. Robbie stared at the concrete retaining wall crusted with white barnacles and small grey oysters.

He gazed across the bay. The gentle breeze produced only a light chop on the water. A single boat circled a quarter-mile away. The captain pulled his net high into the rigging. *It's not shrimp season yet. Next month, I think Sean said. He's probably just checking the net to make sure it's working correctly. Maybe he's sampling to see if there are some shrimp out there. Who cares? Well, he indeed does. Sean may too.*

Robbie got up and walked back over to the Jeep. As he did, he saw a red truck pull up to the seawall. He stopped behind the Jeep and stared. *That looks like Marcia's truck.*

The woman got out first. A man got out from the passenger side. Sean didn't recognize either of them from this distance. He crawled back into the Jeep and dug around for his binoculars. He focused first on the woman. *Yes, that's Marcia. But who is the man? A new beau? Turn around so I can see you.*

Robbie watched as they gathered a few things out of the truck, turned, and walked over to the seawall to sit down. The man turned so he could see his face. He put the binoculars back up to his eyes. Robbie's jaw dropped. *No! It can't be! That's not possible!*

ᚻᚻᚻᚻ

Robbie waited nearly an hour for the man and woman to leave. When they did, he made a beeline toward the Farm. Kim met him at the front door when he walked up. Brenda was in the kitchen getting dinner ready. "You're just in time, Robbie. Sean will be here in about an hour, and dinner will be ready shortly after."

"Good, I have a big announcement to make." The he noticed Brenda's flat stomach. "Looks like you've lost some weight."

Brenda turned around with a big smile, her arms extended outward, showing off her new waistline. "I'll let Sean tell you all about it over dinner. I don't want to spoil it for him."

Christine walked in. "I saw you drive by the Contractors compound and followed you over. I've got a few things I need to discuss with you. Can we go out to the porch?"

Robbie shrugged his shoulders at Brenda and Kim, then followed Christine outside. "Yeah, I've got a few things too. What do you need, Christine?"

"When the Contractor groups were out checking pipelines, cell towers, and well-heads, they came across quite a few families and small groups of people. Most were just barely surviving like animals, and we brought those who wanted our help back here. We have them in isolation at the Hospital, but I don't know what to do with them. What do you think?"

"Have you talked to Sean about this?"

"Yes, but he doesn't know what to do with them either. They would have died if we hadn't found them and brought them here. The men who brought them back did so before asking us. We've since stopped them from bringing people here until we can figure out what to do."

"Have you asked them what they want?"

"No. Our primary concern at this point has been to get them fed and hydrated. We put them up on one of the top floors at the Hospital. I thought we may as well check them out medically too."

"See if they have any skills we can use, especially with phones. Also, if they're willing to work. If they will, offer them citizenship. Explain to them what that means and see if they'd like to stay. Put them to work and see what happens. With the way Corpus is expanding, there'll be jobs opening up everywhere."

"That's true, but we've been having a little trouble with food production. Can we feed them all? There's only a hundred of them now, but I'm guessing there'll be more . . . a lot more. Seafood ran short last year, and so far red meat production is improving but still well down from what it needs to be for our current needs. We grow only so many potatoes, sugar beets, and grains. If we start taking more people in too quickly, we're not going to have enough to go around."

"I'll be here for a couple of days. Sean will be here later, and maybe we can discuss it after dinner. I think we need to start interviewing them to determine their skills. That will get us started with what to do with them. Let's get Brenda and Kim in on the discussion too. They may be able to help us come up with an answer."

They both stood up. "Is there anything else, Christine?"

She smiled. "That was pretty much it. I was going to ask about how your trip up north went, but I'll get that later with Sean. No sense in you having to repeat yourself."

"It feels good to be back in Corpus. I never thought I'd hear myself say that. We've done well here . . . you've done well. We've lost a few along the way, and I miss them, but Corpus will grow and thrive now. I'm proud to say you've been a miracle worker in getting this place in order. With the police force and getting the Farm up and running efficiently . . . you've done a marvelous job."

Christine put her hand on his shoulder. "I only did what needed to be done. There was no one else who was going to step forward."

Robbie extended his hand and Christine gave it a firm shake. He smiled at her grip. "By the way, has Marcia been keeping in line?"

"Yes, she's been doing well. Why do you ask?"

"Something else we need to talk about, but it can wait until after dinner. Until then, I have a surprise announcement for all of you over dinner."

Christine looked at him questioningly. "You're such a tease, Robbie."

Robbie responded with a grin that was like a wave on a mudhole.

They headed back inside and met Sean in the kitchen coming in from the opposite direction.

Robbie hurried over with his hand out, and when Sean grabbed hold, he gave him a hug. "Good to see you again, Sean. You're looking fit."

He looked over at Brenda and Kim. "These two ladies make certain of that." A twinkle in his eye made that quite obvious.

Robbie smiled. "You up for a short business meeting over drinks on the porch after dinner?"

Sean looked over at Christine. She nodded. "Sure, as long as you don't mind Brenda and Kim joining in."

Robbie eyed the girls in the kitchen. "I already told Christine that they should be a part of the meeting. It seems we have a problem or two and maybe they can help, especially with the refugees."

Kim went to the dining room to start setting places at the table. Brenda took a big pan out of the oven and set it on the cabinet top. Robbie got a whiff of the aroma. "What's for dinner, Brenda?"

"Pot roast with potatoes and plenty of brown gravy. Also, squash, carrots, bread rolls, and a surprise for dessert."

"I'll try to save some room."

Kim walked back in. "Everyone, take a seat in the dining room, and I'll help Brenda bring in the food. Sean, be a darling and get the tea, will you?" She batted her eyes at him, and Sean turned to mush and obeyed immediately.

Robbie caught the exchange. He rolled his eyes as he went through the doorway into the dining room. *Those gals sure have Sean wrapped around their little fingers. Can't blame him though. If I were in the same position, I'd be like a hog in mud.*

As soon as everyone was seated, Robbie tapped his glass with his fork and stood up. "Before we eat, I'd like to announce that Florence had a healthy baby boy the other day. We've named him Lawrence."

Sean grabbed his glass and stood up. "Congratulations." They all clinked glasses and took a sip.

Kim set her glass down and ran out of the room. Brenda got up and followed. "I'm sorry, guys."

Sean sat down and pulled Robbie into his seat alongside. "I'm sorry, Robbie. Even though Brenda and I keep telling her that Benjamin is her son as much as ours, she still has episodes about Abigail."

"Benjamin?"

"Yes, nobody told you?"

"No. Brenda said she wanted you to make the announcement. She knows how proud you are of your son. Fine name."

The girls came back a short while later. "I'm sorry," Kim said.

Robbie got up and gave her a tender hug. "Nothing to apologize about. We all love and miss Abigail. We can't expect you to forget her. None of us will."

After everyone had eaten their fill and no one complained about it being cold, the men and Christine insisted on helping the cooks clean up the mess. They promised to finish the job right after dessert. Brenda brought out the cake and ice cream and dished out a serving for each.

Robbie looked at the cake with the yellow rings on top. "What the hell is this?"

"A pineapple upside-down cake."

Robbie looked at the slice queerly, then took a bite. "Damn, this is good! And this yellow fruit?"

"That's the pineapple. We've never had it before, but the guys in Mexico got some down there somewhere. I don't know where, and I don't care. I found the recipe in an old cookbook. Don't you just love it? This is the third time we've had it this week."

"I can see why."

Sean was almost finished with his dessert before he said anything. "You did good, baby." His eyes started twinkling again, but this time he saw Robbie watching and turned red. He put his head down and finished his cake and ice cream.

Later, while they were doing the dishes, Robbie elbowed Sean in the ribs. "I see the girls have you wrapped around their little pinkies, but don't worry about it. If I were in your position, I'd be doing the same exact thing. You've got a couple of great women there, and don't you ever let them go."

Sean looked over at Robbie with a sheepish grin on his face. "It doesn't bother you?"

"Bother me? Hell no. I'm happy for you. We've been through a lot together, and you deserve Brenda and Kim. No one knows that any better than I do."

"And your son? You and I both know Brenda's baby is your son. And so was little Abigail for that matter; and you, Kim, and Brenda . . ."

"That's ancient history, Sean. My son is in Peaceful Valley. Benjamin Lin. That's a fine name, my friend. But . . . speaking of your son . . . where is he?" He looked around until he locked eyes with Brenda.

"He's asleep," Brenda said. "I fed him just before I took the pot roast out. I have a nurse here to help me take care of him. Kim and I have so much other stuff to do, we can't be changing diapers all day."

Robbie took in a deep breath as he massaged his full stomach. "Lawrence weighed in at eight and a half pounds. It was all Florence could do to get him into this world. How'd Benjamin do?"

Sean looked over at Brenda. "I think Ben came in at just barely eight. He'll be a runner. Larry will never be able to keep up with him."

Robbie turned back toward Sean. "Are we about ready to get the meeting started? Christine?" His mind was obviously not on the meeting though. The gears were churning.

"Yes."

Brenda and Kim nodded, but Brenda held back. "I'm going to put a pot of coffee on, go check on Benjamin, and I'll be right out. Coffee will taste good. We've been out for a long time. Luckily, the plane just brought up a new shipment from Mexico."

Robbie led the procession out to the back porch. As soon as everyone was seated, he started the conversation. "John tells me the cell towers are up and working. They had a terrible time with having to power each tower individually. Now, as soon as they get the cell phones figured out, we should have communications."

Sean nodded. "That's about all I know. People are working on the problem day and night. I know how important it is."

"Speaking of power, Sean, if we're going to grow, how are we going to get more electricity? Everything is from the eight wind turbines."

"It's actually nine, but we're having trouble with two. We're working on the problem with the towers, but hell if I know how we're going to produce more." Sean frowned. "Why is it that when you think you've just about got everything figured out, something else always pops up?"

Robbie reached over and slapped Sean on the knee. "Sorry to throw another problem at you." He looked over at Kim. "How long was Ben? Did you guys measure him?"

Kim nodded. "He was twenty inches."

Robbie stuck out his chest. "Larry was twenty-one. Looks like he'll have to give Benny a boost up from time to time."

Sean sighed and ignored the remark. "Crude oil is coming in, and the refinery is at full production. Shrimp season will be opening before long, and I hear they are plentiful in the bay now. They're small, but lots of them."

Robbie leaned forward. "Good to see the optimist in you. By the way, I told some people in Victoria, Seadrift, and Goliad that we could supply some gas. There is a small refinery somewhere between Victoria and Refugio, I think. They wouldn't tell me exactly where it was. Security, I guess. They have fuel, but they'll need more if we're going to get a police force with plenty of squad cars to patrol the area."

Sean grimaced. "You shouldn't have told them that."

"I know, Sean, but I was trying to get them on our side. That's about all I had to offer them. I knew they needed it."

Sean sighed and looked over at Christine. "What do you think?"

She wasn't smiling. "We can produce a lot of fuel at the refinery. If we can get the crude, it will work . . . I think."

Robbie got up and started pacing the floor. "The Refugio area has a lot of oil . . . a lot of it! I doubt their little refinery can handle all the crude they can produce. There have to be old pipelines between here and there. If the lines haven't all rusted out, then we can get the oil from them and return it in the form of gas and diesel."

Sean got up with Robbie. "That could work." He looked over at Christine. "Right?"

Christine rose, and now they were all pacing the floor. "I don't see why not. We have ten times the refinery potential we're using. Our only problem has been with the availability of the crude."

Sean sat back down. They were all bumping into each other. "All right, one problem solved. What's next?"

Brenda walked out with a tray. "What'd I miss?"

"Not much. Robbie said he offered gas to some of the places he went. We're going to try to get their crude and make them some at the refinery."

Brenda looked at Sean. "That's nice."

He glanced at Robbie. "Robbie's idea."

Kim and Brenda finished pouring everyone a cup, and the girls sat on either side of Sean. He blushed a little when they scooted up close. Robbie gave him a 'thumbs up' sign when he looked his direction.

"So, Robbie, how much hair did your son come into this world with?"

Robbie snickered. "Bald as a river rock. Ben?"

"Ben nearly had a full head when he was born. That's all right, Ben will help little Larry read as he matures."

Kim stood up and put her hands on her hips. "Guys . . . guys! I wish Florence could be here to hear you two."

Robbie leaned back in his chair. "Anything else we need to discuss?"

Sean took a deep breath. "Refugees!"

Before he could get another word out, a faint sound of knocking, then screaming from the house interrupted him. Christine automatically reached for her pistol. Sean followed her toward the door. Robbie drew his gun and fell in line.

Christine opened the back door and stepped inside. "There's someone at the front door."

Sean followed her in. *There shouldn't be anyone coming in here at this time of the night,* he thought. Robbie was right on their heels.

Sean opened the door. It was one of the nurses from the Hospital. Christine knew her from earlier visits there and she'd also been to the Farm a few times. There were tears in her eyes. "What's the matter, Naomi?"

She backed up, down the steps. "Stay back. I may be contagious."

Sean's eyes popped wide open. "What? Contagious?"

Christine pushed Sean back and turned her attention to Naomi. "Contagious with what?"

Naomi shook all over, tears streaming down her blotchy red face. She was difficult to understand. "I d-don't know . . . they're d-dead!"

Sean's mouth gaped open. "Dead? Who's dead?"

Christine turned to look at him, then pushed him back again. "Stay back, Sean. You can't expose yourself. Robbie! Keep him back . . . and you too." Christine turned toward Naomi. "Who's dead?"

"One . . . one of the d-doctors . . . and three of the n-nurses."

Christine backed up a little herself. "How long were they sick?"

"I don't know. Not long. They started c-coughing. It didn't take long."

"Was it something they caught from the refugees?"

"I think so. Some of them are d-dead too."

This looks bad. Can't let it spread. "Go back to the Hospital, Naomi, and stay there. You've already been exposed. We can't have you spreading this thing about. It has to be contained at the Hospital."

Sean tried to pull away from Robbie, but he wouldn't let him go. "Christine, you need to stay back too," Sean warned. "We can't have you exposed either."

She stepped back as well. "Naomi, go back to the Hospital and get everyone a shot of antibiotics. And keep the new people there. I'll send over some officers to help with that. Now get going."

Naomi reluctantly turned and got back in her car. Christine reached in her pocket and pulled out her keys. "I've gotta make certain she goes back to the Hospital."

Now that Naomi was gone, Sean stepped out of the doorway and onto the small porch. "And if she doesn't go back?"

She patted her pistol. "I've gotta go. I'll report back as soon as I can."

✳✳✳

Robbie and Sean found Brenda and Kim sitting in the kitchen. Sean pulled up a chair and grabbed Brenda's hand. "Did you two hear?"

Brenda looked up. "Every word. What do you suppose they have?"

"I don't know, but if it's killing people, it's gotta be something terrible."

"And if it's contagious . . ."

Sean paused a second. "Brenda, will you warm up the coffee?"

Sean followed Robbie back out to the porch, and Kim stayed to help Brenda. Both Sean and Robbie were quiet, deeply engrossed in thought. Directly, Kim and Brenda came out and joined them.

Robbie took a sip of his coffee and turned to look at Sean. "I guess we've got another problem now?"

Sean shook his head. "Things have been going so well lately."

Robbie smiled a sour smirk. "But that's the way it's been all our lives. Nothing ever stays the same. Fix one problem, and another pops up. We'll fix this one just like we have all the others."

Sean looked at the girls. "Fighting people is one thing, and finding solutions for mechanical problems is another, but a disease . . . how . . . how do we fight something we can't even see?"

Robbie patted Sean on the leg. "That'll be up to the doctors, I hope. If they all die . . ." Robbie reached down and put his hand on his pistol.

Kim's eyes followed Robbie's hand. "No! You can't do that . . . can you?"

Robbie shook his head. "I don't want to, but if the doctors can't control this disease, whatever it is, then we may not have a choice."

Sean got up and moved over to where the girls were sitting. They spread apart instinctively to let him sit between them. "Girls, I'm sure the problem will be taken care of at the Hospital. There are some very competent doctors and nurses there. Don't worry, I'm confident they'll handle it in short order."

Everyone sat quietly for a while, sipping their coffee. The mild evening, thanks to the sea breeze, helped cool the tension. Robbie had forgotten the other things he wanted to discuss with Sean, but a thought slammed into his forehead.

"I had something else I wanted to tell you before we were interrupted."

All eyes turned to Robbie.

"Guess who I saw down at the Bayfront this morning before I came here?"

The girls were clueless and stared at Robbie with blank but expectant faces.

Sean's brow wrinkled in thought, but he was perplexed as well. "Who?"

"Sonny."

Sean sat quietly staring at Robbie. Brenda and Kim looked at each other, then at him. Their faces turned from perplexed to disbelief.

"Did you hear me?"

Sean shook his head a bit, then a smile came over his face. "No!" *He's kidding.*

Robbie stared at his old friend.

Sean's smile slipped as he stared back. Robbie was dead serious.

His smile faded. "You're not kidding are you?"

"I'm afraid not."

Brenda and Kim gave each other concerned looks and mouthed words, but no sound came out. They both understood, however, what the other was saying. Kim turned to Robbie. "How?"

He shrugged his shoulders. "I'm not sure, but we have to prepare. Worst case scenario, Sonny and Marcia both know you, Sean, and Brenda tried to kill him, and they are going to kill all of you. Hell, Marcia may even try to take over the city. We both know that she was upset Sandra was killed. She was next in line should Sandra disappear. Sean, you could walk outside tomorrow morning and eat a bullet."

Sean's eyes darted back and forth, trying to keep up with the thoughts inside his head.

Kim hopped up and made the rest of them jump.

Brenda slapped her on the leg. "Don't do that!"

"I'm sorry. I just thought we're going to need more coffee."

Sean smiled. "You've got that right, sweetheart, but move a little slower. I'm a bit jumpy."

Robbie nodded. "Yeah, me too."

Christine returned two hours later. They were all still sitting on the back porch when she came through the kitchen and joined them.

"Everything is secure at the Hospital for now."

Sean waved her into a chair. "Are all the refugees still there?"

She sighed. "Yeah, but five of them are dead. I've posted officers around the perimeter. The doctors separated them into two groups. Most don't appear to be sick, but those who show signs of the illness have been isolated in a separate ward."

Kim pulled her hair over her shoulder. "What do they have?"

Christine took the cup of coffee Brenda offered. "I needed this," she said, smiling at her after a healthy sip. "The doctors aren't sure yet, but it seems highly contagious. The one doctor and the nurses appeared to catch the disease from being in close contact with the refugees.

"One of the doctors suspects pneumonic plague. He's sent samples of blood to the lab, and they are testing for the culprit. The doctor said he was familiar with the plague and researched the disease. He suspects the pneumonic variety because the people who died were coughing severely."

"Can we catch it?" Brenda asked.

"Yes, if it's what the doctor suspects. He said the pneumonic plague is the only one that is highly contagious. That's why he suspected that strain."

Sean put his hand on Christine's arm. "Could we have gotten it from Naomi?"

"I don't think so. She wasn't coughing. When I got back to the Hospital, she complained of a headache, and she obviously had a fever, but she wasn't coughing yet, so she wasn't likely to have been spreading the germ. If she starts, then you can catch it just from being around her. If it is, in fact, pneumonic plague, she'll start coughing as the disease progresses into her lungs. If that happens, she's got a good chance of dying."

Robbie leaned forward. "Can it be treated?"

"Yes. The doctor has already started everyone on antibiotics. I got a shot when I was there, as did all the rest of my officers that I left on duty. If it is the pneumonic bugger, he said antibiotics will work well in curing the disease if caught early. If it has already settled into the lungs, as it has in several of the refugees, he didn't know whether or not they'd pull through.

"Considering the deplorable health of most of the refugees, they may be too weak to fight off the disease even with antibiotics. I'll go back over there in the morning to see what the doc has found out. I'll also bring back some antibiotics for all of you. You know how to give shots don't you, Kim?"

"Yes. I haven't given one in quite a while, but it's like riding a bicycle . . ."

Sean coughed, and everyone looked at him. "I couldn't have caught it already, could I?"

Christine smiled and felt of his forehead. "No, I don't think so. You don't seem to have a fever. If any of you get a headache and become feverish, let me know immediately. Those and weakness are the first symptoms. Hopefully, the antibiotic will stall it from spreading any farther than the hospital."

Sean sighed with relief. "How did they get this disease?"

Brenda leaned forward. "I've read about the bubonic plague in some of Sandra's books years ago. It was caused by rats. It was transmitted by fleas usually. We don't have many rats around here."

Sean got up. "The newcomers were living in filth. They could have gotten the disease from rats or fleas." He headed for the back door. "I've gotta pee."

Robbie got up too. "Yeah, I'll join you."

Brenda refilled everyone's cups. "You were at the Hospital, Christine. Could you transmit the disease?"

"I don't think so. The doctor I talked to and one of the nurses were the only persons I came in contact with. They didn't appear to have the disease, and she gave me the antibiotics, so probably not."

Kim frowned. "Probably?"

Christine smirked. "I guess there is an outside chance. Maybe I should quarantine the city. No one leaves, and anyone coming in goes straight to the Hospital. I'll talk to Sean about this when he and Robbie get back."

Chapter 17

Marcia packed her clothes, as did little Lola, and loaded their belongings into the truck. Lola was a bit fussy. "I don't know why we can't stay here! I like staying with Aunt Janelle."

"Your daddy is home now, and we need to join him at our house."

"But . . ."

Marcia cut her off. "No buts about it, little girl. That's home, and that's where we're going."

Lola pouted all the way to their house. Sonny was sitting on the porch when they pulled up. He jumped to his feet the minute he spotted them. Lola grabbed her suitcase. He came over to help them unload their stuff. "So, you're back home to stay?"

"Yes, now that you have recovered most of your memory, it seemed right. This is where we belong. Have you eaten breakfast?"

"No, not yet. I fixed some coffee but wasn't very hungry."

"I brought some eggs and fish. What is left in the icebox?"

"It's empty. Most of the stuff was ruined, and I didn't know what to do about restocking it. There's nothing in the garden either."

"After I fix you something to eat, I'll go over to the seafood plant, Farm, and meat plant to stock up a little. Looks like the chickens are still around."

"Yeah, I thought about eating one for dinner. They're not staying in the chicken pen, so I didn't find any eggs."

"I'll pick up some feed too. If we start feeding them again, they'll stay a little closer to home and should start laying some eggs where we can find them."

Lola had eaten breakfast, as did Marcia at her sister's house, and they weren't hungry. Lola was standoffish and chose to lock herself in her room to pout some more.

Marcia grilled the fish in a skillet and stirred the eggs in. When they were done, she set the plate in front of Sonny and took the seat across from him. "We've got to figure out what to do about Sean."

"That little bastard's got to die, for sure."

"Yes, he does." Marcia propped up her chin on her arm. "And we've got to get things back to the way they were . . . only this time I'll be giving the orders. That bitch, Christine, has been a pain in the ass ever since she started pushing her weight around. We'll bury her too!"

"And they sank my goddamn boat. I'll never forgive them for that."

"Don't you worry, honey, we'll take care of them all. Every last one of them."

"The question is how? We don't have guns, and they do. And we can't do it all ourselves."

"I know some people at the seafood plant and some of the shrimpers will help too. I've already talked to a few I thought I could trust. They're appalled at the fact they tried to kill you and sank your boat. Two of the men said they had pistols and some ammunition.

"There aren't a lot of people at the Police Station most of the time. If we can take care of them there . . . they won't expect it. We can get all the guns and ammunition we need. And we'll have cars too. Most of the shrimpers don't have anything to drive."

Sonny smiled. "When?"

"Soon." Marcia's face was serious, thoughts churning in her head. She nodded at Sonny. "Yes, soon."

—|\-|\-|\-|\-

Robbie tossed and turned for quite a while after he went to bed, but awoke late and well rested. He got up, showered, and joined the girls for breakfast. They had already fixed breakfast for Christine and Sean, and they left early. Brenda smiled when Robbie walked into the kitchen. "Well, good morning, sleepy-head."

Robbie returned the smile. "Good morning, ladies."

Brenda set the bacon on the table. "How do you like your eggs this morning?"

"Over easy will be fine. Where's Sean?"

"He went over to the Contractors. He wanted to check on the progress with the phones. Christine went back over to the Hospital to set up the security-rotations schedule and pick up the antibiotics for us. She'll be back late this morning. I don't think Sean will be gone long either. He said he'd try to be back before noon."

Robbie was enjoying the breakfast, especially the bacon, but his mind was churning. "What am I going to do for the next week? I'll go stir crazy. I need to get back out on the road. I have people to see."

Kim brought over a glass of strawberry juice and set it down in front of Robbie. "You know Christine had to quarantine the city."

Robbie held the glass up to the light and took a sip. "Yeah. Guess you're right. This stuff is good."

Kim patted him on the shoulder. "Christine and Sean will keep you busy. It's better that you don't go spreading germs all over the country just in case you picked up the bug. You certainly don't want to take anything back to Peaceful Valley. Besides, it's only a week or so. Just until we're sure you're not carrying the plague."

Robbie finished up the last of his breakfast and went out to the porch to have a little peace and quiet. Kim refilled his glass on the way out. *Okay, so I'm not going anywhere for at least a week. Christine is right, the quarantine is necessary. If this little bugger gets hold of the community, no telling how many people might die. Wouldn't be so bad if Sonny and Marcia were to kick the bucket.*

Robbie's mind then drifted home. *Can't be giving this disease to Flo and Lawrence, or anyone else for that matter. Okay, so if I have to stay in Corpus, what am I going to do?* Then his mind drifted to Charlize. When she bent over, exposing her jewels, he took a good look. He remembered how his mouth started watering. It was all he could do not to reach out and touch her succulence. *What was she laughing about when I drove away? She had to have known what she was doing.*

Robbie could feel the boner coming on strong and adjusted himself. He shook his head, trying to force the vision out, but then Freya crept in. She was much more than a vision. He had tasted of her nectar.

Robbie almost let his glass slip through his hand, spilling a little on his shirt and britches. He got up and walked to the edge of the porch. *Get your mind off of sex. You're already in a heap of trouble for that night with Freya.* He focused on the women out in the field. He decided to join them, and headed to where they were working.

A couple of the ladies looked up and smiled. "Hi, Robbie. How are you this morning?"

Robbie was surprised they knew his name, though he really shouldn't have been. They considered him a hero. He freed them from the brutal work conditions that were in place when Sandra Hawkins ruled the roost. No, he shouldn't have been surprised, yet he was. Robbie never considered himself a hero or even important at all. He was just doing a job. He was just doing what needed to be done.

Robbie smiled at the women. "I'm doing good, ladies. Just stretching my legs. How about you?"

One of the women wiped the sweat from her brow. "We're doing fine. Putting in a little overtime. Sean says we've got to produce more."

The ladies continued their work, and Robbie strolled back over to the porch. *These women work hard. Maybe not as hard as they did under Sandra, but still extremely hard. I need to talk to Sean about getting more workers out here. Perhaps some of the refugees, once the doctors clear them to work.*

Christine and Kim came out. Kim held up a syringe.

Robbie frowned. "You know I don't like those things?"

Kim waved him up onto the porch. "None of us do, but you're a tough guy. It won't hurt a bit."

Robbie pulled up his shirt sleeve, but Kim shook her head. "This one goes in the butt, my friend."

Christine looked at Kim and started to say something, but caught herself.

Kim laughed. "Get over here, Robbie, and bend over. Let me see that ass!"

Robbie undid his britches and bent over the table. Kim looked at his white butt. "More!"

Robbie pulled at his trousers and Kim grabbed them and gave them a yank. She giggled and stabbed him.

"Owww!"

Kim and Christine both laughed.

Robbie pulled his pants back up and turned around. "You happy now?"

Kim nodded. "That wasn't so bad, was it?"

Robbie limped over and sat down. He grabbed his glass and emptied the contents. "I guess not."

Christine leaned over to Kim. "You know that could have gone in the arm, don't you?"

"Yeah, I know."

Robbie looked over with a raised eyebrow. "What are you two whispering about?"

Kim handed the syringe to Christine, and she headed for the door. "That really didn't have to go in your butt."

Robbie hopped up. "What?"

Kim stepped over to him. "You heard what she said. I just wanted to get another look at your fine white ass." She burst out laughing.

Robbie turned red. "Damn you, Kim." Robbie headed for the door.

"Where you going?"

"I need another drink."

"Will you bring me one back?"

"You want it with or without strychnine?"

Sean arrived back at the Farm just after lunch. Brenda had leftovers from the previous evening in the oven keeping them warm. She met him at the door when he arrived, smearing him with a juicy welcome kiss and a butt-grab.

He looked at her with his longing eyes. "Has it been that long?"

"You know it. Kim's getting a little horny too."

She escorted Sean into the kitchen and hollered out the back door. "If you're hungry, get in here."

Sean gave Robbie a fist-bump, and they helped the girls set the table. Sean handed Robbie a phone.

"Does it work?" he asked in surprise.

"It did when we tested it at the shop. I talked to John back home. The reception was weak, but it worked."

"You'll have to show me how to operate it. I've never used one before."

Sean took the phone back, but Kim broke in. "You guys eat first; then when you finish with the dishes, you can fiddle with that thing."

Both guys frowned but didn't say a word. They took their seats. The girls brought the food and drinks and joined the men.

Between bites, Kim informed Sean that she had a shot for him when he got finished.

Robbie hurried up and swallowed what he had in his mouth. "And don't let her give it to you in the butt like she did me."

Sean looked over at Kim. She cocked her head and grinned. "I just wanted to get another look at his ass. I don't need a shot as an excuse to see yours," she teased Sean.

Both guys were red in the face by now. They didn't say another word throughout the meal.

After lunch, the guys cleaned up the dishes, then went out to the porch. Sean pulled a phone out and showed it to Robbie. "The people working on these things finally figured out what the problem was. The programming has to be exact."

Sean leaned over to demonstrate how to use it properly. The thing only had two bars, but Sean was able to complete a call to John. "We have a little problem here. We seem to have the plague. Some refugees that were brought in had it. We've contained it at the Hospital, and I don't think there is anything to worry about, but we've quarantine the area. So, would you pass this information on to everyone else there?"

Sean passed the phone to Robbie. "John, will you make sure Florence knows I'll be running a little late getting back home?"

"You know I will. Anything else?"

"Yeah, how is Lawrence? Has he grown much?"

John laughed. "You've only been gone a few days."

"I know . . . but I miss him and Flo."

"I'll tell them that."

"Thanks. And how is the airstrip coming along?"

"I don't know. I haven't seen your dad for a few days. Call back tomorrow, and I'll have an update for you."

"Okay, John, I'll talk to you tomorrow."

Robbie hung up the phone and handed it back to Sean.

"No, Robbie, this is your phone."

He grinned. "Really?"

"Yes. Look here." Sean punched a button. "Look at the contact list. All you have to do is punch this button to bring up the list. See, there's Florence, me, your dad, John, and Reggie. Just touch their names, and it'll make the call. I have a box of phones in the living room by the door on the table. When you go back home, take them, and you can call them anytime you want. There's a label on each for who they belong to."

"Cool! But I can't use it except when I'm here or somewhere between here and Peaceful Valley, right?"

"Right. Just where the cell towers are active. When it's safe, and I'll let you be the judge of that, I'll send out crews to work on the other towers toward Victoria and beyond."

"Good job, Sean." Robbie clapped him on the shoulder.

"There were a lot of people working on this project. John and his boys did a lot on the other end of the string between here and Peaceful Valley. I did very little."

"You got them out there."

Sean nodded. "Yeah, I guess I did."

"Now tell me about the plane."

Sean took a sip of his drink and leaned forward. "I think the plane is ready. The men have it out at the Airport in the new hangar. They've run it around on the tarmac a few times, and it seems to be operating fine as far as I can tell. They say it's mechanically sound, but no one's flown it. I told everyone that I wanted you to be the first one to take it up. If you're not busy, maybe you can take me up tomorrow."

Robbie's eyes opened wide with a grin to match. "Let me check my schedule." Robbie rolled his eyes skyward. "Nope! My agenda is open. Shall we take to the skies?"

"How about I take you out there, and you can have a look at it. We can make sure it's ready for first thing in the morning."

"I'd like that, Sean."

Robbie hopped up like his butt was on fire. Sean followed him inside, and Robbie grabbed a couple of leftover pieces of bacon off the stove as he passed. Sean went into the living room where Brenda and Kim were sitting and reading.

He gave each lady a kiss on the forehead. "I'm going to take Robbie to the Airport to show him the Cessna. He's going to take it up in the morning, and we're going to make sure it's ready."

Brenda put her book down. "Can we go?"

"I'd rather you didn't go up in the plane until we're sure it'll stay in the air. You can come along if you'd like though."

Kim smirked. "If we can't fly in the damn thing, we may as well stay here."

"I'm sorry. I'm only thinking of you. If anyone is going to die, it'll be Robbie or me."

Brenda grabbed his arm and pulled him over so she could give him a sloppy kiss. "If you're going to die, I want a good kiss before you leave."

Kim grabbed him by the other arm and nearly sucked his face off. "Just a preview of what you'll get tonight."

Robbie smiled, shook his head, and dragged his friend out the door.

Robbie ran his hand along the wing of the bright yellow plane. "Damn, this thing is a beauty." He and Sean climbed in, and he grabbed the wheel. Robbie turned it and watched the flaps.

"Can I crank her up?"

Sean leaned over so he could see the men outside the plane. "Is this thing ready to go?"

The guys nodded.

"Then stand back and open the hangar doors."

When the men were out of the way, Robbie hit the starter. The engine fired up immediately. He listened to it hum. "Sounds just like the other one."

Sean nodded. "It's almost the same exact plane."

Robbie looked at the instrument panel, and everything appeared to be functioning. He eased the throttle up, and the yellow bird crept forward. When he got it out of the hangar, he made the engine hum. The plane lurched forward.

Robbie made a big circle in front of the hanger, working the flaps and wiggling back and forth just like he did when he was first learning how to fly. He looked over at Sean. His friend flashed him an excited grin. Robbie thought back. *Sean looks just like he did the first time he got into the plane.*

He turned his attention forward. *Damn, this feels good. Tomorrow, me and Sean. And no one shooting at us this time . . . I hope. Better get Christine out here."*

Robbie pulled back to just inside the hangar doors. They both got out and gave each other a high-five.

"Sean, I'm going to get Christine to check the runway. You remember I told you that Sandra had Mathew Helms posted out there when Beka, Florence, and I escaped? I don't want us to get shot at again. And maybe later, we can get some men to clear the brush out there so we can see better."

"I'll assign some contractors to it the next time I'm in the office."

Sean turned to the men standing there waiting for them. "Have it ready for us in the morning. Robbie and I are going to take it up."

The head mechanic nodded. "Yes, Sir."

〜〜〜

Both girls were showered and dressed comfortably when Sean and Robbie arrived back at the house. Brenda grabbed Sean by the hand and led him toward the bathroom. "You guys had your fun, now it's our turn. Robbie, you'll have to self-amuse the rest of the evening."

Sean grinned over his shoulder. "See you in the morning, buddy."

Robbie stood alone in the middle of the living room. *It's too early to go to bed.* He moseyed into the kitchen and opened the fridge. He found a banana and soda, then headed out to the back porch. He sat down in the glider and gave it a push as he peeled the banana.

It'll be fun taking Sean up in the morning. He only got to ride around on the tarmac before. I hope everything works okay. I'll teach Lawrence how to fly. Yes, he'll be an exceptional pilot.

Can't have people shooting at planes. Never again. Sonny and Marcia don't know that we're going up. No, they can't know. Christine will see . . . can't take the chance.

We should have put a bullet in Marcia when we had the opportunity. Now she's back to haunt us again. I know it wouldn't have been right, but sometimes that's the best thing to do.

Maybe she and Sonny won't cause a problem. But, if someone had tried to kill me like Sean did Sonny, I'd want revenge. And Marcia . . . Marcia! If Lola hadn't been in the picture, it would have been a lot easier. Can't change the past though.

Robbie got up and headed across the compound to the nursery. *I haven't seen the ladies back there in quite a while.*

He knocked on the door and heard a friendly 'come in'. He turned the knob and went inside. Several ladies were scattered about, but he didn't see the one he wanted. "Where's Nancy?"

"She's probably out in one of the barns. I'm Julie. Can I help you?"

"I just thought . . . I know Nancy. I have some free time."

"She had her baby and is back to work." Julie got up and stepped around the desk. "She had a girl. That's her over there," she said pointing. "The one with the blonde curls."

Robbie walked over to the crib. She was sound asleep. He sighed. *Beautiful girl . . . just like her mama.*

Robbie turned back to the other girls. He'd forgotten their names again, and they introduced themselves. One of the girls dragged Robbie to the sofa, and another brought one of his sons over and sat him on his lap. Robbie immediately felt a connection. He made noises with his mouth. His eyes lit up when the baby smiled at him. The girls were thrilled.

Robbie bounced little Jared on his knee. "You have a brand new brother back in Peaceful Valley. You'll have to meet him one day."

Robbie laughed and chatted with the girls and held several of the babies. One was a newborn, and they ranged up to two years of age. They weren't all his, but he loved them equally.

Robbie got so wrapped up with the girls and their sons and daughters that it was nearly two hours before he made it back to the main house. Christine was sitting in the kitchen, nibbling on some strawberries.

"I was wondering where everyone got off to."

"I was out in the nursery. It felt good to take a little break from all the problems we seem to be experiencing. Sean, Brenda, and Kim are having a date night. They won't be back out until morning."

Christine smiled. "How about you, Robbie. You up for a date night?"

Robbie's eyes opened wide, and his chin sagged. Christine laughed. "I was just kidding."

Robbie let out a sigh of relief. *Christine's not a bad-looking gal . . . No . . . Florence . . . I've already . . . one too many times . . . dammit, you're with Florence now . . . forever!*

Robbie took a deep breath and tried to focus. "Sean and I are taking the Cessna up in the morning. Would you mind checking the ends of the runway for snipers? Probably no one out there . . . I'm just remembering the last time I flew out of here and Mathew taking some shots at us."

"Not a problem. What time are you guys leaving?"

"Just whenever. I don't know what time Sean will get up. I'll probably get up when the roosters start crowing."

"Okay, I'll be ready then. Breakfast first?"

"Of course. Can't go flying on an empty stomach."

Robbie hit the starter, and the engine sprang to life. He pointed to Sean's seatbelt while he buckled his. The hangar doors opened, letting in the morning sun. He looked over and nodded to the man at the control box.

Rays streaked through the opening of the sliding hangar doors. The sun was bright, and the moisture in the air glistened. A hint of ground fog shrouded the landscape, but nothing to keep them from flying. Robbie eased the throttle forward.

Just like the last time Sean was in the plane, he jumped up and down in his seat as much as the harness would allow. Robbie swatted him on the arm. He grinned, and Robbie couldn't help but feel his excitement.

He focused his attention back on the asphalt ahead. Sean settled down and looked out over the tarmac. Robbie kept his eyes on the gauges as he steered the plane down the taxiway. The wind was virtually non-existent, and the aircraft rolled along smoothly.

Robbie turned the plane to the south and stopped. He took a last look at Sean, took a deep breath, and eased the throttle forward. He held the plane on the broad white stripe and opened the throttle up. *Hold her straight. Throttle and flaps . . . that's all there is to it. Remember last time. Should be a piece of cake without Sandra and the Jeep in the way.*

Robbie eyed the car toward the end of the runway. *That's Christine. She's standing alongside. No problems!* The plane vibrated and the bump, bump, bump of the tires hitting the joints in the cement echoed in his ears.

He eased back on the steering wheel. When the speed was right, the Cessna lifted off. All the ground noise disappeared, and the little plane climbed. He took a quick look at Sean. His eyes were closed.

Robbie looked out of the side window. The ground was getting farther and farther away. He was flying. Another quick glance at Sean. He was looking out the window. When the altimeter read 5,000 feet, Robbie leveled the plane off and cut back on the throttle. "We're okay, Sean. You can relax now."

Sean turned and grinned, then brought his attention back to the view.

Robbie jerked the steering wheel back and forth and pointed the plane down a little. "Oh, no!"

Sean stiffened up, grabbed his seat, and turned to Robbie with fear written all over his face. "What's wrong?!"

Robbie laughed and straightened out the Cessna. "I should have peed before we left."

Sean swatted him on the arm. "Damn you!"

Robbie made a pass over the Bayfront and a wide swing over the bay. He then turned and did a fly-over at the Farm, wiggling the wings in a wave in case the girls were watching. He set the plane in a tight circle, then pulled up, making the engine strain a little. "Enjoying yourself, Sean?"

"Nice, but we better head back to the Airport. Wouldn't want you to piss your britches."

Robbie smiled and turned the plane to the southwest. *Damn, it feels good to fly again!* The airstrip lay ahead. It wasn't that far from the Farm and only took a minute to get there in the plane. He cut the throttle back, pointed the plane down, and lined up with the runway. Just before touching down, he cut the throttle and gently bounced on the concrete.

Sean looked over. "Nice landing."

"The wind is still light. That helps. Well, what did you think?"

"No more joking around and I'll definitely go up with you again. Everything certainly looks different from up there . . . makes the world look smaller."

"Indeed, it does. It will be smaller from now on. If Dad has the runway ready at home soon, maybe I can start running the plane back and forth."

"It's your plane. Maybe it'll help you with Victoria, Seadrift, and some of the other towns on your route too."

Robbie smiled. "I hope so, and maybe even farther afield. The sky's the limit now, Sean!"

Chapter 18

Marcia slammed the truck door when she and Sonny got back home. "Dammit! Those guys owe me! Now they won't help pay Sean back for what he did to you . . . and me and Lola. Goddammit, shrimpers stick together!

"They had weeks to work on their boats, but nooo! They sat around on their lazy asses when they should have been working. Now that shrimping season is here, they scurry around like the rats they are, trying to catch up on what they should have done a long time ago. The sorry bastards!"

Marcia walked to the front of the truck and pounded her fist on the hood. Sonny shut his door and walked around to where Marcia stood, steaming and staring off into the distance. "Can you blame them? Fuel production is up. Ice production is up. Shrimp season will be open next week, and they get all the fuel they need. They can shrimp every day. I would be happy about that if I still had a boat."

"But you don't, dammit, thanks to Sean and those two bitches. They tried to kill you. They can't get away with that."

Sonny wrapped his arms around Marcia. "And they won't get away with it. We'll make sure . . . even if it's just you and me, babe."

⎯⎮⎮⎮⎮⎯

By the third day of the city quarantine, Robbie was getting stir crazy. The plane sitting ready didn't help. He wanted to get back out there. Sean spent most of his time at the Contractors and Robbie tagged along the first couple of days. He was pleased with how quickly Sean had taken to the job of mayor and how well all the people in Corpus Christi accepted him as their leader.

On the third morning after Sean left, Robbie made another trip out to the nursery, then got in the Jeep and drove around for a while. He spent a couple of hours at the meat packing plant before heading over to the checkpoint toward home. Charlize was on guard and Trish was there again as her partner on duty. He explained the situation with the refugees and how busy Sean and Christine were. He didn't have anything to do and couldn't go anywhere for a few more days.

Charlize grinned and leaned over the door frame. "Well, I'll be here every day. You can come to see me. Trish and I will keep you company. Can't have you bored and all."

Robbie looked over to his right. Trish was leaning inside the passenger window.

"We can certainly make sure it doesn't get monotonous." The smile on her face said it all.

Robbie opened his door and got out. Charlize immediately hooked her arm in his and led him over to the outpost shack. Trish followed.

Robbie ate an afternoon snack with the girls. After they were done, Trish grabbed the plates while Charlize went for a deck of cards. She held them up with a grin. "How about a game of strip poker?"

"Well, you do know Florence and I are getting married soon, and she just had my son?"

Trish cocked her head. "That doesn't mean you have to be boring."

Robbie rolled his eyes. "You're willing to do anything to get me out of my pants, aren't you? We play back home. I hardly ever lose," he snickered.

They giggled and started to deal. A half-hour later, Robbie was down to his underwear while Charlize still had her bra and panties. Trish was nearly fully dressed.

Robbie stood up and checked his phone. "My, where did the time go? I promised Sean I'd be at the Farm when he got home. We have plans to make."

Charlize pulled at his shirt sleeve while he pulled on his jeans. "Spoilsport. So close to seeing that sweet ass."

He grinned. "I'm a little sorry I didn't get to see a bit of skin myself."

Trish slapped him on the butt. "Rematch tomorrow?"

He shrugged. "Unless Sean comes up with something, I guess I can oblige you, ladies."

Charlize gave him a stern look. "We'll damn well finish the match then." She looked over at Trish, and they nodded at each other.

"We'll see, ladies."

He gave them each a kiss on the cheek and headed for the Jeep. The sun was behind the trees when Robbie pulled away from the guard shack. *Damn, how did time get away from me? Those two girls are hot, is how! Have a little fun, but don't forget Florence.*

Robbie drove back to the Farm and took a cold shower. Sean dragged in an hour late. The girls gave him their standard 'welcome home', which in front of Robbie, embarrassed him every time. The girls then pushed Sean toward the bathroom, telling him he had thirty minutes to shower and get his sweet ass to the table for dinner.

The girls wouldn't let Robbie do anything. They pushed him into a chair at the table.

"I can help," he offered.

Brenda gave him a gentle slap on the arm. "This is our home, and you do what we say, you hear?"

He gave her a defeated smile. "Yes, Ma'am."

Sean must have been hungry, because he was out of the bathroom and to the table in record time.

"Isn't Christine joining us?" Robbie asked.

Sean had already dished up his plate. He swallowed the bite he had in his mouth and wiped his lips with the napkin. "I saw her earlier. She said she'd be late tonight and for us not to wait for her. I told Kim when I came in. You didn't hear me?"

"No. I guess I was a little preoccupied."

"So, what did you do today?"

"Not much. Just drove around here and there." Robbie quickly changed the subject. "Have you made any decisions about the refugees?"

"Yes. We need to help them. There will be more, and I've instructed the laboratory staff to produce additional antibiotics.

"It was just luck that we decided to take them all to the Hospital. They were in such poor shape. I found out today that some of the contractors came down with the disease. They have been quarantined as well. So far, there haven't been any additional illnesses outside of the Hospital. Keep your fingers crossed."

Robbie took the bite off his fork and waved the fork in the air, his eyebrows sliding inward in thought. "If some of the contractors had caught the disease, then went to the Compound, they could have spread it further."

"True, but that's why Christine is working late. She's trying to get everyone inoculated. As long as the Hospital lab can keep up with antibiotic production, then we should be safe. But with stuff like this, you just never know."

On the morning of the tenth day, since they'd found out about the disease, Christine gave Robbie the go-ahead to leave. "There have been no new cases outside of the Hospital. I'm sorry to say, though, that seven more died there."

Robbie gave Sean and the girls a big hug each. "I hate to be leaving you, but I'm certainly glad to be able to get back to work again."

Sean walked him to his Jeep.

Robbie opened the door, hung on the door frame, and turned back. "Is what I'm doing the right thing to do? Life has gotten so complicated. Things were simple back in Peaceful Valley. We worked, played, and enjoyed life. Now, life is full of roadblocks."

Sean put his hand on Robbie's. "This is what you and Ronnie wanted. I don't think you can stop now."

"Maybe my brother and I were a little too naïve. We never thought how difficult this would be. Now I've lost him. Life has always been hard, but this is brain-racking."

"I know. But it will get easier."

"You think?"

"I know. You just have to keep at it." Sean patted him on the shoulder. "Where are you heading to first?"

"Over the harbor bridge. There was someone in Portland the last two times I've been through there. He's been on the overpass each time. He could have shot at me twice . . . but he didn't. I need to find out why. Could be another good ally there."

"You want me to find someone to go with you?"

"I think I'll be all right."

Sean gave him a fist-bump. "Okay, have it your way. Good luck . . . and keep your head down."

Robbie smiled and nodded, then eased the gearshift into forward.

Fifteen minutes later, Judy climbed down from her lookout position at the harbor bridge to open the gate for him. She didn't keep him long. She was lost for words about his brother. She just gave him a brief hug and wished him well.

He drove slowly over the causeway, admiring the nearly flat green waters. Halfway across, he stopped and got out, walked over to the edge, and looked down. The water was clear and not all that deep. He could see the shells on the bottom. Just like Sean, being near the water relaxed him. He sighed, stretched his arms, looked up and down the long bridge, and got back in his Jeep.

Robbie stopped a half-mile from the overpass and got out his binoculars. He couldn't see anyone on top. He pulled up a couple of hundred yards and stopped again. This time, a head appeared. He spotted the guy clearly with the binoculars. He was looking through the scope on his gun. Robbie grabbed the flag and waved it back and forth.

He put the binoculars back up to his face with the flag in the other hand. *Is he going to shoot or what? What's he waiting for?*

A second man came into view. He scurried over to the first, and they appeared to be discussing the situation. Robbie kept watching. The men stood up and waved him over. He eased forward and took the off-ramp to the overpass.

At the top of the hill, he stopped, killed the engine, and got out. He had his pistol handy but left his AR-15 in the rack. He raised his hands in the air and waited for the men.

He stood patiently as the men, with their rifles trained on him, slowly made their way in his direction.

When they got to within twenty feet, Robbie smiled. "Howdy!"

"What do you want?" the taller of the two men asked.

"Peace . . . friendship . . . democracy. Want me to name more?"

The two men glanced at one another, puzzled.

Robbie's eyes turned to their rifles. "You don't need those. I'm a peaceful guy."

Neither man lowered his gun.

Robbie took a deep breath. "Do you guys know Sandra Hawkins over in Corpus?" He turned his head in that direction and pointed. The two men turned their heads as well.

"We know of her," the taller of the two said.

"No one who goes there ever comes back," the shorter one broke in.

"Except you," the other said.

"Is that why you didn't shoot at me?"

"You caught me off guard the first time, you flew through here so fast. You got my curiosity up when you made it out of Corpus."

"Things are a lot different there now. Sandra Hawkins, the wicked witch, is dead. We have a new mayor now, and democracy is well-established. People have rights. We aim to see they get them.

"You two aren't much older than I am. You don't remember how life was before the country went to hell. I don't either, but my parents and grandparents have told me how it was back then. I'm going from town to town to try to make that happen. See the American flag on my Jeep?" he said, turning and extending his arm in that direction.

Robbie watched as their eyes jerked toward the Jeep, but then immediately back at him. "That is the symbol of the old America. It is also my symbol of what I'm doing. If you see the flag, it means peace. Tell the folks around here what I'm doing. If they want to be a part of the new America, hang a flag from this overpass. I'll be back around this way in a month or so."

The men were quiet. Robbie wasn't sure what to make of them. "Will you tell the others here?"

They looked at each other. "We kinda like things like they are," the tall guy said, "but yeah, we'll tell them."

"You like what you have? You don't need more food? How about gasoline?"

The two glanced at each other. "We have all we need. There's a price tag to having more, I'd bet."

Robbie felt like he was getting nowhere. "Okay, I'm going to go now." He slowly turned around and headed back to the Jeep. He hoped he wasn't going to get shot in the back.

Halfway back to the Jeep, one of the men said, "Mighty brave of you to turn your back on armed men."

He didn't turn around, but twisted his hand about his head in a half-wave. "Thanks for not shooting me."

━╫━╫━╫━

Robbie made stops in Aransas Pass, Rockport, Austwell, Tivoli, and Seadrift. At the edge of each, the American flag was flying high. Robbie was making headway, but there was still a lot to be done. They had questions, a lot of them, and Robbie didn't have all the answers.

Robbie signaled with a wolf howl at the edge of Phillip's place in Austwell. He came out of his shop carrying a chunk of iron and returned with his barking signal. They met at the forge. Phillip dropped the metal and reached for his knife. Robbie had his pistol out and aimed in a heartbeat. "Mighty good with that pistol, Robbie." Phillip gave out a roaring laugh and stuck his knife back in his arm-sheath.

"I come all this way to bring you some gas, and you pull a knife on me. Maybe I should just go on my way." Robbie turned and acted like he was leaving.

"Wait! You know I didn't mean it."

"I'm not so sure. You answer my signal, then the knife . . ."

Phillip took a couple of steps in Robbie's direction. "Jeanne made a pie."

Robbie turned and smiled. "Well, that's more like it." They both had a big laugh.

Robbie ran and grabbed the can of gas out of the Jeep, then followed Phillip to the house. Over pie, they discussed more trading. "We built a new church back home. My brother's fiancée decided to build it when Ronnie died. It needs a bell. A gift for Brooke and a tribute to my brother."

"Say no more. The next time you come around, I'll have one for you."

"And I'll bring more gas." Robbie grinned. "Maybe you and Jeanne would like to come to Peaceful Valley and help install it . . . stay for a church service."

"A vacation?"

"Yeah."

The dishes stopped rattling at the sink.

Phillip pulled at his beard and looked over to Jeanne. "We haven't been to a real church in decades. I'd love that. How about you, Jeanne?"

She looked over. "I'd like that, but it's probably too long a trip for us. That's a really long drive there and back. We're not as young . . ."

"An hour and a half each way."

Phillip laughed. "What are you gonna do, stick a rocket up our asses?"

Robbie joined in on the laughter. "No. We can fly there. Sean has my Cessna ready, and the next time I come here, we can zip up there and back."

Phillip's eyes widened. "You have a plane?"

He nodded. "The only reason I didn't fly this time is that I need to make sure I have a place to land everywhere I want to go. There can't be any old cross-wires on the old power poles, either."

Robbie nodded with a pleased look on his face. They sealed the deal with a handshake. Jeanne insisted he stay the night.

⊣⊢⊣⊢⊣⊢⊣⊢

Robbie made it to Tivoli in time for morning coffee. He was surprised to see Hank there.

Arlene set a fresh cup in front of him and refilled Hank's. "Yeah, the old coot showed up back over here a few days after you dropped him off in Seadrift. Can't seem to get the bastard to leave."

Hank pinched her on the leg. "You know you wouldn't have it any other way, darlin'."

"Yeah, yeah," she said as she walked over to help other customers.

"She loves me." Hank giggled.

"So, you going to stay here?"

"Where you headed?"

"Seadrift."

"I could use a ride over there. A guy's working on a car for me. I'll stay here as long as Arlene will have me, but I need to keep in touch with Clara and the other folks in Seadrift too."

"Say no more."

After coffee, Hank gave Arlene a peck on the cheek, and a pinch on the butt, and they were off.

Each locale had a few more cell tower locations, and Robbie marked them on his map. He was only halfway around the circuit, but it appeared he had enough towers to make a connection to Seadrift. Their primary concern was fuel. He'd have to talk to Sean about getting a transport truck ready to make the loop as soon as they could get enough crude filtering in.

Robbie assured everyone that their needs would be met and that they should be picking people to join the police force. As soon as they could get a steady supply of gas, the top priority would be security. They would all get phones, and they were working on CB radios for the cars so they could converse locally as well.

It took four days to make half the circuit to Seadrift. He spent most of his time answering questions but also making sure the citizens of each town knew their responsibilities too. This included manpower for the police, processing and storage of trade products, and communication of any problems or needs. He didn't want misunderstandings to develop between the communities.

Hank had tears in his eyes when Robbie left Seadrift. "I owe you more than I can ever repay you for making it possible for me to meet Arlene . . . and Clara. If ever there is anything you want or need . . ."

Robbie smiled. "You've done your share, old friend. If not for you, I'd have had problems getting Seadrift to go along with me. They might even have killed me. Hell, I owe you big time for introducing me to oysters alone."

They held a long embrace, both sniffling. Robbie left Seadrift reasonably comfortable with what he had achieved. Everyone so far was on his side. Victoria still remained the biggest obstacle. It was the largest city on the route with a substantial population and a lot of resources. They really didn't need Corpus Christi or the rest of the smaller towns. They seemed to be heading in the right direction, but they could change their minds. They had been taking care of themselves for a long time. But, just like Robbie and his brother, people always wanted more. More fuel was first, but also seafood, maybe a little trip to see places they'd never seen before, and pineapple came to mind. He had to be very careful in everything he said or did.

Robbie thought he saw someone in Bloomington on the last run through there but never found anyone upon closer inspection. He decided one person wasn't really worth looking for.

Robbie hung a right at Bloomington to take a different route into Victoria this time. He discovered a train and thought that was worth investigating. It was parked on the tracks about a mile outside of town.

The engines, of which there were actually three, were intact and undamaged, from what he could tell. He tried to count the cars, but lost track about midway through and gave up.

Tankers stood stoically along the tracks with faded chemical warnings painted on the sides. Cars made for hauling stuff mingled with the tankers. Locked doors indicated there might be something inside—raw materials, perhaps, that could be used for something. The same might be true with the tankers. *This could be a great find.*

He climbed in, around, and through the front engine. Years of dust covered everything. He searched for a starter switch, but not knowing what it might look like, he soon gave up on the idea of getting it running and headed back to the Jeep. He made a mental note for the library in Victoria. He needed to search for a book on trains.

The trees devoured the sun as he made it to the city limit. He had a difficult time finding Freya's house, coming into town from a different direction. Though he figured he could get into Victoria safely on his own, that may or may not be a good bet. Freya certainly could help him get in a little safer. He could also get a good night's sleep.

He walked through the trees until he reached the far side of the grove where Freya's home was located. A light was on. He made his way to the porch and knocked. Without an ounce of fear, she opened the door. She wore her contagious smile as if she'd known it was him. She took a whiff of Robbie and pushed him toward the bathroom.

When he finished his shower, they ate, and Freya showed him the same bedroom he stayed in last time. She followed him to the bed and started helping him take off his clothes.

He grabbed her arms. "I'm sorry, but we can't do this again. Florence had my son last week. I love her."

Freya pulled back, her effervescent face wilting at his words. He reached out and tilted her face up until their eyes met. "Last time was . . . I'll never forget it, or you, but it can't happen again." He wrapped her up in his arms. "There'll always be a special place in my heart for you, but we can only be friends."

She slipped out of his arms and sat down on the bed. Robbie sat beside her and waited. When her breathing slowed, he looked over.

She squeezed his hand and had her smile back on. "I can do that. I'm sorry I forced myself . . . last time. I didn't mean it to turn out . . ." She leaned over and gave him a shoulder bump. "You're the one who came walking in here like that."

He squeezed her hand back. "I guess we were both a little vulnerable at the time."

Freya insisted she fix breakfast for him. She wouldn't let him touch the dirty dishes either. "You have important business in town. I'll clean up. Now go on. I'll see you later."

"No escort?"

"Not this time. You'll see."

Robbie headed on into Victoria. A mile ahead he stopped and stared at the American flag hanging from a wire stretched across the roadway. He couldn't help but smile.

He hit the horn, sat, and waited to see if someone would come out to greet him. He was right. Two men came out of a building to his right. He heard a noise, and there were two more to his left, but they held their position.

"I'm Robbie."

The men didn't point their guns at him like the ones at Portland did. They laid the rifles across their arms and approached. The taller of the two smiled. "Yeah, Robbie, we know who you are. There's been quite a buzz about you since you left last time."

He couldn't contain his smile. "Yeah? What about?"

The shorter man opened the passenger door. "You don't mind if I get in, do you?"

"Err . . . no, I guess not."

He closed the door behind him. "I hear you're from Corpus Christi. There are a lot of us who like the idea of a Unified South Texas."

Robbie nodded. "What now?"

"Our standing orders are to take you to the Chief of Police. He will, in turn, take you to see the mayor and the City Council. If you drive, I'll show you where to go."

Fifteen minutes later, Robbie stood in front of the Police Station. The man pointed and put his rifle on his shoulder, business end in the air. "This way."

As usual, the chief didn't get up when he came in. "Welcome back, Robbie."

Chief Hayes dismissed the man who'd brought him in.

"Thank you, Sir. It's good to be back."

"I'm sorry, but I'll need your pistol. Regulations."

Robbie smirked. "All in the name of progress."

The chief laughed, picked up the phone, and punched a speed-dial number. "Robbie Lindgren is here, Sir. Yes, Sir, we'll be there."

He hung up the phone and stood up. "Are you hungry? I didn't get breakfast."

"I'm fine, but I'll tag along if you don't mind."

The chief strode down a hallway to their dining hall. Robbie hurried to keep up. "Do you have cell phones too?"

"No, just the landlines. We haven't had the need to call out anywhere."

"How about an airstrip?"

The chief snapped his head in Robbie's direction. "An airstrip?"

"Yeah. I have a light plane and thought the next time I come here, it might be by air. Much faster and safer that way."

"We have an old airport out to the east of here, but no planes. They were all destroyed decades ago. So, you have an airplane?"

Robbie followed the chief into the empty dining hall and sat down at the table he directed. "Actually, I have a couple of them. My friend, Sean, the mayor of Corpus Christi, found them in an abandoned warehouse, and a couple of the mechanics fixed them up."

The chief laid the menu down and turned his attention back to Robbie. "That's gonna be convenient for travel."

"I haven't flown them anywhere yet. Sean and I took one on a test flight last week. I need to find places to land them before I start using the planes for trips. I don't want to take the chance of wrecking one, trying to land it in a field or on a road with overhanging wires." Robbie's mind flashed a picture of the last plane he flew. "Maybe I can take you up next time I come to Victoria."

The cook came over. Hayes ordered waffles. He looked over at Robbie.

"Just milk will be fine," he said, remembering the first time he had it back at the Farm in Corpus.

"You sure? Pete here makes the best waffles around."

Robbie didn't want to make waves. "One will be plenty."

Chief turned his attention back to Robbie. "So, who taught you how to fly?"

"I was forced to teach myself. Sean and I got trapped in Corpus Christi a couple of years ago. I finally escaped in one of their planes. That was the first time I'd actually flown."

"So you've been flying for a couple of years now?"

"Actually, the other day was only the second time. I crashed, and the plane burned the first time."

"So, you've only flown twice, and you crashed the first time?" The chief looked hard at Robbie. "And you want me to fly with you?"

Robbie smiled. "These little planes are really easy to fly. They practically fly themselves." He tried to reassure Chief Hayes. "I only crashed because someone shot at us and damaged the plane."

"I'll have to think about it a little." The chief smiled and looked down at the plate the server set in front of him. He grabbed the bottle of honey and drowned the waffle in the amber liquid.

Robbie took a sip of his milk. It was just as he remembered. "So, where do you get coffee?"

"One of our locals got some plants going in his greenhouse years ago. It gets a little too cold in the wintertime here, but in the greenhouses, we have coffee and a few other things we couldn't ordinarily grow."

Robbie poured the honey on his waffle. "You have anything to trade?"

"We have a lot of excess citrus fruit of all kinds. You have citrus?"

"Not much. A bad winter killed most of ours."

Hayes smiled. "The advantage of greenhouses!"

Robbie looked over toward the kitchen. Pete was standing in the doorway. Robbie held up his fork with a piece of waffle dripping in liquid sugar and gave him a nod.

He turned his attention back to the chief. "Before we can do anything, we need to get some of your crude oil to Corpus. To do that, we need to find a pipeline between here and there. We should assign someone to check out the full length of it . . . make sure it's in good enough condition for use."

Chief took the last bite of his waffle and pushed his plate back. "We'll talk to the mayor about getting started on that first thing."

"We already have men looking for sources near Corpus. I'll talk to Sean when I get back. We'll see if we can get a crew to start checking it from our end."

The chief nodded and looked at his watch. "We better get going. We don't want to be late. The mayor gets a little testy when someone doesn't show up on time."

⊣⊢⊣⊢⊣⊢⊣⊢

Robbie followed the chief up the steps to Mayor Rodriguez's office at a near jog. They just barely made the appointment on time. The mayor motioned him and the chief up front. For this meeting, a single large table with chairs all around sat in the middle of the room. The mayor sat in the center on one side and directed Robbie to sit directly across from him. The remainder of the council filled all but one chair. The idea of sitting across from the man who might one day be the governor of his proposed new democracy made his waffle flip in his stomach.

The mayor smiled and asked one of his aides to bring him some water. Rodriguez spoke in a gentler voice this time. This set Robbie at ease, but when a priest came in and sat down in the last empty seat at the table, the butterflies came back.

Robbie took a sip of his water. The mayor introduced him to Father Michael, the only member of the group he hadn't already met. Robbie stood up. He motioned for Robbie to sit back down.

During the first meeting, Robbie and the mayor discussed 'what ifs', for the most part. Now, they got down to brass tacks—a crew for checking out a pipeline to Corpus Christi, specific items to be traded back and forth, police officers for the expanding police force, communications, and a more in-depth discussion of values.

The conversation got to religion quickly, and Robbie focused on the priest. "We recently built a church in Peaceful Valley. One member of our community is a preacher and holds services for those who want to attend. We all worship in our own way, some more than others, but it is not a requirement that you 'believe' in our valley." Robbie glanced over at the mayor.

Mayor Rodriguez looked at Father Michael, then around the table at the other attendees. He then focused back on Robbie. "We have three churches here. Most of the residents go to church at least once a month. I don't go as often as I'd like, but I do make time when my workload permits."

Robbie sat and stared. The look of uncertainty on his face had to be noticeable.

The mayor smiled. "Church is not a requirement in our city either. You and your family appear to be good, honest, and hard-working people. Maybe now that you have an opportunity, if things aren't quite so tough on you in the coming years, you'll give one of our churches a try."

Robbie sighed, forced a smile, and nodded. "That may very well be possible, Sir."

"Either way though, I think we'll get along working together for our mutual benefit. A safer and more prosperous world is more important than whether or not you go to church. And some trade. I'm already looking forward to having seafood on a regular basis. That's one thing I've really missed over the years."

"I've only recently learned of a fruit called pineapple. I think you might like them as well. They make a scrumptious cake."

"We'll look forward to that."

Nearly five hours later, the meeting was adjourned. Robbie got up and fiddled with his chair. "Something the matter?" the mayor asked.

Robbie looked up. "No. Nice folding chairs. Just thinking how handy one of these things would be out on the road. Compact, but comfortable.

"I think we can spare one. It's yours."

Robbie folded the chair, nodded, and thanked the mayor for his generosity. He and the chief left the office fully engaged in conversation.

"Normally, Robbie, I'd have one of my men chauffeur you around, but I'd like to take you to the airport myself. It's been a long time since I've been out that way. I haven't seen my daughter for a while either, and maybe we can stop by her place."

Robbie nodded his agreement. A smile grew on his face with the mention of Freya. "That sounds good, Sir."

"That's enough with the 'Sirs', Robbie. Just call me Chief like everyone else."

"Does your daughter call you Chief?"

He smiled. "In public, but that is rare."

The farther out of town they drove, the brush began to infiltrate the sides of the road, and dilapidated buildings appeared. But, Robbie was pleased to see that the occupants of Victoria had made an effort to keep the road in decent shape.

The chief drove onto the tarmac, and he and Robbie got out to look around. Weeds grew in the cracks in the pavement, but otherwise, it seemed okay. Robbie eyed what was left of the buildings, and the control tower was not distinguishable from the rest of the piles of debris. "Can we drive out to the runway, Chief?"

They piled back into the car. Only a few potholes in the asphalt spoiled the taxiway, but when they got out to the main runways, the concrete was sound. Robbie could see no holes. Grass and weeds grew from the cracks, but there was nothing to prevent him from landing and taking off here.

"Looks like this will work, Chief. Next time I come here, I'll fly in. It's a long way back into town though."

Chief smiled. "No problem. Freya's house is not far from here." He turned the car around and headed south. "She can drive you to wherever you need to go."

Robbie smiled and observed where they were driving. He needed to remember the route. It wasn't far. A mile at most. When they pulled up to the front of the picket fence, Robbie got out and looked around. He followed the chief to the back of the house.

Freya's face lit up when she saw him. She gave her daddy a kiss on the cheek but surprised the hell out of Robbie when she brushed the chief off quickly and moved over to him. Though the kiss and embrace were innocent, they were indeed long enough to significantly change the color of Robbie's face.

Robbie looked at the chief. He couldn't look him in the eyes, but the look on his face was of concern more so than anger. Robbie's face flushed scarlet. His eyes darted between the chief's concerned face and Freya's eyes, sparkling with mischief.

He turned away, blushing madly and struggling to find something—anything—else to talk about. "Um…y-your garden looks nice," he stammered, haphazardly gesturing in its direction.

Freya smirked and dragged him inside, her daddy following. She went to the kitchen and poured drinks.

Robbie and the chief sat down at the kitchen table and waited for Freya. He squirmed in his seat, afraid to say anything, but more concerned that the chief might say something. He didn't feel this uncomfortable in front of the mayor. He sat quietly for fear of putting his foot in his mouth.

Freya handed the men their fruit juice and sat down. "What brings you two out this way?"

"Robbie is going to fly in the next time he comes. We were checking out the airport. I thought he could walk here and you could drive him into town next time he comes."

She looked over at Robbie. "I guess I can do that." She smiled, and he could feel the flush returning. He had no control over his smile. It popped up every time Freya looked at him or said something.

They finished their drinks, got up, and went to the back door. The chief gave his daughter a big hug. "We've got to get back to town, sweetheart. It's good to see you again and looking so well. I still don't like you living way out here, but it looks good on you."

Freya smirked, but the smile crept in. "It's good to see you too, Daddy. I like it here. You know how noisy it is in town. I like the peace and quiet."

"I know. I just wish . . ."

Freya turned to Robbie for a hug, which he gave her, but before she could kiss him, he turned his head. On the drive back into town, he stared out the window, and his mind drifted. He knew things would be a little more difficult with the chief from here on out, but if he could keep his relationship with Freya non-sexual, it would help. *I've got a new baby at home . . . and Florence. I can't be forgetting them . . . Florence and I are going to be married soon. Freya can only get me deeper and deeper in shit! Like the old days at Sandra's. Dammit!*

Robbie snapped back to reality when the car pulled up to the front of the Police Station. He got out and noticed his Jeep parked nearby.

The chief walked around to where Robbie stood. "You want to stay the night?"

Robbie looked back over at the Jeep. "I appreciate the offer, but I think I'd like to get back out on the road. I still have a lot of people to talk to, and we've got a lot of work to do yet. Best I get at it."

"You're doing a good thing, Robbie." He waved at a passing officer and whispered something in his ear. He then turned back to Robbie. "If you succeed at organizing the state, one day there will be a monument erected somewhere around here with your name on it."

Robbie smiled but shook his head. "Not what I'm looking for. Just doing a job."

The officer the chief spoke to came running back out with something wrapped in aluminum foil. He handed it to the chief, who in turn gave it to Robbie. "A little meat for the road. It's already cooked. Just warm it up, or it's good cold too."

Robbie gave the chief a firm handshake, then headed for the Jeep.

Chief yelled after him. "Keep up the good work. The sentries know you now. You won't have any problem going in and out of town. Just keep flying the flag."

Robbie put his arm on the Jeep and turned to give Chief Hayes a final wave. *He's a good man.*

He double-checked the map to make sure he was on the right road. The next stop was Goliad. He looked over at the empty passenger seat. *We're doing it, Brother!*

Robbie easily found the same spot where he stayed last time. He grabbed a bottle of water and the package wrapped in aluminum. He sat in his new folding chair and gazed at the western sky—yellow streaks of clouds laced with red, orange, and gold against a bright blue backdrop folding into the encroaching darkness. He peeled the foil back and breathed in the heavenly scent of the three beef ribs. *Two for tonight; one for breakfast.*

Chapter 19

Sonny sat looking at the pistol in his hand. He slowly turned the cylinder. *Click, click, click.*

He looked up toward the window when he heard the door shut on the pickup. He checked the clock. Marcia wanted to leave at four o'clock. By the time they got to the Farm, Sean would be there, and with a little luck, so would Christine.

Seconds later Marcia opened the door. She came around the table to sit beside him. "Lola will be fine at my sister's."

Sonny sat staring at the gun in his hand. *Click, click, click.*

Marcia reached over and put her hand on his arm. "You having second thoughts?"

"I am. I've never shot a gun. I don't even like guns. I know we carried one on the shrimp boat, but we never had to use it . . . not against people. We killed a few varmints and sometimes a shark that we caught on the boat so we could bring it aboard, but you always did the shooting."

Marcia grabbed the gun out of Sonny's hand. "I can do it. Damn right, I can do it!"

Sonny looked into her face . . . her eyes. Her face was red, and her eyes had no fear in them. She had the look of revenge written all over her and more . . . hunger . . . hunger for power.

I've known this woman half of my life. She's always been a little headstrong, but she's been gentle too. She's been a loving wife and mother, but I guess she's the reason we've been successful . . . the reason we've always had plenty of food on the table and a beautiful home. Her strength as Sandra's right-hand gal . . .

Marcia got up, stuck the pistol in her pocket, and grabbed a drink out of the fridge. She tossed a bottle of water to Sonny. "Let's do this," she said.

Sonny climbed in the passenger side of the truck. *She always drives. She's always told me where to shrimp. What to do. It's like I'm her slave or something.* Sonny shook his head, frowning. *No, not her slave. Of course not. Besides, it's easier that way, right? I do what she says; we succeed. It's worked for twenty years. It will always work.*

Marcia looked over at the quiet Sonny. "Don't forget what you're supposed to do."

"I won't."

They drove in silence for quite some time before Marcia pulled up in front of a house. He didn't recognize the place or the men who came ambling out. Their muscular arms were evident, as were their well-worn clothes. They crawled in the bed of the truck. One was carrying a gun.

"Not much of an army," Sonny said.

Marcia shook her head and crammed the truck into gear. "It is what it is! I can't believe these are the only two I could get to help us. I had to promise them the moon to get them to come along. One will be the Chief of Police, and the other will run the fleet of boats and the processing plant."

Sonny turned and looked out of the rear window. *Looks like they'd make great employees for the sewer plant . . . Chief of Police! . . .*

Marcia pulled up to the front of the Police Station. Sonny got out and waved at the man on the roof. "Ahoy!"

He recognized Sonny and stood up. "What's up?"

"Marcia has some business with Christine."

"Christine's not here. And who are those men?"

"Maybe someone else can help, and they're part of the business."

He didn't argue the point, and Sonny chatted with him while Marcia led her two thugs inside. Seconds later, Sonny jumped at the sound of Marcia's pistol. The man on the roof turned and tried to get back to his bunker. He caught a bullet in the face from Marcia's man with a pistol. He scurried up the staircase to the roof when she cut down the two women inside. They didn't know what hit them.

Marcia waved Sonny inside while the man on the roof kept an eye out. Sonny grabbed an AK-47, a Glock, and a satchel full of ammo. Marcia tossed her revolver and took the automatic pistol off one of the dead girls. Her thug grabbed automatic weapons for himself and the man on the roof.

They got back in the truck. Marcia gave Sonny a loving smile. "Piece of cake!"

He found it difficult to return her smile, but managed to force a distressed one-sided curl of his lip. *I don't like this . . . it's too late to turn back now. I've got to do what Marcia wants . . . needs . . . we've got to finish what we've started. Be strong, you weakling bastard! Where's your backbone?*

Sonny took some deep breaths. He forced a more intense look on his face as he stared at the road ahead.

Marcia looked over. "You okay?"

"Damn right, I'm okay! Let's go kill that son-of-a-bitch that tried to kill me!"

Marcia smiled, but she also squinted her eyes at Sonny. "What the hell is going on over there?" He didn't say anything. Sonny hadn't entirely been himself since they were reunited, but he wasn't anything like himself before he went missing either. She put a hand on his shoulder. "Just remember the plan."

Sonny looked over, and his smile came a little easier this time. "Don't worry about me."

The plan was that the two men in back would remain in the truck and shoot anyone who approached the house. Marcia and Sonny would go inside. If Christine were there, it would only be her, Sean, and his two women. Maybe a cook, but no one else to be concerned about. They would not be expected, but there would be little to concern them until it was too late. They would only take their pistols inside.

Marcia pulled up to the farmhouse and saw Christine and Sean's cars parked nearby. "Yes! They're both here. Sonny, keep your gun behind you until the target is close."

Sonny took a deep breath. *This is it!*

<div align="center">~~~~~~~~</div>

Marcia marched up and knocked. Sonny stood only a couple of steps behind her. She started to knock again when the door opened. It was Christine.

"What are you two doing here?"

"We have a situation down at the Bayfront that requires yours and Sean's immediate attention."

Christine looked over at Sonny, then back at Marcia. "What is it?"

"Is Sean here?"

Christine turned and looked over her shoulder when she heard Sean's voice. "What is it, Christine?"

"I don't know yet, but it seems we have a problem."

When Marcia saw Sean, she shoved her way past Christine, catching her off-guard. Christine fell to the floor. Marcia drew her pistol. Sonny was right on her heels with his gun in hand. Christine saw Marcia's pistol and reached for hers. Marcia made a lunge at Sean frantically trying to steady her aim.

Sean spotted the pistol and ducked back into the kitchen. A bullet splintered the doorframe next to his head.

Sonny didn't have a shot at him, so he turned his gun on Christine. Reggie Carston had trained her and her ladies well after he and the Lindgrens took down Sandra's regime. Christine had her pistol trained on Sonny's chest long before he could target her. She squeezed two quick shots. Sonny's eyes bulged as the bullets tore through his sternum. He was dead before he hit the floor.

Sean made a dive for the butcher's block with all the knives. He slipped on the floor mat in front of the sink and fell to the floor. He rolled over on his side to see Marcia coming around the corner, her pistol homing in on his head. He scrambled to get up, but his hands and feet only slipped on the floor.

Sean focused on Marcia's eyes staring at him straight down the barrel of the pistol. He closed his eyes. The bullet whizzed by his head, and the report echoed in his ears.

Sean opened his eyes. He watched as the scene seemed to play out in slow motion. Marcia's eyes were wide, her face a map of pain and shock. Her gun arm slowly slipped downward. Brenda stepped forward from the shadows of the hallway and plucked the pistol from her hand as her knees buckled and she continued her fall toward the floor. A thud and moan followed.

Sean gaped at the knife sticking out of Marcia's ribcage. He tried to struggle to his feet, but he had injured his leg in the fall. To his knees was as far as he was going to get without help.

Brenda rushed over and helped him to his feet as Kim emerged from the hallway.

Christine made her way to the kitchen door. She sidestepped Sonny's body and pointed her pistol at Marcia. "She's still breathing."

Marcia's body struggled for air, spurting blood from her mouth, the pool spreading across the floor.

Sean looked at the placement of the knife. "Brenda got her good. Lungs and close to the heart. She won't last long."

He looked into Brenda's eyes. "A knife?"

"I always keep one in the nightstand by the bed. You just never know."

Kim stepped forward. "We have both kept one handy for years. We prefer them to guns."

They froze when they heard the truck start outside. Sean grabbed Marcia's pistol. Christine was already headed for the front door. By the time she got there, all she could see was a trail of dust. Sean hobbled out onto the porch, following his head of police.

Christine turned to him. "Looks like she had an accomplice or two. It'll be dark soon, but first thing in the morning, I'll have my team search for the truck until we find it. Maybe we can get some fingerprints off it and make an arrest."

Sean nodded.

They turned and walked back to the kitchen. "We have a mess to clean up here," Christine said.

Kim stepped over and nudged Marcia with her foot. She didn't move. She reached down, wiggled the knife, and pulled it out of her ribs. Kim looked over at Brenda "You did good, girl."

Sean hugged Brenda. "I love you girls. All of you. You too, Christine."

Chapter 20

Robbie lay in his bedroll watching the brightening sky to the east. Today he would go into Goliad and meet with Joey. He hoped that he would have secured a vehicle, a couple of guns, and that one or two of his friends were ready to initiate Robbie's plan.

He ran his tongue around inside his mouth trying to get a little moisture going. Then he felt a sharp pain in his britches. He rolled out of bed, grabbing at his crotch, tearing at his underwear. Something fell to the ground, and he stomped it. He leaned over to take a closer look. *Goddamn spider.* He hunkered over a bit and looked down to examine himself. *Of all the places for that son-of-a-bitch to bite me. That's going to leave a mark!*

Robbie peed, then closed his britches. He couldn't help but scratch. He looked to the east. The sky had lightened up significantly, and he packed up his gear and climbed into the Jeep. He pulled out the foil package and finished off the beef rib he'd saved for this morning. He rinsed his mouth and swallowed the water. He couldn't help but scratch again. *Dammit!*

He went over his options before cranking up the Jeep. First, he had to check on Joey. Next, he would make his way past the lepers in Beeville to Sinton. *I've got to get back to Corpus Christi. Maybe the doctors at the Hospital will have something for this. Damn, this hurts. What kind of spider was that?*

Robbie looked around, cranked up the Jeep, and pulled out to the highway. He rolled to a stop at the checkpoint and cleared his entry into Goliad. He smiled at the American flag hanging in a nearby tree.

Joey showed off his new-to-him Ford Mustang as soon as Robbie made his way to his house. "I've got two buddies ready to go. We all have guns and bullets, sleepin' bags, water cans, gas cans, and food. We couldn't get a lot of gas though. We have a full tank, but only half a can extra. Where can we get more?"

"I've got a portable pump. You'll have to find one for yourself. I have a tough enough time finding gas for my own needs. It's not always easy."

Joey frowned and scratched his head in thought. "I'll do what I can."

"Did you find a map?"

Joey opened the car door and reached inside and pulled out a fold-up Texas map. Robbie showed him the area he wanted Joey and his men to cover.

"I thought I was going with you."

"No, not yet. You need to secure the area around Goliad first. If you find people, they all need to know what's coming. You also need to scout for any resources that we can use, especially gas or diesel."

The smile was gone from Joey's face, but he listened to Robbie as he explained how things needed to go down.

"Keep an eye out for cell towers too."

The young man listened and agreed to all Robbie's demands. He wasn't too happy that he wasn't going with Robbie, but he accepted the fact that the area around Goliad needed to be secure first.

"What about Refugio? Did you go over there?"

"No, but one of our traders went last week to get supplies. I told him to talk to the people there about what you're doing. He said they listened, but were skeptical about whether or not it could work."

"Now that you have transportation, will you go back there and work on them?"

"Yeah, and maybe I can get a line on some extra gas there too."

Robbie's penis was hurting badly now. He stepped in to tell Josephine hi and bye, then headed on his way. Just outside of town, he stopped to pee again. The swelling made it difficult.

Robbie crammed the gearshift into forward and smoked the tires a bit taking off. He got the shivers every time he thought about not being able to pee at all. This scared him. So much so, that he decided he'd stop in Sinton for only a few minutes, then head straight to Corpus.

There he told the man he'd met on his last trip that he had a medical problem and needed to hurry to Corpus. Of course, he had to ask.

"Don't be embarrassed. Let me see."

Robbie showed him.

"You say a spider did this? We have a damn good doctor here, if you'd like him to take a look at it."

Robbie was surprised. "Really?"

The man got in the passenger side of the Jeep, and Robbie got back behind the wheel. "You know, we never really properly introduced ourselves."

Robbie looked over. "No, we haven't. I'm Robbie—Robbie Lindgren."

The man extended his hand. 'I'm Harley—just Harley."

Robbie smiled. "Nice to meet you."

Harley nodded and pointed to a green building. Robbie pulled up in front of the reasonably maintained commercial property at the far end of the main drag.

Harley got out, came around to Robbie's side, and stepped up to the front door. He gave it a firm couple of raps, turned the knob, and pushed the door open. "Yo, Doc!"

The room was lit only by an oil lamp on the front reception desk. No one was in the office. Seconds later, an elderly man stepped in from the hallway. "Good to see you, Harley. And who do you have here?"

"This is Robbie. He seems to have a problem. Something up your alley. Show him, Robbie."

Robbie looked at the Doc, then back at Harley.

Harley snickered. "I've already seen it. The Doc is the only one here."

Robbie ignored the flush in his face and pulled his britches down. "A spider was in my bedroll this morning."

The Doc reached over and grabbed the lamp and held it close. "Looks to be swollen shut?

"Yes, Sir."

"I'll have to put a tube in it. I'll give you some salve, and if the swelling goes down, it'll be okay."

"And if it doesn't?"

"Let's be optimistic."

Robbie pulled up his britches while the Doc went to the back room. He didn't have anything to say to Harley, and they both stood in silence.

The Doc returned with a jar of salve and a clear plastic tube. "This tube will allow you to urinate. The salve should help with the swelling, but don't expect a miracle. Spider bites are slow to heal."

Robbie thanked the Doc. "Sorry, I don't have anything to pay you for your services."

"I'll put it on your tab. We'll think of something, son." He smiled. "Harley's told me about what you're doing. I think it's an admirable plan and I wish you luck."

Robbie returned his smile.

Harley gave the Doc a nod and followed Robbie out to the Jeep. "I can't thank you enough, Harley. I thought I was going to die before I got to Corpus."

Robbie headed back to where he'd picked Harley up. On the way back, Harley told him about their visits to the surrounding towns, spreading the word about what he was trying to accomplish.

"We've outfitted two more vehicles and have been to Mathis and Robstown. There's a good-sized group of people at Mathis. They're protective of their resources there with the lake and all, but I think they understand what you're trying to do. We'll keep working on them.

"Robstown was quite a large city at one time, but the place looked like a run-down burnt out skeleton. Only saw a few people and some of them shot at us. The few that did won't be bothering us anymore."

Robbie gave Harley a finger to the eyebrow salute and thanked him for helping his cause. "With people like you and your men, I believe this is going to work. I knew my plan was going to take a lot of effort and, as hard as I wanted it to work, I wasn't quite sure it would all pan out."

"That reminds me, you were here with your brother last time. Where is he?"

Robbie felt the moisture building in his eyes and fought it off. He sniffled and wiped his nose. "After we saw you last time, someone took shots at us from a water tower. He caught a bullet."

"I'm sorry to hear that. My condolences."

"Thanks. We knew this was going to be a dangerous undertaking when we first started out. I guess you just never think something bad will happen to you." He paused a second, still trying to fight back the tears. "I'm missing him a lot, but I'm going to finish this job for him if it kills me."

Harley put his hand on his shoulder. "You're a brave young man."

He forced a bit of a smile. "Thank you. I guess I'd better get going. It's a long drive back home from here, and I probably won't make it all the way today. I've got some thinking to do."

"You have someone back home?"

"At the moment, but this is going to complicate things." He waved toward his crotch, and then with resignation, got back in the Jeep. "We haven't been close lately with all my traveling. Looks like it's going to be a while longer." He forced another smile before he cranked up the Jeep. "Thanks again, Harley."

Chapter 21

It was almost dark by the time Robbie found a place to spend the night. He pulled to a secluded spot in the brush. He didn't care about the hunger that gnawed at his gut. He didn't care about his horrible thirst. If he drank more, he'd pee more. The tube helped, but it was still excruciating.

Robbie gathered some wood in the waning light. He decided to sleep in the back seat of the Jeep. It was a little more uncomfortable, but he didn't want to take the chance of getting bitten by something again.

Robbie sat watching the fire burn for an hour. He found a soda under the seat that he picked up in Corpus and sipped on the fizzy drink. He thought about Sandra's big twat, and how good his first real sexual encounter felt despite her size.

Jade held his attention for quite a while, but then the others crept in—Nancy, Brenda, Barbara, Kim, and Joy. There were so many he couldn't remember all their names. They each had their individual talents and peculiar quirks, but none of them like Jade.

Then there was Florence. He fell in love with her when they first met, and that love grew later when Sandra tortured her and threw her in a cell. That love faded a bit after he got her back to Peaceful Valley and he strayed a bit, first to Beka, then to Charlotte.

Nothing bad ever happened to me when I was with them, but now that I'm committed to Florence . . . maybe there's a higher power at work . . . I'm being punished. Freya! One little incident and now my dick's about to explode. Freya can't happen again. I've gotta be loyal to Flo.

Robbie finally dozed off, but he had a restless night. He had to get up to pee in the middle of the night and was reminded again of his dilemma. It took nearly an hour for him to fall back asleep. When he woke up again, the sun was already up.

The road home was a long and painful trip. He didn't know how he was going to explain Freya, but if they were to be husband and wife, he didn't have a choice. They couldn't keep secrets. He looked down at the speedometer, and it was sitting at thirty mph. He pressed down on the accelerator. *No sense putting off the inevitable.*

When he got to the church, he stopped and killed the engine. He sat and stared at the empty structure. Even if he believed in God, He wasn't going to help him now.

He started the Jeep and headed on toward the house, detouring around his mom and dad's home. He didn't see anyone outside. It didn't matter, he needed to see Florence first.

Mutt started barking the minute he spotted his Jeep. Florence came running out of the house. She plowed into him as soon as his feet hit the dirt. She tried to lock him up in a tight embrace to give him a kiss, but he gently pushed her away before she could.

"What the hell's the matter?"

He pushed at Mutt too, as the dog vied for his attention. "Down, Mutt." He gave the dog a quick scratch, then stood back up and stared into Florence's angry face. "Something happened while I was gone. We need to talk."

"Well, can't you give me a kiss first? It's been so long . . ."

He gave her a little peck.

Florence took a step back, and her eyes focused intensely on him. Her breaths grew short and amplified. The confusion on her face was evident.

Robbie reached down and took hold of her shirt sleeve. "Let's go down to the pier."

He tugged on her arm, and though she was a bit resistant at first, she trailed along. Robbie led her to one of the chairs, and she sat down.

He pulled up the other in front of her, but before he sat down, he opened his britches.

Florence's eyes bulged as she stared at the discolored organ with a tube sticking out. "What the hell!"

He closed his drawers and sat down so he could look directly in her face. "I saw a doctor while I was in Sinton. He put the tube in so I could pee. A spider bit me the other night."

She looked up. "Holy shit!"

"But that's not what I want to talk to you about. I think this is my punishment for something else."

Her eyebrows slid together, and he could almost hear the gears turning in her head.

"I've been unfaithful."

Robbie watched the first tear trickle down her cheek, followed by another and another. Still, she didn't say anything.

"It only happened once. It won't happen again."

Florence stood up, and Robbie did the same. He took a step closer. Her face turned pale, and her whole body trembled as she processed the implications of what he had told her.

"Once or a dozen. There's no difference." Then her hurt turned into anger . . . violent anger. "You son-of-a-bitch!" she screamed over and over, her fists swinging wildly at his face.

Robbie protected his face but didn't try to stop her from hitting him. He knew he deserved everything she could dish out.

Brooke heard Florence screaming and came out of the back door, running to the pier. "What's the matter?"

Florence stopped hitting him and sat back down in her chair, sobbing. She was shaking by now and couldn't answer Brooke. Brooke looked at Robbie, but he didn't offer an explanation either.

Florence looked up and wiped her face. "Tell her, you bastard! Tell her!" she screamed.

Brooke looked back and forth between the two.

"Tell her you've been fucking every bitch you could find out there!" Florence hissed at him as tears crested her cheeks.

Florence put her face in her hands and wept louder, her whole body shaking. Brooke knelt down by her, put her arm around her shoulder, and glared at Robbie.

He sat back down and couldn't look at either of them. "It was only that one time. Being on the road, after Ronnie . . . alone. I was weak, and I'm sorry. It just happened. It'll never happen again."

Florence jumped up and screamed at him. "Get out of my sight, you son-of-a-bitch! I don't want to ever see you again!" She turned and stomped toward the house. Brooke followed. Halfway to the house, Brooke turned and threw a look at Robbie. If looks could kill . . .

Robbie turned his chair with the back against the house and stared at the water. A few minutes later, Brooke came out. "You'd better leave, Robbie. I had to talk her out of shooting you. I wasn't sure I could take the rifle away from her, but I managed this time. I may not be able to next time."

Brooke headed back up toward the house. Robbie took a deep breath and walked around to the Jeep. He pounded his hand on the steering wheel, cranked up the engine, and headed out. He eyed his parents' house when he drove by. Again, he didn't see anyone outside. Robbie had no intention of stopping anyway. The tears, the knot in his stomach, nausea . . .

He drove by the church and didn't stop until he reached the highway. He closed his eyes and leaned his head on the steering wheel. *I've done it this time. I can't stay here anymore.*

He got the gas can out and emptied it in the tank. He winced at the burning pain in his groin that reminded him of his indiscretions. *Better get used to it. He turned the ignition switch and looked at the gas gauge. Three-quarters. That's enough to get me back to Corpus. If I hurry, I can make it there by dark.*

The horizon gobbled up the sun, but it was still plenty light enough to see without his headlights when Robbie pulled into the checkpoint. Trish was the first one out. "Charlize will be out in a minute. She's in the lady's room."

Robbie smiled, the first time he'd smiled at anything for a couple of days. He looked over when he heard the hinge squeak. Charlize came over and opened the passenger side of the Jeep and climbed in. "You back for our rematch?"

Robbie sighed. "Maybe next time. A spider got me."

"Where?"

He looked down. "In a bad place."

"Let me see."

"No."

"Come on." She reached over and pulled at his britches.

"Don't, that hurts."

"Then let me see."

Robbie huffed and pulled his trousers open. "Feels like I dropped some hot coals down my britches. Dammit, it hurts!"

Charlize gasped. "That's not good!"

Trish patted his arm. "It'll get better, right?"

Robbie shook his head. "I hope."

Trish looked over at Charlize. "It was just a spider. Of course, it will."

"Where are you going to stay the night?" Charlize asked.

"It's getting late. I don't want to bother Sean this evening. I guess I'll sleep in the Jeep."

Trish grabbed him by the arm. "Nonsense. There's a bunk in the lookout shack. You're welcome to stay here."

Robbie nodded. "Let me pull off the road." He moved the Jeep around to the side of the building and got out.

Trish pointed the way. "After you, Robbie."

Charlize stepped in behind him. "We've got a little food here if you're hungry."

"Thanks, but I nibbled on some jerky on the way. I'm okay."

Trish lit a candle. The cabin was quite dark inside. Charlize took a position at the lookout window while Trish showed him the bunk. "It doesn't look like much, but it's comfortable enough."

Robbie put his backpack on it but took a chair. "I don't think I can go to sleep quite yet. Too much stuff on my mind."

Trish smiled. "Like what?"

Robbie sighed and held his head down. "I had a little transgression in Victoria. The spider is my punishment."

Charlize glanced over. "Juicy. You're going to have to tell us all about it. Nothing ever happens around here."

"I told Florence. She ran me off."

⊣⊢⊣⊢⊣⊢⊣⊢

Brooke warmed up the pot of stew she'd made earlier in the day while Florence fed the baby. After she burped him, he went right back to sleep. "Good," she whispered. "I need to talk to you, Brooke."

Brooke fixed herself and Florence a bowl, and they both sat down at the kitchen table. Brooke smiled. "What are you going to do?"

"I can't be with Robbie if he's going to be sleeping with every bitch he runs into. I'll go over to the Carston's tomorrow if you'll keep an eye on the baby. They need to know he was here and that I ran him off. I'll see his mom and dad in a few days. I don't want to run into him in case he went there. Maybe the bastard will go back to Corpus."

"So what are you going to do about it?"

"Robbie and I will never get married, that's for sure. I guess I'll have to let him see Lawrence from time to time, but for the most part, he'll have to stay away."

"And you?"

"I don't need a man. You lost Ronnie . . . well, I lost Robbie too. I don't know about you, but men are nothing but trouble. I can do without them. I'll have Lawrence."

"I've thought about that a lot. I don't think I could ever love anyone again like I loved Ronnie. There are no other men around here now anyway. I'm certainly not going anywhere else looking. Unless God drops someone here in my lap . . .

"It's different for you. Robbie's not dead. I don't think you should be so quick to throw him away. He's the father of your child. You need to make it work for you and Lawrence. Make him suffer a bit . . . make him crawl, but eventually, for your own good, take him back. It's a hard world to be in without a man. He honestly sounded sorry for what he did. Maybe it was just one time."

Florence got up and dipped herself some more stew. "I'll think on it." Then she changed the subject. "I was hoping you'd have a girl for a long time, but now I hope it's a boy."

Brooke smiled. "Yeah, me too. It was easy to pick a boy's name after Daddy. I'll call him Johnny though, so everyone will know who I'm talking about. How about you, you going to keep calling yours Lawrence—or Larry?"

"I think, Lawrence. I like the sound of it. When he grows up, I'll let him decide."

Florence took a bite of her stew and sipped her water. "But . . . if you have a girl, she'll probably be a tomboy. Guess it really doesn't matter. Look at Debra. She grew up the only girl in the valley. Best of both worlds, huh, Brooke? Great stew, by the way. You're the best cook."

Chapter 22

Robbie got an early start and made the short drive to the Farm. Sean's car still sat in front. Christine's was gone.

He was surprised to see a new check-in station constructed next to the driveway to the farmhouse and main barn. He recognized the gal sitting in the chair who patiently waited for him to come over to what looked more like a lemonade stand than a checkpoint. "What's going on?"

She handed him a clipboard with a sign-in sheet and pen. "Sean thought it best to keep better tabs on who was coming and going around here. I think the incident with Marcia and Sonny sparked this addition."

"What incident is that?"

"They came here the other night and tried to kill Sean."

"What!"

"Yeah. Just before dark, they showed up with guns. Luckily Christine was here. But it was Brenda who saved the day. Stuck her with a knife."

"And Sonny?"

"Christine shot him."

"Holy shit!" Robbie glanced up toward the house. "Anyone else get hurt?"

"No, just Sonny and Marcia. They had someone with them, but they stayed in the truck. They took off afterward. Christine is still trying to track them down."

"Do you have a gun?"

She reached under the counter and pulled out a sawed-off shotgun. "If I hadn't recognized you, you'd have seen this already."

Robbie smiled. "I'm sorry, I remember your face, but your name eludes me."

"Stacey."

"Yes, I should have remembered. We talked in the nursery a while back."

"Yes. It's back to duty now. There is always a shortage of women, it seems these days. And with the new hours . . . well, we've all got to do our part, don't we?"

"Can I go in now?"

"Of course, I see Sean is coming out." She thumbed at her boss over her shoulder.

Robbie turned and smiled. His genital pain kept him from running over. Robbie gave his old buddy a fist-bump when he reached him. "Sean, can we talk . . . in private?"

"Sure, we can go out on the back porch."

Robbie followed him through the house. He spotted some leftover bacon on the stove and picked up a couple of strips.

Sean sat down alongside him in the glider. He noticed his limp.

"You all right, Robbie?"

"Yeah. I'll get to that, but I want to hear about Marcia and Sonny first."

He laid out the whole story.

Robbie couldn't contain his delight. "Good ol' Brenda."

Sean nodded. "Now, what's going on with you?"

He squirmed in his seat. "Sean, I'll just come right out and tell you. I've done some terrible things in my life, but now I've gone and topped everything."

Sean's eyes widened, and he turned to focus directly on Robbie.

"I got hooked up with a gal in Victoria. Just a one-night stand, but I told Florence. She threw me out of the house."

"That doesn't explain your limp."

"That's a spider bite. I thought it was a warning. Now, with Florence and a new baby at home . . . it shouldn't have happened . . . nothing I planned . . . I didn't think, I guess. I thought I had to tell Flo.

"She threw me out of the house, so I came back here. The only thing I have left now is my plan to fix this country. I've screwed up my life, but maybe I can still fix south Texas."

"I don't know what I'd do without Brenda, Kim, and Benjamin. They make my job worthwhile. Florence may be mad now, but she'll calm down. She still loves you. You've got to go back and make things right—for Lawrence, if for no one else. The job isn't enough . . . you need family."

Robbie sniffled. "We'll see."

"Whatever happens, you've got the girls and me. We won't desert you."

Robbie put his hand on his shoulder. "I know."

"Can I see it?"

"What? Oh, the spider bite . . . you sure?"

Sean nodded, and Robbie stood up, glanced around, and pulled his britches open.

Sean jumped up when he saw the tube. "Crap, Robbie!"

"That's so I can piss. It hurts as bad as it looks too."

They sat back down. Sean took a breath of the fresh air. "So, what are you going to do now?"

"I dunno. Get back out on the road and see what I can do about getting this country whipped into shape."

"I've got some good news for you. I talked to your dad, and he's got the airstrip ready for you in Peaceful Valley whenever you're ready to fly home."

"When did you talk to him?"

"Day before yesterday."

"I'm not sure I can . . . not for a while anyway. Everyone will know about Flo and me in a day or so. That's not something you can keep quiet back home."

"Guess not." Sean paused. "How about you stay here for a couple of days. I've got a new shrimp boat. We can go out on the water."

Robbie raised his head up. "I think I'd like that. Maybe I'll get lucky and fall overboard."

Sean frowned. "I've been there, Robbie. Way back when we first came here, I almost did just that. Just let the crabs have me. But you know what? No matter how bad things may seem, and I'm pretty sure tomorrow looks mighty dim to you right now, it'll get better. Death is permanent."

"I hurt though. Inside and out."

"You've hurt before, but you're tough. Your dick will heal, and Florence . . . if you really want her, you need to fight for her. I thought I'd never have sex again, but now I'm a father, thanks to you. Losing my nuts was bad, but it wasn't the end of the world . . . not even close. I now have not just one, but two wonderful women in my life. Shit happens; you know that, but you never know what lies in your future."

Robbie sighed and got up. He knew Sean was right. Regardless of how he felt now, over time, he would heal.

Sean gave him a shove on the shoulder. "How about you follow me around today? I've got work to do, and I need to get going. I'll show you my new shrimp boat."

Robbie followed Sean inside and back through the kitchen. Sean grabbed the sack lunch off the table and ran back to one of the bedrooms to tell Brenda and Kim goodbye. Robbie didn't need to see them just yet.

Sean got in the Jeep with Robbie. "If I'm going to work with you, the least I can do is chauffeur you around."

〜〜〜〜

Sean walked into the conference room at the Contractors with Robbie on his heels. "Sorry I'm late, guys." Sean indicated a seat for Robbie, then headed on up to the podium.

Sean pointed to a man, and he stood up. "I'll need my shrimp boat ready to go out in the morning. Take care of that, will you?"

The man nodded and scurried out.

Sean pointed to another man. The representative from the Airport stood up and waited for Sean's directions. "This is Robbie," he said pointing. "I don't think you've met yet. Robbie, this is our Airport manager."

Robbie nodded. Sean turned his attention back to the man. "Robbie is the owner of the newly refurbished Cessna. Whatever he says, goes. The Cessna is to be kept ready at all times."

"Yes, Sir."

One by one, Sean called upon his crew leaders for reports and to give them further directions. He would glance over at Robbie from time to time. He was paying attention and gathering information about the progress of all the operations in and around Corpus Christi.

Robbie was especially interested in the plight of the refugees at the Hospital. Six more died, but the antibiotics seemed to be helping. There were no more cases outside of the Hospital, which indeed was good news.

When Sean was finished, he asked Robbie up to deliver a report on his progress in Seadrift, Victoria, and all the other cities he'd visited.

The meeting ran well after lunchtime due to the lateness of Sean and Robbie's arrival, but no one complained—publicly, anyway.

Robbie drove them down to the Bayfront. Sean pointed to where his boat was parked. It was in a stall away from the other boats. Sean grabbed the sack lunch and shared half his lunch with Robbie while they looked over the vessel.

"This is brand new. How'd you rate a new boat?"

"Being mayor has its perks. There'll be a crew who will run the boat most of the time. It will still need to contribute to the economy, but I'll be able to use it whenever I have the need to go out on the water. That probably won't be often, but like today, when I want a boat to take friends out, I'll have one."

Sean lifted the lid on the ice box. It was full. He checked the fuel level and found it to be full as well. "It never hurts to check." He smiled at Robbie. "Well, let's head over to the Airport."

The Airport manager greeted them when they arrived. The transport was on the tarmac with men scurrying around getting it ready for another trip to Brownsville in the morning. When Sean was comfortable that everything was being taken care of, he led Robbie over to a small hangar with the Cessna inside. "This is where you'll find your plane. It will always be ready when you need it."

Robbie ran his hand along the smooth surface of the propeller. Sean watched as the smile formed on his face. *He'll be all right. Life is always a struggle.*

You can't just give up. Robbie will learn to live again, hopefully with Florence back in his life. It may be tough for a while, but Robbie's a tough man.

Florence fed Lawrence, then dressed him in his best clothes. This was the jumpsuit Emily had made for him. Brooke was already dressed. Florence handed her son off while she hurried and slipped into her best dress. She didn't want to be late for her first church service.

"I shouldn't have let you talk me into this, Brooke."

"You need to tell James and Melissa about Robbie. Now is just as good a time as any. I don't know what you know about church services, but Daddy is not like most preachers I've known. He will help you get over your ordeal with Robbie if you'll just let him. He will not ask you to do anything that you don't want to do. He'll only support you."

Florence didn't say anything. She only shook her head and sighed. She didn't really want to go to church, but Brooke was right. Flo needed to tell James and Melissa, and now was the first opportunity. It would only get harder if she waited.

Florence sat in the back row with Brooke and behind James and Melissa. She was surprised that everyone was there except the Lins and Carstons. She remembered that Emily had said Reggie was feeling a little under the weather a couple of days ago. Probably the reason they weren't present. *I'll ask about the Lins after the service . . . and after I talk to James and Melissa.*

Florence flipped through the hymn book that John had made. There was a dozen of the little books, all handwritten with Kathy's help. There was no music, only the words written out as best as they could remember them.

John's words seemed to float by her and disappear off into the distance. She was deep in thought about Robbie and how she would explain the situation to his parents. She would pick up an occasional word from time to time when John emphasized a phrase.

Kathy got up and joined John ever so often to help him lead the congregation in a song. She would then sit back down, and John would continue. "We cannot always understand why God does things, but He has a plan. Maybe we are being tested . . ."

The words faded like they were deflected off the side of her head. Florence couldn't maintain her attention on John. *Did Brooke tell John about Robbie?* She looked over at Brooke, who noticed the movement, then turned and smiled. Florence smiled back and turned her head away. *She only hugged her daddy when we got here. This is the first time she's seen John since Robbie left. He can't know . . . but his sermon . . .*

Florence looked over at Beka and Lance. They sat close, almost like they were sewn together at the hips. Zack and Debra sat a little farther apart, but they were holding hands. She felt a tear trickle down her cheek. *Robbie and I will never be together again. We can't, with him sleeping with every woman he meets.* "That son-of-a-bitch!"

John stopped talking, and a quiet developed that got Florence's attention. She looked at all the eyes staring at her. *Did I say that out loud? Dammit!*

Florence jumped up and ran out of the door as fast as she could with Lawrence in her arms. He started crying. She couldn't run far. She found a nearby stump and sat down. She pulled her blouse open and directed the nipple into his mouth.

Brooke strolled over and knelt beside her. She put her hand on Florence's arm. "Don't worry. I told them what happened."

Florence couldn't look Brooke in the face. She just rocked back and forth, humming, trying to soothe Lawrence. "I didn't mean to say that out loud. I couldn't get my mind off Robbie, and it just festered up."

"I know. Don't worry about it. It's not your fault."

Lawrence didn't eat much and dozed off. Brooke helped her to her feet.

"Come on back inside. It sounds like Daddy's finished with the service."

Florence followed Brooke back in and sat down where she was sitting before. "I'm sorry."

Everyone immediately accepted her apology; then she spelled out what had happened with Robbie. John only said 'God is testing you . . . be strong', and he let it go at that. Melissa carried Lawrence back home while Florence and Brooke trailed behind, hand in hand.

Beka and Debra gave Florence long hugs, then peeled off and headed home with Lance and Zack. It was Sunday, but they still had a full day of chores waiting for them back home.

Florence and Brooke followed the Lindgrens back to their place and sat down on the porch. Melissa handed Lawrence back to Flo. James went around to the smokehouse, grabbed some meat, and went inside to help Melissa make lunch.

He brought drinks out to the girls, then went back inside. He threw Florence a smile of understanding.

Brooke took a sip. "When Ronnie died, I wanted to die along with him. Daddy and the church have helped me see that you can't give up. Life is supposed to be tough. God tests us. He helps us become strong.

"You can only become strong if you're tested. Our bodies have become strong because we work hard. Our minds are the same way. You hardly cry at all anymore. I remember when we first met, you were crying all the time."

Florence smiled. "I couldn't help myself this time. At least now, I don't cry long."

"That's right, and tomorrow you won't cry at all. Tomorrow we get back to work doing what we need to do to make life better for you, me, and Lawrence."

Florence reached for her water. "And for Rudolph."

Brooke smiled. "You changing my baby's name now?"

"Well, you didn't seem to be so dead set on Johnathan. I thought I'd try out one I remembered a while back. If you decide for sure, I'll stop changing his name."

"You know, I do like the name, if it's a boy . . . after Rudolph Valentino. I read about him in one of Lars's books. Great actor in the silent movie era. I think he played in *The Four Horsemen of the Apocalypse* and a few others I can't remember. I remember this one because of our own apocalypse."

"Is it okay if I call him Rudy then?"

Brooke nodded. "I guess we have a fifty-fifty chance his name will be Rudy. You'll have to help me pick out a girl's name if I need to."

"Of course."

Melissa and James brought out lunch. They fixed their plates, and all eyes turned to Florence.

Melissa poked a potato, but paused and laid her fork down. She needed answers. "So, Florence, tell me more about my son."

Florence looked up. "I told Robbie to leave. I wanted to kill him, but Brooke stopped me." Florence looked over at Brooke. "I don't know what he's going to do. I don't even know where he's gone. I just know he left. I'm sorry."

Melissa didn't have a mean bone in her body, and she'd always been loving and caring for Florence, but her son had disappeared, and she was concerned. "Florence, you and Robbie should have come to us . . ."

Florence picked up on Melissa's condescending tone. She stopped chewing and glared at her. Florence's blood boiled. She wasn't in the mood to talk about Robbie. She hopped out of her chair the best she could while holding onto Lawrence and threw her fork down. "You can't fix this!" she yelled, blowing food on the others. She stormed down the steps, headed for home.

Brooke stood up. "I'm sorry, Melissa. I better go with her."

Brooke grabbed her stomach and stepped off the porch. "Wait up, Flo."

Bright and early the next morning, Robbie and Sean arrived at the boat all set for a day on the water. Sean started it up and let the engine warm. "You're going to like this. It looks like it's going to be a nice day. No wind. Usually, there's a breeze even at this time of the morning. Maybe you won't get seasick."

Robbie smiled. "I don't think I'd get sick. I think that would have to be a mental thing."

"I don't know. Brenda got sick when she, Kim, and I took Sonny's boat. It didn't bother Kim at all, but Brenda threw up her guts. I don't think she was afraid of the boat or the water, or even thought about getting seasick. She just did and couldn't help it. There's gotta be more to it than that."

Sean steered the boat out of the slip and toward the opening in the harbor jetty. When he turned the corner, Robbie looked out across the bay to the east. A hint of light stretched across the horizon.

Sean steered the boat across the bay for nearly a half-hour. The eastern sky was bright, and the sun would peek up in seconds. He slowed the boat and let down the sampling net. "This boat will pretty much run itself. See," he said pointing, "I have a steering wheel and controls back here too by the winch. I can run the boat alone, but this is a dangerous job. Anything can happen, and it's always better to have someone along. Besides, it's easier with two, especially after you haul up the catch."

Sean pulled up the sampling net, and while there were not a lot of shrimp, he guessed it would be okay for a pleasure trip. He let the main net down, and they were off, zig-zagging around at just over one mile per hour. That was towing speed.

"We'll make this drag for an hour. I'll cull the shrimp, and we'll make another for an hour and a half. That should be enough for our day. This is only a pleasure trip, after all."

"Works for me, Sean."

Robbie filled Sean in on his progress in Victoria—the need to get a crew out locating and repairing pipelines between Corpus and there, Victoria's desire for seafood, and the train he'd located with a hundred boxcars and tankers, some filled with something. He'd have to get back to him on what.

"So, Robbie, tell me about this lady in Victoria."

"Trouble."

"Aren't all women, but such a nice problem."

Robbie snickered. "Every man's dream, but . . ."

"But what?"

"I've gotta learn to keep my britches up. That's enough, okay?" He left it at that and climbed up on top of the cabin and into the rigging to get a better look at the bay. The wind was light, and the sky was clear. He could see for miles.

Robbie gazed back at the city. Corpus Christi looked much cleaner from out here. He knew better though. This once *Sparkling City by the Sea* was in comparison a cesspool. There were exceptions though. The Farm was quite lovely, and the Airport was well-kept. The Contractors compound was junky, as expected. The harbor was okay too, though it always smelled like dead fish.

Robbie climbed down and helped Sean dump the first catch on the culling table. Many of the crabs climbed over the sides and fell onto the deck. They jumped at him, their pincers grabbing at air, as he and Sean worked to get the net back into the water for another drag.

After they were going again, Robbie helped Sean pick the trash out of the shrimp. There was more shrimp than other stuff, and this was the easier option. "Looks like a good catch. How are the other boats doing?"

"I think it's going to be a good year. We'll be able to share a few with Victoria."

"They have greenhouses too. They have citrus and coffee. Maybe you should think of more greenhouses for the Farm."

"Brownsville has provided most of what we've needed so far, but if we're going to be trading with other places, you're right, we'll need more."

Robbie played with the creatures and asked Sean about each variety he didn't know, which was almost all of them. They had squid, croaker, shad, mantis shrimp, several kinds of small jellyfish, and a few things even Sean didn't know.

A small crab managed to get the best of Robbie and brought some blood, and a small hardhead catfish poked him in another finger. He learned first-hand about the poison on their fins. He squeezed all the blood he could get out of the puncture at Sean's direction.

"If you don't squeeze the blood out to wash the poison away, it'll be sore tomorrow. It won't hurt nearly as much if you get it all out."

"It hurts, but it's getting numb too. Not enough to stop the pain, but just squeezing the blood out makes it feel better already."

Now that Robbie was experienced at separating out the shrimp, Sean drove in after they'd pulled in their second batch and cleaned out the net. They got nearly a bushel on the first tow, which Sean estimated at fifty pounds and a heaping full bushel on the second. In all, Sean guessed they'd caught a hundred and twenty-five pounds. They also kept four crabs, two each, which Sean put in a pot to boil on the way back in.

By the time the shrimp were iced down, and the boat cleaned up, the crabs were done and had cooled enough to eat. They sat on the railing at the back of the boat and ate the crabs, Sean showing Robbie how to get at the tiny pieces of meat.

"I like the pincers best. I could starve to death eating the bodies. The meat is so hard to pick out."

Sean laughed. "You'll get better and faster in time, but you're right, without the pincers, most people would starve on just the crab bodies."

Robbie stopped by the seafood processing plant on the way back to the Farm. Sean hopped out and told them about the shrimp iced down on the boat. The shrimp were a little too small for eating, in his opinion, but they would be perfect for bait or even in shrimp salad.

Robbie decided he'd head out tomorrow, but after dinner, he'd have a long talk with his friends. They needed to know about Florence. Sean said he'd wait and let Robbie tell the girls himself.

⎯⎞⎟⎛⎯⎞⎟⎛⎯

Robbie got up early and said his goodbyes. He headed for the harbor bridge. He would make Portland his first stop. It was time to get back to work on their plan. Sean would concentrate their work on communications and pipeline location and refurbishing.

Robbie pulled up to the checkpoint on the top of the harbor bridge, and Judy's smiling face greeted him. "Making any progress?"

He stayed in the Jeep, leaning out of the window so he could see and hear her better. "Things are moving along well. Maybe before long, we won't need our barricades."

"That's good news." She walked over and swung the gate open. "You keep your wits about you and your head down."

"I'll be back through in a little while. I'm just going over to Portland. I'll be flying out a little later."

Robbie smiled and stuck his arm out the window. He gave her a 'thumbs up' as he drove by.

Over the next three months, Robbie put his nose to the grindstone and made trip after trip to all the cities and towns he had visited before. Most of these trips, however, were in the Cessna. It was faster and safer, and he no longer spent nights in the woods alone. He secured accommodations in each of the places on his route.

A few hours were often all he needed in one place, so he could cover two or three towns in a single day. A full circuit generally took only three days, and he was back in Corpus Christi again.

Each town built its own police force, all connected by cell phone service as well as CB radio for local communication. Each city expanded their police patrol area and was only limited by communications. With the help of crews from Corpus Christi, cell towers were located, refurbished, and connected.

Crews worked to locate sturdy pipelines all the way to Refugio and Victoria. Soon oil was pumping from these two locations to Corpus Christi. Due to a shortage of pipelines, it was necessary to haul the gas in tanker trucks. There were several terminals with tankers that had sat idle for eons. The contractors overhauled the engines and replaced deteriorated parts as needed. They did what they had to do for the short-term, then worked even harder to improve operations for the long-term.

At the end of nearly three months, everything was going fine. They only had one setback. Static electricity arced and ignited a tanker full of gasoline while unloading near Refugio. Two men died in the explosion, and another while trying to put the fire out.

The mayor of Victoria scheduled a memorial service for their fallen heroes in a local church. People came from miles around to honor these men, even though they did not know them. They gathered in the most prominent church in Victoria, and there was standing room only.

Robbie flew Sean to Victoria for the service. This was their first look inside a real church. Robbie stared at the stained glass windows and the body of Christ nailed to a huge cross, as they made their way to the front. The organ pipes huffed and puffed a soothing song.

Father Michael opened the ceremony with a prayer for each of the men who had died. The organist began to play, and Robbie stood in awe of the sound that emanated from the pipes.

When the song was over, the priest called Robbie up to the dais. He stood and gazed over the congregation. His heart pounded in his ears. "For those of you who don't know me, I'm Robbie Lindgren. With the help of your mayor and Mayor Sean Lin from Corpus Christi—" He waved his arm in his direction. "—we are going to rebuild this country starting with south Texas. You never expect it, but it was inevitable that people would die. We have lost three brave pioneers in our quest for a new democracy . . ."

When he finished, Robbie motioned to Sean. "I think Mayor Lin would like to say a few words."

Sean stepped up. "There will always be bumps along the road of life, but we cannot give up . . ." He glanced over at Robbie. "Perseverance will get us to where we want to go . . ."

Mayor Rodriguez closed the ceremony. "I would like to add that Robbie had a twin brother. A gunman took his life not long ago, yet Robbie pushes on with his quest. I wish I'd have met Ronnie Lindgren. I know he was as great a young man as his brother is proving to be. Let's show him that we are behind him. Let's show everyone that we can be a great country again. We do not have to fight each other. We must love our brother . . ."

Many were in tears long before the mayor finished his speech. The applause roared inside the church as he stepped down.

Father Michael said another prayer for their lost workers and welcomed their souls into Heaven. He closed with another prayer for Sean, Robbie, and Ronnie.

⎯╂╀╂╁⎯

The crews had expanded the service area from Corpus Christi to Port Lavaca along the coast, to Cuero and Yoakum north of Victoria, to Floresville up near San Antonio, and south and west to Harlingen and Kingsville.

They had built eight crews over the area for expansion. Three teams basically replaced what Robbie was doing in searching out new areas. The other five crews worked on communication restoration, fuel production, and police training. They all needed to be in uniform and a cohesive group for everything to work. Under the leadership of Sean Lin and the field operations of Robbie Lindgren, thus far everything was at least working. There were exceptions, however.

When one of the lead crews pulled into Falls City up toward San Antonio, they were fired upon. One man was killed, another shot; however, the third, luckily the driver, managed to get them out.

The driver drove south until he could get some cell service, then called in the incident to Corpus Christi. Sean relayed the problem to Robbie, who was only a short drive out of Corpus. Robbie had driven to nearby Portland to talk to the people there. As hard as he tried, he could not sway this community to come over to his side. There had to be a reason, but the leaders were tight-lipped about what was actually going on.

Robbie wrapped up his meeting and returned to Corpus. Sean had three well-armed members of their newly formed SWAT team meet him at the Airport. They loaded up in the Cessna, and Robbie followed the roads back to Falls City, landing on the roadway where the driver of the scout vehicle waited.

Robbie checked on the wounded man. He was shot in the arm and leg. He would be okay, but he needed to get to the hospital. Robbie and one of the other men helped him into the plane.

The driver of the scout vehicle explained the situation to the SWAT team. "They just started shooting at us. They didn't even let us finish explaining what we were doing. They just wanted us out of there."

The team leader turned to Robbie. "We'll take care of the problem. You get that man some medical attention."

Robbie put his hand on the driver's shoulder to settle him. His best friend died in the ordeal. "Roger, is your SUV okay?"

"Yeah. A few holes and a busted side mirror. Everything else seems to be fine."

"Okay, you'll be the driver for the team. When they're finished here, bring them back to Corpus. I'll tell Sean what's going on. I'm sure he'll want to assign you a new crew so you can get back on the road if you're up to it."

Robbie had moved up to a management position, not by choice, but by necessity. He didn't seem to notice the transition, but merely gravitated into it. He always stayed so busy, he didn't have time to think about it. The plane became a necessity rather than a convenience, and Robbie was getting quite adept at flying. He was learning the area so he could navigate to where he was needed quickly.

As Robbie and his crews expanded their democracy over a more extensive territory, more planes were found abandoned in some rural airports and crop dusting services. Some were in decent enough shape that Robbie sent repair crews to see if they could salvage some of them. It wasn't long before five more planes were recovered and, one by one, Robbie took them back to Corpus for further repairs.

Robbie instructed the pilot there to begin training more pilots in between their trips to Brownsville. A couple of the members of the special forces team were also directed to train the pilots in SWAT tactics. Sean and Robbie decided the new planes were most needed for the police force and quick response teams. They also might be required for the transportation of medical supplies.

Robbie's spider bite caused him a great deal of pain for the first week, but finally, the swelling went down enough that he was able to remove the tube. The itching nearly drove him crazy, but at least it kept his mind off sex. He kept applying the salve and managed to function when he was needed.

At the end of three weeks, however, he was mostly healed up, and his sexual urges returned, but he had no contact with women. Though he could have had Charlize or Trish, he imagined, he stayed away. He forced himself to stay busy, but with all the demands upon his time, this was no chore.

Mostly, mentally he was punishing himself for his weakness and the one-night stand with Freya. He had a soon-to-be wife and a baby. He knew better, but he couldn't contain his animal urges when he was away from Florence on the long trips. It might have been easier for him if their sex life before the baby had been better, but still, that was no excuse for his indiscretion.

He still loved Florence and his son very much. He thought long and hard about how he was going to win Florence back. He wasn't sure it was possible, but he had to think of a way. Another indiscretion and he would lose her forever, if he hadn't already. Maybe she could forgive him for one incident, but never two.

Maybe if I go to church. Show her I'm a changed man. And get down on my knees and beg. Mutt always gets his way when he begs.

Robbie was at the Farm with Sean one afternoon when the special forces team returned from Falls City. Sean told them he'd meet them in his office at the Contractors compound. He tried to keep all outside business away from the Farm for the sake of Brenda and Kim mostly, but also for the many other ladies there, especially those at the nursery.

Sean was sitting at a table next to the podium talking to Robbie when the men came in. "Let's keep this casual, guys." Sean pointed to chairs across the table from him and Robbie. He waited for them to sit. "Okay, let's hear it."

The spokesman for the group instinctively started to get up, but Sean waved him back down. "Casual."

The officer smiled. "There were thirty-seven men, women, and children at Falls City. Only six of them were hostile. They had a few hunting rifles and pistols. They basically held the others hostage. They had their rules, and the others did their bidding.

"They wouldn't listen to me. I waved the American flag followed by the white flag, and they shot at me. I took that as an act of war, but they were no match for our firepower. We quickly eliminated the six targets and then had a long talk with the remaining citizens. They were relieved to be out from under their little dictatorship, but were also concerned about their protection.

"I explained our new system of government and our police force. I told them they could stay where they were at, or they could come to Corpus. Most wanted to come here. A spokeswoman for the group is waiting outside. She's been checked out at the Hospital."

Sean looked over at Robbie, then back at the officer. "More refugees," he sighed. "Okay, bring her in. Let's see what she has to say."

The officer nodded at one of his men. When he pointed to Sean, the woman ran over and grabbed his hand. She dropped to her knees, not able to control her tears. "We won't be any trouble. We'll work for our keep. Just give us some food and a place to stay. We . . . thank you . . . we would have all died."

Sean pulled her to her feet. He looked at the others, then back to the woman. "What's your name?"

"S-Susan."

Sean pulled his handkerchief out and handed it to her.

"They beat us and made us work like slaves. They raped my thirteen-year-old daughter. They were animals. Thank you . . . thank you for rescuing us. We want to be a part of your new Texas. We'll help . . . whatever we can do . . . please!"

Sean turned to the officer. "Where are the rest?"

"They're locked up at the Police Station. We didn't have enough men to guard them at the Hospital, but backup is on its way."

Sean turned back to the woman. "You'll have to be quarantined for a while. We've had some disease problems."

"You're going to lock us up?"

"No, we'll take you to the Hospital. You'll be confined, but not like at the jail. It'll only be for a short while. You've already been checked out there. We'll check out the rest of the group and keep you there for a while longer to make sure. There we can get you some food, and you'll have beds to sleep in. No, it won't be like the jail, and it will give us time to interview you all and determine where you can fit into our community here in Corpus. Everyone has a job to help us build the new south Texas. It will also allow us time to find you suitable housing. There are a lot of empty homes, but they all need repairs."

Susan sighed. She grabbed at Sean's hand. "Thank you."

The woman was escorted back out. Sean took a deep breath and turned to the officer. "Well, I guess we'd better get them to the Hospital. Let me know if you have any problems."

"Yes, Sir." The officer saluted and started to head out.

Sean held out his hand. "What kind of shape are they in?"

"They've apparently been eating, and none of them appeared sick or feeble. I think they're better than most of the ones that were brought in before by the contractors."

Sean sighed. "Okay, see to it."

The officer saluted again, and he and his men turned and walked out.

Sean smiled. "I just love it when they do that."

Robbie gave him a shove. "You letting this job go to your head, Mr. Mayor?"

"I'm definitely getting used to it."

Chapter 23

One day there was a lull in the action, so Robbie decided to drive down to the Bayfront. He found a shady spot along the seawall and stared at the water. *It's been over three months since I've been home. I miss seeing Mom and Dad, but more importantly, I miss Florence. I'll never get her back if I stay here. I'm missing seeing my son grow up. I've only seen him twice. He's got to be a big fella by now. Benjamin has grown by leaps and bounds since I came here.*

Sean keeps telling me Dad is maintaining the airstrip there. I know him; he'll do that until I go home. I need to have a long talk with Ronnie. Damn, I miss him. I've gotta make time to go back. Yeah, maybe tomorrow.

Two more months went by, and Robbie never made the time to get back to Peaceful Valley. He stayed away from the Farm for most of that time as well. Sean invited him to dinner numerous times, but he seldom showed up.

Robbie dropped by Sean's office at the Contractors compound when he had business with him, but spent most of his time to himself. He made a few quick flights to some of the cities, but most days he worked on his new residence.

He moved into an abandoned house near the Bayfront where he could easily walk down to the water when he wanted. It was rundown and needed a lot of work, but he scrounged materials from surrounding properties to fix it up to where it was livable.

When he didn't have business to conduct, which was getting thinner and thinner all the time just like his waistline, he enjoyed sitting on the seawall to watch the gulls and listen to the sound of waves slapping up against the concrete.

Men scurried around on the T-head, making final preparations to their shrimp boats. Boats moved around the harbor between the fuel docks and the ice truck, waiting to load. Tomorrow was the first day of the Fall season, and he looked forward to a steady supply of big white shrimp. Sean had told him about the green-tails, another name for white shrimp because of the green coloring on their tails, and how big and sweet they were. Sean especially liked them on the barbecue.

The boats had been doing some sampling the past few days to try to determine where the best shrimping places were, and he managed to procure a few off the boats. The next couple of months though, he could have fresh white shrimp any day he wanted.

Late in the afternoon after the sun went behind the trees, Robbie headed down to the seawall like he did two or three times a week these days. He enjoyed the tumbling afternoon temperatures when the August heat of the day turned into a refreshing coolness thanks to the breeze off the water.

He watched as all the shrimpers worked late, making sure their boats were in perfect shape for the opening day of the season. He opened up his backpack and took out his soda and the piece of bread he'd brought to feed the gulls. Robbie loved the fruity sodas he'd tasted for the first time in Corpus. They were not always available, but when he could get them, he stocked up.

He sipped his soda and fed the birds. He was about to get up and head home when his phone rang. He pulled it out and looked at the screen. It was Sean. "Hey, Sean."

"Robbie, your dad called a couple of hours ago. He said he couldn't get hold of you."

"Yeah, I had my phone charging. What's up?"

"Your grandpa's not feeling well. He's asking for you." The phone was quiet. "Robbie?"

"Yeah, I heard you."

"You going home then?"

"I don't have a choice now." *I've gotta see what's wrong with Grandpa. I was too little to remember Grandpa Lars. Reggie is the only one I have left. I can't not see him before he dies, if that's what's happening.* "I'll make sure the plane is ready this afternoon, and I'll pack and leave first thing in the morning."

"Let me know what's going on, you hear?"

"I will. I'll call you tomorrow."

Robbie hung up and walked back home where his Jeep was parked. He picked up a few things at the house and headed for the Airport.

He was anxious that he was going to get to see his son and Florence again. He was also mad at himself for not going sooner. As upset as he was that he hadn't tried to fix things between himself and Florence, he was even angrier that he hadn't seen his parents and grandparents. *Dammit, I should have made time. What the hell is wrong with me?*

Robbie lifted off the Airport runway just as the sun peeked above the horizon. The trip home was only an hour. He eased off on the throttle and eyed the grassy runway at Peaceful Valley. His dad had maintained the strip perfectly, just as he thought he would. He smiled when he saw the homemade windsock. It was a pair of pajamas Florence had worn many times. The familiarity of the red flower pattern rushed forward in his mind. *Could this be a signal from Flo?*

Robbie turned and lined up with the runway into the light wind. His concentration was piqued. The landing was always the tough part. One little mistake and he could lose his plane again. Or worse, he could die, which didn't scare him so much these days. But if Florence would give him a second chance, life might mean a little more. He'd pondered death many times over the past few months, but the thought of now seeing his son and even the slightest chance that he and Florence could be a family again gave him hope.

The light plane hit the turf and bounced. Robbie's mind suddenly jerked back into reality. *Pay attention, dammit!* He grasped the wheel tighter, and the plane settled down on the reasonably smooth surface. Robbie cut the throttle all the way and coasted to a stop near the back of the church. He smiled. *Good job on the runway, Dad.*

Robbie grabbed the screw-anchors and put them into the ground under the wings and attached the tie-down straps. His stomach knotted up when he heard voices. He reached into the plane and grabbed his backpack. A long, deep breath, and he headed toward the church. His eyes teared up as soon as he spotted his mom and dad there.

He winced, Melissa squeezed him so tight. "Air, Mom."

"Well, maybe if you'd come home more often." She pushed him back. "And you still need to eat better, young man."

James wrapped them up in a group hug. Robbie had difficulty talking through the tears. "I've missed you so much!"

Melissa wiped her tears. "Then are you going to make more of an effort now?"

"That depends a lot on Florence, but I promise I won't stay gone so long next time."

Robbie turned and headed toward the house. "How's Grandpa?"

Melissa and James caught up with him. She grabbed hold of his arm. "Slow down. He's okay."

"And Flo and Lawrence?"

"You two have a lot to talk about."

Robbie stopped. "I'm not sure I can, but I'm going to try."

Melissa smiled. "You can build a new country; you can put your family back together. You'll work your way through this. The important thing is that you're here."

James broke in. "Let's go see your grandpa first. He's been asking for you. You can talk with Florence after."

⊣⊢⊣⊢⊣⊢⊣⊢

Robbie opened the car door for Melissa, then hopped in the back. He couldn't help the smile that came over his face, seeing the familiar woods to his place. He looked to see if Florence was around when his dad pulled up in front of the house. He didn't see her. Mutt barked and ran out from under the porch. He gave Mutt a scratch on the back, then darted off toward his grandpa's.

Robbie stopped and looked back again just before he went into the trees.

"Don't wait on us," James yelled. "We'll be along shortly."

Melissa waved at Brooke, standing at the front door. "James, I think I'll wait here." She gave him a peck on the cheek. James followed his son.

Robbie automatically howled his arrival when he got to his Grandpa's place. Emily came to the door and returned the signal. He folded his grandmother up in a big bear hug. He had to take a moment for her too. He would see his grandfather soon enough.

Emily released him when James came running up. She led Robbie into the bedroom where Reggie lay.

Robbie gasped. "Grandpa."

His eyes lit up when he saw his grandson. "Robbie." The surprised look on the boy's face at his grandfather's condition must have registered with Reggie. "Don't look so worried. I'll be up and at 'em in no time."

Robbie smiled and looked over at Emily. She came over and sat down on the edge of the bed. "I think it's his heart. He's just getting too old to be doing the things he's been doing. I keep telling him he's got to slow down a bit, but the old coot won't listen to me." She reached down and squeezed his hand.

"There are some excellent doctors in Corpus, Grandpa. I can have you there this afternoon before dark, and they can have you fixed up tomorrow morning."

Reggie smiled and looked into his grandson's eyes. "Nonsense, boy. I'm just getting old. There's no cure for that. It'll be my time when it's my time. I'm ready."

Robbie stood up and turned his back to his grandpa. "That's not the grandpa I know." He looked at Emily, then his mom and dad standing in the doorway. "My grandpa would have fought for his life just like he did against Sandra Hawkins. My grandpa would never give up. *My* grandpa would want to see his great grandson grow up and help teach him how to fish and hunt."

Robbie stepped toward the door.

"Robbie."

Robbie turned around. "What?"

"Do you really think the doctors there in Corpus can fix me?"

"I can't guarantee it, but they're damn good doctors. It's worth a shot if you're up for it. Besides, you might even like the flight. I'm getting pretty damned good at landing these days." He grinned. "Haven't crashed once."

Reggie chuckled and grabbed at his chest. "Laughing might kill me too, Son. Better lay off the humor until after your doc fixes me up."

"Yes, Sir."

After a little more coaxing, Reggie agreed, and they had him on an old travois in no time. Luckily, there was still one lying around. James and Robbie dragged the travois through the woods to Florence's, where the car was parked. Emily followed.

"Grandpa, if you'd let us build a road to your place, this would certainly be a lot easier . . . and quicker."

Reggie snorted. "I'll think about it."

At least they only had to go the mile to his house, unlike before where they'd have had to go the full two miles to the Lindgrens'. James and Robbie helped Reggie into the back seat of the car.

Florence came out carrying their son while James and Melissa got Reggie situated. Robbie ran up to the porch. "Lawrence sure is getting big."

Florence forced a smile. "He eats like you do . . . or did. Looks like you've lost a few pounds."

"Been busy."

James tooted the horn. "We're ready, Robbie."

He turned back to Florence. "Can we talk when I get back?"

"We'll see." That was all she said.

Robbie hurried back to the car.

They made a quick stop so Melissa could grab a few things. Since other than Reggie, Robbie could only take one additional passenger, Melissa insisted she should go. She took only a few minutes to get her stuff. They were on the plane and ready to go in no time.

Reggie lay curled up in back as comfortable as they could make him. "You sure you can get this thing off the ground with me? I'm pretty heavy, you know."

"No problem, Grandpa. I've done this with more weight in the past."

Robbie looked over at his mother. The look on her face was of sheer terror. "What's the matter, Mom?"

"I didn't think this through first. I've never been on a plane before."

He reached over and placed his hand on his mother's. "Don't worry, I'll get us there safely."

〜�〜

Robbie made it to Corpus just as he said he would and had his grandpa in the hospital thirty minutes after landing. He'd seen the doctor before, and she smiled when she saw him. A nurse led Reggie into an examining room. The doctor pointed to a waiting room for Robbie and Melissa.

Robbie got up three times to pace. When his mother looked worriedly at him, he sat back down. "What's taking so long?"

Melissa graced him with a loving smile. "You said they were good doctors. They're thorough. Have a little patience." She patted him on the hand. "You've been gone a long time, Robbie. You can't stay gone that long anymore. You and Florence have to work things out."

"I want that, Mom, but I really messed up this time. All she said was 'we'll see' before we left."

"She's been going to church. Maybe her heart has changed a little. It's not good for a son to grow up without a father.

"You've been gallivanting all over Texas trying to fix this country. So far, it's gotten your brother killed and torn you and Florence apart. It's time you thought of yourself and your family, not the country for a change."

"I know, Mom, but we've made a lot of progress. I know Ronnie wouldn't have wanted me to quit. This was his dream too.

"Other men have died as well, but it's worth it. We're saving lives too. We've connected communities as far north as Port Lavaca and halfway to Brownsville to the south along the coast. Inland, we've gone to Gonzales to the north and over to Floresville near San Antonio and as far south as Kingsville.

"People are still killing each other over food, fuel, and just for the hell of it. We're putting a stop to it. South Texas is already safer. Soon, you won't even need to carry a gun to be safe."

"And when are you going to make time for family? That was what you and Ronnie said when you first started this campaign . . . that you wanted to do it for the future. For your family and children."

"I'm doing that. We've trained men to do many of the things Sean and I have been doing. I'll bring Sean home again soon to see his parents. And maybe before long, if Florence and I can get back together, I can stay home permanently. If I go somewhere, maybe it will be to take Grandpa around to see the new country. I'm sure he'd like that. He's only seen Corpus, and that was no picnic."

"You promise?"

The doctor stepped in. Robbie and Melissa stood up and took a couple of steps toward her with hopeful eyes.

"It looks like he's got a blockage in one of the vessels to the heart."

Robbie looked at his mom and then back to the doctor. "Can you fix it?"

"It will require a minimal surgery procedure called angioplasty. I trained for the procedure way back early in Sandra's reign at the beginning of my career, but I've never performed one. Sandra Hawkins wouldn't allow us. If a person was old enough to need one, in her book, they weren't worth the effort to save. Old guys with heart problems were left to die."

Melissa reached out to the doctor. "You've got to save him . . . he's my dad . . . he's not that old . . . sixty-something, I think."

"And he's my grandpa. We need him. You're not operating under the rules of Sandra Hawkins anymore. You've got to save him."

The doctor smiled. "That's what I intend on doing. They're prepping him now."

Robbie looked at his mom and back to the doctor. "Now?"

"Yes. This is something that needs to be taken care of quickly. You two relax. I'll be back in a couple of hours."

Before Robbie or Melissa could say another word, the doctor turned and headed out of the waiting room. They gravitated back over to their chairs, and he sat down beside her. He reached over and took his mother's hand.

Melissa turned her palm up to Robbie's and gave it a squeeze. "John tricked your dad and grandpa into going to church. Reggie only went that one time, but I've been able to get your dad to go most Sundays.

"John is a Baptist preacher, but he's mellowed, I think. Not anything like the hard-core Baptist preachers I knew when I was a teenager."

Melissa smiled and shook her head. *That seemed so long ago.* "We talk about our gardens a lot and sing songs. I really like that. It's more like a community holiday party than a church service. John usually reads a couple of passages from the bible that he feels are relevant to the day, but other than that, it's more like a family get-together. We sing a lot of songs too. John made some song-books . . . I really like singing."

Robbie got up and walked around the room. He wasn't used to sitting for so long at a time, not even when he was eating a meal. "That reminds me, I have a surprise for Peaceful Valley."

"What's that?"

"I'm not going to tell you. You can't keep a secret any longer than Florence or Brooke. I met some new friends, and you will meet them soon, but that's not the surprise. I'll try to bring them the next time I come."

"And when might that be?"

"Soon. That's all I can say. I told you I'm going to make the time to come home."

Robbie walked across the room and stood with his face to the wall. He butted his head against the surface.

"Quit that! Come back over here and sit down. Patience, remember?"

Robbie scooted his feet across the floor to the chair beside his mother and sat down again. This time, he leaned over with his elbows on his knees and his face in his hands.

Melissa massaged the back of his neck. "You know, Son, Lawrence will be crawling before you know it. He's growing so fast. He rolls over and scoots around. He's a lot like you. You certainly don't want to miss his first steps."

Robbie sighed but didn't raise up.

"Your grandpa and James were hunting just before the heart problems started. Maybe Dad overdid it a little. They got a really nice hog. Biggest one I've seen in the valley. It had to weigh over four-hundred pounds. I remember your grandpa saying he thought it was one of Sam's tame hogs."

It was nearly three hours later when the doctor came out to see Robbie and Melissa. "I've got good news for you. The procedure went well. I used a balloon to spread the vessel and put a stent in to keep it that way. It looks like he only had one blockage."

Robbie hugged the doctor. "Thank you. Can we see him?"

Melissa nodded, her eyes hopeful.

"Not for another hour or so. He's still groggy from the anesthesia. We need to keep a close eye on him for a little while to make sure his vitals stay where they're at. Then you can see him."

"How soon before he can travel? Fly back to Peaceful Valley?"

"If he does well, three days, four at most. I'll come to get you when you can see him."

Once again, Robbie and Melissa sat down.

Melissa smiled. "He'll be his old crotchety self in no time."

Sean, Brenda, and Kim came by and visited with Reggie for a while two of the days he was in the hospital. Robbie and Melissa spent about half of their time there. The other half, Robbie took Melissa on tours to different parts of the city.

Reggie was much better on the second morning, and insisted he could go home immediately. Three things kept him there. Both the primary nurse and the doctor being relatively good looking were the main two reasons. The third was the fact that the doctor threatened to strap him down to the bed and gag him. She reminded him several times that she meant business.

Melissa didn't care for the smell of the bay, but she loved the taste of the white shrimp served at the Farm one evening. Sean promised he'd see to it that they took back thirty pounds of the green-tails so everyone at home could have some. They were only a few days into the Fall shrimp season, but record numbers of the tasty crustacean were coming in daily.

The only fruits and vegetables Sean could offer were some tomatoes and a few others from the greenhouses. This was the hot time of the year, and most of the crops were in except the cotton, but that would be in soon too. What they had to offer from the greenhouses, the Lindgrens already had back home. Unfortunately, there was nothing special available.

One afternoon, Melissa noticed that Brenda and Kim made regular trips to a building in back of the main barn and decided to stroll out there. Julie introduced her to Nancy and the rest of the ladies.

"I'm Melissa, Melissa Lindgren."

Julie frowned. "Any relation to Robbie Lindgren?"

"Yes, I'm his mother."

All eyes focused on her. Julie stepped from behind the desk and wrapped her arms around her. "Nice to meet you, Melissa. Would you like to meet some of your grandkids?"

"What?"

Nancy took Melissa by the hand. "Yes, half the kids in here are Robbie's."

Nancy pulled on her arm a bit, but Melissa held her ground. Nancy gave her a warm smile and pulled again. "When Sandra captured Robbie, she made him perform. If he hadn't, she would have killed him. He was the primary source for . . . er . . . babies."

Melissa followed along beside Nancy. She introduced her to each of her grandkids.

"Can I pick them up?"

"Absolutely."

Melissa picked up Theresa and held her close. She didn't try to stop the tears. "I can't believe I have so many grandchildren. Robbie never said anything."

She picked up each of the toddlers and infants and held them close. *This is grandmother heaven! My, my, why didn't he say anything? I can't let him know that I know. He will tell me in good time. Won't he?*

After Nancy had introduced her to all the bundles of joy that were Robbie's, Julie handed her a handkerchief. "Well?"

"I had no idea. Robbie never said a word. What does he think about you and the babies?"

Nancy put her hand on Melissa's shoulder. "He loves his kids. He's proven that." She looked over at Julie. "As far as us, we know he will never marry us. He can't be a real father to the children, but he comes around often to visit. We were just doing the job Sandra demanded of us. Now that Sandra is gone, we all accept the situation as it is."

"Please don't tell Robbie that I know. If he accepts his children like you say, he will come to me and his dad and tell us. Promise you won't tell."

The girls nodded and crossed their hearts with their fingers.

Melissa looked around the room. "Thank you. I don't know when, but I'll be back. Maybe Robbie will bring me someday."

The last day before they were scheduled to head back to Peaceful Valley, Sean and Robbie discussed business most of the day. Melissa tired quickly of listening to them talking about tank batteries, distillation processes at the refinery, cell-phone tower problems, and crop planting charts. Christine happened over and stayed the afternoon. She kept Melissa occupied. She was a welcome relief.

Christine prepared a pitcher of tea, and she and Melissa spent most of the afternoon on the porch, where they could have some privacy.

"So, Christine, how long have you been in Corpus Christi?"

"I was born here. I ran away when I was fourteen though. Not far. Just far enough to get away from my mom and dad. I stayed with a friend in Portland, just on the other side of the causeway from here," she said pointing to the north. "When the grid shut down, I came back. It was too dangerous over there."

Melissa noticed the tear on her cheek. "What is it?"

She put her face in her hands and stared at the planks. "I had twin sons."

"Had?"

"There was a terrible gunfight one day . . ."

Christine's body began to tremble. "They didn't have a chance."

Melissa put her arm around her. Thoughts of Ronnie came rushing back. "Ronnie . . ."

"Yeah, I miss him too, right along with my boys."

Christine raised up and sniffled. She took a deep breath and wiped her face. "I got a job at the Farm. I've been here ever since. It's much better now that Sandra is gone. Your son and Sean have worked miracles."

"You okay?"

Christine nodded.

Melissa gave her a sympathetic hug. "It seems quite nice around here now."

"Yes."

Melissa sighed. "I ran away when I was young too. I was in Waco. I got out when all hell broke loose and made my way back to my parents in Peaceful Valley. You should have seen the surprise on their faces. Do you have parents?"

"No, they were dead when I came back."

Melissa put her hand on Christine's arm. "I'm sorry."

"Thanks. That was a long time ago. Anyway, Sandra needed help at the Farm and took me in."

"Did Sandra?"

"No. I don't know who killed them. I couldn't have worked for Sandra if she had. I did what I was told, and she was reasonably good to me. More so than everyone else. Then Robbie came along. He changed everything. He's such a good boy . . . man."

⎁⎁⎁⎁⎁

Robbie assured Sean he'd be back in a few days that last day before he left. Reggie had a hefty supply of aspirins to keep his blood thinned to prevent clotting around the stent, and for the first time in the past few days, was relatively quiet when he got on the plane. Melissa didn't have a lot to say on the way back either. She mostly stared out the window, watching the miniature version of the landscape.

Her mind was churning, however. She tried to remember the names of all the new grandkids, but there were too many. *Christine is a good woman. She'll keep an eye on Robbie when I can't. It's sad about her sons and parents. Maybe Robbie is right. There has been too much killing. It was peaceful in Corpus. I never heard a shot while we were there.*

James had cleared a roadway all the way to Reggie and Emily's while they were gone. After they'd taken Reggie home, Melissa and James sat down on their porch to discuss the trip.

James leaned over and gave her a kiss. "So, how was Corpus Christi, sweetheart?"

"Interesting, to say the least." She grinned. "I'd like to go back. Maybe Robbie can take us there, and we can have a little vacation."

James squeezed her hand. "You liked it that much?"

She couldn't shake the grin. "You have no idea."

This drew a frown from James. "I'm all ears."

"Grandbabies. Lots and lots of them . . ."

Chapter 24

After James helped him get his grandpa home, Robbie stayed the night with Reggie and Emily. He loved his grandparents to no end. They were the only ones he had left, and he was glad that for now at least, they would be around a while longer.

Reggie was tired and went to bed before it got dark, just after sunset. Robbie was tired too, but he sat in the dining room, talking to his grandmother for several hours.

"I don't know what's going to happen between you and Florence, but you've got to try to make it work. Promise me you will, Robbie."

Robbie sighed. "Yeah, I'm going over there first thing in the morning, and we'll see if we can get this settled."

"You still love her, don't you?"

"Yes, Grandmother. I just don't know if she'll listen."

"She still loves you, Robbie. True love doesn't die so quickly."

Emily reached out and put her hand on his. "Whatever happens, promise me too that you'll come back often to visit your grandpa and me. We're not going to be around here forever. I thought I was going to die when you stayed away so long. Reggie almost did."

"Since I have the plane, I'll be coming back this way often. I know you guys would like to have some real coffee for a change . . . and tea."

Emily smiled. "That's nice, Robbie. Just remember . . . what's important is you. You come to see us when you can. Your grandpa and I love you more than you'll ever know."

Robbie's lungs shuddered as he drew in a sharp breath of air, struggling to fight back the tears that wouldn't stop coming. It had been a hard few days. He had come close to losing his grandpa, and he missed home so much. "I think I need to go to bed now, Grandma."

Robbie sat on a stump at the edge of the clearing to his house. He got there just before sunup and was quiet so he wouldn't draw the attention of Mutt. He wanted to enjoy the coolness of the morning, though the morning low was near eighty degrees. The moisture in the air made it feel cooler.

What the hell am I going to tell her? Florence thinks I was sleeping with everyone. I've got to convince her that Freya was the only one. It's not like we're married. We may as well have been married and her with my baby. She'll see it that way. All I can do is beg for mercy. If we're married . . .

The door opened to the cabin, and Florence stepped out and whistled. Mutt crawled out from underneath the house and waited for the bowl she had in her hand.

She set it down and looked around. She looked right at him, but he was too well concealed. He knew better than to flinch. She wasn't the same woman he'd met way back then in Corpus. She could shoot and clean what she killed. After the ordeal with Sandra Hawkins and her army, Florence learned to take care of herself, and she toughened up just like she was told she had to if she was going to live out here. Florence was a country gal now.

Robbie waited until she started back up the steps before he got up and signaled with a wolf howl. He got butterflies in his stomach when she turned and returned the signal.

Mutt waited until he got halfway to the house before he ran out and greeted him. Robbie gave him a pat on the back, and he followed him back to the porch where Florence was waiting, but stopped at his bowl and resumed his breakfast.

Florence stood firm on the steps with her arms crossed over her chest. The look on her face was one of somewhere between disgust that he could come back after such a long time and pure hatred, or at least that's what he imagined.

She turned, and Robbie followed her up the steps. She turned back just before she pushed the door open. "Be quiet; the babies are sleeping."

Brooke was sitting at the kitchen table sipping a drink when they walked in. She got up and excused herself as soon as she saw Robbie, knowing they needed some privacy. He noticed the flatter belly immediately. He didn't say anything. She just quietly went into her room and closed the door.

Robbie followed Florence's lead and sat across the table from her. He glanced toward Brooke's bedroom. "Boy or girl?"

"Boy."

"Name?"

"She finally settled on Johnathan."

"You're looking good."

Florence didn't reply. *She's not going to make this easy.* Robbie squirmed in his seat. "I still love you, Florence. I'd like to come back home. I made a mistake . . . it'll never happen again."

Florence sat rigidly, her tense eyes focused on him. "No, it won't happen again," she said sternly.

Robbie reached over to touch her hand, and she quickly pulled away. Robbie pulled his hand back. "I'm sorry."

Florence's eyes were as dry as he'd ever seen them. She took a deep breath. "You care more about south Texas than you do your son and me."

"That's not true."

"Then why did you stay gone so long? You left me here to do everything. It's not easy taking care of a baby, then add on top of that, everything else that needs to be done around here. You don't care about us."

"If I didn't care about you and Lawrence, I wouldn't be here now."

There was a long silence. Robbie reached out to take her hand again. "I do love you. If you let me come back, I'll never cheat on you again."

"Was she pretty?"

"Hell no. Not as pretty as you. She was convenient—and you and me, well . . . we hadn't for a long time."

"That's no excuse."

"No, it's not, but it's the only one I have. I was weak."

"And what's going to keep you from being weak again?"

"We'll be married."

One tear, followed by another. "When?"

"Now . . . tomorrow . . . as soon as John can. Before I have to go back to Corpus."

Florence was trembling by now. Robbie got up and pulled her to her feet. He wrapped her up in his arms and kissed her like never before. The kiss was salty, wet, and lasted an eternity, it seemed. He could feel her heart racing.

Florence pushed him back. "If you ever do anything like this again, I will kill you."

"I know."

"So?"

"So what?"

"You've got wedding plans to discuss with John."

✛╍╂╍╂╍╂╍╂╍╂

Robbie walked back to his mom and dad's place. He had nothing to drive, but he didn't mind. He loved these woods. And he was coming home. He breathed in the fresh air. *You don't notice the fragrance from inside a vehicle.* The walk gave him more time to think.

I worked hard to help Florence grow up into the woman she needed to be to live in Peaceful Valley. There was much to learn, and she was a good student. She paid attention to what I told her, and she learned much on her own, especially at the hands of Sandra.

She's tougher now. I wasn't sure she'd give me a second chance. I've got to earn her trust all over again. She made that perfectly clear. Florence and I will take care of our son. Flo will grow even stronger and tougher in time. She reminds me a lot of Grandma Eileen. Grandpa taught her everything she needed to learn to live out here, and Grandpa taught her well. Yes, Florence is a lot like her. She'll not give me another chance.

Halfway to the Lindgren homestead, Robbie paused to watch a doe and her baby. *So peaceful out here! Thank you, Florence, for giving me another chance.* He squinted and forced away the tears.

I'll stop by and tell Mom and Dad, then on to the Wimberleys'. I'll tell Grandma and Grandpa in the morning. I'll tell Debra and Lance when I find out when John can perform the service.

Robbie signaled when he reached the Lindgrens'. He ran up. His mom and dad were waiting on the porch. "I'm on the way to John's. I need to find out when he can perform a wedding ceremony."

Melissa immediately broke out in happy tears. "I am so happy for you, Son."

Robbie smiled. "She forgave me."

His mom and dad wrapped him up in a tight embrace.

Robbie pulled away. "I've got to get going. I'm going to see if John can marry us tomorrow."

Melissa grabbed his shirtsleeve. "No, no, no. We haven't had a wedding around here in ages. These things take time. We've gotta do this right. Dresses need to be made, the church fixed up, food prepared. You don't even have a ring, do you?"

"No, Ma'am."

"I didn't think so. You go set things up with John, then tell the neighbors, but no sooner than two weeks."

Robbie sighed, shook his head at the foiled plans, then darted off. He stayed in the woods when he passed Zack and Debra's place. Robbie was out of breath when he got to the Wimberleys'. He signaled, and John waved him in. "What brings you around, Robbie?"

"Florence and I are getting married. Can you perform the service?"

"I would be proud to. When?"

"I stopped by Mom and Dad's on the way. I told them tomorrow, but she nixed that idea. She said it needed to be at least two weeks."

Kathy laughed. "Your mother's right. These things take time to plan."

"How about two weeks from today?"

Kathy glanced over at the calendar. "Two weeks and a day. Friday, the fourteenth?"

Robbie glanced at John. "That works for me."

"What time?"

"Noon."

John couldn't contain his glee. "The first wedding in the new church. I can't wait."

Robbie gave them a hug and was out the door in a flash. He stopped by Debra's and told them the news, and was back at his parents' in record time. "The wedding will be Friday in two weeks."

He checked his phone. He had three bars. "Sean."

"Yeah, what's up, Robbie?"

"Florence and I are getting married."

"When?"

"Two weeks and a day. I'll be back there tomorrow. I've got stuff to do. Don't tell the girls. I want to tell them."

Sean laughed. "I'll try to keep the secret. I'm happy for you, Robbie."

"See you tomorrow."

Robbie made it back to his house at sunset. Florence met him on the porch. "Noon, in two weeks."

"But you said tomorrow."

Florence huffed and went back inside. He followed. Brooke was sitting on the sofa, reading.

"That's what I told Mom. She said absolutely not, that there hasn't been a wedding around here in ages."

Brooke put her book down. "She's right, Flo. We need to make this a big deal. Hell, it is a big deal!"

Florence sighed. "I guess you're right.

"I'll go back to Corpus tomorrow. I need to clear up some stuff back there. I'll be back in a few days; then I'll pick Sean and the girls up just before the wedding."

Reggie was nearly back to his old self when Robbie stopped by the next morning. He moved a little slower and grumbled as he fumbled with the bottle of aspirins. "Dammit!"

He plopped one in his mouth and chased it down with water, then headed over to the recliner. Robbie and Emily joined him on the sofa. "Don't ever get old, Robbie."

"I don't think I can stop the process, Grandpa."

"Yeah, I know you can't. I'm just saying enjoy life while you're young. I want to thank you for saving my life."

Emily looked over. "Yes, thank you. It would have been tough around here without this old coot."

Reggie smiled. "Yeah, she can't do anything without me these days." He blew a kiss toward Emily, then returned his attention back to Robbie. "People shouldn't let themselves get too old. Too many problems. Don't get me wrong though, I'm certainly happy you took me to Corpus, but people just shouldn't get too old."

"You're not that old, Grandpa."

"I know. I feel a few years younger now, thanks to you; but before, I felt like I was ready to meet my maker. Arthritis, muscle deterioration, digestive problems, and the like. Nothing serious yet, but now that you've saved my life, I'm going to need to think about how long I want to live again. A person just shouldn't have to suffer too much before he leaves this world."

Emily butted in again. "You keep taking your pills, and you won't have to worry about it so much for a few years. The aspirins should help your general aches and pains as well as your heart. You overdo things though, and you could drop dead tomorrow. We can get some of the boys over to help with the heavy chores, particularly firewood. That will make life a little easier for you."

"Grandpa, I'm sorry we didn't ask your permission to build the new road into your place. We just thought it would be a little easier if we had to get you out again. We've rounded up most of the marauders around the area. We now have a bona fide police force, and things are much safer for us all now. As time goes by, we will tighten security even more."

"I wasn't so sure your plan would work, Robbie, but you've done a fine job. I guess it was time for a road in here. One day when they start writing history books again, you'll be in there."

Robbie smiled. "No one will remember me by then. I'll be dead and gone before there are new history books written."

Reggie reached over and patted Robbie on the hand. "Don't be so sure of that. Maybe I'll just do a little writing myself."

Emily laughed. "That's funny, old man!"

"What! I could do it."

"I know you could, but your perspective of things isn't quite normal. In fact, a good deal away from ordinary."

"What are you saying, darlin'? I could write history."

"I know you could, but Robbie would only get a paragraph or two. The rest of the book would be how you built Peaceful Valley, destroyed the dictatorship in Corpus, and saved our little community from Sandra Hawkins. If I know you, you'd be the reason Sean and Robbie turned this country around and created the new democracy."

Robbie smiled. "You write the history book, Grandpa. In my book, you're the hero anyway. I don't need to be remembered."

Emily noticed Robbie was squirming. "Something bothering you?"

"No, just the opposite. Florence and I are getting married."

She clapped her hands together in glee. "When?"

"Two weeks."

"Come here and give your grandma a hug. My, Son, it must be a madhouse over at your moms."

"Not yet, but I'm sure it will be starting tomorrow."

"I'm sure. You should have told us as soon as you walked in the door."

"I needed to see how Grandpa was doing. Then I didn't want to interrupt him."

Emily smirked. "I guess I'll forgive you this time." She looked over at Reggie. "You talk too much. Maybe you do need to do a little writing."

Emily hopped up. "I've got to get busy too. I hope you'll still fit in your suit, old man."

"I wouldn't worry about me, honey, I still weigh the same as when we got hitched."

Robbie got up too. "You guys haven't changed a bit, as long as I can remember."

Emily threw him a grateful smile. "You're sweet, Robbie."

⌁⌁⌁⌁

Robbie slept in for the first time in a long time after a fulfilling night with Florence. Florence kissed him, and he was off to Corpus.

Robbie went back to the Farm and had dinner with Sean and the girls. They served up stingray, another first for him, in honor of the impending wedding. He frowned as he watched Sean filet the steaks off the ugly creatures. He was doubtful that something so ugly could be edible, much less taste as good as they did, but just like the shrimp, he loved the tender meat.

Sean insisted he stay there that night, and Kim and Brenda prepared a bedroom for him. When the girls came back in, he bid his friends goodnight. "You ladies did a great job with the stingray. Thanks so much for the excellent dinner."

Kim blew him a kiss. Brenda gave him a hug. "When you get hungry for something a little different, this is the place to come."

Robbie spent one morning out on the shrimp boat with Sean. He took some time away from his chores, which grew less demanding every day. The alone time with Sean gave them the solitude to talk about the more complex details of getting south Texas in order, but also for some man-bonding, which they both needed badly.

Sean fired up the grill each evening and put some shrimp on. After dinner, Brenda got out the cards, and the others taught Robbie how to play Pinochle.

One day, Robbie went to see Charlize and Trish after he and Sean had finished their business. Charlize pulled out the deck of cards. "We never did finish that game of strip poker."

"And we're not going to. Florence and I set the date—two weeks. I won't be seeing you ladies much from here on out. I'll be flying most places I need to go. Mostly, however, I'll be staying home."

Trish pouted. "Awww. We're going to miss you."

"I'm looking forward to being a married man. We can still be friends, can't we? You lovely ladies were great when I was depressed."

Charlize gave him a kiss on the cheek. "Congratulations on the marriage. Don't be a stranger, you hear? We've grown fond of you."

Robbie cocked his head. "I won't."

He went to the Farm, took a shower, and lay in bed, thinking. *Charlize and Trish are sweet gals. I'm glad they understood that we could only be friends. I've got to be faithful to Florence. I can't mess that up again.*

The girls in the nursery may rub Flo the wrong way. I have to get her here often to show her that she doesn't have anything to worry about. We were just doing what was demanded of us. That's over now. There's no real connection, except that they are the mothers of my sons and daughters.

The next morning, a crack of thunder jolted Robbie out of bed. By the time he'd finished breakfast, the morning shower was long gone. He walked out to the back porch. It was cooler than the previous morning, but the humidity hit him in the face.

The sun streaked through the air, and the fields at the back of the house were shrouded in steam. *It's going to be another hot day. Not just hot, but sticky.*

Sean joined him on the porch when he finished up in the bathroom. "What are you going to do today, Robbie?"

"I'm going to fly up to Austwell. A man by the name of Phillip is making a bell for the church back home. I told him I'd take him and his wife there to install the bell and attend a service. Tomorrow's Sunday, right?"

"Yeah, I think so."

"I'll stay the night in Austwell and fly them out early tomorrow. I should get there plenty early for John's Sunday service. It'll surprise the hell out of Florence. After the service, we can install the bell, and I'll fly them back home.

"From there, I'll check in at Tivoli and on to Seadrift to touch base with those folks. Joey over in Goliad wants me to take him up in the plane. I need to check on his progress too.

"I'll swing by here after that to pick up some shrimp for the mayor in Victoria. Victoria is key to our success, and I've got to keep him happy. I'll probably spend a day or two there."

He didn't tell Sean about Freya. He knew for sure that she'd never had shrimp and he'd take a second little package for her. He wanted to grill her some and have dinner with her. It was important to him that he remain friends with Freya, and he thought she felt the same way. He hoped she would be happy to hear the news of his impending marriage.

She was not like any of the other girls he'd met around Corpus. She was mysterious and seductive. Smart too. Freya loved to read. She spent an hour talking about the wonderful library in Victoria the first time he visited her. It was one of the few places that survived virtually unscathed by the apocalypse.

He hadn't seen her since her father took him there after they'd checked out the airport. It was a long walk into town the last few times he went to Victoria, but he wasn't ready to see Freya again just yet. He tried to put her out of his life and his mind until after he saw Florence. Now, he had a most challenging chore, he imagined

Sean handed Robbie a hand-drawn map he'd made. "If you have time, I'd like you to drop in here," he said, pointing.

Robbie scrutinized the map.

"There's a pump station that should be up and running by now. There's a good stretch of road where you can land and taxi right up to the front door."

Robbie nodded.

Sean ran his finger around in a circle in another area. "There should be a cell tower or two somewhere around here. There's a whole lot of nothing out toward Yorktown, and our crews haven't found any towers out that direction. Maybe you can spot them from the air."

"Anything else?"

"No, just watch out for pop-up thunderstorms. With this daytime heating, there are bound to be a couple later on this afternoon when it heats up. Your light plane won't take the winds those things sometimes generate."

Robbie smiled. "I'll be careful."

✶✶✶

Robbie touched down on the outskirts of Austwell. He noticed some power lines near town and set down about a mile out. He taxied to within a quarter-mile of Phillip's place and got out. Immediately, he could hear the clanging of metal. *Does this guy work all the time?*

Robbie signaled with a wolf howl as he neared the junkyard. Phillip returned with barking and Robbie headed that direction.

"Good to see you again, Phillip."

"You too, Robbie. Come around here. I've got something to show you."

Sitting on top of a stack of pallets was a shiny new bell. Robbie peered closer. On the side was the inscription *In Loving Memory of Ronnie Lindgren.* "You even got the spelling right."

"I'm good at remembering names. I was going to blacken it later this afternoon. The lettering will stand out better."

"Is that gold?"

"Nothing but the best around here. I had some old coins. They weren't doing me any good."

"I appreciate the thought, but if you have any more, I'd hold on to them. When I get this country going again, you might need some for spending money. Outside of bartering, gold, silver, and a few precious stones will claim a high value."

"So, you come to pick up the bell?"

"And you and Jeanne. Tomorrow's Sunday. I thought I'd take you guys to church, then afterward we can install the bell."

"You bring the plane?"

"Yep. Want to see it?"

They walked the quarter-mile to the Cessna.

"This is a mighty fine plane, young man."

"Hop in the other side. I'll take it closer to your house."

Robbie hit the starter. The engine hummed. He looked over at Phillip. His teeth shined in the sunlight.

Robbie parked the plane and got out the anchors. While he was tying the plane down, Jeanne came around the side of the house. "I didn't think that sounded like a lawnmower."

Phillip waved her over. "Go get your favorite dress, Hon. We're going to church in the morning. And you best prepare the guest bedroom. Robbie is spendin' the night."

Phillip showed Robbie how to blacken metal, then polished the engraving. "This thing will last almost forever."

"I really appreciate you doing this. I haven't told anyone back home. Our preacher, John, will especially be surprised. I will be getting married in the new church in a couple of weeks. It will be John's first wedding in the valley. You and Jeanne will get a chance to meet my fiancée, Florence, tomorrow."

"Well, congratulations, Robbie." Phillip gave him a firm handshake. "Let's get this thing boxed up and put it in your plane. Then we'll tell Jeanne the good news."

⊣⊢⊣⊢⊣⊢⊣⊢

The next morning after an early breakfast, Robbie, Phillip, and Jeanne piled into the plane. Jeanne insisted on sitting in the back seat. She squealed when they hit a bump in the road on take-off, but she was fine after that.

Phillip looked outside for a few minutes, then eyed the gauges. "How fast are we going?"

"About a hundred and fifty. Give or take a few. We'll be in Peaceful Valley before you know it." He looked over his shoulder. "How are you doing back there, Jeanne?"

"I'm fine. It's been so long since I've been in a plane. Nothing as small as this, but I used to travel quite a bit. Then I met Phillip. That grounded me. I never wanted to leave his side, and he always stayed so busy."

It was an hour and fifteen minutes from take-off to touch-down. They were early. The two men carried the crate with the bell and set it in front of the church. John caught them in the act.

Robbie waved him over. "This is Phillip, and this is his lovely wife, Jeanne. They're from Austwell. I thought I'd bring them to Peaceful Valley." He turned back to his guests. "This is John Wimberley, our pastor."

John shook their hands, then eyed the crate. "What do you have in the box?"

"A surprise. You'll find out soon enough."

John led them inside. "Have a seat. Everyone else will be along soon."

Kathy Wimberley, and her and John's sons, Lance and Zack, came in directly with their significant others, Beka and Debra. Robbie introduced each to Phillip and Jeanne. The rest were not far behind.

Florence squealed when she saw the plane and ran inside. She nearly twisted his neck off when she hugged him. "I didn't know you were going to be here."

"I thought I'd surprise you." He turned to Phillip and Jeanne. "These are some new friends I met from Austwell. You'll see why they're here a little later."

When everyone was seated, John and Kathy led them in a song and prayer. Robbie then ran outside and got the box. "A while back, I asked Phillip to make something special for me. Not that we need something to remember Ronnie by, but for future generations, I thought it would be nice if there were something special to commemorate him and the work that he and I were doing to create a new era for south Texas."

Robbie opened the box. On a wooden yolk in a sturdy wood frame sat the twelve-inch bell with the inscription. Oohs and aahs echoed through the room. "Every time this bell tolls, Ronnie will be remembered. He will be remembered for his ultimate sacrifice in something he and I believed in so strongly."

He looked over at Phillip. "You did a wonderful job in creating this everlasting token to my brother. Thank you."

Phillip nodded.

Robbie rocked the yolk and chanted Ronnie's name each time the bell rang. Everyone joined in. "Ron-nie! Ron-nie!"

There was a round of applause, everyone's eyes glued to Phillip.

Robbie motioned for Brooke to come up front, and he sat down next to Florence. She handed Lawrence to Melissa, and he scooted closer. He gave her a peck on the cheek and pulled her hand onto his lap.

Brooke glanced over to Phillip and Jeanne. "Ronnie was to be my husband. Thank you for the bell. It will remind me of him and the love we shared for as long as I live."

She turned to Robbie. "Thank you for your thoughtfulness. You two took on a dangerous job. I knew that, but I supported you 100%. I still do. What you and Ronnie were doing was worth the effort and the sacrifice." She looked over at Johnathan and smiled. "Your efforts and Ronnie's will make this world safe for us all. Our kids will know of that when they grow up."

The boys mounted the bell on the roof while Phillip helped from the ground. "I'm sorry, boys, but I don't do ladders."

John stood alongside. "Yeah, ladders are made for the younger generation."

The bell wasn't all that hard to install, and they had the task done in no time. James came running back from home with a length of rope. The boys attached it to the chain. John stepped over and pulled the rope. The boys began to chant 'Ron-nie' again.

The crew strolled back to the Lindgrens' and had a light lunch. Melissa made sure Robbie ate well. She didn't know when she would see him again, so she tried her best to get all the calories in him that she could.

Everyone thanked Phillip for the bell again and headed to their respective homes. Florence gave Robbie a kiss that he wouldn't soon forget, and she and Brooke headed home.

James drove Robbie and his new friends to the plane. "You two are welcome here anytime. I hope you'll be up this way again."

Robbie gave his dad a big hug. "I'll be back soon. Thanks again for the runway. I'll try to keep the grass worn down."

"I'll expect that, Son."

Robbie had Phillip and Jeanne back in Austwell in no time. They insisted he stay the night and get an early start in the morning. He didn't argue.

Robbie swapped a couple of new cell phones and extra batteries for a few new CB radios with the folks in Seadrift. He asked about Hank, but he was gone. "He got him a gal over in Tivoli. We don't see him around here much," one of the men said.

"Okay, thanks. I'll catch him over there."

Robbie headed on toward Refugio. He landed on the road just outside of town where the pump station Sean told him about was located. The guard led him to the office.

The man at the desk leaned forward. "I'm Red."

"I'm Robbie. Sean wanted me to check your progress in returning the station to production."

Red leaned back in his chair and crossed his arms over his big belly. "You know what happens when you pump air into a tire with a hole in it, Sonny?"

His heavy Texas accent brought a smile to Robbie's face. "Yeah, the air blows out, and the tire doesn't air up."

"Ever' time we crank up the pumps, we blow crude all ov'r the ground. I've got my crews out working on the problem on this end, but it's a long way to Corpus. You tell Sean if he wants the oil, he'd better get his crews working on the leaks from his end. We got four tanks full of crude an' as soon as we can get all the leaks fixed, we'll have the black gold squirtin' over his way. Right now though, it's just squirtin' in the dirt."

"I'll tell him what you said. We need the oil now."

"Tell him we have it and if he wants it, the leaks gotta be fixed. We can't be wasting the stuff."

"I'll tell him."

Red grinned. "You need some rattlesnakes, son? Mighty good eatin', and we got ourselves a ton of 'em 'round here," he said, chuckling.

Robbie forced a tight-lipped smile. "Maybe next time."

"Okay, have it your way, but they're mighty good fried just like chickin."

Robbie got up to leave and extended his hand. Red took it in a firm grip. "Maybe next time you're here."

"Maybe," Robbie replied.

Robbie walked back to the plane and got in the air before he tried to call Sean. He had no service in this location on the ground.

"Sean, we've got a problem with the Refugio pump station. They say they have the oil, but there are so many leaks in the pipeline that they can't pump it."

"I already have a crew out that way."

"Apparently, one crew isn't enough. Do you have any more men you can send out?"

"No, they're all working on other jobs."

"How bad do you want the Refugio oil?"

"Bad. Okay. Don't worry about it. I'll see if I can round up a couple more crews. I'll have to pull them off something else."

"That's up to you. What's more important, Sean?"

"You and I both know the answer to that. Thanks, Robbie. I'll do what I can."

Robbie picked up Joey at Goliad. "Every place I go, there are train tracks."

"Yeah, I see them too. What's your point?"

"I found a train. Near Bloomington. It looked like it was in perfect condition. It had a hundred cars or more and three engines. You know anything about them?"

"About as much as I know about flying planes."

Robbie smirked and backhanded him on the arm. "If we're going to get this country going again, we're going to have to move a lot of supplies. A train can do that."

"So, who you gonna find to run your train?"

"Ask around. See if there's someone here that knows trains. I'll do the same."

"Are we going flying, or not?"

"Patience, Joey." *I guess I could have a little more patience with him too. He's smart . . . and the only person out this way who is helping me.*

Robbie started the engine. Joey jumped up and down in the plane just like Sean. Robbie headed north toward Yorktown. "Sean said we need to find some cell towers out this way so we can get communications going over here. Did you make it up this way like I told you to?"

Joey had his face to the glass. "Yeah. There weren't many people out here though. I did find three families living just outside of town. Yorktown itself was dead. All the buildings burned to the ground and grown up with brush. So why are ya so interested in this place?"

"There have to be more people out here somewhere. For the cell phone to work, we need a continuous line of towers. The signal can only travel ten or twelve miles. If there is one missing tower, the phones won't work farther out."

Robbie kept looking at his map so he'd know where he was in case he spotted a tower. He also made sure he stayed high enough that he wouldn't hit one if they found them.

He flew a grid pattern on all sides of Yorktown. The sky was clear except the cloud building to the west. After three hours, Joey spotted two towers and Robbie, two more. They marked them on the map, and Robbie headed back to Goliad.

The sound of something hitting the plane jolted Robbie and Joey almost out of their seats. Robbie gripped the steering wheel so tight his knuckles turned white. His eyes focused on the instrument panel. The gauges appeared to be normal. He looked over at Joey. His eyes were wide, and his face was a lighter shade than usual.

"What was that?" the boy asked in a whisper.

A feeling of déjà vu came over Robbie. Was he going to crash this plane too? "I don't know. We better get this thing on the ground."

Robbie looked at the map and then the compass. He could feel the hair standing up on the back of his neck. The plane seemed to be functioning normally, but just as with the smoke and fire with the other Cessna, he knew things could change quickly.

Robbie focused on the ground ahead. He could see Goliad off in the distance. He held his breath most of the way except when he was sniffing the air for smoke. *So far, so good.*

Joey pointed. "There's my house."

Robbie lined up with the road, cut the throttle, and pointed the plane down. Then, with his excitement, he realized he was not headed into the wind and throttled the plane back up a bit. He made the half-circle and again pointed the plane downward and cut the throttle. The wind teased the light aircraft. Robbie looked over, and Joey's cheeks were pouched out, and his lips puckered tight. His eyes were wide open and focused on the road ahead. He didn't appear to be breathing, and neither was Robbie.

The plane bounced once, then twice on the pavement, then settled down. Robbie cut the throttle, and they coasted to a stop. He took in a deep breath. He hadn't realized he was holding it. The two boys looked at each other and grinned. They both let out a long sigh.

Robbie undid his seatbelt and crawled out. He walked around the plane, looking for a problem. Feathers stuck onto the cowling at the edge of the windshield. "We hit a bird." He walked over and pulled the feathers off and held them up to Joey. "Looks like a hawk of some sort."

Joey walked over to Robbie and gave him a bump on the shoulder with his fist. "I'm sure glad you didn't crash us."

Robbie huffed his relief. "Me too!"

"You gonna come over for a while? Mama's bound to have dinner ready soon."

Robbie looked to the west. "It's going to be dark before long. I'm staying in Victoria tonight. Can I take a rain check?"

"Mama's gonna have a place set for you for sure."

"I know. Tell her I'm sorry. I have a package to deliver in Victoria and need to go. The ice won't hold up till tomorrow. Tell her I'll be back and I'll definitely stay next time. Keep up the good work around here, and I'll see you soon, okay?"

Joey smiled. "Maybe one day you can get me one of those phones, and we can talk a bit."

Robbie nodded. "I'll see what I can do." Robbie gave him a high-five and headed back to the Cessna. Robbie took off, circled around, and gave Joey a wing wave. He could see Joey's teeth shining in the late afternoon sun.

Chapter 25

Robbie made a quick run to Corpus to pick up the shrimp he wanted for the mayor and Freya. The sun was melting on the horizon when Robbie touched down in Victoria. He parked the plane and hurried it over to Freya's house with his cooler in hand. There was only a hint of light left in the western sky.

He signaled with his wolf howl. *Ooowww!*

Freya opened the back door with a big smile on her face. "It's been a while, stranger!"

"I need a place to stay the night. You know anyone around here that can put me up?"

She put her finger up to her temple in thought. "Maybe!"

Freya pushed the screen door open farther and waved him in. Robbie stepped across the threshold, and she followed. She looked at the cooler. "What do you have there?"

"Shrimp for the mayor."

"The mayor, huh?"

Robbie pulled his backpack off and took out a small package. "Don't worry, I have some for you too. You've never had shrimp before, have you?"

"No."

"Well, you're in for a treat. Do you have some garlic? They're fantastic with a little garlic and salt."

"I have both, but I'll have to get the garlic out of the garden."

She ran outside and pulled a bunch while Robbie opened up the package and got out a skillet. He peeled and veined the shrimp while Freya made a salad and drinks. She noticed the cooler on the floor. "Should I stick this in the freezer overnight?"

He nodded.

Seconds after the green-tails hit the skillet, the aroma filled the air. Robbie nodded with an expectant smile.

She raised her eyebrows. "If those things taste as good as they smell, they're going to be wonderful."

"I told you. You'll think you died and went to heaven when you bite into one of these things."

Freya set the table. Robbie shook the pan and slid the shrimp and garlic around in the butter. He cooked them fast and hot. Minutes later and they were ready. He pushed half onto Freya's plate and the rest on his.

Robbie watched her face as she took her first bite. Her expression said it all. They finished the meal in silence, both savoring every bite.

Robbie helped her clean up the table and kitchen, then asked her to join him on the sofa. "There's something I need to talk to you about."

Freya sat down next to Robbie and turned to face him with the effervescent smile she'd had since her first bite into the shrimp. Her mood dampened when she saw the seriousness in Robbie's face. "What's the matter?"

His face tightened up. He squirmed in his seat and looked around the room to make sure the walls weren't closing in on him. *There's only one way to do this.* He took a deep breath. "Florence and I set the date to get married."

"But I thought . . ."

"Under different circumstances . . . you've been wonderful, especially that one night, but that's all we have. I've told you about Florence. We have a long history, and I still love her. I can't live without Flo and my son."

Freya sniffled. "Since we're honest here, I've got something else to tell you."

Robbie focused on her words, his smile trailing off into oblivion. "What's that?"

She looked down, and he reached up and pulled her chin back up until her eyes met his. She forced a smile. "I had an abortion when I was sixteen. They botched the job, and I had to have a hysterectomy. I almost died. The only problem is I can't have kids. Without you, I'll have no one."

"That's not true. You'll still have me, but only as friends. I'll be the best friend you've ever had. We just can't have sex."

"But I want kids. We could adopt one if we were together. I can't do that alone."

His smile turned to laughter.

"What's so funny?"

"I don't see why that's a problem."

"I've got lots of kids. Maybe too many. I can share them with you."

"She gave him a quizzical look. "How many?"

"Maybe a hundred or more. I don't know for sure. They're mostly in Corpus Christi. I have one son back in Peaceful Valley."

Freya sat with her mouth open in disbelief. "How . . ."

"It's a long story."

"I have the time."

Robbie turned and got comfortable. "When my friend, Sean, and I were captured by Sandra Hawkins in Corpus a few years ago, she liked me. Said I'd be good for her breeding program. She put me to work at the Airport, but weekends I spent at the Farm with her girls . . ."

⌇⌇⌇⌇

Robbie strolled into the Chief of Police's office with Freya at his side and the cooler in the other hand. He put the cooler on a chair. There was no room on the desk. "The shrimp I promised you and the mayor, Sir."

The chief got up, walked around, and opened the cooler. "I've got to hide these until I can get them home. On second thought, maybe I should run them there now. I'll drop some by the mayor on the way." He scribbled on a couple of pieces of paper and stuck them in the outbox. "What are you kids up to today?"

"I thought I'd show Robbie more of our city. I figured I'd start with the library."

"Good choice. You like to read, Robbie?"

"Yes, Sir. I haven't had time for reading lately, but yes when I get the chance . . ."

The chief grabbed the cooler. He didn't seem to care about Robbie's reading habits after all. He never looked over. "I guess I'll get these things home before they walk off. I'll see you kids later, right?"

"Yes, Daddy." She gave him a peck on the cheek.

Freya looked over at Robbie. "Shall we?"

"The library?"

She smiled and pulled on his arm.

⌇⌇⌇⌇

Freya stood and waited for Robbie to open the big glass door for her. He did so promptly and followed her inside. The door was not locked, but there was no one inside that Robbie could see. As soon as she got through the door, she held her arms up high over her head and twirled around in circles until she got dizzy. "Books . . . wonderful books." She whirled back toward him, and the look on her face was that of a child in a candy store.

Robbie heard a shush and looked over. A woman, apparently the librarian, had come back up front from a side room. He smiled and nodded.

Freya grabbed him by the arm and pulled him along as they quietly strolled down aisles and aisles of books, starting with the fiction section. She ran her fingers along the spines. "Prince Charming, Sir Lancelot, Black Beauty, Tom Sawyer," she whispered. "Stories you can fall in love with. Stories that whisk you away to another land, another time . . . hours of pure reading pleasure."

Robbie followed her along, noticing all the labels—romance, mystery, action and adventure, and more. He thought back to his grandpa Lars's collection. His books were sufficient for him, and he'd read every one of them, never imagining there were so many authors, so many books in the world.

They moved on to non-fiction where he found self-help books and periodicals where, if he had the time, he could learn how to do most anything, or catch up on current events—from a time long ago.

After they'd made the rounds through all the aisles, Freya led him back through the non-fiction aisles where she picked up a copy of a gardening book and one on healing herbs, then down one of the fantasy aisles where she grabbed a couple new books she hadn't read.

"Would you like one to read, Robbie?"

"Maybe. Do they have any about trains?"

"I don't know. Let's see what we can find."

She led him back to the fiction aisles. "Here's one about a train robbery. Midnight Train . . ."

"No, not stories. Something about how trains work."

She sighed. "Well, why didn't you say so?" She led him back to the non-fiction books. She walked down the aisle, running her fingers along the spines. When she stopped, she pulled out the book her finger stopped on. She quickly glanced at the cover. "Here you go," she said, smiling, and handed him the book.

He turned through the pages. "This is still a story. I need something that tells how to start and operate them."

They went to the front desk. The little old lady pushed her black-framed glasses up from the tip of her nose and eyed Robbie.

Freya laid the books down that she wanted. "Do you have any books on the workings of trains?"

"Technical stuff," Robbie added.

The librarian walked around the counter. They followed her. She pointed to a section, turned around, and headed back up front. Robbie watched as she walked out of sight around the end of the bookshelves. "She doesn't say much." He then turned his attention to the books.

Robbie found one book that had to have weighed ten pounds. It had schematics, graphs, and photos of pieces of trains. He found a picture page with train routes across Texas. He eyed the area around Corpus Christi, San Antonio, and Victoria. *Trains used to run everywhere. If I can get a train going and the tracks repaired, we can haul a shitload of stuff wherever we need it.* He turned to Freya. "This will do."

He and Freya returned to the front desk. The lady squinted at him, giving him a good once-over before she put her stamp of approval for his book. "These books have to be back in thirty days," she said looking at Freya. "You know that, dearie."

She turned back to Robbie. "Mind your time well, young man. I don't tolerate late returns."

He smiled. "Yes, Ma'am."

Robbie and Freya headed toward the door, Freya skipping along in front of him. He opened the car door for her, then ran around and got in the passenger side. "Thank you, dear sir."

"What do we do now?"

"I'd like to see your airplane."

"All right! Off to the airport. By the way, what happens if I return the book late?"

"I don't know. I always take mine back on time. Maybe she'll have you arrested."

"What?"

Freya laughed. "Yeah, she's my step-mom."

Robbie frowned. Then the light clicked on in his head. "The chief's wife?"

"Yes."

It should have been a twenty-minute ride there, but the speed Freya drove, it only took ten.

She couldn't contain her excitement when she saw the bright yellow Cessna. "I've never flown in a plane." She turned to him, her eyebrows raised a bit. "Will you take me? Please!"

Robbie couldn't resist her. He helped her get into her seat and told her to buckle up. He unclipped the tie-downs and got in. Robbie could see the excitement in her eyes, but unlike Joey and Sean, she didn't jump up and down. She just sat, calmly eyeing every detail of the interior of the cockpit.

At the end of the runway, they exchanged grins, and he hit the throttle. The wind was light, and there were only a few puffy clouds scattered around. The plane lifted off smoothly, and Robbie climbed to five-thousand feet. Freya leaned over and kissed him on the cheek.

The rest of the trip, she mostly looked at Victoria below as he made a full circle over the city. "It looks so much cleaner from up here."

Suddenly, the plane hit an air current, and the Cessna jumped. It was much like running over a speed bump a little too fast. Freya screamed and grabbed the handhold.

Robbie looked over at the fear in her face. "It's all right. Just a little turbulence. Happens all the time."

Her tension eased, and she put on her best puppy dog face. "I love you, Robbie."

"And I love you too . . . as a friend."

She put on her pouting face. "Right . . ."

Later that evening, Freya pulled some steaks out of the freezer and Robbie put them on the barbecue. They sat at the table with drinks, discussing their futures while the potatoes and steaks cooked.

"Tell me more about your kids, Robbie."

"I don't know any of them. It was just a job. Not something I'm proud of, but it's what I had to do to survive.

"Don't get me wrong, I love the little tykes, and the gals are lovely. I have a connection to them in the back of my heart, but there is no love there. Maybe a little fatherly love for the kiddos.

"And the girls told me they never expected me to be a father to their children. Again, we were all just doing our jobs."

He turned the steaks and sat back down. Freya reached over and took hold of his hand. "So, you wouldn't want to marry any of them?"

"There was one, Jade . . . I would have married her if I had a chance, but Sandra executed her. I still have a place in my heart for her, but it's a dead end road."

Robbie got up to check the meat. "How do you like your steak?"

"Medium well. I like a hint of char."

Robbie smiled. "You don't have to worry about that. I think the fire was still a little too hot when I put them on."

She ran in and got a couple of plates. Robbie put his hands together and his elbows on the table. He stared at Freya. She stared at him. He smiled. "Bless the meat, damn the skin, open up your mouth and cram it in."

Freya chuckled.

"That's about as religious as I can get."

"I'm not religious either."

Robbie pulled the foil off his potatoes and looked up. "I didn't think you were, but that's one thing we haven't discussed yet. I'm glad you're not."

She cocked her head. "I do believe there is a higher power out there somewhere, and if God were to walk in the door and introduce himself and could prove his claim, I'd follow. But until then, we don't have to discuss the matter again. Now let's eat before our steaks get cold."

"No argument there."

⎯⋀⎯⋀⎯⋀⎯⋀⎯

Robbie helped her clean up, and they sat on the sofa and talked for a while to let their food settle a bit. "We forgot to go back to the precinct to see your dad."

"I'll run by there after I take you to the airport and explain that we went flying and were hungry when we got back, that we just let time get away from us. He'll understand. He always does."

"Tell him I'm sorry too."

"So, even if we have a new arrangement, you'll still stop by from time to time, won't you?"

"Yes, I'll need a place to stay when I make my rounds. I'd love to visit then, if that's okay."

"So, I'm just a place to stay now?"

"No, you're my friend." Robbie grinned. "—and my ride too."

She smacked him across the arm. "I'll need more shrimp next time you come for that, mister."

⎯⋀⎯⋀⎯⋀⎯⋀⎯

After a full breakfast of scrambled eggs and a couple of pieces of leftover steak sliced up in the eggs, Freya dropped Robbie off at the airport. He made a circle and gave her a wing wave. She waved back. He knew she was sad to see him go, but they needed time apart. He needed the idea of them being just friends to sink in. He'd be back in a few days after he took care of the business he had in Corpus.

Robbie touched down in Corpus Christi mid-morning. He headed straight for the Contractor compound where he figured Sean would be.

The mayor had his head down when Robbie peeked around the corner of the door. He was buried in paperwork, but he looked good behind a desk. He had always had a sharp mind and seemed to love the work he did, especially since he got the chance to go shrimping regularly.

Robbie tapped on the doorframe. "Got time for an old friend?"

Sean jumped out of his intense train of thought and looked up. "Thanks for giving me an excuse to get out of the rat race for a few minutes."

He got up, and Robbie stepped over to the desk and set the CB radios in the chair alongside. Robbie held out his fist for a proper greeting—a fist-bump. "The guys in Seadrift were sure happy to get the extra phones."

"How's Hank doing?"

"I didn't get to see him. He's staying in Tivoli now. I'll catch him next round. Looks like he and Arlene hooked up."

"That was a match made in Heaven—her cooking and the way he can put it away. Yep, they'll get along just fine. We better get this country back on its feet quick, though. Arlene is going to need more customers, or he'll eat up all the profits."

They both laughed.

"Then we better get to business, Sean. Are all the towers between here and there working yet?"

"Yes, we got them going yesterday, and not just to Seadrift, but to Port Lavaca, as well. I had a long talk with the mayor over there. They were pleased with how fast things are progressing. Before you know it, all of south Texas will be connected, and we'll have a formidable police force to keep everyone safe.

"We got a tanker loaded with gasoline headed to Seadrift yesterday too. I told the driver that if he had some extra, to take the rest to Port Lavaca. A little token of our sincerity. When the truck gets back, I'll send a load of diesel later in the week."

"The plan's coming together then?"

"Yes, only one problem though."

Robbie frowned. "What's that?"

"We should have had the pipeline from Refugio connected by now. I only found one crew to send out to help with the repairs. I'm still looking for another. Until it's completed, we're dead in the water."

"I talked to Red at the pump station. He has a crew or two working on the problem too, but there were a lot of leaks. They have four tanks full of oil sitting and waiting on getting the line fixed. If you can find one more crew, everything should be fine. If you want though, I'll drop by there again and double check."

"That's probably the best thing to do. Just to make sure."

Robbie grinned. "Consider it done. I'll give you a call when I find out something. Having a little trouble with cell coverage in the area too, but from the plane, it's been working fine."

"You look like you're doing a lot better, considering your condition."

"What condition is that?"

"Impending marriage."

Robbie smirked but didn't comment. He reached into his backpack and pulled out the book he found in Victoria. He turned to the page with the rail locations. "If we can get a train going and the tracks repaired, we can haul a lot of stuff anywhere we want. It'll give us a backup for moving crude too."

Sean was all ears. "They go everywhere."

"I know. That train I found in Bloomington is perfect for the job if I can get it going. It seems like there was a big terminal here in Corpus at one time too. Lot of tracks on the other side of the ship channel. I've never been over that way. Maybe you'd like to take a little drive with me tomorrow."

"You never know. We might even find another train."

"Wouldn't that be a stroke of luck?"

"Yeah, let's do take a little ride."

He nodded, but the smile disappeared from Sean's face. He looked back at the stack of papers on his desk. "I've gotta get back at the reports if we're going out on an excursion tomorrow."

"No problem. I'm going down to the Bayfront for a while; then I'll meet you back at the Farm later."

"That works for me."

"What time will you be there?"

"No later than six. Tell Kim and Brenda I'll be running a little late, will ya?"

"You got it."

⌁╴╎╴╎╴╎╴⌁

Robbie, Kim, and Brenda with little Benjamin in her lap chatted in the living room while they waited for Sean to get in. Kim played patty cake with Ben while Brenda bounced him up and down. He was a happy baby.

I wonder if Lawrence is happy. I've got to get back home. I can't be spending too much time away. Florence was so happy when I surprised her by coming home with the bell. We've gotta get this country moving forward under its own steam.

Robbie got up and walked over to the desk in the corner. There were sketches of a little girl and an infant. A partially burned candle, ribbons, and a small cross.

Kim walked over and grabbed his hand. "A memorial to Abigail. Getting back to her grave is difficult. I can remember her from right here."

"The pictures?"

"I drew the infant first. Then, I wondered what she would look like if she had grown up a bit."

Robbie put his hand over her shoulder. "We all miss her."

She reached up and placed her hand over his. "You're a good friend, Robbie."

When Sean came in. Kim ran over and wrapped her arms around him. "Dinner's ready. All we need to do is set it out. If you get your shower, we'll have it on the table by the time you get done."

A barely noticeable smile developed on Robbie's face. *It sure is good to see Sean so happy. He deserves it.* He yelled at Sean. "Your boy is growing like a weed. He's going to be a big one."

"All that good tiddy!"

Brenda's head jerked around, her face turning red. "Damn you, Sean! You can do without dessert tonight. You could stand to miss a few, in fact."

Robbie couldn't stop laughing, but managed to shut it off when Brenda turned on him and gave him a raised-eyebrow.

Brenda stuck Benjamin on Robbie's lap and grinned mischievously. "We've got to set the table. And I hope he pisses on you too."

Robbie found himself sitting alone in the living room. He turned Benjamin around so he could look him in the face. "You wouldn't pee on your Uncle Robbie, would you?"

⌁⌁⌁

Freya was just putting up her breakfast dishes when she heard a knock on the door. She looked through the peephole. It was one of the maintenance men who came by often. She opened the door. "Billy, what are you doing here?"

"I heard you had a faucet leak."

"I don't know where you heard that. I don't have any leaks."

"Best if I check them out for you while I'm here." He pushed his way into the house.

Freya huffed. "I told you I didn't have any leaks!"

As soon as Freya pushed the door closed, Billy turned his attention back to her. "Okay, so you don't have a leak. Well, if you don't have anything that needs fixin', maybe you can fix something for me."

"What's that?"

He pushed her back against the door and tried to kiss her. She clawed at his face and pushed at him, but he didn't budge. "Don't!" she screamed.

"Come on, baby," he said and pawed at her breasts. "I need some TLC."

"Not anymore, Billy!" and she shoved at him with all her might.

Billy stepped back and wiped his hand across his face. He looked at his bloody arm. "You humpin' that flyboy? I've seen him around. You know I can take better care of you than he can. You know I'm really good with my hands . . . and after that, I can make you squeal."

"That's not going to happen anymore, now you get out of my damn house!"

Billy took a deep breath and slowly stepped back toward her. His tone turned to begging. "Come on, baby. You know I love you. Haven't I shown you that you an' me are made for each other? That flyboy will take what he can; then he'll fly away, and you'll never see him again."

"We're not sleeping together. He's just a friend."

He chuckled. "That's bullshit. I know you better than that."

"He's none of your business anyway. Now get out!"

Freya moved over, out from between him and the door. He took a step forward. In the blink of an eye though, he turned and with a balled-up fist, hit her hard square between the eyes. Freya folded up like a chair and fell to the floor. She didn't move.

Billy waited for her to get up, but she just lay there. Then he saw the blood spreading from under her head. He knelt down and looked at her face. Her blank eyes stared back.

Chapter 26

Sean hopped in shotgun and Robbie cranked up the Jeep. Judy let them through the checkpoint on the harbor bridge. Robbie glanced at the smooth bay waters. "Looks like it's going to be a great day, Sean."

Sean looked over briefly. "Out of the office is always a great day."

They both laughed.

Sean pointed, and Robbie steered off the main highway onto connecting roads leading to the ship channel. The tracks were easy enough to find. Robbie followed the road that paralleled them. "Looks to be a yard up ahead with some cars."

He pulled to the side of the road, and they got out. Most of the cars were tankers. Robbie picked up a rock and tapped on each one as they walked through the train graveyard. "The tracks are in bad shape, the tanks all sound dry, and the few boxcars are open and empty."

"It's a long channel. Maybe we'll have better luck up the way."

They got back in the Jeep and drove on. Robbie stopped when he spotted the ship. "I wonder what might be on that thing." Then he saw some movement. "Get out and behind the Jeep," he yelled to Sean.

Robbie grabbed his AR-15 as they both scrambled. He looked through the scope. There were three men now, and they all had guns. "Sean, they're not pointing their rifles at us. Wave the flag at them and let's see what they do."

Robbie put his rifle back up. One of the men waved his hat. Robbie exchanged his gun for the binoculars. He waved the men down. They gave him a 'thumbs up' and motioned for him to come over.

Robbie and Sean got back in and drove to the ship's ramp. Robbie got out and held up his hands. One man came out while the others stood guard.

"I'm Robbie Lindgren. This is Sean Lin, the Mayor of Corpus Christi."

"We're from Portland. We have jurisdiction around here." The man didn't offer his name.

"This is still a part of Corpus."

"Not anymore. We've been told about you, Robbie, and what you're doing. I believe you've been told that we aren't going to be a part of your new regime. You stick to the highway and the other side of the ship channel, and you'll be okay, but if you come scrounging around our territory, someone's going to get hurt."

"We're looking for a train and some cars, and checking the tracks."

"The only train engine is burned. All the cars are ours, and as far as the tracks go, you don't need them if you don't have no train."

Robbie whispered to Sean. "Have your crews said anything about running into anyone along the pipeline?"

"No, the pipeline is a few miles west of here . . . near the refinery. Maybe they don't know about it and what we're doing. Better not tell them either."

Robbie turned his attention back to the man. "Okay, we'll go back to the other side. You guys have a great day."

Robbie and Sean got back in the Jeep and headed for the harbor bridge.

"Robbie, let's see if we can set up another meeting with the guys in Portland. You didn't seem to have much luck in bringing them over to our side last time. Maybe if we show them we're making progress, they'll be more willing to listen."

Robbie hung a left at the highway and buzzed across the causeway to Portland. He stopped within a quarter-mile of the overpass where he'd been seeing the guards. Sean waved the flag and Robbie sat looking through the binoculars. A man waved him in.

Robbie eased forward. "I'm going to fly home tomorrow to see Florence for a few days. Let's see if we can set up a meeting sometime next week. What's a good day for you?"

"How about Wednesday? It breaks up the week nicely."

※

Robbie arrived back in Corpus after several days at home. Florence was ecstatic to see him, but the whole valley was a whirlwind with wedding preparations. He was happy to kiss her goodbye, wish her well on the planning, and get out of there.

He knew he'd find Sean at his office. His job as mayor, and his drive to do the best possible job, led to him becoming a workaholic.

"What's up, Sean?"

"We still haven't got the crude in from Refugio."

Robbie shook his head. "Guess I better go see what's going on."

Sean nodded.

Robbie dropped him off at the Farm, and he ran out to check on the airplane to make sure it would be ready first thing in the morning.

Sean said dinner would be ready when he got back. "Grilled shrimp okay with you?" he asked.

"Any day, any time!"

It was 6:00 p.m. when Robbie pulled up to the farmhouse. He could see the smoke billowing up above the roof. He strolled around back where he found Sean hard at work. "What's that in your mouth?" he asked laughing.

He hurried up and swallowed the bite. "Gotta make sure they're seasoned right." He forked one of the orange crescents and held it out for Robbie. "I'm not sure these are seasoned quite right. What do you think?"

Robbie rolled his eyes. "Is there a wrong way to season them?"

"So, how are things back home?"

"Good. I really needed the time with Flo and Lawrence."

"Yep, you've gotta keep a little wood on the fire, or the flames of love will go out."

"Yeah, I was concerned about Lawrence too. I saw how happy Ben was when Brenda and Kim played with him. I've gotta make sure my son grows up happy. I know you won't have that problem."

They both laughed, but quickly cut it off and turned around when they heard the door slam. Brenda came out with a platter in her hand for the cooked shrimp when they were finished. "Don't you guys be eating up all our meal," she scolded.

"Gotta make sure they're done right, Honey!"

She handed the platter to Sean. "Don't spoil your dinner."

"Yes, dear."

Brenda went back inside to help Kim finish the trimmings and set the table. Sean started taking the shrimp off the pit.

Robbie followed him inside and they gathered around the table.

The girls didn't want to hear about business, and they'd already caught up on their goings on. Everyone dug in and ate in silence. Sean looked around the table. "Mom always said if it got quiet during dinner it was because the food was good."

"Your mom was right," Brenda said around a mouthful of shrimp.

Sean grabbed the dessert out of the fridge, and after the cobbler was demolished, they adjourned to the living room for coffee and a little music. He set the volume on the stereo and got in his recliner.

Robbie stretched out on the sofa. "I overate."

"Yeah, me too." Sean unbuttoned the top button of his pants.

"When I get finished up in Refugio, I'll probably stay in Victoria a few days. Then I'll make another run to Peaceful Valley after that. Anything you need from home?"

"Not really." His mind drifted off in thought briefly. "How much trouble would it be for you to make a pass by here before you go home?"

Robbie sat up on the sofa. "Not much."

"I haven't seen Mom and Dad in ages. I know they're worried about me. I just thought I'd like to see them." He turned to Brenda and Kim. "How about you two? Would you like to take a trip to Peaceful Valley?"

They looked at each other and shook their heads. "I think we're good here," Brenda said. "Besides, we'll go for the wedding."

While Brenda and Kim knew everyone there and had stayed there for a while, they were Corpus gals. They didn't have family in Peaceful Valley.

Sean nodded. "Looks like it's just you and me, if you can make the time to swing by here."

"That's not a problem. I'll be making more passenger runs from now on. You can be my first recreational commuter."

⌁⌁⌁⌁

Robbie cranked up the Cessna and got an early start back toward Refugio. No sooner than he was off the ground, he received a phone call from Sean. "The crude from there started coming in."

With that, he made a beeline toward Victoria. A bit of a tailwind shortened the flight to forty-five minutes. He tied the plane down and hoofed it over to Freya's.

Robbie knocked on the door, but there was no answer. He tried the doorknob. It was locked. He walked to the garage and looked inside. Freya's car was parked there where it always was. *What's going on?*

He checked the ignition. No keys. Then he checked the ice on the shrimp in the cooler. It would last another day in the shade. He didn't want to carry it all the way into town if he didn't have to. He left the cooler in the garage and went outside to look around. No one. Nothing unusual.

Maybe she's staying the night with a friend. She could have walked somewhere. Perhaps her daddy came and picked her up.

Robbie decided he needed to hotfoot it to town for some answers. He didn't know exactly how far it was to the station, but it felt like ten miles at least. *I'm spending so much time flying and driving, I'm getting out of shape. I need to spend much more time with Flo and Lawrence. Chopping wood alone will keep me fit.*

One of the officers led Robbie to the chief's office. He was sitting behind his desk as usual. He stood up, and Robbie stepped forward. "I just got back and stopped by Freya's . . ."

Chief Hayes held up his hand. He then nodded to the officer who'd accompanied Robbie inside. Robbie turned to look at the officer, and he had his pistol aimed at him.

"What . . ."

"Shut up!" the chief said in a high tone. "Put your damn hands up."

Robbie complied, and the chief removed his gun belt and patted him down. He pulled his handcuffs out, then turned Robbie to face the gun while he pulled his arms around behind him. He snapped the cuffs on.

"I haven't done anything," Robbie insisted, his eyes darting back and forth between the officer and the chief. They didn't respond.

The chief nodded to the officer. "Take him away."

The big brute pushed him through the doorway, and before he knew it, he was locked in a cell. He went over and sat on the side of the bunk.

His mind raced to try to come up with an answer. *What the hell am I supposed to have done? Did something happen to Freya?*

Robbie rattled the door of his cell. "Hey! Hey! I want to talk to the chief."

One, two, three days went by. Robbie was fed three meager meals a day, but no one would say a word to him. He asked politely at first, but no one would get him the chief or tell him anything about Freya. He also thought it suspicious that Freya didn't come to visit him. He spent a lot of time worrying.

By the third day, he yelled, trying to get some answers. Still, no one said a word to him. He wasn't even scolded for yelling. All he received was silence.

Just after breakfast on the fourth morning, the chief showed up at Robbie's cell. He unlocked the door and motioned for Robbie to come out. Robbie held out his hands.

Chief Hayes shook his head. "We don't need the cuffs."

He followed the chief who led him to his office. He pointed to a chair, and Robbie sat down. The chief then sat down behind the desk. "Robbie, I'm sorry. I didn't think it was your fault, but I had to make sure."

Robbie had a confused look on his face. "What's not my fault? Did something happen to Freya?" It was the only rational thing he had come up with since they locked him up three days ago. His mind didn't want to go there. Something was really troubling the chief. "What?"

Hayes sniffled. "Freya is dead."

Robbie's mouth dropped open, but he was lost for words. *Dead . . . Dead! No!!* He could feel the water instantly building in his eyes. He managed to get two words out: "What happened?"

"She was murdered." There was a long pause. Both had difficulty with words. "My men brought the guy in who did it a couple of days ago . . . I could have let you out then, but I was just so mad. You are the reason . . . the reason it happened, but it wasn't your fault. I could see that Freya loved you . . . dammit!"

"Who did it?"

"A jealous boyfriend. One of his friends who also liked Freya came to me. He said Billy went ballistic and went to see her after he saw you with her in town . . . if you'd have been here, he'd have gone after you . . . but he went to confront Freya. I took an officer over there, but it was too late. She had a piece of Billy's shirt in her hand . . . and there was other evidence."

Billy. I don't know a Billy.

The chief took a deep breath. "Anyway, we tracked him down. He had scratches on his face and arms."

Robbie leaned over and put his head in his hands. He was hurt deeply, but maybe more than that, he was mad . . . *Dammit, why didn't Billy come at me? I'd have fixed the sorry shit.*

Robbie looked up. "What's going to happen to Billy?"

"I'll fry his ass."

Robbie smiled. He was confident of that. "Can I go?"

The chief's face was sad. "Of course."

Robbie didn't say another word. He walked out but stopped on the front steps. He looked around but didn't see anyone he recognized. He headed over to a line of squad cars and when almost there, an officer he knew got out of his car. He was stunned to see Robbie. "Good to see you out. Horrible what happened to Freya."

"Can you do something for me?"

"What's that?"

"I left some shrimp in Freya's garage in a cooler. I know it won't help much, but the chief really likes shrimp. Can you . . ."

"Say no more. Hop in."

They retrieved the cooler and Robbie checked the shrimp. The ice was gone, but they were still cold enough to be safe. They hurried back to the station. Robbie knocked on the chief's door. Hayes motioned for him to come in.

He set the cooler beside the desk. "I brought these for you. You should have trusted me more and not locked me up. I wish I had been here for Freya, but I wasn't. We need to put this behind us and move on for the good of south Texas."

The chief forced a weak smile. "Thanks, son."

"These things have been sitting in Freya's garage for a while. They need to be refrigerated."

Hayes got up and opened the cooler. "Let's go to the kitchen." He put the lid back on and picked up the shrimp. Robbie followed alongside him down a long corridor. "Freya was special, but you know."

He nodded. "I could see how she looked at you. You gonna be okay?"

"No, not for a while, but maybe one day."

Hayes put the shrimp in the refrigerator. Robbie didn't have any more to say. He turned to head out but stopped at the door when he heard the chief.

"I'm going to put Billy in front of a firing squad next week. You want to be here?"

"Thanks, but no thanks. I've been down that road before."

Robbie headed back toward the airport. He wanted to walk. He had the daylight, and he'd spend the night out there.

Engrossed in thought, the walk to the airport only seemed like minutes. He checked out the Cessna, and it hadn't been tampered with. He found a comfortable place in the building where he'd parked the plane and set up camp.

He squeezed his eyes shut, and tears rolled down his face onto his bedroll. He fell asleep with Freya's sweet smile gracing his dreams.

Chapter 27

Robbie got back to Corpus mid-morning and found Sean at the Contractors compound. Sean gave a couple of the men instructions about things that needed attention while he was in Peaceful Valley for a few days. The guys went to the Farm to grab his bag, and they headed to the Airport.

Robbie wasn't his usual cheery self, and Sean quickly picked up on his somber mood. His friend told him the story about Freya on the trip home.

"I'm sorry to hear that, man. If there's anything I can do . . ."

"I'll be okay."

"It sure will be good to see everyone back home, won't it. Give Florence and Brooke a hug for me. Mom will be mad if I don't head straight over."

They touched down in Peaceful Valley just after lunchtime. Robbie took care not to fly over his house so Florence wouldn't hear the plane. He wanted to surprise her.

Sean grabbed his bag. "This sure beats the three-hour drive."

He grabbed his stuff, and the boys headed to the Lindgrens'. Robbie let out his signature wolf howl, and his mom and dad immediately appeared on the front porch.

Melissa was all smiles. "Come on in, we're having a late lunch."

Sean bowed out. "I'd love to, but I'd like to get on to Mom and Dad's. I'll grab a bite there. Thanks for the offer."

Robbie gave his mom a hug and followed her and James into the house. The food was on the table, and Melissa poured her son a glass of juice. "It's good to see you again, Robbie."

He smiled but didn't answer. This immediately got Melissa's attention. "Something wrong?"

"Nah."

Melissa knew otherwise and cocked her head at him with an inquiring look. "I know better, young man."

"Just a lot of stuff happening. Business."

James looked up from his plate. "Everything okay?"

"Yeah, everything's fine. Just a lot of stress getting everything going with the oil and refinery. Then there's still some communications problems."

James snickered. "I can certainly attest to that. I've been having some problems with my phone for a while. John's been in touch with Sean a few times, but he doesn't know what the problem is either. Maybe Sean can shed some light on things in that department tomorrow."

"Maybe so. We could be expanding a little too fast. There are crews scattered out from here to Port Lavaca, to Gonzales, and almost to San Antonio. There's even a crew or two down toward Kingsville."

"That far?"

"Yes, Sir. There were a few small pockets of resistance, but mostly everything is going along fine. If we can't get the kinks out of the communications system, things may fall apart though."

James smiled. "I know you've worked hard, and you and Sean will get everything figured out and running like a finely tuned machine before long."

"Thanks for your confidence."

After they finished eating, they went out to the porch to continue their conversation. Melissa gave her son a loving smile. "You need a haircut."

Robbie nodded. She ran inside to get some scissors. As bad as he wanted to see Florence and his son, he was hesitant, mainly since his mother picked up on his mood. James ran out to the garden to let Melissa have some alone time with Robbie.

Melissa took a chair down to the ground and raised her eyebrows. "So, you coming to church with us in the morning?"

"I don't think so, Mom."

"Your dad is going."

"Really?"

"Yeah, he's been going every Sunday. I think he closes his ears when John starts going on a little too long about God, but I think, for the most part, he likes it. John's an excellent preacher. He mostly tells stories about current events and a few of the hardships they faced getting here from San Antonio. Come with Florence and your son. They seldom miss a Sunday."

Robbie sat quietly while his mother snipped away at his hair. He wasn't sure whether he wanted to go or not. His mother gave him a shove in the back. "Well?"

"I guess it won't hurt." *It's going to be a change, but you're in for the long haul, buddy. Flo and I can work this out just like mom and dad.*

James came strolling back to the porch with a handful of peanut plants with little goober pods hanging down from the roots. He held them up for Robbie to see.

"Where'd you get those?"

"John brought them back from Corpus a few months back. He likes peanuts a lot, and when he found them, he asked if I'd grow some. Their garden is a lot smaller than ours. There's a sandy spot on the far corner that's perfect for them."

Melissa went inside to get him a bowl for the peanuts and to put the scissors away. When she came out, she handed the bowl to James. "You guys get those things off the plants, and I'll roast them." She turned and went back inside.

James and Robbie got quiet while they filled the bowl with peanuts. When they finished, Robbie stood up and stretched his legs. "Grandpa going to church?"

James pulled out a smoke. "He went a couple of times. That first time when John tricked your grandpa and me. Reggie went one more time but hasn't been since. He probably won't be going tomorrow."

Melissa came back out to the porch. "My, don't you look better. Need a shave though."

Robbie smirked. "I'll get one in the mornin'. I'm gonna run over to see Flo and then on to Grandma and Grandpa's. See how he's doing after the heart surgery. I guess I'll see you guys in church . . . and thanks for the haircut, Mom."

⊣⊢⊣⊢⊣⊢⊣⊢

Robbie jumped out of bed at daylight, despite staying up with Florence. The baby was in a playful mood last night, and he did some bonding with his family.

He took a deep breath, got dressed, and headed out to the woodshed. He got a good workout before breakfast. He'd missed Florence's cooking. It tasted better than he remembered.

When he finished his shower, they headed toward the little church. They met up with his mom and dad. James and Robbie lagged behind Melissa and Florence a bit, discussing the weather.

"The cistern is almost dry," James said. "Maybe you can help me haul some water this afternoon."

"Sure, Dad."

Melissa looked back. "You guys come on. Enough about the weather. Looks like everyone else is already here. Maybe you can ask John to pray for a little rain."

After church, Melissa invited everyone back to the house for lunch. After they'd had their fill, James and Lance went out to the porch to have a smoke. Robbie tagged along. Beka came out a short while later. "Robbie, you going to take us flying? You know we've been wanting to for a while."

Robbie smiled. "I was going to ask Mom and Dad if they'd like to take a flight with me."

"How many can you take at a time?" James asked.

"Three. Dad, you can come with Zack and Deb or Lance and Beka."

Melissa came out to refill their glasses and caught the conversation. "I've already been up. I don't need to go again. Honey, you go up with the kids."

Robbie turned back to his dad. "Come on Dad. Who else?"

Debra looked at Beka, and she didn't immediately hold her hand up, so Debra held up hers. "Zack and I will go."

Beka yelled for Florence. "Robbie, I want you, me, and Flo to go up together. I'd like it to be like the first time, without the crashing and burning, of course. And definitely without being shot. I couldn't enjoy the last time, my leg hurt so much."

Florence came out. "I'm going to pass this time. I'll do it another day." She leaned over and whispered in Robbie's ear. "When you get finished, I'll be waiting for you at home. Your mom is going to keep Lawrence tonight." She kissed him on the cheek and went back inside.

Everyone followed Robbie and James to the plane. "I'm sure proud of you son for learning a new skill. You sure about this?"

"I've been up and down more than a couple of dozen times without any problems. This little plane is easy to fly. It doesn't take a stiff wind, but it's fine in the air. I try to stay on the ground when it's windy, but in Corpus Christi, it's breezy a lot in the afternoons."

Robbie unclipped the tie-downs and climbed in. Zack and Debra took the back seat while James took shotgun. Robbie looked over at his dad. "Buckle up tight."

James watched everything as they picked up speed. He gripped the hold bar until his knuckles turned white. He took a deep breath when they lifted off. "Not as bad as I expected, Son. You did good."

"I'm getting better. Nice runway."

Robbie made a couple of circles around the valley. He looked back at Lance and Debra. Lance had a big grin on his face. Debra looked a little green. "You okay, Deb?"

"I'm fine."

He cut the flight a little short. He didn't want Debra to get sick. As soon as she got out, she gave Robbie a hug for taking her up, then threw up on his leg. "So this is how you thank someone?"

Robbie cleaned up the best he could with a rag from the cockpit and a bottle of water, then climbed back in to take Beka and Lance up.

Beka took the passenger side, and Lance loosened his seatbelt enough to lean between the seats.

Robbie circled over the Lins' and Wimberleys'. "You okay back there, Lance?"

"Yeah, this is fun. Thanks for taking us."

"I'm happy to. How about you, Beka?"

"It's much better when you're not shot, and the plane's not burning."

Robbie laughed. "We don't want to do that again."

"Hell no!"

Back on the ground, they all thanked him for the ride. "I wish you didn't have to go back to Corpus so soon, Robbie."

"There's still a lot of work to do. It won't be long until the wedding. I'll spend most of my time home after that as long as Dad keeps up the runway."

James patted him on the shoulder. "I'll do just that."

Robbie told everyone bye and headed home. When he walked in, Florence was stretched out in the recliner wearing nothing but a smile.

✛✛✛✛✛

Sean met Robbie at the plane at mid-morning. They had a lot to talk about on the way back to Corpus Christi. "So next Friday is the big day, Robbie."

"Yes, it is. We've got to get everything fine-tuned this coming week, so I won't have to worry about taking some time off. I talked to one of the pilots on the Brownsville run. He got me a room with a real nice family there who have a beach house. I thought I'd take Florence there on our honeymoon. Pina Coladas, swimming, and all the bedtime I can get; some of it sleeping."

They both laughed.

As soon as Robbie set the plane down, the boys geared up for work. The mechanic assured Robbie the plane would be ready again first thing in the morning. Robbie drove Sean by the Farm so he could tell the girls he was home. A quick kiss and the guys headed to the Contractors.

Robbie dropped Sean off. "I'll get your reports tonight over dinner. I'm going over to the Police Station to check in with Christine."

"Okay, I'll see you later. Tell her about the guys across the ship channel. We don't want them interfering with the pipelines over toward the refinery. And I want her, or at least a couple of her best officers, with us when we meet up with their elders in Portland on Wednesday."

"Will do."

Robbie made a stop by the seafood plant to order some packages of shrimp for tomorrow's trip. He then drove to the Police Station. A smile spread over Christine's face as soon as she saw him. "Good to see you again, Robbie."

"You too. It's been a while. So, I see you've become a paper pusher too."

She sighed. "Someone's got to do it."

Robbie pulled up a chair and looked at the officer's reports, vehicle reports, and he especially scrutinized the coverage map. "You're moving into San Antonio?"

"Yes. There are resources there we can use. When we started looking at the medical and manufacturing aspects the city once had, we found it to be a treasure trove of assets."

"Is there enough fuel for this?"

"We're managing. The crews have worked miracles with the wells and pipelines out west of here. The folks at the refinery are getting the crude from up north as well. We seem to be overloaded with oil now. They're working on getting another frack-unit going. Soon there will be plenty of gas."

"Frack?"

"Fractional distillation. To turn the crude into gas, diesel, and byproducts."

"Got it. You having dinner with us at the Farm later?"

"I'll be there."

"We'll talk more then. I've got an early flight in the morning."

"Later!"

⌇⌇⌇⌇⌇

Robbie made a quick stop in Austwell to deliver a batch of shrimp and a couple of cans of gas to Phillip.

"I found a train over in Bloomington that appears to be in good shape."

Phillip's eyes lit up. "I used to run a train for a while. Seems like a hundred years ago now."

"Really? I was going to ask you about parts to fix the track, but maybe you can help with the engine."

"They're not hard to run. Just gotta know what you're doing."

"I've got a friend, Joey, in Goliad. I'm going to get him to clean it up a bit. Maybe one day I can get you two together and see if we can get it going."

"I'd like that."

"Okay, I have a long way to go today and a short time to get there. I'll see you soon."

Next stop was to see Red at the pump station just outside of Refugio. "We got 'er pumpin' part-time," he said with a big grin on his red freckled face. "Shore want to thank ya for the cell phones. I've gotta get up on top of the building to get service, but those things really helped us to connect with the crews in the field. Tell Sean thanks for the extra crews too."

"So everything's working?"

"We got all the big leaks fixed. We'll run twelve hours on and twelve hours off. We'll find all the smaller leaks and get those repaired. Then we can run around the clock. Like I told you before, we can't be wastin' this stuff."

Robbie smiled. "I'll be right back."

He ran to the plane and grabbed one of the packages of shrimp out of the cooler.

"What ya got there?"

"A little token of our appreciation for all your hard work."

Red opened up the package. He grinned. "I got somethin' for you too." He set Robbie's package in the fridge and pulled out another and handed it to him. "Fry these up nice and crispy. You'll love 'em."

"Snake?"

"Prime rattlesnake, Sonny."

Robbie thanked him, gave him a high-five, and headed back to the plane.

He met up with Joey and delivered the last bundle of shrimp to Josephine.

"Lawdy, it's been a long time since I've had these. Thank you, Son."

Robbie gave her a hug and went outside to talk to Joey. "I found a man in Austwell who knows about trains. I've got some gas for you and a book about them. I want you to get up to Bloomington and clean the engine up. Don't worry about the cars, just the engine for now. You can read, can't you?"

"I do okay."

"Good. Study up and make sure everything that's supposed to move works. I'll get you and Phillip together and see if you guys can get the thing going. Also, check the tracks and see what we need to get started on those too. Phillip can make parts if need be."

Robbie made it back to Corpus late on Tuesday. He, Sean, and Christine made the meeting in Portland on Wednesday. They were a stubborn bunch. They avoided most of their questions and kept changing the subject. They wanted to talk more about what Robbie and Sean were doing than what they were doing. In the end, all that was settled was that they would meet again.

Christine got in the back seat. "They're hiding something. I don't know what, but there's something they don't want us to know."

They were quiet as Robbie drove to the freeway. He looked over at Sean. "Secrets can't be kept forever. We'll find out what they're up to one day."

Sean and Christine agreed.

It was a busy week, and before Robbie knew it, his wedding day was here. After a shrimp dinner on Thursday night, and a good night's sleep, Sean rounded up the girls, and they made their way to the Airport on Friday morning. Robbie had the plane ready when they got there.

Flo fed Lawrence, then helped Brooke. They weren't sure they could get the wedding off on time, but they were going to give it their best effort.

Brooke fired the stove up early while Florence fed the chickens and brought in more firewood. Brooke worked on icing while the wedding cake baked. In between tasks, they laid out their clothes. Florence bathed both kids and got them dressed.

She checked her phone for the time. "We've got to hurry, Brooke. Melissa said James will be here by 10:30."

Brooke took the cake out. She had to let it cool a bit before she could put the icing on. She cleaned up the dirty dishes while Florence got her shower. Little Johnathan started crying. She fed him again, then passed him off to Florence while she went for her shower.

Flo checked the time. "James will be here any second. We've got to hurry."

Mutt started barking, followed by the sound of the horn. She opened the door. James was already headed up to the porch. "Come on in, James. We're about ready."

James grabbed the cake and took it out, then returned to help with the baby's stuff. "My, don't you ladies look nice."

Mutt followed the car back to the Lindgren's. It was a madhouse there.

Beka and Debra fussed over Flo and Lawrence. Sally scooped up little Johnathan as soon as Brooke came through the door. Melissa dropped what she was doing and wrapped her arms around Florence. "It's about time you officially become my daughter-in-law. You look fantastic."

Florence blushed. "Thank you, Melissa."

"Call me Mom now, will you, Flo?"

"Of course." They squeezed each other tighter, and the happy tears flowed freely.

James set the cake on the table, and in minutes the place was empty except for Florence and her bridesmaids. Everyone headed for the church to finish preparations there. James was the last out. "I'll pick you ladies up as soon as Robbie takes his place at the altar."

Beka made a ribbon for Florence's hair while Debra worked on her nails. Brooke rummaged through Melissa's bathroom and found a tube of lipstick.

When they'd finished with the last minute details, Florence pulled out her phone and checked the time. It was 11:15. *What's keeping them? Robbie should have been back by 11:00.* She walked over and opened the door.

Brooke came up beside her. "It's a glorious day for a wedding. Not a cloud in the sky. Nothing's going to rain on this parade."

Florence forced a smile.

Brooke closed the door. "James will be here any minute. Come on over and sit on the couch."

Beka and Debra gathered around. Florence looked at Debra's tummy. "So, you're definitely pregnant now?"

"Yes. No doubt about it."

She looked over at Beka. She shook her head. "Not yet."

She turned back to Debra. "So, when are you and Zack getting married?"

"Around Christmas, I think. We've been talking about it. Probably just after the holidays. I love wintertime. January maybe. The baby will be here in February."

"Have you thought of names?"

"Constantly. Maybe Charles or Dennis if it's a boy. I'm hoping for a girl though. All you guys have boys. Maybe Marissa or Chastity if it's a girl."

Florence rechecked the time. It was 11:45. She got up and walked back over to the door. She could feel the tears starting to form. *No, dammit. I'm not going to cry. There's a reasonable explanation . . .*

She walked over to the sink and drew a glass of water. Her hand was visibly shaking. She took a sip and walked over to the couch.

Brooke got up. "I'm sure there's a good reason why they're late. Don't worry. They'll be here anytime. Come on. Sit back down."

Florence plopped down on the sofa. Beka reached out and took her hand. "Flo, we've been through a lot together. Everything always turns out just fine."

She looked up, but the smile was hard coming. "Why does everything have to be so tough though?"

"That's life, girl. I thought you'd have learned that by now. You dealt with your daddy, and things got better. You survived Sandra, and life got easier. You and Robbie have had problems, but it has always gotten better. You'll see. This time is no different. By tonight you'll be the happiest gal on the planet."

Beka gave her a shove. "Just wait and see."

Florence got up and rechecked the time. It was after noon, and she went back to the door. *He could have crashed the plane. I'll never see him again.*

She opened the door. There was no sign of James, and she slammed it shut. *Robbie wouldn't have been late if humanly possible. He's dead. He crashed.*

She couldn't hold the tears back this time. She grabbed a dish towel off the counter.

Beep . . . beep.

Her knees almost buckled, and she grabbed the back of one of the dining room chairs. Brooke hurried to the door and flung it open. James was nearly to the porch.

"Well, come on ladies. We've got a wedding to attend."

Beka and Debra grabbed Florence's arms and helped her to the car. She kept the dish towel. She couldn't control the tears now, but they were nervous tears of happiness.

When they pulled up to the church, James hopped out to check to see if they were ready inside. He then took Florence's arm. The bridesmaids led the procession and took their places. James gave Florence a kiss on the cheek. "Welcome to the family."

Florence smiled, took another swipe with the dish towel, and he pulled the veil over her face. The applause was almost deafening in the tiny church when James led Florence inside. The girls sang the wedding processional as he walked her down the aisle.

The grin on Robbie's face set her at ease. Reggie stood alongside him as best man.

John stood front center. "Who giveth this woman?"

James stood proudly. "I do." He placed Florence's hand in Robbie's and took his seat alongside Melissa.

John opened his bible. "Dearly beloved. We are gathered here today to unite this man and this woman in holy matrimony. If there be anyone who can show just cause as to why this union should not take place, may he speak now or forever hold his peace."

He took a brief second to gaze across the room. "Robbie and Florence have written their own vows. Florence."

She turned to face Robbie. "I promise to love, honor, and cherish you until death do us part, but first I want to know why you were so damn late for our wedding."

Robbie grinned. "I'm sorry. I didn't have a wedding ring. Sean and I ran back to the Farm, and we rummaged around until we found one. Those things are hard to come by."

She glanced over at Sean and he nodded.

"Okay, I'll accept that." Her cheeks turned a rosy red. "Everyone here knows we have had problems. You have destroyed a lot of my faith in you. I will question that trust often until you prove that you deserve it. If I have doubt, I will be hard on you. Show me that you are worthy of my love and we'll be as happy as I can make you." She turned to John. "I have no more to say."

"Robbie."

He cleared his throat. "I know I made a mistake. It will never happen again. I do love you. I will always love you. I believe I have shown that from the day we met. I promise, from this day forward, I will never give you a reason not to trust me. I will work hard to make the rest of your life the fairy tale you want and deserve.

"We will have many kids. They will be strong and take care of us when we grow old. Yes, we will grow old together. The world we live in will be safe, and we will travel to places you never imagined. That will start with our honeymoon. I'll tell you all about it after we're hitched."

He looked back at John.

Reggie stepped up and handed Robbie the ring. "With this ring, I thee wed." He slipped the ring on her finger. "Sorry, it's a little loose. Grandpa can tighten it up." He looked over at Reggie.

"No problem, Son."

Florence turned to her bridesmaids. Brooke handed her the ring.

Florence placed the ring on his finger. "This was your Grandpa Lars's ring. Your mother had it tucked away. Lars was a gentle and loving man. I'm sure Eileen conveyed that to you many times. Every time you look at this ring, I want you to think of his strength. Lars only had love for Eileen, and their bond was stronger than the roots of the sycamore tree under which they now reside. May this ring give you the strength you need to remain loyal only unto me."

John looked over the crowd. There wasn't a dry eye in the bunch. "With the power vested in me, I now pronounce you man and wife. You may kiss your bride."

Robbie pulled up her veil and kissed her like he hadn't in a very long time.

The bridesmaids squealed and gathered around. Reggie gave his grandson a firm handshake and hug. Kathy led the group in a song. When they'd finished, Melissa announced there was cake waiting back at the house.

Robbie and Florence drank a little too much of Reggie's wine, which neither were accustomed to having. Brooke minded Lawrence for the evening and made arrangements to stay with Debra and Beka. James and Melissa drove the newly-weds home. Robbie gazed at his parents' smiling faces as he picked up Florence. James backed the car out.

Robbie carried his bride across the threshold. When he put Florence down, she pushed him toward the bathroom. She almost tore his clothes off. She adjusted the shower temperature, and they both stepped in. She lathered him up from his chin to his toes, rubbing her body into the suds. She didn't miss a spot. She twirled him in the rinse cycle, and before they knew it, they were both squeaky clean.

They dried off as they walked over to the bedroom. Robbie asked her to lie on her back perfectly still. He looked over the curves of her body for a few seconds before mounting his charge. It wasn't the charge of the light brigade though. It was more like the serpent sneaking its way through the leaves in the forest—quiet, slithering, methodical, and stealthy . . . searching. He examined every square inch of Florence's smooth body.

She giggled from time to time, and he nibbled away the goosebumps on her belly. While he was in the neighborhood, he moved downward, searching carefully with his tongue for the little valley he longed for as he caressed her legs. By the time he'd finished there, the valley was as wet as if there had been a spring shower.

There was a little rumbling in the distance as Florence moaned and begged for him to put her out of her misery. She reached down and touched him and massaged his hardness. He moved into position, and she led him into the prom-ised land.

Robbie worked his magic, taking turns at who was king of the mountain, both erupting in multiple orgasms.

Epilogue

The months went by lightning fast, and Christmas was here before they knew it. The new State of Texas had steamrolled into reality, communications stretched from corner to corner, and all the opposing hostile forces had been eliminated.

Robbie's original plan had been to help get Sean elected as the new governor of Texas as soon as the reconstruction had been completed. Plans for relocating the central government back in Austin as it had been many years ago, however, turned Sean off of the proposition.

He now loved Corpus Christi mainly due to the prospect of going shrimping every week, but even more so because he loved Kim and Brenda and his life there. Robbie didn't want the job either, and Christine declined. "I like my job in law enforcement."

Mayor Rodriguez from Victoria was more than happy to move his career forward in Austin. He was energetic, and they knew they could trust him to develop a system of government similar to the one they had built in Corpus Christi.

Joey had a yearning to get away from Goliad and to see more of the country. He ended up as the chief engineer of their new train system. Many of the black citizens had segregated themselves, and he was instrumental in rallying them around getting the new railway system functional. They became an integral part in the success of the new economy.

It was a glorious day for Robbie when Hank and Arlene got married right after Christmas. He loved the old man for the oysters he'd opened for him and Sean the first time they met in Corpus. He also liked the quirky stories he told about the 'good ol' days'. He was also instrumental in getting the citizens of Seadrift to join the cause. Robbie was his best man.

The damage to Austin was so extensive that much rebuilding was necessary to make the city habitable. So, in the meantime, it was decided that it was best that the central government be moved to Victoria until Austin could be rebuilt.

Christine agreed to move to Austin mainly because tight security was needed with the reconstruction. With Robbie's help, she moved to Austin to get the project underway. Fourteen months later, the new government was moved there.

Robbie, Florence, and their son settled into a comfortable life in Peaceful Valley. Robbie still made weekly trips to all the surrounding areas, but he spent most of his time making sure Flo and Lawrence were happy. He had three more sons and two daughters.

Robbie spent hours visiting the graves next to the old sycamore tree after each church service. He had long talks with his brother especially, but also with his Grandmother Eileen. Though Robbie didn't remember his Grandfather Lars, he always thanked him for the skills he entrenched into his grandmother which she, in turn, passed along to him. He seldom missed one of John's sermons. While he never became a true believer, he loved listening and sharing in the stories of family.

He didn't forget Charlotte, little Abigail, or his childhood buddy, Buster. He always placed at least one flower on each grave before he left.

James and Melissa got to where they didn't miss a Sunday church service. Despite their beliefs, Reggie and Emily often attended as well. John and Kathy were happy to have them. No one ever said a word about Reggie not being able to carry a tune in a bucket when they sang. He lost some weight, changed his lifestyle a bit, and didn't have any more problems with his heart.

Robbie finally told his parents about all his kids in Corpus Christi like his mother knew he would. He took James and Melissa there on monthly trips along with Florence so they could all get to know their extended family a little better. Flo welcomed the kids and their mothers into their fold.

Robbie also took regular trips to Brownsville and beyond with Florence. Brooke was always ready and willing to take care of the kids while they were gone. They found a small inn there that served up the most exquisite margaritas. They always brought back fresh pineapple for pineapple upside-down cake. Florence got the recipe from Brenda.

Even though he loved Florence dearly, there remained a small place tucked away in the back of his heart for Freya. Every so often, he'd take a trip to Victoria alone to see Chief Hayes and put a few flowers on her grave. He imagined that she flew with him often.

Robbie also made a short stop to visit Jade's grave and to place flowers on hers as well. Visions of the two ladies haunted him for the rest of his life.

Sean eventually trained others to take care of much of his workload and went shrimping more, but mostly concentrated on taking care of Brenda, Kim, and their son, Benjamin. He went to Peaceful Valley to visit his parents regularly. Brenda and Kim never went there again.

Folks gathered from miles around on the steps of the Founders Circle Memorial in Corpus Christi. Sean, with Brenda and Kim on either side and Robbie and Florence next to them, took the front center position in the rows of chairs. James, Melissa, and many of the remaining residents of Peaceful Valley shared the front row.

Benjamin Lin stepped to the microphone. "We gathered here two short years ago to commemorate the statue of my father, Sean Lin, the first mayor of the free Corpus Christi." He waved his hand toward the statue of his father. "He couldn't have done what he did without the person we are gathered here today to honor, Robbie Lindgren, the true founding father of United South Texas."

Lawrence Lindgren stepped to the microphone. "The collapse of Texas sixty years ago cost the lives of ninety-five percent of the population. For twenty-five years, what was left of the citizens struggle to survive.

"They were the tough ones in many cases, but for the most part, they were the lucky ones—lucky like Robbie Lindgren, that they had a man like his Grandpa Reggie. His knowledge and resources allowed them to protect themselves. Robbie's Grandpa Lars was the ultimate survivor who taught my great-grandma Eileen all the skills he could.

"Somewhere along the line, Robbie and Uncle Ronnie, who I unfortunately never got to meet, were instilled with the insight and drive to rebuild the country. After only a few short years, they gave people hope that they and their kids could live productive lives in relative safety, that the land now had time to heal, and that the same mistakes would not be made again.

"There were a few pockets of resistance here and there, however, like the citizens of Portland. They put up a sign *Don't Stop - Don't Get Shot!* And others did the same. Robbie left them alone. They never shot at anyone passing through, and Robbie figured they were good people, they just didn't trust or believe the world could be reunited. Robbie hoped that in time, they would see his dream was possible and join the rest of the human race. The happy news is that all these signs are now gone.

"In most of the communities Robbie visited, he found good people who remembered what it was like before the grid shut down. When there are good people, there is always hope, but for twenty-five years, it had been lost. Thanks to a couple of brave young men, hope is now here to stay. Their dream has now ballooned into the New United States. While the country does not stretch from sea to shining sea yet, it is well on its way."

Lawrence gave Benjamin a nod, and he pulled the covering off the statue. Robbie's figure had one hand on Sean's shoulder, the other pointing to the sky.

Lawrence walked over and gave Robbie a hug. "Thank you, Dad. I love you."

The End? Let's call it the End of the Beginning!

About the Author

Larry Landgraf was born and raised in and around the swamp country of the Guadalupe River Delta on the Texas Gulf Coast. After four years of college, not wanting to spend the rest of his life in an office or classroom, he became a commercial fisherman. That played out in the late '80s, and he became a general contractor for another twenty-plus years. Due to a death-defying injury on the job, he turned to writing.

Trying to save his commercial fishing career, Larry wrote his first book in 1986. The career and book were a failure. He didn't write again until he published his second book, *How to be a Smart SOB Like Me*, in 2012. Then he got serious about writing and in 2015 published *Into Autumn* to launch his *Four Seasons* series. The release dates for *Into Spring* and *Into Winter* are 2017, and 2018 for *Into Summer*.

Larry divorced in 2006 when his wife of 38 years decided to walk out. This marriage produced three kids, all grown now. Larry met Ellen in January 2009 after a long search which spanned the globe. They now live together in the swamp where Larry has lived all his life. Much like Eileen Branson in *Into Autumn*, Ellen is a city gal, but loves Larry's swamp. Larry, much like Lars Lindgren in the story, wouldn't have it any other way. He teaches her the ways of the swamp, and she has plenty to teach Larry, as well.

Fresh Ink Group

Independent Publisher

&

Hardcovers
Softcovers
All Ebook Platforms
Worldwide Distribution

&

Indie Author Services
Book Development, Editing, Proofing
Graphic/Cover Design
Video/Trailer Production
Website Creation
Social Media Management
Writing Contests
Writers' Blogs
Podcasts

&

Authors
Editors
Artists
Experts
Professionals

&

FreshInkGroup.com
Email: info@FreshInkGroup.com
Twitter: @FreshInkGroup
Google+: Fresh Ink Group
Facebook.com/FreshInkGroup
LinkedIn: Fresh Ink Group

Fresh Ink Group

Four Seasons Series
Larry Landgraf

INTO SPRING
The Next Generation

Twenty years after *Into Autumn*, Sean and Robbie leave Peaceful Valley for Corpus Christi, hoping to find women who will join their fiercely protective group back home. What they find is a fight to survive the violent dictatorship of ruthless Sandra Hawkins. Meanwhile, a new family joins the group in the Valley, except that what seems like a safe addition might bring the worst kinds of change. *Into Spring* continues the Four Seasons saga about building a new life in Texas after the collapse of civilization.

Paper-cover ISBN-13: 978-1-936442-44-7
Hardcover ISBN-13: 978-1-936442-43-0
Ebook ISBN-13: 978-1-936442-45-4

INTO WINTER
The Armed Invasion

The ruthless dictator of Corpus Christi, Sandra Hawkins has blood in her eyes as she plans revenge against Peaceful Valley. Sean Lin discovers her plan, but does the small community stand a chance against her heavily armed and well-trained army? The valley's residents are wary hunters skilled at camouflage and stealth, but will toughness and smarts be enough to save their way of life from overwhelming force?

Hardcover ISBN-13: 978-1-936442-56-0

Paper-cover ISBN-13: 978-1-936442-57-7

Ebook ISBN-13: 978-1-936442-58-4

How To Be A Smart SOB
Like Me

Work, money, food, relationships, life in general—these are the everyday struggles for billions crowded into our challenging world. Larry Landgraf tells us his story and the many lessons he's learned for finding extraordinary happiness. *How to Be a Smart SOB Like Me* is a stark but heartfelt examination of a life well-lived. You might like him, and you might not, but you can't help but learn ways you, too, can achieve your best.

Paper-cover ISBN-13: 978-1-936442-51-5
Hardcover ISBN-13: 978-1-936442-50-8
Ebook ISBN-13: 978-1-936442-52-2